SAPPHIRE
PAVILION

SAPPHIRE PAVILION

A STEVE STILWELL THRILLER

―❦―

DAVID E. GROGAN

Seattle, WA

Camel Press
PO Box 70515
Seattle, WA 98127

For more information go to: www.camelpress.com
www.davidegrogan.com

Cover design by Sabrina Sun

Sapphire Pavilion
Copyright © 2017 by David E. Grogan

ISBN: 978-1-60381-603-8 (Trade Paper)
ISBN: 978-1-60381-604-5 (eBook)

Library of Congress Control Number: 2017930925

Printed in the United States of America

To all Wounded Warriors and Vietnam War veterans, and especially those heroes still waiting to come home.

Also by the author

The Siegel Dispositions

ACKNOWLEDGMENTS

———∿∿———

D URING MY LAST EIGHTEEN MONTHS IN the Navy, I commuted from my family's home in Virginia Beach to Northern Virginia to work at the Pentagon. I left Virginia Beach around eight p.m. every Sunday night and arrived between eleven p.m. and midnight just outside the Washington D.C. beltway, where I rented a room from a retired nuclear submarine skipper. I worked at the Pentagon all week and then left for Virginia Beach around eight p.m. on Friday night, hyped up on a Venti Starbucks coffee and thrilled to have missed the rush hour traffic normally clogging Interstate 95 South between the Capitol and Fredericksburg.

Since I got up on workdays quite early to be prepared for the Judge Advocate General's arrival in the office each morning, staying alert on the Friday night trips home posed a challenge. Loud music helped, but I soon learned nothing worked better than listening to podcasts. At the risk of revealing how much of a history nerd I am, I confess that my favorite podcasts were the speeches of President John F. Kennedy and Veterans Chronicles. Former NBC broadcast journalist and Voice of America Director Gene Pell hosted Veterans Chronicles, which featured interviews with U.S. veterans from every major armed conflict of the twentieth and twenty-first centuries.

Although I enjoyed all the interviews, I found those involving Vietnam veterans most intriguing. Despite having "watched" the Vietnam War on the nightly news growing up, I found I knew very little about the war and even less about the Americans who fought in it. The solution was Audible.com and Stanley Karnow's *Vietnam: A History*. Listening to Karnow's book became the mainstay of my Sunday and Friday night drives, with splashes of Veterans

Chronicles and loud music thrown in when I reached my saturation point on the war.

The concept for *Sapphire Pavilion* grew out of one of those history-laden commutes. I wanted to write something that would honor Vietnam veterans in a very real way, while still entertaining and engaging the reader. The story line developed over the course of several weeks, with each commute adding characters and layers to the plot until I was just about ready to start writing. There was one significant impediment: I had never been to Vietnam. That not only made it difficult to picture the country's sights and sounds, but I had no sense of the Vietnamese people.

I remedied that problem by traveling to Vietnam in July of 2014. I visited Ho Chi Minh City (formerly Saigon), Da Lat, Hue City and Khe Sanh. During the day, I toured each destination and the surrounding countryside with tourists from around the world, and at night I sat in an empty hotel restaurant with an iPad, a portable keyboard, and a Diet Coke, and wrote the story. I should say, once I dove into Saigon and walked its streets, ate at its restaurants, visited its historical sites, and talked to its people, the story wrote itself. By the time I left Vietnam, I had a solid start on the manuscript, a camera overflowing with pictures to help inspire later chapters, and a host of memories from all the people I met while I was there.

I am indebted to a number of people who helped me shape the manuscript to make sure *Sapphire Pavilion*'s story got told. First and foremost is the editing team at Camel Press, Jennifer McCord and Catherine Treadgold. Like alchemists of old, through the judicious application of science and magic, they turn ordinary text into gold. I am also especially indebted to my friend and international relations mentor, retired ambassador Marisa Lino (U.S. Ambassador to Albania from 1996-1999), who took time from her busy schedule to review the State Department-related content of the manuscript to keep me from straying too far from diplomatic reality. Joe Galietta and Michael Coblin did the same for me with regard to the FBI material. Remarkably, they did so even though they did not know me. I connected with them through a network of former judge advocates from all the military services. I am grateful for their feedback and advice.

Two Vietnam veterans warrant special mention, not only because they assisted me with the accuracy of the flight sequence, but also because they both flew C-130s in Vietnam during the war. Both former Captain Alan Baker and retired Lt. Col. Jay Van Cleeff provided incisive comments and direction on Chapter 2. For that, I give them my thanks. For their wartime service to the United States, I salute them.

Last, but certainly not least, I would like to thank my family for putting up with my writing and for providing incredibly valuable feedback on the drafts that I incessantly asked them to critique. My father, himself a former Air Force pilot, was the first to read the manuscript and gave me critical comments, as did my sister Jenny Scharner. My wife, Sharon, also gave me honest feedback (as only a spouse can do) and my daughter Chelsea helped with some of the supporting material. It may take a village to raise a child, but it takes a family to produce a novel. For their support and love throughout the process, I am forever grateful.

—*David E. Grogan*

1

Thursday, 18 January 1968
Ubon Air Base, Thailand

Two jet-black Cadillacs raced along the tarmac toward the hazy silhouette of an aircraft up ahead. Neither vehicle had its lights on; they didn't need lights with the jungle moon casting its incandescent glow across the runway. They zoomed past the terminal and the apron where all the other aircraft nestled for the evening. Ignoring bold-lettered warning signs, they sped onto the ramp, chasing a giant C-130A "Hercules" transport lumbering to the point where it would turn onto the main runway and launch into the torrid air rising above the Thai airfield.

The C-130 paused before taxiing onto the runway, allowing the lead Cadillac to approach. It parked twenty-five feet behind the aircraft, perpendicular to the left wing. There were two figures in the front seat, one a fashionable strawberry blonde in her late twenties with flipped hair. Her lithe figure was perfectly complemented by her light cotton business suit. She opened her window to look at the other car, but the exhaust from the C-130's roaring turbos was too much for the driver. He asked her to close her window and she did. She twisted backward, looking over her shoulder, gently pressing her cheek against the cool glass. It was too late and she knew it. What she had to tell him would have to wait until he returned.

The second Cadillac followed closely behind the first. It angled to the right of the plane until it was parallel to the wing. Only the driver was visible through the window in the front seat. When the vehicle stopped, a sturdy man in his late thirties emerged from the driver's side rear door. He wore a dark business suit, starched white shirt, and a pencil-thin black tie. His non-regulation haircut branded him as a civilian. Hands occupied—he carried his hat in one hand and a briefcase in the other—he shoved the car door closed with his polished wingtip shoe. He walked toward the rear of the aircraft, the blast from the propellers forcing him to lean into the wind. His suit coat flapped so violently, it looked like it would rip from his body. Pausing at the base of the plane's lowered cargo ramp, he glanced over at the first Cadillac.

She could see him looking in her direction. She started to open the car door but the driver reached over and held her arm, so she closed it. She wanted desperately to run to him, but it wasn't to be. She had to let him go for now.

The man switched the briefcase to his left hand, which still clung to his hat. Then he smiled and waved to the woman. She waved back from inside the car, but had no idea whether he could see her. He walked briskly up the ramp, which lifted until it merged with the aircraft's fuselage.

Her driver didn't wait for the ramp to close all the way. He began a slow curve to the left to retrace his tracks toward the terminal building and beyond. The woman sank into her seat, staring out the front window. She hated unfinished business; that was just the way she was. As the two cars sped away, she swore to herself she would fix the situation as soon as he returned. She was already counting the days.

2

---〜〜---

"**H**EY PIKES, YOU STILL GOT THE sealed orders?" asked Lieutenant Colonel Ray Eversall, his hand guiding the yoke of the C-130A cruising in the night sky over Laos.

"Nav's got 'em, sir," replied Captain John "Pikes" Peke, the plane's copilot. Nav was short for navigator, another U.S. Air Force Captain working just behind the two pilots. A short but stocky Italian-American with jet-black hair and a Napoleon complex, Nav kept the crew entertained with his trooper's vocabulary, having elevated profanity to an art form.

Eversall activated his mic with a press of a button. "Nav, you got the orders?"

"Yeah, I got 'em, Skipper, but I still say it's bullshit we can't open 'em till we get over the waypoint. Who the hell we gonna tell, anyway? I mean we're flying a night mission in radio silence. What the hell?"

"You've flown enough spook missions to know how the game goes," Eversall chided. "Besides, it gives us something to look forward to."

"Yeah, Skipper, but usually the game doesn't go like this. Nobody drives out to the runway to stop a take-off, let alone some stiff in a suit with Top Secret orders. And why can't we open 'em until we're flying over some godforsaken point in the middle of nowhere? That's fubar, Skipper. I don't care what anybody says."

"Roger that, Nav," Eversall replied, "but maybe that's why they asked for volunteers to fly this mission. Besides, General Rollins didn't think it was fubar. He thought I was fubar for balking at taking the passenger on board, and he radioed all the way from Japan to tell me. I'm just hoping I still have a job when we get back to Thailand."

"I wouldn't sweat it, Skipper," Pikes said. "I mean, we did bring the guy onboard, we've got the orders in hand, and we're back on schedule. The General got what he wanted."

"I like the way you think," Eversall replied, looking over at Pikes and smiling. "But I'm guessing the General may not see it that way. Generals get a little bent out of shape when you question their orders, and they all seem to have long memories."

Pikes nodded and shrugged. As good as Pikes was, Eversall knew he still had plenty to learn about how things worked in the Air Force.

"I show us crossing into South Vietnam now," Nav reported a few minutes later.

"I say we go ahead and open those orders, Skipper. That way, if we gotta make a course change, we can be ready to execute it as soon as we arrive. Besides," Nav added, "who the hell'll know if we open 'em a little early?"

Eversall turned around in his seat and winked at Nav. "I suppose I don't see any problem with you bringing the envelope here so I'll be ready to open it when we get to the waypoint."

"You got it, Skipper," Nav replied, grinning at his boss's malleability. He handed the envelope to Eversall. It was the size of a normal sheet of paper, manila on one side and marked with two-inch diagonal orange stripes on the other. Block letters printed on the striped side said TOP SECRET—OPEN AT WAYPOINT. Nav rubbed his hands together like someone waiting for a choice slice of beef at a buffet line carving station.

"Skipper," Pikes interrupted as he took control of the aircraft from the autopilot. "Looks like we've got some company coming from the north at ten o'clock. It's moving pretty fast."

Eversall rested the orders on his lap and leaned forward, squinting to get a better look. "Yeah, I see it. I don't recall anyone briefing anything about an escort. Take it down to fifteen thousand feet at two hundred sixty knots and come right fifteen degrees just in case. Nav, be ready to get us back on course. I'll get these orders open and see what they say. I'll bet they indicate we get an escort for whatever it is we're supposed to be doing."

"Wilco, Skipper," Pikes replied, tightening his grip on the yoke and pushing it forward to take the plane down to fifteen thousand feet. "It's got to be a friendly. I can't imagine an NV fighter being this close to the DMZ, let alone at night."

Eversall knew Pikes was right. The North Vietnamese, or NV as the aircrew called them, rarely risked their fighters in night actions. Having an NV fighter stray all the way down to the Demilitarized Zone between North and South Vietnam was even more unheard of, so this had to be a U.S. fighter escort or a U.S. plane returning from a mission over North Vietnam. Still, Eversall wasn't ready to concede the point. He wanted to see how the unidentified aircraft reacted to his own plane's maneuvering.

"Four minutes to waypoint," Nav shouted.

The loadmaster's voice broke over the intercom. "Skipper, our guest would like to be up there with you when you open the orders. You want me to bring him up?"

"Not now," Eversall barked, tearing open the Top-Secret envelope. "We've got an unidentified aircraft up here with us. Now's not the time to play show and tell. Tell him I'll talk to him later."

"Copy all," the loadmaster replied as the plane buffeted through turbulence on the way down to the target altitude.

Eversall blew into the envelope to make it easier to remove its contents. As he started to pull out the papers, which were covered with another orange TOP SECRET cover sheet, Pikes reported again.

"Skipper, our friend made a compensating course change and is heading toward us. Hard to tell the distance at night, but I estimate he'll be on top of us in a little over a minute."

"Okay, boys," Eversall said as he folded back the Top-Secret cover sheet from the orders and started to scan them. "Nav, give Pikes a course change to put us right over the way … holy shit!" Eversall rarely swore unprovoked with real obscenities, so his word choice told everyone this was something big. "You're not going to—"

"Missile inbound!" shrieked Pikes, not believing what he was seeing. "That bogey just launched on us!"

"I got it from here," Eversall yelled, dropping the Top-Secret orders, which scattered on the flight deck floor. He grabbed the yoke and turned the plane hard to port to close the distance between it and the other aircraft. The head-on approach would help mask the exhaust from the engines in case the inbound missile was a heat-seeker.

The loadmaster hopped on the intercom again, his voice animated after Pikes' missile broadcast. "Skipper, what should I do with the passenger? He won't stand a chance if we get hit."

"Get him in a parachute," Eversall yelled, pissed at the distraction. He needed to focus his full attention on evading the attack.

"Missile just went over us by a hundred feet!" Pikes exclaimed, relief apparent in his voice. Sweat covered his face and his hands dripped perspiration onto the flight console. "Skipper, you want me to get on the radio to tell this guy we're a friendly? He's got to be one of us."

"No," Eversall said bluntly. "We're under radio silence and still have a mission to complete. Plus, this guy sure isn't acting like a friendly. He's got to be a stray NV."

"Radio silence doesn't do us much good if we're dead," replied Pikes, pushing back on Eversall's uncompromising adherence to orders. "Shit!" Now it was Pikes' turn to swear. "Missile two inbound at two o'clock."

"I'm taking us down to the deck," Eversall exclaimed.

"There are mountains down there," Nav warned. "Don't go below nine thousand feet or the ground will get us even if the missiles don't!"

Eversall said nothing. He turned the nose of the plane toward the incoming missile and put the plane into a dive.

"Brace for missile impact," Pikes screamed into his microphone.

This time the missile didn't miss. It slammed into the inboard engine on the right wing but miraculously didn't explode. The supersonic missile was too much for the wing's frame, though, and the impact sheared off the wing just beyond where the missile hit. The remaining two engines on the left wing continued to drive forward, but with the outboard engine and half the right wing gone, the plane started to spin toward the ground.

"Bail out, bail out," Eversall commanded over the microphone. He looked to Pikes, knowing this would be the last time he'd see him this side of eternity. "Get the hell out of here, Pikes. I'll call in our position and I'll be right behind you."

"You'll need my help holding her together," Pikes yelled over the violent shaking in the doomed aircraft.

"I said, get the hell out of here. That's an order. Now get going." Eversall looked over at Pikes with a smile and the courage of someone ready to stare down death to the end. "I said, get going."

As Pikes unbuckled from his seat, he struggled to make his way aft, given the plane's downward spiral. He briefly looked back at Eversall, who was fighting the controls and getting ready to broadcast over the radio. Pikes didn't look back again as he grappled his way to the cargo bay.

"Mayday, Mayday," Eversall broadcast over the emergency circuit. He no longer had any regard for radio silence. They were well beyond the point of no return. His job now was to stay in the air long enough for the crew to get out and to make their position known to would-be rescuers. The altimeter told him he had only a few seconds left over the mountainous terrain. "This is *Lion One*. We've been hit by enemy fire and are going down. Last known position was Waypoint One on mission flight plan. Repeat, Mayday, Mayday."

Seconds later, the plane crashed into the side of a tree-covered mountain. Eversall had been able to steer the plane just enough so it wasn't a head-on blow, and the plane hit the ground near the base of the mountain and started careening through the virgin forest. Both wings and the tail ripped off as the fuselage continued forward, until a jagged rock protruding from the undergrowth tore it open. The plane's flight deck was obliterated and there was no sign of Eversall—only blood and the shattered glass of the windshield littered across what had been his seat, moments before. The engines smoldered two hundred feet behind the airplane but didn't catch fire. Everything in what was left of the fuselage lay still; and the mountain rendered a moment of silence.

3

Sunday, 14 May 2000
Ho Chi Minh City, Vietnam

R IC STOKES STRAINED TO LIFT HIS head. It felt like a force greater than
gravity was grabbing him around the neck and pulling his head to the
ground. He raised it an inch or so before it fell back, planting his right cheek
against the slimy stone pavement. He tried to open his eyes, but his left eye
felt puffy and he couldn't see out of it. Fear shot through his veins. Where the
hell was he and what the hell had happened? Pain pulsed with every heartbeat
from the tip of his forehead to the back of his skull. He gathered all his strength
to pick himself up, using his hands to do a pushup until he contorted himself
into a sitting position. With his right cheek no longer resting on the stones,
he looked around.

Despite the darkness, he could tell he was in a narrow, ancient alley,
bounded by weathered wooden walls, barely wide enough for two people
to walk down side by side. A combination of raw sewage and rotting food,
baked in a subtropical oven, putrefied the night air, making it difficult to
breathe. In front of him, about twenty-five yards, a street crossed the alley.
Motorbikes zipped past the opening in both directions, their high-pitched
buzz reverberating off the walls long after the offending machines disappeared.

Above him, a slit of cloudy sky followed the alley's contours. Corrugated
tin roofs overhanging the windowless walls flanked the slit on both sides.
None of this meant anything, for he had no idea how he'd gotten there. He
heard something coming from behind him and saw two rats running at him
with something in their mouths. Oblivious to his pain, he shot to his feet to

defend himself. His six-foot three-inch athlete's frame suddenly rising from the darkness didn't deter the cat-sized rats. They ran by him, disappearing into a hole under the wall with whatever it was they were carrying between them.

Ric probed the back of his head with his right hand and felt a knot the size of a golf ball. Now he knew why he had a headache, but how did it happen? He checked his fingers for blood, but there was none, at least none he could feel or see in the ambient light in the alley. That was the first good news he'd had since coming to. He went to check his wristwatch to see what time it was, but his watch was missing. Then he groped his sport coat pockets for his wallet, but that was missing too. He'd been rolled! How could this have happened? And where was Ryan?

Dizzy and nauseated, he reached over to the wall to steady himself. He sucked in a gulp of the dripping, pungent air to marshal his strength. After a few tentative steps down the alley toward the street, he took his hand off the wall and balanced on his own. Every step required concentration and effort.

Once he reached the street, he leaned up against the corner of the building to assess his surroundings. Storefronts with filthy, soot-stained retractable metal doors rolled down, their paint a mere shadow of the original colors, told him he was in a dilapidated shopping district. Some of the stores also had security gates, although from the establishments' appearance, it didn't look like there could be much inside worth protecting. Most of the stores' names were Vietnamese, but he was able to recognize a few because they included English words or phrases like *pharmacy* or *market*, or *Made in America*. Not that it mattered; all the shops were closed.

Above the stores were three or four stories of ramshackle tenements, remnants of French Colonial architecture with louvered doors and window coverings, hanging plants and tattered awnings. Many had clothes still hanging over railings outside windows to dry, although drying at night in this humidity was more an aspiration than a reality. Almost all the apartments were dark—it had to be late.

After gathering his strength in the relative safety of an iridescent sign under a shopkeeper's overhang, he started walking down the street to look for a cab. He had no way to call and saw no one on the street to ask for help, so he kept walking until he finally found an open shop. In the window under a torn red awning hung plucked chickens tied by their legs, with a couple more roasting on what passed for a rotisserie grill. On the other side of the entrance, a red and yellow neon sign advertised a beer with a name he hadn't seen before. The aroma drifting out of the store was a blend of cooked chicken and some other animal he didn't recognize or want to identify. Based on smell alone, he would have skipped the store, were he just looking for something to eat. But he had no other options tonight, so he walked inside and made his way to the counter, forgetting his left eye was swollen shut and he had no money.

"Taxi?" he said to the weathered black-haired shopkeeper standing behind the cash register. The man either spoke no English or was afraid to respond, given the battered appearance of his latest customer. He did come out from behind the counter and walk outside to point toward an intersection farther up the street in the direction Ric had been walking. He thanked the man and started trudging toward the intersection. As he neared the corner, a young Vietnamese man wearing a golf shirt, loose-fitting khaki cargo shorts, and flip flops pulled up to him on one of the buzzing motorbikes.

"You need ride?" he asked, smiling like someone about to make big money.

"Yeah, I do," Ric replied, wondering how he and the young man would fit on a bike that small.

"Where you going?"

"The Mountain Flower Hotel. Do you know where that is?"

"I know where everything is," the young man replied, grinning proudly. "You got address?"

Ric didn't bother asking why the young man needed an address if he knew where everything was. He started rummaging through his pockets for his wallet and room key, only to remember both had been stolen. He did find one of the hotel's business cards and gave it to the young man, who nodded in recognition. It also hit him that he had no way to pay for the ride without his wallet, but he figured he'd deal with that once he got to the hotel. Ryan would take care of it. Besides, the young man hadn't said anything about money yet. Maybe he was just a Good Samaritan.

As Ric approached the bike, the young man stared at his face. "What happen your eye? It messed up. I take you to hospital."

"No, take me to hotel," Ric countered, now dropping his own articles. His eye was not his immediate problem. He needed to get back to Ryan to figure out what had happened. There would be time for the hospital later.

"Okay, boss," the young man said, his tone conveying Ric was making a mistake. "You get on bike, hold tight, we go."

"You got it," Ric said as he wedged his forty-eight-year-old American-sized rump on the tiny seat behind the young man. No sooner had he wrapped his arms around his benefactor's chest than the motorcycle jumped to life, tearing toward the intersection. Ric locked his arms, squeezing the young man as he did, and held on for dear life. He planted his feet on the pedals behind the flip-flopped feet of the young man and watched his life flash before his eyes as they turned onto a busy nighttime street still filled with traffic and people. It would be just his luck to survive a beating and robbery only to be killed on a motorcycle on his way back to the hotel.

On both sides of the street, colorful signs lit up clubs interspersed with shops, their dirty metal security doors pulled down to the sidewalk and locked for the evening. Parked motorbikes overflowed from every nook and cranny on the sidewalk, and young "butterfly girls" in tank tops and miniskirts flirted with Vietnamese and foreign men stopping in cars and on motor scooters at street corners. The young man weaved his bike in, around, and through the traffic, gunning it any time he found an opening, only to have to slow down again when the hole disappeared a little farther down the road. Ric closed his good eye, reasoning that if he was going to die, it was better not to see it coming.

After about ten minutes of warp speed and bugs bouncing off Ric's face like rain on a windshield, the young man slowed his motorcycle and veered out of traffic to a temporary parking place in front of the Mountain Flower Hotel on Lý Tự Trọng Street. Ric loosened his death grip around the young man's midsection and dismounted, his head still aching and his stomach queasy from the zigzagging and careening around the many near misses en route. The young man looked at him and smiled.

"This your hotel. You okay now?"

"Yeah, I'm okay now," Ric lied. "That was quite a ride."

"You like my driving?"

"Yeah, you drive great," Rick lied again. "How much do I owe you?"

"Twenty bucks."

Ric knew the price was way too high, but he was in no condition to haggle, and at this point, he really didn't care. He just wanted to talk to Ryan and find out what was going on. "Okay, twenty dollars sounds good. I need to go into the hotel to get some money because someone stole my wallet. I'll be right back out."

"Big American, you don't cheat me," the young man implored. "I help you when you hurt. You pay me, I wait."

"I won't cheat you," Ric promised. "I'll be right back."

Ric turned and walked toward the front door of the Mountain Flower Hotel. He managed a shallow smile when the doorman said hello, but his focus was on getting twenty dollars for the driver and on stopping the throbbing pain emanating from the knot on the back of his head. So he sailed past the doorman and walked straight to the front desk without uttering a word. When he reached the counter, a bespectacled, middle-aged desk clerk tapping an unsharpened yellow pencil on the counter was waiting for him. The desk clerk's eyes filled the oversized lenses of the glasses he wore, making them appear bulbous and exaggerated.

"May I help you?" the desk clerk asked, glaring at Ric's swollen eye and the bedraggled state of his clothing. He spoke without a hint of a Vietnamese accent.

"Yes, you certainly can," Ric replied, noticing the clerk scrutinizing his appearance. "I'm Ric Stokes and I'm staying in Room 1004. As I'm sure you can tell, I've had a rough night. Someone hit me over the head and robbed me, so I've lost my wallet and my room key, and my passport is in my luggage in my room. A young man gave me a ride back to the hotel on his motorbike and I owe him twenty-five dollars." Ric checked his pockets in front of the clerk to prove his assertions. "Can you give me twenty-five dollars and charge it to my room, please?"

"I'm not supposed to do that," the clerk replied matter-of-factly.

"Do I look like someone who's trying to steal twenty-five dollars?"

"Actually, you don't look very good," the clerk remarked. "Do you need a doctor or want me to call the police?"

Ric thought for a second. Although he didn't want to see a doctor, having the clerk call the police would buttress his credibility. After all, what thief would ask for the police to be called if he were trying to steal money?

"I can see a doctor in the morning," Ric replied, "but I would like you to call the police so I can report the robbery and maybe get my wallet back. While we're waiting for them to come, can you give me the twenty-five dollars so I can pay my driver?"

The clerk looked around and saw no one else in the lobby other than the doorman, who was watching the back and forth of the dialogue. He opened the cash drawer and, from underneath the Vietnamese money tray, pulled out a twenty-dollar bill and a five-dollar bill. He placed the money on the counter, and with his hand still on the cash, said, "You'll see a charge equal to thirty-five U.S. dollars on your bill. I'm sure that will be fine, won't it Mr. Stokes?" The clerk smiled, knowing his guest had no other options.

"I guess it will have to be," Ric replied, taking the money and folding the bills in half. "Thanks for your help." He made no attempt to hide his disdain for the clerk's successful extortion. The clerk's smile also went unanswered.

With money in hand, Ric headed back for the door, handing the doorman the five spot as he walked by. The gesture prompted a big grin and guaranteed Ric good service for the rest of his stay. He then approached the young man, who was sitting sidesaddle on his motorcycle, waiting for Ric to return.

"Here's your twenty," Ric announced, handing the young man the bill. "I told you I wouldn't cheat you."

"You good American," the young man beamed. "I like you." He reached into his pocket, pulled out some heavily creased but readable business cards, and handed one to Ric. "If you need ride while you in Ho Chi Minh City, you call me and I give you ride. No other driver as good as me. I always give you best price."

"I'll do that," Ric assured the young man. "And thanks for helping me tonight."

The young man nodded and smiled, then mounted his motorcycle and disappeared with a deafening buzz as he zipped into the city's late-night traffic. Ric headed back toward the hotel, where his new friend, the doorman, held the door wide open for him. Ric saluted as he passed and returned to the front desk.

"Can I get a key to my room, please?"

"There is a ten-dollar charge for a lost key," the clerk said, realizing he had Ric over a barrel for the second time in less than ten minutes.

"Fine." Ric set the young man's business card on the counter and watched as the clerk made a new room key card. Taking the room key, he reminded the clerk to call the police for him. "And please, send them up to my room. My head is really hurting and I want to lay down."

Ric made his way to the elevator and took it to the tenth floor. He walked down the hall to Room 1004 on the corner and put his key in the door. As he opened the door, he thought he heard a woman gasp, so he started to close the door, thinking he might be entering the wrong room. He looked again at the number on the door, 1004, confirming he was in the right place. He pushed the door open and turned on the light.

"Ryan, what the hell is going on?" Ric yelled. A topless Vietnamese woman in bed with Ryan pulled the sheets up over her, covering her breasts. Ric couldn't believe his eyes; the room was trashed. Ryan's and the woman's clothes littered the floor. A lamp near the window lay on its side, the lampshade bent upward at a forty-five-degree angle and the bulb broken. Someone had left the bathroom light on and the closet door open, and white powder covered the table next to the bed. An open baggy containing more white powder spilled its contents onto the brown carpet under the table. Ric could see the tip of an open bottle of Jack Daniels under the chair opposite the desk, and the entire room reeked of alcohol.

"Ryan, I said what the hell is going on here?" Ric stepped over the debris on the floor, and walked around the bed to rouse Ryan. When he got to Ryan's side of the bed by the powder-covered table, he grabbed him by the shoulder and started to shake him to wake him up. The woman, who looked to be no more than twenty, slid to the other side of the bed, still clinging to the sheet to cover her nude body. As she moved, the covers came off Ryan and he lay there, naked and blue.

"My God!" Ric screamed, shaking Ryan with both hands now. "Call an ambulance!" he yelled to the woman, but she either didn't understand English or ignored him. She hopped off the bed, pulling the sheet with her, and began picking up her clothes. Ric left Ryan and pushed the woman back onto the bed on his way to the hallway door. "Help, help!" he screamed down the hall, but none of the other rooms' doors opened. Panic stricken, Ric ran back to the still-naked woman and started to shake her by her shoulders. "What did you do? Answer me! What did you do?"

Ric pushed the girl down on the bed again and rushed back to Ryan, who was now even bluer than when Ric first saw him. He pulled Ryan's mouth open, tilted his head back, and started to perform mouth-to-mouth resuscitation, but Ryan didn't respond. Ric looked up to get the woman to help him with chest compressions, but she had gathered her clothes and slipped out the door while he attended to Ryan. "My God, please don't let him die," Ric prayed out loud. "Help, help!" he yelled again, while starting chest compressions on his own.

After the second cry for help, two policemen in dark green security police uniforms ran into the room. Both officers were half Ric's size. "Get on floor," the first one yelled, pulling a baton from his belt.

"You've got to help him," Ric begged, pointing at Ryan. "He's dying."

"Get on floor," the officer repeated, raising his baton and threatening to club Ric if he didn't comply.

Recognizing he had no choice, Ric dropped to the floor on all fours, leaving Ryan to die. "Please," Ric pleaded, looking up at the policeman brandishing the baton, "call an ambulance."

"Passport," the policemen demanded. "Give me your passport now."

"It's in my suitcase in the closet. If you let me get up, I'll get it for you. But please, call an ambulance."

The lead policeman spoke to his partner in Vietnamese, who then made a call on his radio. Ric hoped he was calling an ambulance, but he had no way of knowing.

"You get up and get passport," the lead policeman said, poking Ric in the lower back with the baton.

Ric did as instructed, moving slowly and deliberately so the policeman wouldn't mistake his movements for aggression. Ric looked over at Ryan—he had to be dead by now. When Ric reached the closet, he pointed to one of the two suitcases and said, "This is mine. I'll need to open it to get my passport."

"You hurry up," the policeman commanded. His partner, baton also drawn, was watching Ric as well.

Ric pulled his suitcase out of the closet, noticing it felt heavier than when he had stowed it there, empty, earlier in the day. He left the suitcase in an upright position and unzipped the cover, allowing it to open so he could reach into one of the pockets. As the suitcase opened, a large, white, powder-filled plastic-wrapped package fell out onto the floor.

"Holy shit," Ric exclaimed, "where the hell did that come from?"

The lead policeman cracked him on the back with his baton. "You get on floor, you get on floor," he demanded, "or I mess you up."

"It's not mine," Ric declared as he fell on all fours. "I swear to God; I don't know what it is or where it came from."

"You shut up," the policeman yelled, stepping on Ric's back and driving him to the floor until he lay flat and face down on the carpet. He grabbed Ric's left arm and wrenched it behind his back. With Ric's arm bent as far behind his back as it would go, the policeman pulled handcuffs from his belt and put them on his left wrist. Then he took the baton and bludgeoned Ric's right tricep, causing him to screech in pain. "You give me other arm," he shouted.

"Please don't do this to me," Ric implored with the side of his face shoved deep into the coarse stiff pile of the carpet. "I swear to God I've done nothing wrong."

The policeman yanked Ric's right arm behind his back and Ric felt something pop, followed by excruciating pain. The policeman locked the handcuffs around Ric's right wrist. "Get up!" the policeman yelled, pulling him backward by the handcuff chain. "You get up now. Get up!"

Ric screamed in agony, trying to bring his body up to a kneeling position, but his barrel chest and high center of gravity wouldn't let it happen. His failure caused the policemen to pull all the harder on the handcuff chain, tearing muscle, sinew, and tendon. Ric tried to roll onto his side to make the pain stop, but the force of his weight shifting pulled the much smaller policemen to the floor, cursing in Vietnamese as he went. That's when the second policemen thumped Ric across the back of his head with his baton, ending Ric's evening.

4

～～

Friday, 26 May 2000
Williamsburg, Virginia

STEVE STILWELL TOOK THE SCHEDULE HIS office manager, Marjorie
Weldman, prepared for him out of his inbox to see what the day had in
store. Since today was a Friday, Marjorie had booked the afternoon solid with
potential new clients visiting his solo law practice in Colonial Williamsburg
for the first time to discuss whether they needed a will or other estate
planning services. All he had on the calendar this morning, however, was an
interview at 9:00 a.m. with a new attorney, Ms. Casey Pantel, who sent him an
unsolicited letter asking for a job.

Steve tucked the schedule into his day planner and slid a thin manila
folder in front of him. The un-labeled folder included Ms. Pantel's résumé
and cover letter, as well as some articles about her Marjorie pulled from the
Internet. Her credentials were impressive—she attended Penn State on an
Army ROTC scholarship, majoring in history with a minor in French. She
graduated in the top ten percent of her class. She then served as an Army
helicopter pilot, participating in Operation Provide Comfort II in northern
Iraq, helping the Kurds after the Gulf War. She used her GI Bill to attend the
College of William & Mary School of Law, graduating fourth in her class, high
enough to earn a follow-on clerkship with a distinguished federal district
court judge in Norfolk, Virginia. Now, her cover letter said, she was ready to
enter the competitive world of private practice.

With about fifteen minutes to go before the interview, Steve grabbed his
coffee cup and wandered out to the lobby, where his office manager normally

sat. Anyone wanting to visit his office had to get by Marjorie first. That was no easy feat, as she controlled access like an armed sentry at a nuclear facility. She was watering plants by the front window with her back to Steve when he strolled into the room.

Although nearly forty-three, Marjorie was dressed in a short taupe skirt, a rose-colored blouse, and beige heels. Contact lenses and shoulder-length tinted blonde hair in a loosely tied updo completed the ensemble. A year ago, she would have looked like an older woman trying unsuccessfully to squeeze into a younger woman's clothes, but a divorce, a new diet, and Steve's flexibility in accommodating her workout schedule allowed her to carry off her new look with panache. Steve told her he was certain the office received better and more frequent service from the office supply store, the mailman, and the overnight delivery trucks as a result of her makeover, an observation with which Marjorie blushingly agreed. She held her skirt close to the back of her legs for modesty as she leaned forward to pour water from a blue, quart-sized plastic sprinkling can.

"Are you making sure the plants are healthy for Ms. Pantel's visit?" Steve asked, tongue in cheek.

"Plants are funny, Mr. Stilwell," Marjorie answered, keeping her back to him while continuing to water a leafy palm near the corner of the bay window looking out over North Henry Street. "If you don't water them, they die. Kind of like the ones in your office." Marjorie turned around, raised her eyebrows and smirked, like Steve's mother used to do when saying I told you so.

"I never liked those plants anyway," Steve retorted, amused by Marjorie's jab. "I'm gonna grab a quick cup of coffee before the interview. When Ms. Pantel arrives, please show her in."

"Certainly," Marjorie replied, turning back to the plants.

Steve walked to the kitchen and poured himself his first cup of coffee of the morning, adding vanilla-flavored non-dairy creamer. He wasn't sure if the mixture tasted like vanilla, but it was better than black coffee or coffee with milk. Walking back to his office, he heard a woman speaking to Marjorie in the reception area. No sooner had he sat down at his desk than Marjorie escorted Ms. Pantel into his office.

"Mr. Stilwell, Ms. Casey Pantel is here to see you." Marjorie walked just in front of the visitor but retreated behind her as they neared two cream-shaded leather tub chairs—recent additions to Steve's remodeled office—in front of his desk. Casey looked professional but plain, sporting a navy-blue pantsuit and matching flats. Her auburn hair was pulled back into a bun, while a single-strand gold necklace accentuated her fair skin against her dark business suit. Steve assessed the simplicity of her attire and her obvious physical fitness as likely carryovers from her days in the Army.

"Thanks, Marjorie," Steve replied, walking around his desk to shake Casey's hand. "I'm very pleased to meet you."

"It's my pleasure, Mr. Stilwell." Casey gripped Steve's hand and shook it firmly—another Army carryover. "I really appreciate you meeting with me."

"Given your résumé, I'd have been a fool to pass you up," Steve admitted, still standing in front of his desk. "Why don't we have a seat at my conference table?" He motioned in the direction of a round cherry table and its four chairs, also products of the recent remodeling. "It's much easier than both of us trying to look at each other over my cluttered desk."

Steve took a seat at the table in the back of his office, while Casey went for the chair opposite him. He noticed she was favoring her right leg, particularly when she pulled out the chair to sit down. He was going to ask if she had recently injured herself, but thought better of it just in case it was more than a temporary condition.

"Can I get you anything to drink before we start—coffee, water?"

"No, I'm fine, thanks. I had a Starbucks before I came over."

"Well, I hope you don't mind if I drink my coffee while we talk. If I don't get my morning caffeine, I'll pay for it later."

Casey nodded and smiled.

"Okay, then. Why don't we get right to it."

"That sounds good, Mr. Stilwell. Where would you like me to start?"

Steve picked up Casey's résumé, perusing it as he began to speak. "Like I said, very impressive. You did well at Penn State, you were a successful Army helo pilot, and you blew the curve at William and Mary. On top of that, you had a clerkship with a well-respected federal judge in Norfolk. It seems like you could work anywhere you want. So my big question is, why here?"

"That's pretty simple, Mr. Stilwell," Casey began matter-of-factly. "I wrote you the letter because I really want to work for you. I've been in Norfolk for the last two years, so I read about you in the newspaper when you saved that old German man. That's when I told myself I needed to meet you."

"Meeting me and working with me are two completely different things, Casey. Can you elaborate on the working part?" Steve set Casey's résumé aside in anticipation of her response.

"Sure," Casey replied, not skipping a beat. "You've got a great reputation as a trust and estates attorney, but you need a litigator to round out your practice. I can do that for you."

Steve liked her answer—it showed she had chutzpah. She wasn't afraid to be honest with him and call things the way she saw them. He pressed her to see how she would respond to even more probing questions.

"I don't see where you've got litigation experience, though. You've clerked for a trial judge, but you haven't tried cases. What makes you think you can jump right into court with some of the complex probate cases I take in?"

Casey didn't flinch. "I've studied lawyers in the courtroom up close and personal for the last two years, and I've watched my judge directing litigation like a maestro directs a symphony. I know I can do it. If I can fly helicopters for the Army in Iraq, I can certainly take a probate case into court."

"I like your confidence," Steve replied. "I've seen attorneys settle cases for less than they're worth because they're afraid to argue in front of a jury. But there's more to these cases than meets the eye, so you can't expect to start off trying complex cases by yourself. It'll take some time." Steve knew, though, that once Casey's experience matched her self-confidence, she would be a real weapon in the courtroom. He'd have to mentor her, but so far, she looked like a good investment.

"That's no problem, Mr. Stilwell," Casey replied. "I want you to teach me." She paused for a moment. "And, there is one more thing ...."

"What's that?"

"It's the other major reason I want to work for you. I know you'll understand my veteran's status."

"Well, of course I do. I really admire your military service."

"You know when you said there is more to litigating than meets the eye? Well, there's actually more to my veteran's status than meets the eye."

"I'm not sure I know what you mean. You'll have to give me a little more than that." Steve knew Casey received an honorable discharge from the Army, so he wasn't worried about misconduct. He figured she was still in the Reserves and would need to be out of the office to drill with her unit one weekend a month and two weeks a year. He supported the Reserves and could deal with that as long as she scheduled her legal commitments around her military duties.

"Well, as I mentioned, I was an Army helo pilot."

"Sure, I believe you were part of Operation Provide Comfort II in Iraq."

"That's right. Well, on my last mission, we had an engine malfunction and we couldn't save it. The helo crashed and my copilot was killed. It all happened so fast." For the first time, Casey hesitated. Steve wondered if she was changing her mind about telling him what happened, but she picked up her story where she left off.

"The rescue team literally had to cut me from the wreckage. I lost my right leg below the knee. The investigation concluded it was a mechanical failure and not pilot error, but that didn't bring my copilot back. So in the spirit of full disclosure, sometimes I need to schedule appointments with the VA hospital in Hampton, either for my leg or to help me deal with the aftermath of the crash. I figured you'd understand my situation better than someone who hadn't served in the military." Casey's face creased around her eyes as she spoke, her tension palpable. Steve could tell this was not an easy disclosure.

"Listen, Casey …. May I call you Casey?"

"Sure," Casey said, nodding. She looked at him with sad but hopeful eyes. Steve sensed she needed him to reach out to her.

"I understand and I'm proud of your service in the Army. I'd be honored to have you join my practice. Just plan your schedule to minimize conflicts and we'll make it work. How does that sound?"

"That's sounds great, Mr. Stilwell," Casey replied, the sparkle returning to her eyes. "But I don't want you to hire me out of pity."

"First of all, I don't feel sorry for you. I admire you. Second, with your résumé, the only way I wasn't going to hire you was if you bombed the interview, and you certainly haven't done that. So now that we're past the preliminaries, let's talk salary. I can start you off at fifty thousand dollars. Once your billings exceed that, we can talk about a raise. I'll also make sure you get the vacation you need and time to work out, just like in the Army. Those are things the big firms won't offer but I can. What do you think?"

"Wow, I didn't expect an offer right here and now, but I accept!" Casey's face broke into a wide smile. "I really appreciate you giving me this opportunity. I promise you won't regret it."

"You've earned it, Casey, and I'm looking forward to having you in the office. Along those lines, when would you be able to start?"

"I can start right away if you need me to. I'll just commute from Norfolk until I can find a place to live in Williamsburg."

Before Steve could continue, Marjorie knocked on the door.

"Mr. Stilwell, I'm sorry to interrupt y'all, but Noriko Stokes is here to see you. She says she's a friend of yours and needs to speak to you right away. She says it's an emergency." Marjorie mouthed, "She's crying," so Steve and Casey could see what she was saying, but Noriko Stokes, who was somewhere behind her in the lobby, could not.

"Got it, Marjorie," Steve replied. "Please tell Mrs. Stokes I'll be right with her. Casey and I just need to finish up."

"Okay, Mr. Stilwell." Marjorie turned and scurried back into the lobby.

"Sorry to cut our meeting short, Casey, but it sounds like this is something I need to take. We'll have plenty of time to continue our discussion."

"That's no problem, Mr. Stilwell. I understand completely. The only thing we didn't settle was when you want me to start."

"Oh yeah, that's where we were. You'll see that's one of the problems with working with me; I tend to forget things every now and then. If it weren't for Marjorie keeping track for me, I'd have lost my law license a long time ago." Then, finally getting back to the point, he added, "How about you start next

Thursday, June first? That's after Memorial Day and it'll give you a little time for the transition. Does that work?"

"That works fine, Mr. Stilwell. Thanks so much for giving me this opportunity."

Steve put his hands on the table and pushed back his chair, giving him room to stand. Casey followed suit. They shook hands as they made their way to the door.

"Oh, there are a couple more things," Steve remembered, pausing before they went out into the lobby.

"What do you need, Mr. Stilwell?"

"First, now that you're working here, please call me Steve, not Mr. Stilwell. I didn't insist on that early enough with Marjorie and now she refuses to change, so I want to start right with you. Okay?"

"Okay, I can do that … with a little practice."

"Great. Second, see Marjorie on the way out, let her know I've hired you, and give her your contact info. She may need some additional information to make sure we're ready for you on Thursday."

"That's easy," Casey replied.

"All right then. Have a great holiday weekend and I'll look forward to seeing you next week."

"You, too, Mr. Stilwell … I mean, Steve." Casey smiled awkwardly as she left his office and walked toward Marjorie's desk.

Steve was pleased with his decision to hire Casey. Although the offer was spontaneous and he knew Marjorie would scold him because he hadn't spoken to Casey's references, he already sensed a professional chemistry between them. Just based upon her answers, he felt she would add vigor and enthusiasm to a law practice that was starting to drift toward the mundane. He couldn't let himself get stuck in a rut, and now he had the added responsibility of keeping the practice interesting and challenging for Casey. He didn't have time to revel in his hiring decision, however, for Marjorie returned to the door just moments after Casey departed.

"Here's Mrs. Stokes, Mr. Stilwell," Marjorie said as she escorted Noriko Stokes into his office. "Is there anything else you need?"

"No thanks, Marjorie," Steve replied, walking to greet Noriko. As he approached the well-dressed Japanese woman in her mid-forties, she burst into tears and dropped to the floor, crying uncontrollably. His concerns about being stuck in a mundane law practice were about to evaporate.

5

Same day—Friday, 26 May 2000
Williamsburg, Virginia

STEVE RUSHED TO NORIKO'S SIDE, GOT down on his knees, and held her by her shoulders to steady her. "Noriko, what's the matter?" He presumed the news wasn't good, but his mind wouldn't let him speculate on what might be wrong. Marjorie also heard Noriko crying and rushed into the room to help.

"Mr. Stilwell, what's the matter? Did she fall? Should I call an ambulance?"

"No, that won't be necessary, Marjorie. But can you help me get Noriko to a chair?"

"Sure," Marjorie responded, bending down to take one of Noriko's arms. Noriko was short and slender, but her emotional collapse made her unable to stand, so Steve and Marjorie had to take her by the arms and pull her upright. At six feet one and 175 pounds, Steve was in great shape, albeit with a little gray hair around the edges, and Marjorie was a forty-three-year-old fitness buff, but when the two tugged on Noriko, she was like a leaf bag filled with sand. The two struggled to get her to her feet. Only when Steve wriggled his head under Noriko's arm so he could use his shoulder as leverage were they able to bring her to her feet and pour her into one of the chairs in front of his desk.

"I'll go get Mrs. Stokes a glass of water," Marjorie declared. "Are you okay staying with her?"

"Yes," Steve answered. "I'll be fine until you get back."

"Steve," a voice called from the door of his office. "Is there anything I can do to help?" Casey poked her head in just as Marjorie was leaving to get the water. "I heard crying and didn't know whether to come back. But it looks like you can use another woman here, so if there is something I can do, please let me help."

"Please, Casey, come on in. Let me introduce you to Noriko Stokes. She's the wife of one of my best friends from my days in the Navy JAG Corps." Steve thought Casey's arrival might be just the distraction Noriko needed to regain her composure.

"Noriko, this is Casey Pantel. She's a former Army helo pilot. She's working with me now and I think you might enjoy meeting her."

"Hello, Noriko," Casey said, kneeling in front of Noriko and gently gathering both of her hands in her own. As she did, Marjorie walked back into the office with a glass of ice water. Casey reached up and took the water from Marjorie and held it out for Noriko. "Noriko, Marjorie's brought you a glass of ice-cold water. You'll feel a lot better if you take a sip." As she offered the water, Casey guided Noriko's hands to the glass. Noriko took the glass with two shaky hands and slowly sipped as Casey stayed close by.

The cool water injected life into Noriko's features and the color started to return to her skin. Steve stepped back and half sat on the corner of his desk, relieved Casey had come in and calmed Noriko.

"Thanks for bringing the water, Marjorie," Steve said, acknowledging her contribution. "I think Mrs. Stokes is going to be okay now, so we can take it from here." Turning his attention back to Noriko, he added, "if you're okay with it, I'd like to have Casey stay here while we talk. As you can see, she's a pretty special person."

Steve winked at Casey and telegraphed a small grin. Casey smiled back and eased her way up until she was able to sit in the other chair in front of Steve's desk. A small table with a brass lamp separated her and Noriko, so Casey sat on the edge of the chair where she could maintain eye contact.

"Do you think you can talk now, Noriko?" Steve asked. "If not, just let me know when you're ready. We've got all the time you need."

Noriko looked up at Steve and took a deep breath, then wiped the tears from her eyes. "I think I'm okay for now," she replied in the perfect English of a second-generation Japanese-American, or Nisei, born in California. "Thank you both for being so patient with me. I've had a very hard week."

"So what's going on?" Steve asked, interpreting Noriko's statement as an invitation to explore what she meant.

"Ric's in a lot of trouble." Noriko started to sob, interrupting her progress, but she caught herself. "You've got to help him, Steve." Tears again welled up in her eyes. "He would never do what they said he did."

"Who's *they*?" Steve asked.

"The Vietnamese police."

"The Vietnamese police?" Steve asked. "I take it he was in Vietnam?"

"Yes, that's where he was. I mean, that's where he is now, too."

"What in the world is he doing in Vietnam?"

"A man from Houston asked Ric to go with him to Vietnam after they exchanged some emails. He paid Ric twenty-five thousand dollars and promised another twenty-five when they got back. It had something to do with an article Ric wrote a few years ago."

The large amount of cash sounded suspicious to Steve. Ric was an experienced attorney and a respected former Navy JAG Corps officer, so he assumed he could look out for himself. Still, the story didn't sound promising. He needed to cut to the chase and find out what was going on.

"So, what do the Vietnamese police say Ric did?" he asked, steering the conversation back to where it was before his questioning took it off on a tangent.

"They said they found heroin in his suitcase. Ric swears he doesn't know how it got there."

Steve's heart sank. Drugs were what immediately came to mind when he put Vietnam together with the large cash payments, but he just couldn't fathom Ric Stokes being involved with drugs. He suppressed the thought, hoping Noriko's answers would lead to a plausible—and defensible—explanation.

"What about the man he was traveling with? Could he have put it there? I mean, it doesn't sound like Ric knew this guy before they went on the trip."

"That's the worst part," Noriko added, again forcing back the tears. "The man he went with is dead."

"Wait a minute," Steve interrupted, not believing what he'd just heard. He thought drugs were as bad as it was going to get. This took the situation to an entirely different, and exponentially more serious, level. "Did you say the man he traveled with is dead?"

"That's what they told me. The Vietnamese police said he died of a heroin overdose. They found him dead in their hotel room. Ric told the Vietnamese police he found the man in bed with a prostitute, but she left before the police got there, so they don't believe Ric about that either. And they found heroin in Ric's suitcase. Now Ric's in jail in Vietnam and they're telling me they can't get him out."

"Who's the 'they' you've been talking to?" Casey asked, inserting herself into the conversation. "Have you spoken to the Vietnamese police?"

"No," Noriko replied, the questions helping her to maintain her composure. "The State Department in Washington called. They've been talking to the U.S. Embassy in Hanoi and passing information to me. The embassy said they've been allowed to visit Ric once. They said he's doing okay, but he was pretty beat up when he was arrested. Ric won't say how that happened. I'm sure he's afraid the police will hurt him if he says anything bad about them."

"I still can't believe Ric had anything to do with drugs," Steve asserted. "Something has to be going on here." He stood up and started walking around his desk to his chair, talking as he went. "I know I shouldn't speculate, but maybe he got duped by the guy he went over there with. Maybe the guy thought a former senior Navy officer would provide the cover he needed to bring drugs back into the United States without U.S. Customs getting suspicious."

Steve paused. His theory didn't wash. Ric wouldn't be so easily fooled. He was too smart. There had to be more to the story, which just didn't add up. Talking to someone at the State Department might get him ground truth. Noriko was too emotional at this point anyway, and it was clear she only had second-hand information.

"Steve, can you help Ric, please?" Noriko begged. "Can you go over there and bring him back?"

"Of course I'll help, Noriko, don't worry about that," Steve assured her, stopping short of promising to bring Ric back. "First I'd like to make some calls before committing to going over there. I want to speak with the State Department. They may not speak with me, though, unless you and Ric retain me as your lawyer. I won't charge you anything, of course, but we should draw up the paperwork so it'll be official."

"I can't thank you enough, Steve," Noriko replied, cupping her face in her hands and starting to cry again. "I just … I just … I just didn't know what to do or who to turn to. I wish I'd thought to call you as soon as I found out."

"When did you find out?" Casey asked.

"Last week. Ric was arrested on May fourteenth and I found out two days later. Is that a problem?"

"Don't worry about it," Steve reassured her. "I'm sure the additional time allowed the embassy and the State Department to figure out what happened. I'll make the call this afternoon. Casey and I will be sure to keep you informed. Does that work for you, Noriko?"

"It does," she said, nodding her head in an exaggerated manner, conveying that her emotions were still in control. Still, she looked like a different woman than the one who'd walked into his office twenty minutes earlier. Now she stood up from her chair under her own power. Casey rose with her and took her by the arm, helping her toward the door.

"We can stop and talk with Marjorie on the way out and get the paperwork Steve mentioned taken care of," Casey said, still guiding Noriko by the arm. "Then Steve and I will work this matter for you, I promise. I can't imagine how hard this must be, but we'll do everything humanly possible to get to the bottom of it."

Noriko didn't say anything; she just locked eyes with Casey and forced a small but grateful smile.

"I'll get back to you soon," Steve reiterated as Casey led Noriko through the door. He just hoped he'd have something positive to report. Being arrested for possession of heroin in Vietnam couldn't be good, and the fact that Ric was in Vietnamese custody was even worse. Possession was nine tenths of the law when it came to avoiding trial in a foreign country. Steve couldn't fathom Vietnamese authorities releasing Ric on his own recognizance or allowing him to post bail—if Vietnam even had such a thing. He and Casey had some research to do, and he had to call the State Department to try and get the full scoop.

One thing was for sure, though: he was glad he'd hired Casey. She'd proved her mettle with her masterful handling of Noriko, and that was just the tip of the iceberg. He'd need lots of help doing research and juggling his other cases. But one aspect of their work arrangement already needed to be changed: he couldn't wait until next Thursday for her to start. Her first day with the firm was already well underway.

6

━━∿━━

Same day—Friday, 26 May 2000
Williamsburg, Virginia

AFTER NORIKO LEFT, STEVE, CASEY, AND Marjorie regrouped around the
conference table in Steve's office. The story of Ric Stokes' ordeal hit Steve
harder than Casey or Marjorie because only he knew the man. He simply
couldn't picture him having anything to do with drugs, other than prosecuting
drug offenders during his early days as a Navy JAG. Steve was still shaking his
head in denial when he started the conversation.

"I'm in absolute shock," he declared. "I can't thank you both enough for
helping me get through that. It would have been a disaster without you." Steve
fought to keep his emotions under control now that Noriko was gone. Though
determined to help his dear friend, he felt powerless. Ric was locked in a cell
halfway around the world. Conditions had to be godawful. Worse yet, nothing
he could do would bring immediate relief.

"I'm glad we could help," Casey replied, as if sensing Steve's struggle. "Have
you ever handled a case like this before?"

"Believe it or not, lots of 'em. When I was stationed overseas, I used to
work with foreign police and prosecutors all the time trying to get our sailors
out of jail. But I never had to do it for my best friend."

"At least that's a start," Casey said, remaining positive. "So what do you
need us to do?"

Steve wasn't ready to answer that yet. He needed to reconcile what he
knew about Ric with what Noriko told him. "I'll tell you why this situation
doesn't make sense to me. Ric used to prosecute drug cases in the Navy with a

vengeance. He hated everything about drugs because he saw growing up how they ravaged the lives of his friends. In fact, that was one of the main reasons he went to the inner city to teach instead of going to work for a big law firm after he retired from the JAG Corps a few years ago. Every day he carried on his own personal crusade against the drug culture teaching high school, and I know his students respected him for it because he'd been a senior officer in the Navy. He wanted to show them a good education offered more than drugs. He'd never do anything to jeopardize that work, or more important, his personal example as a retired African-American Naval officer. Never."

Neither Casey nor Marjorie said anything. Steve needed to work this out for himself. He sat quietly for a moment, resting his elbows on the table and massaging his temples with his fingers as he looked at his glass-covered shadow box on the wall. The rectangular maple display case, given to him when he retired, contained an American flag folded into a triangle at one corner. The remainder of the box housed all his military decorations, mounted on a dark-blue felt background. To those who knew what they meant, the medals and awards recounted his Navy career. To Steve, they symbolized his military bond with Ric and his duty to help him. The box also reminded him to be strong.

"All right, here are my thoughts for the way ahead," Steve pronounced, sounding once again like the Navy captain memorialized in the shadow box. "And feel free to chime in if you have any suggestions. Casey, instead of starting next Thursday, let's consider today your first day. After you sign whatever paperwork Marjorie needs, I'd like you to research Vietnamese drug-trafficking laws. We need to know what we're up against. Once you get that done, see if there are any treaties between the U.S. and Vietnam that might come into play here, like an extradition treaty or a drug-trafficking treaty. One of them might allow the U.S. government to intervene. Can you do that?"

"I'm on it," Casey said. "I'll need a place to work, a telephone and computer access, and a couple of minutes to get oriented, but I'm in."

"I can set you up in Mr. Smyth's old office," Marjorie offered, referring to the partner Steve bought out a little over a year after joining the trusts and estates practice. "It'll take an hour or so. I'll have to update the computer and clean up a little, but you'll be up and running in no time."

"Perfect," Steve proclaimed. "I'll leave that to you two. In the meantime, I'm gonna see if I can talk to someone at the State Department to find out what's really going on here."

"Do you need me to arrange the call?" Marjorie asked.

"Thanks, but I'd rather have you get Casey up and running as soon as possible. I had an assignment at the State Department a few years ago, so I've got someone I can call to see if I can extract information. If that works for everyone, I say we get started."

Marjorie smiled and rendered Steve a quick salute. "Aye, aye, Captain!" she said. "Follow me, Casey, and I'll show you your new office." Casey nodded and trailed after Marjorie, leaving Steve to make his call.

Steve logged on to his computer and navigated to the State Department's website. One option was to contact the Vietnam desk officer in the East Asian and Pacific Affairs Bureau. The desk officer would have, or could get, the latest information about Ric's arrest directly from the embassy in Hanoi. The problem was, Steve didn't know the desk officer, who might well blow him off. What he needed was someone on the inside who could either introduce him to the desk officer or glean every bit of available information about the case and then relay it to him.

Steve's ticket was Tad Schwartz. Tall, gangly, disheveled, and utterly brilliant, Tad was the Assistant Legal Adviser in charge of advising the East Asian and Pacific Affairs Bureau. His legal team was known by its State Department office designation, "L/EAP", for Legal/East Asian and Pacific Affairs. Steve worked for Tad for a couple of years on loan from the Navy, so Tad knew Steve well and would trust him. Of course, Tad would never disclose anything confidential, but he also wouldn't hold anything back if it was permissible to release the information, even it if was sensitive. Harvard Law educated and an international lawyer with over twenty years of diplomatic experience, Tad was a key person to get in Steve's corner.

After a little more digging, Steve found a telephone directory on the State Department website listing Tad Schwartz's office telephone number. He pulled out a yellow legal pad from the second drawer on the right side of his new Amish-made cherry executive desk and grabbed a pen to take notes. Then he called Tad Schwartz. Someone answered on the third ring.

"L/EAP, may I help you, please?" The female voice sounded pleasant and sincere.

"Yes, may I please speak with Tad Schwartz?"

"May I tell him who's calling?"

"Yes, it's Steve Stilwell."

"One moment, please."

"Steve Stilwell, is that really you?"

"It sure is, Tad. How are things going?"

"Great, just as busy as ever. Things just never seem to slow down. So what's up with you?"

"Well, I retired from the Navy and went into private practice in Williamsburg, Virginia, a couple of years ago. That's actually why I'm calling.

I've got a case I'm hoping you can give me information on or point me to someone who can."

"I'll do what I can. What's the case?"

"It involves an old Navy JAG Corps buddy of mine, Ric Stokes. It looks like he's been arrested in Vietnam on drug-trafficking charges."

"Yep, I'm familiar with the case. The Vietnam desk's consulted me, so there's not too much I can say without talking to my client first. I can say that the Vietnamese authorities think they have a solid case. He was found with a kilo of pure heroin in his suitcase and the guy he was traveling with died of a heroin overdose. Doesn't sound too good to me. Do you know why he was over there?"

"All I know is it had something to do with an article Ric published a few years back. If it's the paper I'm thinking of, it involved military aircraft shot down during the Cold War. Not sure how that ties in with the trip, though." Steve held back on disclosing Ric's compensation arrangement. He didn't want to say anything that might make matters worse for Ric. He also wasn't sure what Tad already knew but couldn't talk about. "Any thoughts on what I should do?"

"If you've got the time and money, I'd get over there as soon as possible to try and meet with him. He'll definitely need a local attorney if he hasn't already gotten one, and you can help him arrange that. The consulate can help with that as well. If the local attorney knows you're involved, it'll help ensure your friend gets a good defense."

"That's great advice, Tad, thanks. I'll start packing my bags."

"I'll give the desk officer a heads-up you'll be traveling. She can help expedite a visa from the Vietnamese Embassy and can give you a consulate point of contact in Ho Chi Minh City. Any idea of when you'll be able to travel?"

"Tomorrow, if I can get the visa," Steve replied. "I really appreciate your help with this, Tad. I know Ric Stokes will appreciate it, too."

"No problem, but I need to give you a word of caution. The drug cartels in Vietnam are notoriously violent. If they think you pose a danger, they won't hesitate to slit your throat in broad daylight and publicize your death as a warning to others. They've penetrated the local government, so you won't know if you're talking to a policeman or a judge who's on the take until it's too late. The consulate may be able to help, but I'd be wary of trusting anyone."

"Thanks, Tad. I'll watch my back," Steve promised. "The last thing I want is to spend the rest of my retirement in a Vietnamese jail. I'll give you a call once I get back."

"Good luck, Steve."

"Thanks. I think I'm really going to need it this time."

7

―――

Monday, 29 May 2000
Williamsburg, Virginia

Casey opened the front door to Steve Stilwell's law office building on North Henry Street. It was just a few minutes before eight a.m. on Memorial Day, and Marjorie was already seated at her desk, ready for the holiday work routine to begin. Casey painted a smile on her face and struggled to be outwardly excited about her first full day on the job. She wasn't sure if she could pull it off. Although she had come a long way since her helicopter crash, Memorial Day triggered painful memories.

"Hello, Marjorie," Casey announced, stopping in front of the receptionist's desk. "How was your weekend?"

"Hi, Casey." Marjorie swiveled on her chair to look up at the firm's new associate. "It was nice, but a little too short. Have you heard from Mr. Stilwell?"

"Not yet, but I think he's still en route. As I recall, he gets in very early on Tuesday morning Vietnam time, which is eleven hours ahead of us. That means he'll arrive this afternoon our time. I wouldn't be surprised if he checks in to see if we've found out anything new." Casey started moving in the direction of her office. She wanted to sit by herself for a while before trying to be more sociable.

"You look like you're moving a little slowly this morning, Casey." The concern was evident in Marjorie's voice. "Are you sure your weekend went okay?"

"It was a little hectic," Casey admitted, pivoting on her natural leg to face Marjorie again. "I checked out a bunch of apartments and found a place to live off Ironbound Road. The lease starts this weekend, so I can move in on Saturday."

"Why don't you let me help you?" Marjorie asked. "Moving's a tough job, and I imagine with your leg, it's difficult to carry heavy stuff."

Marjorie's comment surprised Casey. She'd worked with her for less than a day and Marjorie already felt comfortable talking about her leg as if it were routine. Normally people, even family, avoided mentioning her leg because they didn't know how to deal with it. They either looked away or stared; both reactions made her uncomfortable. Occasionally a young child would say something or ask her about it. Embarrassed mothers would try to squelch their child's curiosity, but she never minded answering the kids in an age-appropriate way. She just wanted to be accepted for who she was.

She walked back to Marjorie's desk and rested her fingertips on the desktop. Fighting back tears, she said, "Marjorie, you can't imagine how much I appreciate that."

"Of course I can," Marjorie replied, reaching for some folders in her in box, as if unaware the conversation had taken a deeper turn. "Nobody likes to move by themselves."

"Not just that. You felt comfortable talking about my leg without making it a big deal. That means a lot to me."

"Listen, honey," Marjorie said, her Tidewater accent thickening. She leaned forward over her desk as if she were going to divulge the secret formula to Coca Cola. "I've been the only woman working in this office for over ten years. I've been kind of a mom to the attorneys here. They're men, and God knows, they need the help." Marjorie sat back in her chair with a look of exasperation on her face to drive the point home. "They count on me to tell it like it is and I do. I'll do the same with you."

"Please, Marjorie, treat me just like you do Mr. Stilwell. I don't want to be any different."

"But you *are* different, Casey." Marjorie paused, her expression serious. "You're a woman, and I just want to shout for joy that there's finally another woman in the office to talk to." Marjorie leaned forward again, as if they might be overheard. "We've got to stick together. I'll cover your back and you cover mine. It'll take both of us to cover Mr. Stilwell's. As you can see, he gets caught up in the craziest cases."

"You've got a deal, Marjorie. How about this weekend? You help me move and I'll buy lunch."

"As Mr. Stilwell would say, 'Sounds like a plan.' Now, I've distracted you long enough. Why don't you go ahead and settle into your office? I'll bring you a cup of coffee."

"Thanks, Marjorie ... for everything." Casey grinned as she headed to her office. She'd felt down this morning and her conversation with Marjorie helped. It wasn't so much the loss of her leg that bothered her. She'd learned to cope with that, at least as much as anyone could cope with such a thing. It hadn't been easy, though. Months at Walter Reed Army Medical Center in Washington, DC, as an inpatient, followed by more months of physical therapy and learning to use her prosthetic leg. She wasn't the only one there, though, and having others in the same predicament helped. In fact, she felt fortunate because she saw others whose injuries were much worse.

What she didn't see were other women. She was the only female amputee in the Center. The others were men. They were part of her family now, and they treated her like a sister. But they couldn't understand what it felt like to be a woman who suddenly didn't have a leg below the knee. They didn't have to look at the legs of beautiful models every time they waited in line at a grocery store, realizing they could never, ever look like that again. And they couldn't understand the anguish of never being able to wear a skirt again without displaying a metal leg protruding from a socket strapped to the fragmented remains of a once shapely calf muscle. It was months before she could look into a full-length mirror, and just the thought of shopping for shoes made her cry. So did the burning sensation in her right foot. But when she looked down, there was no foot, only pain. The doctors called it phantom pain, but it was pain, nonetheless.

Ultimately it was her parents, her Army training, and her soldiers that got her past the physical trauma. Her mom and dad were by her bedside as soon as she arrived at Walter Reed. They took shifts making sure the already attentive nurses adjusted her position in bed or brought her whatever she wanted to eat. Her dad left after two weeks to go back to work, but her mom stayed on, reviving her spirit as only a mother could, until she felt confident she could survive in her apartment by herself.

Years of Army training built on her parents' efforts by driving into her the primacy of accomplishing her mission. Her mission now was to get back on her feet, even if one of those feet was artificial, and be mobile and self-sufficient. Soldiers from her former command visited her in the hospital and in her apartment after they returned from their deployment. They encouraged, or more accurately they *directed* her to get back to the Army and flying; failure was not an option.

It wasn't the physical wounds, though, that caused her to take a tack away from the Army. In fact, once she was fitted with her prosthetic leg and learned to walk and even run again, she could have returned to a flying status if she'd wanted to. But she didn't. The possibility of flying reminded her that her former copilot would never fly again, or never see his wife and daughter again, for that matter, because he was dead. There was nothing Casey, her parents, her soldiers, or the Army could do about that.

It wasn't for lack of trying. The Army officer investigating the crash found in his report that Casey was in no way at fault for the accident. The helo experienced a catastrophic dual-engine failure due to a massive hydraulic system breakdown. "There was nothing, repeat, nothing, Captain Pantel could have done to thwart or lessen the severity of the crash once the aircraft started to plunge toward the ground."

Casey understood that the report exonerated her, but that still didn't explain why she survived and her copilot, an officer she was honor bound to protect and defend, didn't. To her, his death was mission failure and her subconscious wouldn't let her forget it. Whenever current events pushed her guilt to some distant recess in her memory, a vivid nightmare would bring it back again, replaying the crash in three-dimensional horror. But instead of depicting what actually transpired in the cockpit—Casey and her copilot calmly executing emergency recovery procedures just as the Army had trained them to do—her dream cemented her behind her pilot's seat, unable to reach the control stick or foot pedals or to take any action to avert the crash, while her copilot looked back at her, screaming, "Do something, Casey. Do something!"

Worse yet, Casey wasn't physically able to attend her copilot's funeral at Arlington National Cemetery in the month following the crash. It was unfinished business, an open wound in her heart even visits to his gravesite hadn't closed, and sometimes nightmares about the funeral drove her into a gloom so deep, she couldn't emerge from it on her own. That's why she needed a job near a VA hospital and a boss who understood the hidden costs of military service.

Marjorie poked her head into Casey's office and knocked with the hand not carrying the steaming cup of black coffee. "Okay to come in?"

"Sure, Marjorie."

Marjorie brought the cup over to Casey and set it on the big cherry desk that used to belong to Steve Stilwell's former partner and mentor, William P. Smythe. As with the previous occupant of Steve's office, Mr. Smythe was from the old school of attorneys, so his office looked prehistoric. Since many of Mr. Smythe's clients were elderly people who had him draft wills and trusts for them before they died, the décor worked just fine. But Casey already had a new look in mind, a brighter ambience that would help her fight her periodic bouts with depression. Upbeat furnishings and state-of-the-art technology would also help her brand herself as competent and relevant to a younger clientele, furthering the youthful shift Steve began when he joined the practice two years before.

"Thanks so much, Marjorie." Casey took a quick sip of coffee and set the cup back down on the saucer. "Would you mind sitting down for a minute so we can think about what we need to do today?"

"Of course, but first let me get my notepad." Marjorie scampered out of the office and was back sitting in one of the two wingback armchairs in front of Casey's desk before Casey finished a second sip of her jet-black brew. "All set," Marjorie announced.

"Okay," Casey began. "To be honest, I'm not really sure what I need to be doing. Last Friday, we found the reference to the 1994 agreement on diplomatic access to American citizens arrested in Vietnam. Steve's already got that, and it didn't offer much help anyway. Today I was going to try and get in touch with the wife of the man who died of the overdose in Saigon and see if she'll talk to me. I also wanted to research the drug trade in Vietnam. Is there anything else I should be doing?"

Marjorie shook her head. "I don't know what else we can do until we hear from Mr. Stilwell."

"Then let me see if I can find the name of the guy who died." Casey dug through the notes of her conversations with Noriko Stokes. In addition to speaking with Noriko in Steve's office last Friday, she'd called her over the weekend for more information. She flipped through the pages of her yellow legal pad until she found the name of the man Ric had traveled with on page four.

"Okay. The guy who died was Ryan Eversall, and he lived in Houston, Texas. All Noriko remembers is that he owned a car dealership and was married—or so she believes. Do you think you can track down his wife, if he has one, and set up a call for me?"

"Unless she's got an unlisted number, I'll find her," Marjorie replied confidently. "In fact, I've got a few tricks up my sleeve even if she has an unlisted number. It just takes a little longer." A mischievous grin broke out on Marjorie's face.

"I don't even want to know," Casey chuckled, giving Marjorie an exaggerated glower of disapproval. But the jovial interlude faded quickly. "Oh, and there's one more call I need to make today."

"Who to?" Marjorie asked, ready to copy the name and number onto her notepad.

"Elizabeth McMichaels."

"Who's that?"

"The wife of my copilot who died in my helicopter crash. I've got her number and I'll call her myself directly from my desk." Casey took a deep breath, the sadness of earlier this morning shadowing her face. Mechanically, she flipped the pages of her yellow legal pad back to their original position and set the pad off to the side of her desk. Suddenly, she felt older, much older. She leaned back in her chair with arms outstretched so she could grab onto the edge of the desk for support. "I couldn't go to my copilot's funeral since I was still in the hospital, so I call his wife every Memorial Day. I don't want her to think I've forgotten her husband. It's the hardest phone call I make all year."

Marjorie got up, aligned her chair with the one on the other side of the table, and started retreating to the door. "It may be hard, Casey, but I'm sure she appreciates it. It's nice of you."

Casey didn't hear her. She was already thinking of what she had to say to Elizabeth McMichaels. She felt an itchy perspiration bead on her forehead just behind her hairline, and her heart beat faster until she thought she could actually hear it. She was on her way to a bad place, like she had been when she got up in the morning after dreaming about the crash. Why did it have to be Memorial Day again? And why did he have to die?

"HELLO, McMICHAELS' RESIDENCE."

"Hi Leeza, this is Miss Pantel. Is your mom there?"

"Hi Miss Pantel. She's hanging her coat in the closet. I'll go get her."

"Thanks, Leeza." Leeza was only four-and-a-half years old when her father died. Casey figured she had little memory of him. The thought made the pit in her stomach grow even deeper. She picked up a pen and set it down again; her phantom right foot tightened and throbbed.

"Hello?" The woman's voice was familiar, soft and calming. It had a soothing effect.

"Liz, hi, it's Casey. I just wanted to call and let you know how proud I am to have served with Jim."

"Casey, it's so good to hear from you!" Liz's voice conveyed genuine excitement and warmth, like she was talking to family.

"Leeza sure sounds grown up. She must be almost eleven by now."

"She is, Casey, you won't believe it when you see her again. She's a beautiful child and she really has her father's eyes. You'd see it right away."

"I'm so sorry about Jim, Liz. It must be hard for you on Memorial Day. I know it is for me."

"Please don't apologize, Casey," Liz reassured her, just as she did every year. "Jim always said you were the best pilot in the squadron and he really admired you. I'm glad you were flying with him that day. I know that gave him peace and it's given me peace, too. So how are you doing?"

Casey hesitated. "Well, I'm actually at work right now. I've started a new job with a small law firm in Williamsburg. My boss is a retired Navy JAG. I think this is exactly what I needed. In fact, I'm moving to Williamsburg on Saturday."

"That sounds great, Casey. I'm so glad to hear it. Now how's your leg? Are you still having problems with it?" This was the second time today her leg was the subject of routine conversation. That also put Casey more at ease.

"Actually, it's doing quite well now. I've even started running again. I think I've finally rounded the corner."

"I'm so happy to hear that, Casey. You deserve more happiness in your life. I hope you find it."

"Well, I better let you get back to Leeza. Please let her know I can't wait to see her again."

"I will, Casey. It was so good talking to you. I really appreciate your calls and your thoughts about Jim. It means a lot to me."

"To me, too, Liz. To me too."

Casey hung up the phone and sat motionless, frozen in time. Liz had been able to deal with Jim's death. Why couldn't she? She had to stand up and get some fresh air before the venerable walls of her new office closed in on her. She walked quickly out and toward the front door.

"Marjorie, I'm going to run over to DoG Street. I'll be back in a few minutes." Casey couldn't hold back her tears.

"Is everything all right?" Marjorie asked, with barely enough time to swivel her chair before Casey bolted outside.

Casey didn't answer. Turning right at the tree-lined brick sidewalk, she strode past the colonial quadrangle on the corner of Prince George Street. She walked faster than usual, which made her limp more pronounced. She fixed her tear-filled eyes on the sidewalk, trying to flush away all painful memories so she could focus on the Stokes case. She wouldn't be successful—she never was—but she needed to go through the motions anyway. She had no choice.

AFTER ANOTHER STRONG DOSE OF COFFEE from one of the shops along the commercial section of the Duke of Gloucester Street—or "DoG" Street (pronounced like the canine) as the locals called the main road in Colonial Williamsburg—Casey worked her way back to the office. She convinced Marjorie she was okay and that the best thing for her was to dive into her work, which she did with gusto.

Getting up from her chair to stretch her muscles after a two-hour research session at her computer, she strolled over to the door with a pen and pad of yellow stickies in hand. She was feeling better now, her call to Liz McMichaels behind her. She attributed her most recent nightmares and anxiety to the buildup for the call, and now that it was over, she could feel her equilibrium returning. Her research was also sucking her deeper into the case, and she hoped her work would return her guilt to its mental cage—at least until something new came along to release it.

"Marjorie, by chance were you able to find out anything about Ryan Eversall's wife in Houston?" Casey leaned up against the doorframe with her left shoulder, shifting most of her weight to her natural leg. The sunshine pouring through the lobby window made her yellow blouse look brighter than when she was hunched over her keyboard at her desk.

"I actually talked to her," Marjorie answered proudly. "Her name is Angela Eversall. I found her name online in Ryan's obituary. She lives in West University Place in Houston, Texas."

"That's fantastic," said Casey, recognizing Marjorie's sense of accomplishment. "Did she say she'd speak with me?"

"Sort of. She's willing to talk to you, but she wants to meet you in person. She's afraid to talk over the phone."

"Did she say why?"

"At first she was afraid we were trying to sue her. I promised that wasn't the case and told her you just wanted to find out about the trip so you could get Mr. Stokes out of jail. When she still hesitated, I added it might also help clear her husband's name. That's when she agreed to talk to you, but not over the phone. She said she has the strangest feeling someone's been watching her."

"Hmmm," Casey murmured, pondering Marjorie's words. "That's certainly odd. Did she say why she thinks so?"

"Nope," Marjorie replied, shaking her head from side to side. "She said she doesn't see anything when she looks outside, but she feels it. She can't explain it."

"Then it looks like I'm going to Houston, doesn't it?"

"I've already made the reservations," Marjorie said with Radar O'Reilly-like efficiency. "I've got you on an eleven thirty flight tomorrow morning. She wants to meet with you tomorrow night at seven thirty. You fly back on Wednesday."

"Perfect."

"Oh, and there is one more thing."

"What's that?" Casey couldn't imagine what it might be.

Marjorie cocked her head to one side and forced a grin, as if preparing to make a proposition Casey would reject. "She wants you to drive around the block before you get there to see if you notice anything suspicious. I hope you don't mind, but I told her you'd be happy to do it."

"I don't mind at all," replied Casey, relieved the request wasn't more complex. "It's a small price to pay for the interview. I just hope she's stable enough to talk to me. She sounds like she's still reeling after her husband's death."

"She probably will be for some time, given the way he died. I mean, I can't imagine getting a call like that. You know, with the prostitute and all."

"I guess I'll find out tomorrow night, won't I?"

"You need to be careful, Casey," Marjorie said, transitioning to her maternal persona. "You don't know what that woman's capable of. I'm sure you and Mr. Stilwell can figure out another way to get the information if y'all really need to."

"Don't worry, Marjorie, I'll be safe. I know what it's like to go through a tough time, so maybe I can help her work her way through it. She might just need someone to talk to."

Dealing with two widows in one day might have dragged Casey deep into the doldrums, but she actually felt a strange sense of accomplishment. Her work was having the therapeutic effect she needed. Now she had to transform feeling better into results for Ric Stokes. That depended upon whether Angela Eversall turned out to be a credible witness or a paranoid widow grieving a possibly cheating husband. For Ric Stokes' sake, she hoped it was the former.

8

Tuesday, 30 May 2000, 8:30 a.m.
Ho Chi Minh City (Saigon)

"MR. STILWELL, YOUR TAXI IS HERE," the bellhop at the Le Dey Hotel announced.

Steve slid forward on the dark-brown leather sofa beneath the circular chandelier in the hotel lobby. Although he'd slept for only four hours, he felt rested. The mosquito netting he'd jury-rigged above his bed gave him the peace of mind he needed to drift off quickly without worrying about some rogue, malaria-infested mosquito with a vendetta against Americans. Also, arriving dead tired early in the morning helped him acclimate quickly to the local time zone. He was ready to sleep when he checked into his hotel, even though Saigon was on the other side of the International Date Line and eleven hours ahead of Williamsburg.

"Thank you," Steve replied, gathering his black leather planner as he stood up to make his way out. The bellhop held the lobby door and then hurried down the steps ahead of him to open the door of the white Toyota sedan waiting at the curb.

As soon as he hit the outside, the heat and humidity attacked his dark-gray wool-blend suit and made his exposed skin feel hot and sticky. At the bottom of the stairs, a short woman with high, round cheekbones, her skin raisined by years of sun, sizzled unknown meats and vegetables on the skillet of her dull, stainless-steel vendor's cart. Prepared dishes decorated the shelves behind a steam-coated glass window on the front of her cart, while two cartons of large brown eggs sat unrefrigerated in boxes on the blistering tile sidewalk. Nothing looked appetizing to Steve, but perhaps the locals thought differently. The woman didn't look up from her cooking when he walked by.

Steve hopped into the waiting cab and asked the driver to hold on for a moment while he reached into his wallet to get a tip for the bellhop. He pulled out a multi-pastel colored ten-thousand Dong note bearing a picture of "Uncle" Ho Chi Minh on the front and handed it to the bellhop, who smiled and said thank you as he closed the car door. This was Steve's first use of Vietnamese Dong, having exchanged one hundred U.S. dollars for over two million Dong at the Le Dey front desk. Not yet comfortable with the Vietnamese currency, he felt like he was parting with his youngest son's college tuition when he handed over the ten-thousand Dong note, but in reality, it wasn't even fifty cents. Still, the tip seemed significant to the bellhop.

"Good morning," Steve said to the driver as the taxi slid into the flow of traffic, or more accurately, motorbikes. The driver waved but didn't say anything. He gripped the steering wheel with both hands and gave the car some gas, repeatedly beeping the horn as he joined the melee. Helmeted riders on motorbikes, sometimes with families of four onboard, passed the slower moving car on both sides.

By the time they arrived in the middle of the first intersection, the light was already green. Countless motorbikes streamed through the intersection, like two unending columns of ants heading to picnics in opposite directions. Without waiting for a break in the oncoming traffic—there might never be one—the driver began a slow left turn, repeatedly beeping his horn as he crept forward directly into the oncoming column. The motorbikes parted like the Red Sea on both sides of the sedan, neither slowing down nor perturbed by the car's intrusion into their lanes. Other motorbikes making the same left turn drove on the left side of Steve's car, taking advantage of the wedge forged through the oncoming traffic. Once through the intersection, the driver drove until he could make a right turn on Nguyễn Thị Minh Khai, a larger road that took them most of the way to the front gate of the U.S. Consulate.

A couple of blocks past Saigon's historic Notre Dame Cathedral, the driver turned right onto a street bordered by a cream-colored security wall about ten feet high, with numerous treetops and green A-shaped roofs visible just inside the wall. Vietnamese police patrolled the sidewalk outside the compound, with security booths placed near the compound's corners. A large U.S. flag, partially obscured from view by the big trees lining the sidewalk, flapped above the compound. The driver pulled up to a pedestrian entrance with several green-trimmed glass doors leading to the inside, flanked on the left by a plaque on the wall that showed the seal of the State Department, its proud eagle indicating the facility belonged to the United States of America.

"Thanks for the ride," Steve said after carefully counting out what he owed in Vietnamese currency. He opened his door and stepped back into the sweltering heat and humidity. He was sweating even before the door closed. As he turned to look at the entrance to the compound, a young man in his late twenties pushed open one of the consulate's glass doors and headed in his direction. He was wearing a lightweight khaki linen suit with a white shirt and brown plaid tie. His dishwater-blond hair, twisted in humidity-enhanced curls, was much longer than Steve's, some of it even drifting over his ears and collar. The Consular officers he'd dealt with in his Navy days assisting wayward sailors overseas looked much more conservative, so Steve assumed the individual was part of the administrative staff.

"You must be Steve Stilwell," the young man said as he approached, extending his hand toward Steve. "I'm Robert Fowler, the consular officer assigned to monitor your client's case." He grasped Steve's hand and shook it vigorously, apparently not at all intimidated by their age difference. Steve concluded Fowler had to be assertive, given his position at the consulate. He couldn't convey weakness or he'd get eaten alive in diplomatic circles.

"Nice to meet you, Robert. And thanks for meeting with me today."

"It's my pleasure, although I'm sorry it's not under better circumstances. There's a coffee shop just around the corner. How about we go there to talk? It's much easier than wasting time getting you through Security at the consulate."

"That's fine with me. I'm on your dime." Steve thought it odd that they weren't going into the consulate. It wasn't like getting through Security would be a problem. He'd done it before, dozens of times, in embassies around the world. He chalked it up to his status as a private attorney, not a senior active duty Navy officer, and the younger generation's more casual way of doing business. He preferred more formality when dealing with important matters like this.

Fowler led him to a small café just around the corner from the consulate. The establishment's walls were lime green with plants jutting onto the sidewalk. Vietnamese customers already occupied the two umbrella-covered tables outside. Fowler weaved between their tables and picked a place set well back inside the café, out of the sun and directly under a wobbly ceiling fan so lethargic it seemed to protest its own rotations. Walking around the table, Steve took off his suit coat, draped it over the back of his chair, and sat down. Fowler was already seated and motioning for the waitress.

"The Vietnamese love their coffee shops," Fowler said. "It's a habit I picked up rather quickly. Meeting in a place like this also gets me out of the consulate every now and then. I hope it's okay."

"It works for me," Steve replied, looking down to place his napkin on his lap so his eyes wouldn't betray his discomfort with the meeting site. "How long—"

Fowler cut him off. The waitress had arrived at their table, and he addressed her in Vietnamese. She nodded and then looked at Steve, saying nothing but apparently waiting for his order.

"I've just ordered a cup of iced Vietnamese coffee with milk. It's actually quite refreshing on a hot day like this. If you haven't tried it, I recommend it."

"I'll have a cup of hot coffee, black," Steve said, irritated at having been interrupted mid-sentence. He wouldn't order an iced coffee now if it were the only item on the menu. He already didn't like Fowler; too much Ivy League arrogance about him. A junior naval officer would never have cut off a more senior person like that. But Fowler was the key to helping Ric Stokes, so he had to be nice. The waitress acknowledged his order and disappeared.

"So, how long have you been assigned in Saigon?" Steve asked, consciously masking his dislike for Fowler.

"Almost three years, now. This is actually my first assignment out of college. That is, after Vietnamese language training."

"Oh, where'd you go to school?"

"Yale."

"Very impressive." Steve gloated to himself at having picked up the Ivy League aura, not to mention the hint of a New York accent. "Do you speak Vietnamese fluently?"

"Actually, I do. Languages are kind of my thing. But I know you didn't come here to talk about me. How about we talk about Ric Stokes." As if on cue, the waitress returned with the coffees and set them down. She then moved on to check the tables outside. Steve's coffee was in a small cup with a metal drip filter on top. He set the filter on the table and took a sip of his coffee. It was piping hot and tasted very strong.

Fowler sipped his iced coffee and then set it on his napkin to soak up the condensation running down the outside of the glass.

"So, what can you tell me about Ric Stokes?" Steve asked. "Where do we stand?"

Fowler pulled a pack of cigarettes from his pocket and tapped one loose. "Another habit I picked up over here," he remarked, frowning. He stuck the smoke into the corner of his mouth and started to speak while digging through his pants pocket for a lighter. "I've got to be honest with you, Steve. It doesn't look good." He brought a green plastic lighter up to the cigarette dangling from his mouth and lit it, inhaling briefly. Turning his head, he blew a small cloud of smoke toward an unoccupied table.

"You know the basic details already," he went on. "Stokes was found with a kilo of heroin in his suitcase. The police say he resisted arrest. Worse yet, the man he was traveling with died of a heroin overdose, and no one's been able to verify Stokes' claim that there was a prostitute in the room at the time of his partner's death. The police view the case as open and shut." Fowler slid the table's square glass ashtray in front of him and rested his cigarette in a groove on one side.

As he reached for his coffee, Steve broke in. "Robert," he said, "I know Ric Stokes, and there has to be more to the story. He prosecuted drug cases in the Navy. Drugs aren't in his DNA."

Fowler finished a long, slow sip of iced coffee before responding. "That may be well and good, Steve, but the Vietnamese police only know the Ric Stokes who had a kilo of heroin in his suitcase."

"Then I guess it's my job to make sure they find out about the real Ric Stokes."

Fowler picked up his iced coffee and pushed out a response half under his breath. "Don't forget you're not in the American justice system anymore." As he sipped, he raised his eyebrows, as if to accentuate the fact.

Now Steve was pissed. "What's that supposed to mean?" Forearms on the table, he stared straight into Fowler's face.

Fowler set his coffee down and leaned back in his chair, putting space between them. "It means the Vietnamese police really don't care about what Ric Stokes was like before they found him. That's not relevant to them, or to the prosecutors, for that matter." He reached for his cigarette and took another drag, holding it near his face as if another puff were imminent. "In other words, Steve, they see this case in black and white. Stokes was found with drugs and he's a foreigner. There won't be any public sympathy for him. In fact, the prosecutors will want to wrap this up as quickly as possible to show they're tough on foreigners who commit crimes in Vietnam."

"Okay, I can buy that," Steve admitted begrudgingly. "So how much time before he goes to trial?"

"A few months, maybe six at most." Fowler exchanged his cigarette for his iced coffee, but didn't drink. "Don't expect much, though. The trial's just window dressing on an outcome that's already determined. Like I said, Steve, the Vietnamese government won't want the people to think it treats foreigners, especially Americans, any better than its own people." Fowler finally sipped his coffee, signaling he'd made his point.

Gloomy as the outlook seemed, Steve wasn't deterred. He knew Ric Stokes, and he knew there was more to the story than what Fowler implied. He would just have to find out what really happened. "So what's the next step?"

"Let me be frank with you, Steve," Fowler replied. "The best thing you can do for Stokes is to meet with him this afternoon and help him get his affairs in order back in the States. There's really nothing you can do for him here."

"No offense, Robert, but this whole thing just doesn't make sense to me." He couldn't believe the consulate entrusted such a serious case to an Ivy

League boy wonder. Normally able to restrain his emotions, Steve barked out his response like an order. "You've got a decorated senior military officer in jail and all you can recommend is that I get his affairs in order? You've got to be kidding me."

Fowler recoiled in his chair, his eyes widening. "I'm just trying to be—"

"I don't care what you're just trying to be. Ric Stokes devoted his entire adult life to serving the United States, fighting drug trafficking in ways you can't even imagine, yet you've already written him off because that's the way things are done in Vietnam. That's unacceptable, Robert."

"I'm sorry you feel that way, Steve." Fowler reached for his cigarette and took another puff, as if trying to look unfazed. "I can assure you, we'll do all we can to help Stokes. But I also feel obligated to be honest with you, even if it's not what you want to hear." Checking his watch and calmly looking into Steve's eyes as if to lob one final challenge, he added, "I want to avoid squandering a lot of time, effort, and money on what looks very much like a foregone conclusion."

Steve didn't take the bait. At least he knew where Fowler, and presumably the consulate, stood. He also knew he could work State Department channels to compel the consulate to help Ric—maybe even remove Fowler from the case. But no one in the State Department—certainly no politician—would support Ric if it looked like he was involved in drug trafficking. He needed to get the facts first, and the best place to start was with Ric himself. Then he could get Fowler removed from the case.

"I certainly appreciate your concern for the U.S. taxpayer," Steve retorted. "And ... so you can get back to your work at the consulate, what are the details for my meeting with Ric?"

"We'll need to leave the consulate at two o'clock. I suggest you meet me in front of the main entrance again, just like you did this morning. Chi Hoa Prison is only a few kilometers away. With traffic, we should be there by two thirty, but no later than two forty-five. You'll get thirty minutes with Ric, starting promptly at three."

Not waiting for a response, Fowler leaned back in his chair and mimed writing a check in the air. Within seconds, the waitress appeared with check in hand and set it on the table. Fowler perused the bill and started to pull his wallet from his jacket pocket.

"We each owe forty thousand Dong," he announced, starting to sort through his bills for the correct denominations.

"I've got it," Steve said, turning around and retrieving his suit coat off the back of the chair. He pulled a hundred-thousand Dong note from his wallet and tucked it into the folder holding the check. "Is there anything else I need to know about the visit?"

"Don't take anything other than a pad to write on and a pen. And you can leave your suit coat and tie at the hotel. It will be too hot this afternoon. Oh, and thanks for the coffee."

The two men stood up. Though Fowler saw his own napkin fall to the floor, he walked away. Steve picked it up for him. It reinforced his view that Fowler thought himself privileged, entitled to have others clean up after him. Steve caught up with Fowler at the front of the café.

"I'm walking back to the consulate from here," Fowler told Steve as he pulled a business card from his pocket. "Here's my card. If you need any help in Saigon, give me a call. Like I said, we'll do whatever we can to help."

Steve took the card and shook Fowler's hand, not because he wanted to, but because that's how meetings like this customarily ended. "I appreciate the offer," he said, already looking around for a cab. "I'll see you this afternoon."

9

———⌇———

Same day—Tuesday, 30 May 2000, 2:43 p.m.
Chi Hoa Prison, Saigon

Steve trailed Fowler and a male Vietnamese police escort wearing a green uniform trimmed with gold buttons and red epaulets into the bowels of Chi Hoa Prison. The three-story octagonal brick building with a faded tile roof reminded him of the Pentagon. Both were built during World War II in geometric shapes. Both had obtuse security requirements that made access difficult, and both had occupants serving long sentences. At least at the Pentagon, there was the chance of escape at the end of a three-year tour of duty. No one escaped from Chi Hoa Prison alive.

The escort led Steve and Fowler through a maze of passageways, cellblocks, and iron gates with spear-tipped pales, to a narrow corridor lit only by a single ancient neon tube affixed to the ceiling. Two prison guards wearing the same style uniform as the escort flanked the corridor's entrance, their assault rifles broadcasting that no one went into or out of that corridor without their approval. One of the guards sat in a chair puffing a cigarette, his rifle resting across his lap. When he saw the group coming, he jammed the butt into an ashtray that was far more ash than tray, and stood with his companion. They held their weapons close to their chests, blocking the entrance to the corridor. Steve's Vietnamese escort rattled off a battery of high-pitched commands, and the guards stood at ease.

"Mr. Stilwell," the escort began, turning toward Steve as he called his name. "You visit prisoner now. Twenty minutes, no more." Then, turning to Fowler, he added, "You wait here."

Steve recalled from his discussion with Fowler at the café that he was supposed to get thirty minutes with Ric. Thirty minutes was barely enough time to see how Ric was doing, let alone find out what had really happened. Twenty minutes seemed untenable, so he decided to pursue the matter with the escort.

"Excuse me, sir, but I believe I'm supposed to speak with Ric Stokes for thirty minutes, not twenty." Fowler grimaced and looked away.

"I'm sorry. Did I say twenty minutes?" The escort smiled at Steve, making him glad he'd raised the issue. "Fifteen minutes." The escort wiped the smile from his face and sneered. "You lucky you get any time with American drug trafficker. We not tolerate him in Vietnam. Now go. You waste my time."

"Where do I go?" Steve asked, afraid the escort would use his question as an excuse for yet another rebuke.

"He take you," the escort snapped, pointing to the shorter of the two guards. The escort barked instructions in Vietnamese to the shorter guard, who nodded, turned, and began to walk down the corridor. Steve followed a few steps after him, leaving Fowler behind.

The corridor was about twenty-five feet long with no windows and a single door at the far end. The dimly lit, yellowed walls looked like they had not been painted since the building was constructed fifty years before. A mist smelling of cigarette smoke and sweat hung near the ceiling. Steve's throat fought to repulse it, but he soon found himself inhaling deeply in search of oxygen. Muffled coughs continued until his throat acclimated. When he got to the far end, the guard opened the door and motioned for him to enter. Once he did, the door slammed behind him.

Steve stood alone in the room. His only companion was a three-legged wooden stool positioned in front of a thick window with a circular metal grating for communicating with the other side. A moment later, a door opened in the other room. In walked a tall black man dressed in all black cotton prison pajamas. The man looked gaunt. His shoulders were slumped, and his head, with its receding hairline and gray tinting above the ears, was tilted toward the floor. It was as if he were determining exactly where each foot needed to land before creeping forward. A prison guard in the same green uniform as the others entered the room with him. When the guard saw Steve waiting by the window, he gave his charge a shove and exited through the door at the back of the room.

When Ric Stokes looked at Steve, his eyes lit up and a wide smile broke across his face. He knelt down in front of the window, his bony knees like chair legs on the filthy tile floor. The metal grating was at just the right level for him to speak.

"Thank God you came, Steve," Ric exclaimed.

Steve pulled the stool up to the window and took a seat. He had to bend down to speak through the grating. "Of course I came," he said as if there were no other option. "As soon as Noriko told me you were in trouble, I made the arrangements to get over here as quickly as I could. How ya holding up, old man?"

"Makin' it," Ric responded, shaking his head and trying to sound upbeat. "One day at a time. I can't tell you how much I appreciate you coming all the way over here, Steve. I owe you, man."

"Listen, Ric. They're only givin' us fifteen minutes, so we've gotta cover some ground here fast. I'm gonna do everything I possibly can to help, but I've gotta know what happened. Level with me, man. What's goin' on here?"

"Look, I swear the whole thing's legit," Ric assured him. "It all started when a guy from Houston named Ryan Eversall called me out of the blue. He said he'd more or less pinpointed a C-130 that crashed during the Vietnam War, and he wanted me to help him find the wreckage. I don't know if you remember it, but he'd read the article I published for my master's thesis about aircraft shot down during the Cold War, so he hired me to help him deal with the red tape. He gave me twenty-five K up front and promised me another twenty-five when we got back to the States."

Steve interrupted with some questions he'd been waiting to ask since Noriko first told him what happened. "Didn't you find that a little strange? I mean, you could have done everything from the States. Why'd you have to go with him?"

Ric nodded. "I had the exact same questions. I think what it came down to was he wanted to travel with somebody that could make shit happen. Since I was a retired Navy officer and an international lawyer, I was his man. I also thought I could use the experience to help my students learn about the Vietnam War. I've got to admit, the fifty big ones did a lot of talkin', too."

"All right, I can buy that," Steve declared. "So what happened once you got over here?"

"We landed in Saigon, where Ryan hired a driver to take us to Dak To in the Central Highlands. It was over five hundred kilometers from Saigon and some of the roads were really bad, so it took us two days to get there."

"Is that where you found the plane?"

"No. In fact, it wasn't until we arrived in Dak To that I found out Ryan didn't know exactly where the plane was. Seems he'd heard a vet in Houston talk about an old Vietnamese man in Dak To who said he knew where a big American plane crashed. So when we arrived in Dak To, Ryan had our driver ask around for the old man. I don't know how the driver did it, but three hours later, the old man appeared at our hotel. He was a Montagnard and said his family supported America during the war."

"Man, were you guys lucky," Steve remarked.

"It gets even better," Ric declared. "The old man led us on a two-day caravan on a couple of old, broken-down horses we rented from a local farmer. We eventually found the C-130's wreckage strewn along the side of a mountain in a narrow valley and completely covered by the forest canopy. The fuselage was intact, but the wings and the tail were torn off and lay some distance behind the plane. The cockpit was crushed, so the pilots must have died. Then we noticed something unusual."

The door flew open behind Steve and the escort came in. "Time up. You come now."

Steve couldn't leave yet; he needed ten more minutes. Taking into account what had happened when he asked for more time before, he knew pleading for mercy wouldn't work. He could think of only one option, and it wasn't good. In fact, if it backfired, he could be sharing a cell with Ric Stokes. But desperate times call for desperate measures, so he took the chance.

"Sir," Steve implored, "I could really use ten more minutes—no more, I promise." He reached into his pocket and pulled out his wallet, searching for a fifty-dollar bill. When he found one, he folded it in half and offered it to the guard. "I realize I'm wasting your valuable time, so maybe this will help you and your family."

When the guard hesitated, Steve froze, his outstretched hand still grasping the folded bill. He started to slowly withdraw his hand as if the offer never happened. Before he could pull it all the way back, the escort reached forward and grabbed his hand, probing Steve's palm for the fifty. Steve looked down at their hands as he fumbled to relinquish the bill. The escort never took his eyes off Steve. When the man finally had control of the money, Steve let his arm drop to his side. Uncrumpling the bill, the man folded it and tucked it into his front pants pocket.

"Ten minutes, no more," he announced, glaring at Steve. Then he turned and went out the door, closing it behind him.

Steve pasted a smile on his face. "That was close," he exclaimed, turning back toward Ric, his hands shaking as he returned his wallet to his pants pocket.

"Thanks for what you just did, Steve, but don't put yourself at risk for me. It's not worth it."

"We'll discuss that later, but we've got to wrap it up quickly," Steve said, pushing the stool aside and joining Ric on the floor in front of his side of the grating. The tile floor felt like it was cutting into his knees, which were worn out from years of running and exercise. But he felt more comfortable looking Ric in the eyes at his level. He shifted his weight to give his right knee some relief. "So, what was it you found so unusual?"

"*Unusual* may not be the right word. *Unexpected* might describe it better. We found five graves about twenty yards from the aircraft. Three had dog tags on the stones used to mark the graves. Ryan took those to prove we found the crash site."

"Okay, so somebody buried the crew."

"Yeah, but it doesn't look like the plane was found until recently."

"So, someone survived the crash and buried the other crewmembers." Steve didn't understand the point Ric was trying to make.

"That makes sense, except for two things. First, C-130s only had five crewmembers, so there must have been a passenger or passengers onboard who buried five people. Second, what happened to the survivors?" Ric paused for a moment and rubbed the scraggly gray-speckled beard now adorning his chin. It made him look even older and more emaciated.

"Now I see where you're going," Steve said. "We'll have to get the Pentagon's MIA recovery team out to the site to answer those questions. How do I tell them where the wreckage is?"

"Ryan wrote everything down in a green notebook, and I mean *everything*. The dude was meticulous. Map coordinates for the crash site, the plane's tail number, measurements for the debris field … it's all in there." Ric looked up at the ceiling before returning his attention to Steve. "Oh yeah, and there was one more kind of unusual thing. We found a leather briefcase inside the fuselage, the kind a businessman would carry. It wasn't something you'd expect to find in the cargo bay of a C-130. Ryan checked it: both clasps were broken off and it was empty. But there was a nameplate on it. I think it had the initials KDH, but I'm not a hundred percent sure."

"Is all that in the notebook?"

"Every last detail. We spent two days cataloguing the site and took a bunch of pictures before we headed back to Dak To. Ryan was really pumped because he thought the crash site would be big news. He gave the old man an extra hundred dollars and then our driver brought us back to Saigon. We got in on a Saturday afternoon—I think it was May thirteenth—and checked into the Mountain Flower Hotel. Our driver recommended the place because it was close to the airport and lots of Westerners stayed there. After we checked in, we cleaned up, made arrangements to fly out the next day, and went out for a late dinner."

"Do you remember the time or where you went?"

"It must have been about nine o'clock when we left the hotel. We were looking for Western food, so we took a cab to a nearby restaurant district and wandered around until we found something that looked good. We were both dead tired, so we ordered a couple of beers to unwind and waited for our food.

"As we were talking, a really attractive blonde, maybe in her early thirties, walked over to our table and asked if she could join us. She said she was a buyer for a woman's clothing supplier and that she rarely saw another American after leaving the airport. She said she just wanted to relax, have a drink, and talk to some Americans. At some point before our food arrived, she offered to buy us a round of drinks for letting her sit with us. While she was at the bar, Ryan warned me not to mention anything about the plane crash and to say only that we were in Vietnam to visit historical sites. When it came to the plane, he didn't trust anyone but me.

"She came back to the table with three glasses of Scotch. She gave one to Ryan and one to me and then proposed a toast. We drank our Scotches over the course of the next few minutes and then it goes blank. The next thing I remember is waking up in an alley after having been robbed and beaten up. I managed to get a kid on a motorcycle to take me back to the hotel, and I'm sure you know what happened after that. But I swear to God, Steve, we didn't have anything to do with drugs. You've got to believe me."

"You know I believe you, Ric. But is there any way Ryan could have planted the drugs on you hoping you'd be able to get them through Customs? I mean, you're a retired Navy officer. He might have thought your baggage would be less likely to be searched."

Ric shook his head emphatically. "No way. If that's what he was trying to do, he would've waited until I was done packing. I'm sure it was a set-up, but not by Ryan. He got set up too, but for some reason they killed him. I don't know why—maybe somebody thought he knew too much about the plane."

Rubbing his chin, Steve said, "Could the answer be in the notebook? I mean, why was Ryan so secretive about it? I wonder if the police will let me have a look."

Ric snapped his fingers and pointed at Steve. "Maybe you won't have to ask."

"Whaddya mean?"

"Ryan didn't want to carry the notebook with him when we went out to dinner, so he asked the hotel desk clerk to lock it up behind the front desk. You're the only person I've told about it, so maybe the police don't know and it's still at the hotel. It might be worth a try."

The door behind Ric flew open and a guard barged into the room. He yelled something in Vietnamese, signaling the meeting was over. Grabbing Ric by the shoulder, he pulled him to his feet. Ric moved slowly, prolonging their meeting just long enough for a quick goodbye.

"Steve, tell Noriko I love her and that I'm innocent," he declared as the guard tugged him toward the door. "And thanks for helping me."

"Hang in there, old man," Steve shouted, putting his mouth up to the grating to make sure Ric could hear. "I'll get to—" The door slammed behind Ric before Steve had a chance to finish.

ALTHOUGH HE HATED LEAVING RIC BEHIND, Steve didn't want to spend a second longer than he had to in Chi Hoa Prison's octagonal hell. Fowler must have sensed his claustrophobia, or felt it himself, as he prodded their escort to get them back to their vehicle. Neither American spoke until their vehicle emerged from the prison grounds and they were safely on their way back to Steve's hotel.

"A pretty nasty place, isn't it?" Fowler began.

"Absolutely horrible," Steve concurred. "I can't imagine what the parts we didn't see look like. It's like taking a trip back to the nineteenth century."

"How's Stokes holding up?" Fowler sounded sincere.

"The ordeal's wearing on him. I'd say he's lost at least twenty-five pounds since the last time I saw him. But he's a tough guy and he'll hold on until we get him out." Steve spoke confidently to allay any doubts Fowler might have about Ric's innocence. He wasn't sure Fowler had Ric's best interests in mind.

"So what did he tell you that makes you so sure he's innocent? Did he explain where the drugs in his suitcase came from?" For Steve, Fowler's skepticism confirmed his lack of commitment to helping Ric. Fowler seemed to be taking the path of least resistance, which meant allowing Ric to be convicted so he could move on to the next case. Steve decided not to share what Ric had disclosed.

"It looks like a set-up," Steve replied. "Ric had nothing to do with the drugs and it doesn't sound like Ryan did either. There's more to this story than meets the eye."

"I hate to say it again, but unless he gave you proof, you're wasting your time. Your intuition won't hold any water with the People's Court, just like it wouldn't hold any water in a U.S. court. Without evidence, I'm sorry to say this case will have a predictable outcome. So, I ask you again, did he give you anything to disprove the allegations?"

Fowler's brash questions made Steve dislike him all the more. Steve wasn't some rookie attorney handling his first international criminal case— he'd done this countless times before. No way would he disclose any of his conversation with Ric, especially not the existence of Ryan's notebook. He didn't trust Fowler; it was better to keep the man at a distance where he couldn't undermine his efforts. He deflected Fowler's question with one of his own. "I thought the State Department was supposed to help U.S. citizens wrongly accused of crimes in foreign countries."

"You're assuming Stokes was wrongly accused. Based on what I've seen, that doesn't seem to be the case." Looking away from Steve, he added, "Like

I said, Steve, I recommend you let us handle things here in Saigon. You take care of things stateside. There's a lot you can do for his family, but if you stay here, Stokes will be convicted and his family won't be prepared. I know what I'd do."

"You can at least keep me informed of developments in Ric's case, can't you?" Disdain dripped from Steve's voice.

"I'll do better than that, Steve. I'll visit him to make sure he's being treated properly, help him hire a local attorney, and attend all his court proceedings. I can assure you, there's really nothing more you can do for him here." Fowler paused briefly and added, "So how do you want me to update you?"

The car pulled up to the curb in front of Steve's hotel, signaling a welcome end to the conversation. "I'll shoot you an email when I get back to my office so you'll have my address," Steve replied, somewhat mollified. At least Fowler intended to carry out his consular responsibilities toward Ric as a U.S. citizen in a Vietnamese jail. "And please send me the contact information for Ric's local counsel as soon as Ric selects him. I'll want to touch base with him right away." Steve gave no indication of when he would be leaving Saigon or what his next actions might be. Fowler didn't need to know.

The bellhop from the Le Dey Hotel opened the door for Steve and he exited onto the sidewalk, only to duck his head back into the car to issue a final order. "I expect you and the consulate to take good care of Captain Stokes. Given his long and distinguished military career, he's earned it." His parting shot might make no difference in Fowler's treatment of Ric but Steve needed to say it. Shoving the door closed, he headed up to his hotel room without looking back.

10

Same day—Tuesday, 30 May 2000, 4:36 p.m.
Saigon

STEVE WASTED NO TIME GOING AFTER Ryan's notebook. If the police had listened in on his conversation with Ric Stokes, it might already be too late. He ran up to his room at the Le Dey, snatched some cash from his safe, and took a taxi to the Mountain Flower Hotel. The bellhop raced him up the stairs to open the front door for him.

"Thank you," Steve said, making his way directly to the bespectacled clerk waiting on the other side of the front desk counter. His timing was perfect; there was no one else in the lobby other than the bellhop, who waited at the door. Steve got right down to business, as he didn't know how much time he had.

"May I help you?" the front desk clerk asked, not bothering with the welcoming smile of his counterparts at the Le Dey. Steve hoped he would be cooperative, but the look on the clerk's face was not promising.

"Yes, as a matter of fact, you can." Steve scanned the lobby to reconfirm they were alone. "Do you recall a couple of weeks ago you had a tall black man and a white guy staying at the hotel together?"

"Was one the man who died?"

"Yes, that's the one." Steve chose his words carefully so as not to arouse suspicion. "Their names were Eversall and Stokes and I think they may have left a notebook in your safe behind the front desk. Mr. Stokes asked me to get it for him."

"Isn't Mr. Stokes the black man in jail?"

"Yes," Steve admitted, "and that's why he asked me. He says it has some notes in it that will help him explain things to the police."

"So why didn't he just tell the police about it and have them come and get it?"

Steve was ready for the question. "He was afraid the police wouldn't understand why the notebook was important and might throw it away."

"Maybe I should call the police and tell them it's here and that it's important. What do you think of that idea?" Leaning toward Steve with one elbow on the counter, he whispered, "Or, I could give it to you if you pay me for the time I kept it safe for him." He took off his glasses and folded them, carefully setting them on the desk behind the counter next to a stapler. "Wouldn't that be better?"

"How much would I owe you for the safekeeping?" Steve asked, amazed at how the charade really didn't bother him, given his earlier successful bribe of the prison escort. It seemed like a mutually beneficial way to get business done.

"What do you think it is worth?" the front desk clerk asked, conveying to Steve that this was also not the clerk's first foray into the world of under-the-table payments.

"How about twenty-five dollars?" Steve guessed this was probably close to a month's pay for the clerk.

"How about one hundred dollars?" the clerk countered.

"Wow! That's high," Steve replied, waving his hand as if brushing the counteroffer aside. "I'll give you fifty." He didn't want the clerk to think he was desperate to get the notebook.

The clerk had all the leverage. He had the notebook Steve wanted and he didn't have to give it to Steve unless he got what he wanted. He played his hand with the skill of a professional poker player.

"Now that I think about it, we gave the notebook our very highest level of security. It will cost you one hundred twenty-five dollars. Otherwise I will have to turn the notebook over to the police."

Realizing the situation could only get worse, Steve pulled out his wallet, produced two fifties, a twenty and a five, and handed them to the front desk clerk, who arranged the bills so that the pictures on the front all faced the same way. "I'm sure your security was very good," Steve said, playing along with the dialogue so it sounded like he was paying for a service, not paying a bribe.

"We are proud of our work here." The clerk squatted down on his haunches in a position Steve had seen lots of Vietnamese men and women assume but was unthinkable to him. The clerk retrieved a key hanging under the cash register shelf and unlocked a box somewhere below the counter. When he stood back up, he held a dark-green spiral notebook. It was over an inch thick, with the open end flared from overuse. A tired business card and three sets of dog tags clung to the top of the notebook. Although the dog tags were priceless in that they would finally bring closure to the families of the service members lost in the crash, Steve ignored them so as not to draw attention to their value. He instead focused on the business card.

"What's this?" he asked, pointing to the business card.

"When the black American came into the hotel that night, he left it on the counter before he went to his room. Since I didn't see him again, I just put it with the notebook. I'm giving it and the metal identification chains to you at no extra charge."

In a strange way, Steve admired the clerk's capitalist spirit. He had always been told that while the Americans won every major battle, the Communists won the Vietnam War. The enterprising hotel clerk made him think the Communists might have lost in the long run after all.

"I appreciate your generosity," Steve said, milking the situation for all it was worth. "Do you by chance know what the card is?"

"A young man on a motorbike gave the black American a ride back to the hotel that night. He must have given your friend his card in case he needed another ride."

"Thank you so much—you've been very helpful."

The front desk clerk nodded and rested on a tall stool behind the counter as Steve stuffed the dog tags into his pocket and made his exit to a waiting cab. It had been an emotionally draining day and he was ready to get back to the Le Dey Hotel and dive into the notebook. Maybe, just maybe, it would contain something that would help him get Ric out of jail. If not, he was fresh out of ideas.

11

Same day—Tuesday, 30 May 2000, 6:04 p.m.
Saigon

STEVE SET THE GREEN SPIRAL NOTEBOOK on the narrow black lacquer desk in front of the mirror across from his bed. Dragging over one of the two heavy wooden chairs from the breakfast table in the far corner of the room, he sat down, pulling the gold-beaded chain on the brass lamp just behind the desk's telephone. Even after he'd removed the lamp's shade, the light was yellow and dim, making it difficult to see in his poorly lit, windowless room, so he opened the bathroom door and turned on the light, illuminating the notebook just enough to make it readable. Ryan had kept elaborate cursive notes in diary fashion. He thumbed through the pages to see how extensive the notes were; more than three-quarters of it contained information about the crash.

The first page began with an entry on 29 April 2000 stating "Boarded United Airlines Flight 1029 from Houston, Texas, en route to Ho Chi Minh City." Daily entries chronicled every step of the way from arrival in Ho Chi Minh City on 1 May to discovery of the plane. The chronology tracked what Ric told him, but in much more detail. The first significant entry occurred on 4 May. It stated, "Arrived Dak To and located Nguyen Van Tuan who will escort to crash site. Departure the day after tomorrow by horse." Several more entries documented the preparations for the trek and the trek itself, until they arrived at the crash site, the location of which was identified with geographic map coordinates. The entries then described the debris field, confirming the wreckage was a C-130 with tail number 70467 still visible on the decaying fuselage.

Steve skimmed through the listing of engine, wing, and cockpit parts and their locations relative to the remnant of the main fuselage until he came to the description of the gravesites. Three of the sites were cross-referenced to the dog tags the hotel clerk gave him. Handwritten in big block letters, the names were CAPTAIN JOHN PEKE, CAPTAIN JOE SCALPATO, and MASTER SERGEANT DAVID DUGAN, all U.S. Air Force members. The other gravesites had no names.

Steve picked up the dog tags and pulled the corroded chains through his fingers. Although time had taken its toll on the letters punch-stamped into the aluminum tags, all three names were clearly visible. Steve ran his index finger over the raised letters on one of the tags as if reading Braille. It saddened him to think these men died over thirty years ago, in the prime of their lives, serving their country in a war they probably didn't understand. They did their duty, fought when others chose not to, and paid the ultimate price. Now they were buried on a desolate hillside in Vietnam; no hero's welcome home or even a flag-draped casket for their families to mourn over. Instead, they likely died a terrifying death as their plane collided with a mountain in the middle of nowhere. If they survived the crash, they had to wait, alone and with the hope of rescue fading, until death or the Viet Cong overtook them.

Even more heart-rending, their families never got to experience the joy of a loved one returning home safely from war. Steve couldn't help but put himself in these men's shoes, or even Ric's shoes, for that matter. What if he had never returned from his deployment to the Mediterranean aboard the aircraft carrier USS *Saratoga*? Or what if his family lost him now, without ever knowing what happened? Even worse, what if in the last few precious moments of his life, he realized he would never see his wife and two sons again or have the chance to say goodbye?

The dog tags and Ric's situation drove Steve still deeper into thoughts he was uncomfortable with. He loved his family more than anything, but did they know that? And was it really true? All his sons had seen growing up was a workaholic Navy officer, deploying around the world, going whenever and wherever the Navy called. Missed birthdays, holidays, sporting events, graduations—what were his boys, now in college with their childhoods forever gone, to think?

And what about Sarah? She'd told him she felt like she was second in line when it came to the Navy, and she wasn't sure if, given a choice between the Navy and her, he would choose her. He begged her to understand that she would always come first and that he couldn't live without her. But each time the next career-enhancing assignment came along, he'd promise her his working hours and travel would get better as soon as the tour was over. They never did, and after twenty-two years of being repeatedly uprooted from jobs, friends, and family to help him climb the Navy ladder, Sarah knew better and was tired of lip service. She wanted action. That was the primary reason he'd retired, but here he was, two years later, gallivanting around the globe again while she stayed home alone.

Of course, he had good reason for being in Vietnam—Ric's life hung in the balance. He would never forgive himself if he didn't do everything in his power to help his friend. But there was always a good reason and Sarah, as loving as she was, needed more than the shadow of a husband chasing every good reason. She needed all of him, and more importantly, he needed all of her. He promised himself he would take her out to dinner at her favorite restaurant in New York City once he got back and things settled down. This time he would try something new. He would listen to see what solutions she had to offer rather than placating her with his own self-serving solutions as he had done in the past. He had no idea what the outcome might be, but the dog tags told him he had no choice. After giving them a squeeze, he set the tags on the desk, reluctant to let go. He couldn't help but think that in a twisted world where fate and purpose inexplicably intertwine, perhaps three families' losses thirty years before could be transformed into his family's gain.

12

Same day—Tuesday, 30 May 2000, 6:36 p.m.
Saigon

THE DOG TAGS DREDGED TO THE surface deeply buried doubts about how Steve had balanced his family and Navy career, making it difficult for him to focus on Ric's case. But when he tried to divert his attention to Ric, something in the back of his mind nagged at him. Was Fowler right? As the man so glibly pointed out, the facts surrounding Ric's arrest looked damning. Steve's heart assured him otherwise, but his heart's assurances were worthless without evidence. All he had to work with was Ryan's notebook and three dog tags. The swirl of thoughts proved too much for him. He needed to get outside the four walls of his hotel room to clear his mind and figure out his next move.

He unlocked his room safe and took 500,000 Dong, or about twenty-five dollars, and added it to his wallet. He also added a business card from the Le Dey hotel. That way, if he got lost, all he had to do was show the business card to a taxi driver and he could get home. He left everything else—the rest of his money, his passport, Ryan's notebook, and the dog tags—locked in the room safe.

Steve took one of the Le Dey's two elevators down to the lobby. He gave his room key to the front desk clerk for safekeeping and headed for the large glass-front doors, which the bellhop already held open by an oversized brass handle. Steve half smiled and said "thanks" as he passed, then trotted down the stairs.

The moment his feet touched the sidewalk, a woman in a dingy light brown linen shirt and matching pants approached. Her leather-skinned feet and ankles, dried and tanned after years of a survival existence, looked swollen and painful.

"You buy?" she asked, displaying a selection of cheap beads, fans, and other souvenirs on a tray held in place at her waist by a strap behind her neck. "Very nice gift for wife or girlfriend. You have girlfriend?"

"No thank you," Steve replied as he walked past the woman, feeling guilty for not buying anything but knowing if he did, a hoard of similarly needy vendors would descend on him. The woman would not take no for an answer, though, and started badgering him down the sidewalk, holding up a bracelet made of small, polished, brown-marble beads.

"Very nice for lady. You buy," she insisted. "Forty-thousand Dong." She was working very hard to make a sale worth about two U.S. dollars. Feeling even more hardhearted and insensitive, he again said no, waving his hand to politely add emphasis. This time the woman got the message and wandered off in search of a tourist more willing to part with some money.

Steve turned right at the fifth intersection, entering a street filled with four- and five-story buildings. They were sectioned off like Asian row houses as far down the street as he could see, each section not much wider than an American one-car garage. At street level, the cacophony of activity from the previous street repeated itself, although the side street was smaller than the main artery it jutted off of, forcing the motorbikes and green taxis to press closer together.

As Steve rounded the corner, a man sitting on a motorbike called to him. "Where you going? You want ride? Half-hour, five U.S. dollars."

"No, thank you," Steve replied, waving him away and continuing down the side street.

About ten shops ahead, he saw a pastel-green restaurant on the corner of an alley cutting in from a side street to the right. Above the restaurant was a sign with "ZACCA'S" in raised bold black letters on a banana-yellow background next to the orange and black image of a pumpkin. Steve noticed several Westerners sitting at tables inside. He was always wary of getting sick after eating at restaurants in developing countries. The number of Westerners assured him the food was safe to eat. He wandered over to the menu displayed on a sidewalk pedestal, trying to look uninterested. The trick was to see what ZACCA'S had to offer while still preserving the option of walking away without guilt from any of the all-too-helpful wait staff coaxing him inside. The menu featured reasonably priced Vietnamese and Italian cuisine, so he decided to give it a try.

"You like to come in and eat with us?" asked a smiling young Vietnamese waitress dressed in a black skirt and a yellow sport shirt with a ZACCA'S monogram embroidered in black. She looked no more than twenty.

"I'd love to," Steve replied. The waitress escorted him to a table for four up against a mirrored wall on the right of the restaurant and took away the excess place settings. The room was only wide enough for two rows of six hardwood tables, each with four chairs. The wall opposite the mirrors was open to the alley, allowing a pleasant breeze to caress hanging pots of dangling purple flowers and aerated fish bowls teeming with tiny fish and millions of even tinier bubbles.

As he looked over the menu, an eye-catching brunette walked in. She wore dark sunglasses, a loose-fitting sky-blue tank top, and a short, lacey white skirt that fluttered around her legs. White minimalist sandals accentuated her deep tan. She was a Western woman alone, surely an unusual sight in Vietnam. A waitress seated her one table away in the other row of tables where she could see him and he could see her.

Steve's waitress reappeared from behind him, blocking his view of the woman, and set some French bread toast garnished with diced tomatoes and cilantro on his table.

"You ready to order?" the waitress asked, pen and paper in hand.

"I am," Steve answered, flipping past the Italian items to the third page of the menu. "I'd like to try the chicken stir-fry." This was his first time in Vietnam and he couldn't imagine coming all this way without sampling the local cuisine. Maybe his dinner would allow him to absorb a little Vietnamese culture in between thoughts about Ric's intractable situation. It would also give him something positive to tell Sarah once he returned home.

"You like something to drink?"

"Yes. How about a Huda beer?" It was the cheapest beer on the menu.

"Thank you. I bring it shortly." The waitress entered the kitchen behind Steve, his view of the brunette now blocked by another waitress taking her order. Before his line of sight was restored, his waitress brought him his Huda beer in an open bottle, along with a frosted mug. He picked up the mug in one hand and the Huda bottle in the other and tilted them toward each other, slowly pouring the beer into the mug to minimize the froth. The effervescence and aroma made him glad he'd ordered a beer, a drink he rarely indulged in stateside because he wouldn't drive after drinking. The risks were too great for an attorney in a small town, let alone a former military officer. He watched intently as the frosted mug slowly filled with ice-cold beer.

"You know that's a local beer brewed in Hue City."

The woman's voice startled him. He hadn't noticed her approach.

"I'm sorry, I didn't hear what you said," he replied, sounding more formal than courteous. "I was a little too focused on pouring my beer."

"So I see." The woman put her hand on the back of the chair facing him and flashed a smile. Steve stood to introduce himself, making sure his wedding ring remained visible by placing his left hand on the table as he slid his chair back. He guessed she was ten to fifteen years younger, so he assumed she was just being friendly. Still, he felt more comfortable making his boundaries clear.

Before he could think of what to say next, the woman said, "Please, no need to get up. I just overheard you place your order and you sounded like a fellow American. There are so few of us here, you know." She stepped around the table toward him. "My name is Gallagher, Wendy Gallagher." She extended her hand. "My friends just call me Gallagher." Steve shook her hand; her grasp was firm, conveying confidence and purpose.

"I'm pleased to meet you," Steve said, not quite sure what was going on. "I'm Steve Stilwell." The two stopped shaking hands, and for a second, faced each other in silence.

Gallagher spoke first. "Well, Steve Stilwell, do you think your wife would mind if I joined you for dinner?" The sparkle in her hazel eyes indicated she knew what the answer would be.

"Of course not," Steve said, easing around the table to get her chair. "Please, have a seat." He wanted to be friendly, but no stranger had ever asked to sit with him at a restaurant before, let alone an attractive younger woman. Even though she'd obviously seen his wedding ring, he kept up his guard.

Gallagher paused just long enough for Steve to help her with her chair and then resume his seat on the opposite side of the table. "So, let's get the basics out of the way," she began. As she spoke, the waitress brought a place setting for her and a glass of red wine, which she swirled around several times but did not sip. "Where are you from and what brings you to Vietnam? Oh, and by the way, your beer is what started this conversation. Huda is a local beer brewed in Hue City. Are you familiar with Hue?"

"I am, but I've never been there. There's a U.S. Navy ship named after the city because the Marines had a big battle there in 1968 during the Tet Offensive. I recall watching some of the fighting on TV as a teenager. It made a big impression on me, especially with the draft going on. But I must confess, that had nothing to do with why I bought the beer. I ordered it because I'm hot and sweaty and Huda was the cheapest beer on the menu." He grinned.

"Ah, a connoisseur," she mused. "I thought you were a man of sophistication and fine taste the moment I laid eyes on you." She took a sip of her wine while looking over her glass at him, and then set the glass on the table in front of her. "So, what about the other questions? Where are you from and what are you doing here? It can't be a vacation, or your wife would be here, too, right?" Gallagher leaned forward with her elbows on the table, resting her chin on her clasped hands, eagerly awaiting his answer.

This was the second time Gallagher had asked questions involving his marital status, so Steve decided to oblige her to make his status and intentions clear. "You're right on both counts. If this had been a vacation, I would have brought my wife. I'm afraid, though, that this trip is all business."

Gallagher feigned a frown. "That's too bad. I'm sure she would have enjoyed Vietnam. So what line of business are you in?" She took another sip of wine.

"Well, I'm actually a lawyer from Williamsburg, Virginia. How about you? What brings you to Vietnam?"

Gallagher ignored Steve's questions, backtracking instead to his answer. "So, I'm eating dinner with a colonial lawyer in post-colonial Vietnam. It's kind of poetic, isn't it?"

Steve wasn't feeling the poetry, but thankfully the waitress interrupted their conversation by setting a mammoth helping of stir-fry on a very large dinner plate in front of him. She also brought Gallagher a large, fresh-looking Caesar salad with a small sliced loaf of hot Italian bread and butter. After the waitress left, Gallagher broke off a piece and continued the conversation, apparently no longer concerned with historical rhyme or reason.

"So, what business brings a Williamsburg attorney to Vietnam?" Gallagher took a tiny bite of bread and chewed slowly, waiting for Steve's response.

"Wait a minute," Steve interjected, not so easily distracted. "We never got to where you're from or what you do. And if you don't mind, I'm going to try to put a dent in this stir-fry while you're talking."

"I'm sorry I'm keeping you from your dinner."

"No, not at all. I just don't want you to think I'm not listening when I start eating." He removed the wooden chopsticks from their paper sheath, split them in two, and went to work on his stir-fry.

Gallagher had just speared some lettuce, but she rested her fork on the edge of the bowl and looked at Steve. "Well, I don't think it's that interesting, but I'm a trade agent. In fact, let me give you one of my cards." She rooted through the purse on her lap until she found a gold case and handed a business card to Steve.

"Sure enough, it says Wendy A. Gallagher, Trade Agent." Steve noted the address was a post office box in Potomac, Maryland, outside of Washington, DC. The card contained her mobile telephone number, but no physical address. "So what does a trade agent do?"

"I knew you'd ask that," Gallagher replied. She sat back in her chair and crossed her hands on her lap. "When an American businessman wants to do business or get something done in Asia, he calls me and I make the inroads. I meet with company and government representatives here, get the lay of the land, and then make proper introductions when the American is ready to meet with his Asian counterparts. Relationships are everything in Asian business, and I make sure there are good relationships from the start."

"So how do you arrange the initial meetings? I mean, you just said relationships are important. If they don't know you, why do they meet with you in the first place?"

"It's not really an issue now because I've built a reputation for facilitating good business. But if I'm working with someone who hasn't heard of me, I include a list of local references and success stories. Oh, and there is one more thing." She paused, twisting a strand of her long brunette hair around her index finger. "I always include a photo with my bio. I think Asian men enjoy being seen at a fashionable restaurant with an even more fashionable American brunette." She batted her eyes and added, "Lots of people are smart, Steve. But not as many are smart, devious, and pretty." Gallagher let the hair around her finger unwind and then she eased forward in her chair, again resting her chin in her hands.

Steve wasn't sure how to respond, so he smiled out of conversational habit and then looked down at his stir-fry, pretending to gather his next mouthful. He had to acknowledge that Gallagher was attractive. Any man would notice her, and it was clear she was trying to gauge his level of interest. But he'd just pledged himself to rebuilding his relationship with his wife and he could honestly say he wasn't interested in Gallagher. What did catch his attention, though, was her line of work. She had business and government contacts and she knew Vietnam. Perhaps she would have ideas about how to help Ric or who in the government he needed to talk to. She certainly could do no worse than Fowler had. It was worth a try. All he had to do was channel the conversation in that direction. Gallagher took care of that for him.

"So," Gallagher began, "now it's my turn to eat and your turn to tell why you're here." She retrieved the fork she'd rested on her salad bowl earlier and started working on the lettuce. Steve jumped on the opportunity.

"Unfortunately, a good friend of mine has found himself in a Vietnamese jail, so I'm here to see if I can do anything for him. In fact, I visited him earlier this afternoon. He's in good spirits, but it's a real mess."

"If you don't mind me asking, why was he arrested?"

"I don't mind at all. In fact, I'm hoping you might have some thoughts about how I can help him. Anyway, I'm afraid he's in jail for drugs. I know my friend, though, and there is no way he did what they allege. We're both retired Navy lawyers and we prosecuted sailors involved with drugs all our careers. Ric hated drugs and what they do to people. Based on what he's told me, I think it was a set-up, but I don't know how to prove it."

"So why don't you tell me a little more about your friend and maybe I can help." Gallagher glanced down at her salad, jabbing another leaf with her fork. "Why don't you start with what he told you this afternoon? Did he say why he came over here in the first place? I mean, if he says he was set up, he must have come over here for a reason."

Steve rested his chopsticks on the side of the stir-fry dish. He talked through his cases all the time with Marjorie, but Marjorie wasn't here. Gallagher was his only option, and she seemed willing to help, or was at least pretending to be. He decided to take a chance and lay the situation out. As long as he didn't disclose any client confidences, he'd be in good shape. With a little luck, Gallagher might give him the leads he needed to get Ric out of jail. If not, he'd be no worse off than he was now. The decision wasn't hard.

"So here's the story. Ric came over here with a guy named Ryan—I can't recall his last name off the top of my head—to locate an American plane lost during the Vietnam War. Apparently Ryan was a rich businessman from Houston, and hunting down military aircraft was his hobby. He asked Ric to go because he thought my friend could help him with the red tape if they found the airplane."

Gallagher continued to nibble on her salad, pausing only to ask another question. "Did they find it?"

"They did. It crashed on the side of a mountain. Ric said an old villager led them to the site. It took them several days of trudging on horseback through the jungle to get there. Ric said Ryan scoured the crash site and took lots of pictures, but I don't know what happened to the camera. They also found gravesites, so either someone survived the crash to bury the others, or local people found the crash site and buried them. But for some reason, the U.S. government hasn't explored the site yet. That's where Ric came in. He was going to liaise with the Department of Defense's MIA recovery team. That's the military organization responsible for recovering the remains of U.S. service members lost during the Vietnam War."

Gallagher set her fork on the table and dabbed around her lips with the red cotton napkin from her lap, making sure no salad dressing followed her out of the restaurant. She folded the napkin into a loose triangle, set it next to her salad bowl, and took another sip of wine. Then she sat back in her chair, still holding her wine glass, and pressed Steve for more information.

"Did Ric tell you how to find the plane? I mean, if his story is true, maybe the Vietnamese police would believe him about the drugs if they see he's telling the truth about the plane."

"Ric doesn't know how to find the plane again. He said the Vietnamese names are too hard to remember and he didn't think at the time it was important for him to know."

"So how was he going to tell the recovery team where the plane is? It doesn't sound like his story holds water, Steve."

"Ric may not know how to get back to the plane, but Ryan does—"

"Isn't Ryan dead?"

"He is, but Ric told me Ryan documented everything he saw. He told Ric what they found was going to be big, really big, when he broke the story."

Gallagher raised her eyebrows and sat forward in her chair, setting her wine glass on the table and pushing aside her plate a couple of inches to give her additional room. Her gaze was intense now. Steve wondered what had changed. Was it the possibility that Ryan kept notes?

"So do the police know about Ryan's notes? It sounds like they would really help verify Ric's story." Gallagher leaned even farther forward.

Steve mentally ran back through his conversation with Gallagher. He hadn't said Ryan was dead, only confirmed it after Gallagher made the assertion. Did she know more than she was letting on? Suddenly he had the strangest feeling he was the one being used to get information. A younger, beautiful woman walking up to him and asking to have dinner with him. He believed her at first when she said she just wanted to talk to another Westerner, but now he questioned her motives. He recalled the advice of his contact at the State Department—be careful who you trust. He'd already disclosed a lot of information, perhaps too much. He would be more circumspect with what he disclosed until he was sure he could trust her, and no way would he tell her he already had Ryan's notebook.

"Ryan hid the information the night he died, so the police don't know about it yet."

Gallagher again sat back in her chair. The relaxed, friendly look returned to her features. "So, here's how I can help. Obviously Ryan can't go back and get his notes. But if you tell me where they are, I'll use my contacts and get them for you. Then you can go through the material and share it with the Vietnamese police and American authorities. See how easy it is?" She reached for her wine glass and took a long, slow sip. She looked directly into Steve's eyes before setting her wine glass back on the table.

"I can't recall the name of the place off the top of my head," Steve lied, hoping to buy some time to sort things out. "But I've got it in my notes from my conversation with Ric this afternoon. If you give me the number for your hotel, I'll call you tomorrow and let you know."

"I can make it even easier than that. How about we take care of the bill here and then I can give you a ride back to your hotel. I'm pretty good on a motorbike. Have you ridden on one yet?" She seemed too helpful, and way too interested.

"That's really not necessary. My hotel is just a few blocks around the corner."

"All the more reason for me to give you a ride. I promise I won't get us lost." Gallagher opened her purse and pulled out a red leather designer wallet.

She looked up at Steve and added, "You might even enjoy the ride." Her lips curved into a sly smile.

Steve wasn't sure what the last comment meant. He didn't want to alienate her in case it turned out she could actually help Ric. The motorcycle ride would give him time to think, so he decided to accept Gallagher's offer. "All right, as long as you let me pay for dinner."

"Deal. So, what's the name of your hotel?"

"It's the Le Dey. Do you know where it is?"

"I do. I've stayed there before. I'll get my bike and meet you out front."

Steve paid the bill and went out front, where Gallagher was waiting on her Honda motorbike. She was holding her helmet, her hair flowing over her shoulders and her lacey white skirt pulled tight over the top of her bronzed legs. The bike was already running in a low, quiet rumble.

Gallagher called to him as he neared the bike. "Hop on. I don't have a helmet for you, but I'll go slow so you'll be fine."

Steve straddled the seat behind Gallagher, leaving four or five inches between them. He grabbed the bottom edge of both sides of the seat to hang on.

Gallagher turned and looked over her shoulder as she got ready to put on her helmet. "Slide up right behind me," she instructed. "I promise I won't bite. When someone big like you sits too far back, it makes this thing harder to balance."

Steve did as instructed until he was tucked up right behind her. Unable to hold onto the lower edge of the seat anymore, he braced his hands on the seat behind him.

"That's much better," Gallagher announced. She turned around and laughed, but before he had a chance to react, she leaned back into him and drove the motorbike into the street, merging with the other riders.

After about five minutes of swerving in and out of traffic and turning through a couple of intersections where motorbikes, cars, and buses convulsed in every direction through unmarked lanes, Gallagher pulled up on the sidewalk in front of the Le Dey Hotel. Steve dismounted, thankful he was still alive. After Gallagher stowed her helmet and locked her bike, they walked to the stairs leading to the hotel's front entrance.

"That wasn't so bad, was it?" Gallagher said.

"The traffic was wild. It's even wilder being in it than watching it from the sidewalk."

"I meant riding with me."

"No, it wasn't so bad," Steve admitted, choosing his words carefully. What was her game? Either she was truly a helpful person or she had more at stake than she was letting on. Maybe a little of both. He led her up the stairs and followed her through the open door into the hotel lobby, where they stood in front of the hotel check-in desk.

"Hello, Mr. Steve," two blue-suited young women called out, almost in unison. "Did you have a nice dinner?"

"I did," Steve replied. Both front desk clerks smiled at his response. Steve retrieved his room key from the taller of the two clerks.

"It looks like you're a big hit with the young ladies," Gallagher quipped.

"Not hardly. The people at the front desk are nice to everyone." Steve stopped walking. "How about I run up to my room and get the name of the place? I'll be right back down. You can grab a seat over there in the lobby." Steve pointed in the direction of a gargantuan brown leather sofa and a black lacquer coffee table with a floral arrangement in the center. A Vietnamese man Steve didn't recognize lounged in one of the accompanying chairs. He was dressed nicely in a maroon sport shirt and blue slacks, so Steve assumed he was a guest.

"How about I save you a trip and some time," Gallagher countered. "I'll go up to your room with you, you give me the information, and I'll leave right away."

Warning bells signaled Steve not to let her go to his room. She was pushing too hard, either for the information or for something else. Either way, letting her go up to his room was out of the question. He drew the line at the lobby.

"I don't think that's a good idea. Just wait here and I'll be right back down."

Gallagher looked perturbed. "I'm not going to bite, you know. I'm just trying to save time."

"I appreciate that, so I'll make this quick." The issue wasn't negotiable.

Steve left Gallagher by the front desk and walked over to the waiting elevator. Once inside he pushed the button to the fourth floor. He only had a few minutes to figure out what to do. If he told Gallagher where Ryan hid the notebook and Gallagher followed through on her promise to retrieve it, what would happen when she learned he already had it? If she truly meant to help, she'd feel like he played her and he could forget getting her help with Ric. But if she had some other agenda or was connected to something more sinister—like the Vietnamese drug cartels—then misleading her could have serious consequences. The elevator stopped at his floor.

Steve walked down the hallway, unlocked the door to Room 413, and walked over to the desk. Although he knew the name of Ric and Ryan's hotel, he went through the motions of perusing his notes to confirm the name. As soon as he found it, he turned to leave, but a figure leaning against the doorframe startled him.

"Jeez! Don't sneak up on me like that! What the hell are you doing here?"

Steve made no effort to hide that he was both surprised and pissed. "I asked you to wait in the lobby."

Gallagher tried to disarm him with her smile. "Sometimes men say they'll call and they never do."

"Look, I said I'd be right back down and I meant it." Steve stepped past her out into the hall and shut the door behind him, forcing her to scoot out of the way. He double-checked to make sure the door locked and started walking toward the elevator. Gallagher followed and waited with him for the elevator doors to open.

"I'm sorry," she said. "I should have waited, but I wanted to make sure you knew that I really want to help. Did you find the name of the place?"

Still perturbed, Steve divulged the information, half to get rid of her and half thinking she deserved to be sent on a wild goose chase. "He gave his notebook to the front desk at the Mountain Flower Hotel." The elevator door opened and they both entered, immediately doing an about-face toward the elevator door. Neither looked at the other.

"I'll make arrangements tomorrow to get it," Gallagher promised, now looking over at him. "And I'll let you know as soon as I have it. See how easy that was?"

Gallagher's sincerity made him feel bad. She sounded like she really wanted to help, yet he'd deliberately deceived her to get back at her, and for what? Showing up at his hotel room? More important, his overreaction jeopardized any possible chance of her assisting him with Ric. He had no choice but to rectify the situation. The door to the elevator opened and he followed Gallagher into the center of the lobby, where she stopped to say goodbye.

"I should have something for you by tomorrow night if the notebook is there," Gallagher explained. "I'll call the front desk as soon as I get an update and they can put me through to your room."

Steve gave her an apologetic look. "Listen, Gallagher, I've been thinking. I really appreciate your help, but I don't want you to have anyone get the notebook. Let me tell my contact at the U.S. Consulate about it and he can decide what to do. I don't want to get you or anyone else involved in this—it's bad enough already."

"I really don't mind." Gallagher paused. "You realize, don't you, that this may be your best chance of helping your friend? But if that's what you want, I won't pursue it."

"That's what I want," Steve said. "But thanks for the offer, and it was a pleasure meeting you." Steve reached out to shake Gallagher's hand. Her grip lacked its earlier firmness.

"I enjoyed meeting you too, Steve Stilwell." Then, before he could react, she leaned forward and kissed him on the cheek. "Okay, I lied. Sometimes I bite just a little." She started to walk away, flashing him a mischievous, seductive smile. "Oh," she said, looking back over her shoulder and announcing loud enough for the front desk clerks to hear, "if you change your mind, just give me a call. You've got my number."

Then she vanished out the hotel's front door into the steamy Saigon night.

13

Wednesday, 31 May 2000, 3:24 a.m.
Saigon

T HE FRONT DESK CLERK AT THE Mountain Flower Hotel shuffled papers,
pens, and brochures on the counter one last time in an effort to stay
awake. His twelve-hour shift ended at four a.m. He only had thirty-six minutes
to go. Guests rarely arrived or departed on a weekday at this hour, so he was
surprised when the lobby door swung open.

Two Asian men entered, one completely bald and the other with thick
black hair parted on the side and bangs draping over his forehead. They looked
to be in their mid-thirties. He presumed they were Vietnamese, but he wasn't
sure because both wore collared shirts with a straight hem and decorative
trim running lengthwise down the front. The shirts made them look Filipino.

The men stopped and conferred near the lobby entrance, giving the clerk
time to check for reservations. Although they weren't carrying any luggage
and no one was due to check in before the clerk's shift ended, he flipped
through the index cards he had prepared for guests checking in later in the
day just in case they were early. None of the reservations fit, so he prepared
to dispose of the men as quickly as he could. The last thing he needed was
someone delaying his departure past four.

The clerk glared at the two men, hoping to get their attention. When they
continued to ignore him, he called to them to move things along. Although
neither answered, they finally looked in his direction.

"May I help you?" he asked in Vietnamese, with a tone suggesting he really wasn't interested in doing so. This time, the men stopped talking and the bald man walked over. The other remained by the door.

"Yes," the man said curtly. "Two Americans stayed here several weeks ago and left a notebook at the front desk. I need that notebook."

The front desk clerk, small and spindly compared to the much huskier bald man, was not intimidated. He'd dealt with all kinds of people in his six years at the hotel.

"Do you mean the notebook that belonged to the man who died?"

"Don't give me a hard time," the bald man commanded. "Just give me the notebook."

"Maybe you should talk to the police. One of the Americans died and the other was arrested." The clerk sat back on the stool behind the counter, tilted his head, and looked down his nose at the bald man. He wasn't going to make this easy for him. He hoped the bald man would get discouraged and go away.

The bald man had other plans. Reaching behind his back, he drew a pistol from underneath his loose-fitting shirt and pointed it at the clerk's forehead. "Listen, you little shit," he blustered. "Give me the notebook now or I'll blow your head off."

The front desk clerk's eyes opened wider than his spectacles and his arrogance drained out of him and ran down his legs. Quivering, he stood up and raised one hand in front of his head, as if his hand could protect him from the gun's projectile. "Please don't shoot me," he begged. "I don't have the notebook anymore, I swear."

"You better get it for me now," the bald man growled, shaking the gun, "or you're a dead man."

"An American came by this afternoon and asked for the notebook. He said he was a friend of the Black American arrested by the police. He said the Black American needed it to help with his case, so I gave it to him. I swear that's the truth."

"What's the name of the American you gave it to?"

"I don't remember, I swear. If I had the notebook, I'd give it to you. Please don't shoot me."

The bald man relaxed and put the gun down at his side. "Show me where you kept the notebook. I want to see with my own eyes that it's gone."

"Of course, of course," the clerk spit out, sitting on his haunches as he had when he retrieved the notebook for Steve Stilwell less than twelve hours before. He yanked the key from its hook underneath the cash drawer and unlocked the now empty security box. Still squatting, he pulled the box all the way out so the bald man could see. "See, it's completely empty. I swear I don't have it anymore."

"Next time, keep better records," the bald man quipped. Then he reached over the counter with the pistol and shot the clerk in the head, splattering the floor and back wall with blood and brains. Returning the pistol to the holster behind his back, he joined the other man still waiting by the door. They took one last look around the lobby to confirm they'd left no witnesses, then escaped on motorbikes they'd parked next to a light pole a short distance from the hotel's front door.

14

Tuesday, 30 May 2000, 7:15 p.m. CDT
Houston, Texas

ANGELA EVERSALL AND HER THREE CHILDREN lived in a shutterless two-story brick home with a two-car garage set back about thirty feet from the road. A blue Ford minivan sat in the driveway, the rear obscured by shrubs jutting out from the side of the house. A large oak tree shaded most of the front yard, which looked like it hadn't been mowed in several weeks, and the sidewalks needed to be edged.

Before pulling into the driveway, Casey drove around the block. The other homes in the neighborhood looked well manicured, proper, and affluent. Some yards still had children's toys strewn about. A red bicycle lay on its side near the front steps of one white-painted brick house, while a Cozy Coupe stuck out of a bush at another, their operators nowhere to be seen. Casey checked her watch. It was seven twenty-five on a school night—time for homework, not play.

As Casey rounded the final corner on her way back to Angela Eversall's house, a man walking his dog strolled by. No one else was around. A few cars were parked along both sides of Albans Road, but she saw no indications of overt surveillance. Everything looked normal.

With her scouting mission complete, Casey pulled her rental car into the Eversalls' driveway and parked next to the blue Ford. She grabbed her purse and briefcase and headed for the front door, checking her watch as she approached. She was proud of her Army punctuality; it was seven thirty on the dot. She climbed three stone-slab stairs and rang the doorbell.

About fifteen seconds later, the door eased open until the security chain on the inside stopped its progress. A woman cautiously peered through the gap. Casey couldn't make out her features because it was dark behind her, so her face appeared shadowy.

The woman spoke first. "Hello."

"Angela?" Casey inquired. "It's me, Casey Pantel from Williamsburg. You spoke with my office administrator yesterday about my visit." The woman stepped back, unfastened the chain lock, and pulled open the door, revealing her tall, slender figure and intense red hair. She was wearing white shorts and a red University of Houston t-shirt, making Casey feel overdressed in dark pants, a cream blouse, and flats. Casey thought she saw the woman smile briefly.

"Please, come in." She closed the door as soon as Casey was inside. "I'm Angela, Angela Eversall."

Casey shook Angela's hand, which felt cold and clammy. The woman looked nervous or afraid. She hoped it wasn't because of her.

"I'm pleased to meet you, Angela, and thanks for seeing me on such short notice." The woman didn't answer, but kept holding Casey's hand in both of hers. Her face was tense.

"Were you able to check the neighborhood before you came here?"

Although Angela could not have been more than thirty-seven or thirty-eight, she had bags under her eyes and her hair looked rumpled. Her house was in disarray, with clothes piled in chairs and newspapers still in plastic delivery bags stacked on the floor. The vacuum cleaner was visible in the hallway, and the coat closet door was open. A little farther down the hall, dirty dishes littered the kitchen table and counter. The disorder seemed inconsistent with the décor and the quality of the furnishings. Casey sensed Angela was having a difficult time dealing with her husband's death.

"I drove all around the neighborhood and didn't see anything unusual. It looks nice and peaceful to me."

Angela tightened her grip on Casey's hand. "Thank you so much for doing that. You can't imagine how I've worried. I've even sent my kids to my mom's house until I'm sure it's safe here." She led Casey into the living room, pausing next to a glass-topped coffee table. "Would you like a drink? Water, wine, anything?"

"No thank you. I ate dinner right before I came over. But thanks for asking."

The troubled smile returned to Angela's face as she directed Casey into one of two leather occasional chairs positioned around the coffee table. The leaves on the plant decorating the table were starting to brown.

"I hope you don't mind if I finish my glass of wine," Angela said as she headed for a small mahogany bar at the far corner of the room. A crystal decanter with two empty glasses on a matching tray sat on one end of the bar. An open bottle of wine and a large goblet over-filled with red wine occupied the middle. Angela retrieved the glass without taking a sip.

Before sitting down, she walked to the room's only front-facing window. She pulled back the long edge of the room-darkening shade, doing one final check of the street outside. Apparently satisfied, she sat on the edge of the other occasional chair and leaned forward in Casey's direction. She took a small sip of wine and set her glass on the table. "I'm sorry the place looks a little messy, but so much has been going on lately …."

Casey leaned forward in her chair, clasping Angela's hands and looking deep into her eyes. "I'm so sorry to hear about your husband, Angela. It must be very hard for you and your family."

Angela started to cry, pulling a tissue from a box sitting under the chair. "It was just so unexpected." She wiped the tears from her cheeks with the back of her hand, the sobs growing farther apart as she composed herself. "I knew the trip had risks. We talked about malaria, Dengue fever, tuberculosis, dysentery … but in a million years I never would have suspected drugs." She went on as if this were the first time she had been allowed to tell her story. "I mean, we started dating in college and Ryan never used drugs. That was one of the things that attracted me to him. He was so straight-laced and sweet, just like the good guy in the movies. I really miss him." She started to sob again, patting her eyes with a tissue.

Her voice full of compassion, Casey said, "I'm so sorry to make you go through this, but I'm hoping something you know may help us clear Ryan's and Ric Stokes' names. They both sound like such fine men."

"They were," Angela said emphatically. "I only met Ric once, right before they left for Vietnam. He was just like Ryan, so polite and responsible. Knowing Ric was a Navy veteran made me feel better because I thought he'd help keep Ryan safe. I guess I was wrong …." Her voice trailed off.

"Do you know why Ryan wanted to go to Vietnam?"

"He was looking for his father's plane."

Casey's eyes grew large. "His *father's* plane? What do you mean?" She couldn't hide her astonishment. No one mentioned this connection before and she wondered if Steve knew. It was an incredible twist to the case, even though she couldn't tell why it might be relevant to what happened to Ryan and Ric.

"His father's plane was lost during the Vietnam War when Ryan was ten. His father was listed as Missing in Action. When his mother died seven years ago from cancer, she left him all his father's Air Force memorabilia, including his uniforms and pictures of his father with his squadron in Vietnam. That's when it started."

"What started?"

"Ryan's obsession with finding out what happened to his father. He wrote the Air Force to get his father's service record and anything else they'd give him, which wasn't much. Then he contacted some of the guys in his father's squadron to see if they could tell him about his father's service in Vietnam. From those letters, he was able to piece together when his father's last mission was and the identities of the other crewmembers. He tried using official channels to find out more about his father's last flight, but kept running into dead ends. It seemed there were no official records of the flight. He even attended a couple of squadron reunions and met some guys who were in Vietnam with his father. They were able to confirm the names of the other men on his father's plane, but no one knew what the mission was for. Finding out about his father's last mission started to consume him. I mean, it was all he thought about."

Angela paused, setting her glass on the coffee table. "I'm sorry for droning on. Are you sure you wouldn't like a cup of coffee or a drink? I feel like such a bad host drinking alone."

"I'm fine, Angela, and you're being a very gracious host. I mean, I've dropped in on almost no notice and you've kindly taken me in. I'm very appreciative."

"Then promise me you'll let me know if you need anything."

"I will."

"And if I'm boring you with too much information."

"You're definitely not doing that. In fact, you're giving me exactly what I was looking for. I don't think I told you, but I was an Army helicopter pilot and my boss is a retired naval officer. If you're willing to share the information Ryan collected, we might be able to cut through the red tape and get answers to the questions Ryan came up with during his research. It might help us clear his name and get Ric Stokes out of jail."

"Ryan kept everything locked in a cabinet in his study. I haven't gone into it since he died. In fact, I really wasn't sure if I ever would. He was just so obsessed with it all, especially after he spoke with the veteran here in Houston."

"What veteran was that?"

"He used to speak at Vietnam veterans' meetings in Houston and wherever else they'd let him. He'd tell them about his efforts to find out about his father, just in case someone might know something. At one of the meetings, a vet told him about a trip he'd taken to Vietnam with some other members of his unit. He mentioned that an old Vietnamese man up in the mountains offered to take him to a crash site if he paid him. The vet thought it was a scam and didn't think anything of it again until he spoke with Ryan. But something about the crash convinced Ryan it would lead him to his father."

Casey interrupted to make sure she hadn't missed anything. "That seems like kind of a long shot, doesn't it? There had to be hundreds of crash sites. What made Ryan so sure?"

Angela nodded. "I thought it was, too, but he'd apparently cross-referenced the information against known crash sites and this one wasn't listed anywhere."

"Did the veteran tell him what kind of plane it was?"

"I don't think so. I think Ryan came up with that on his own from all of the research he did."

Casey was skeptical. Looking for a needle in a haystack sounded like a sure thing compared to what Angela was describing. Plus, there were better alternatives to traipsing through the jungle trying to find the plane. Ryan would have known that.

"So why didn't Ryan just notify the Department of Defense? He had to know the military has teams of experts that investigate crash sites in Vietnam."

"He did, but they told him he didn't have enough information to justify an inquiry at this point. So Ryan decided to get more information. Once he found the plane, he intended to tell the military so they could investigate the site. He knew he couldn't navigate all the U.S. and Vietnamese laws, so he asked Ric Stokes to help him. Ric agreed and the two of them decided to go to Vietnam to find the plane. They spent months planning the trip and making the necessary arrangements with the U.S. and Vietnamese governments. They left at the end of April. That was the last time I saw Ryan."

Angela caught herself before the tears started to flow again, dabbing her eyes with a tissue. Although Angela's eyes were red and puffy from crying, Casey thought she saw a glimmer of hope now that she had finally told her story. Her features appeared softer and more relaxed.

"I really appreciate you going through this with me, Angela. I know it must be hard on you. You've already given me a great deal of information that will help us get to what really happened, but if you'd let me take Ryan's papers back with me, I think that would help. Once I copy them, I can send the originals back to you."

"Will they be safe? I mean, I don't want to lose them just in case our kids want to see them when they're older." Angela started to sob again. She had done well talking about herself, but referring to her children was more than she could handle.

Casey steered the conversation back to neutral ground. "I promise they'll be safe. In fact, if you prefer, we'll hand-deliver the originals back to you."

"You'd do that?"

"Certainly. We'll copy them and bring 'em back in a couple days."

Angela stood up and looked down at Casey. "All right then. You can take them with you, but I really would feel better if you brought them back down to me personally." She motioned toward a door at the back of the living room. "Let's go to the study and I'll get you the papers."

"Thank you," Casey answered as she stood up and followed Angela to the study at the back of the house.

The walls of the study were covered with enlarged photos of C-130s. One wall had a four-by-eight-foot blueprint of the side view of a large four-engine transport plane with the designation C-130A in the upper left corner. A white built-in bookshelf ran the full length of the back wall, two of its sections filled with books on the Vietnam War. A framed picture of a smiling Air Force Lieutenant Colonel in a flight suit adorned the desk in front of the bookshelf. The picture was angled so that anyone seated at the desk or walking into the study would see it. In the back-left corner of the room, under a large green map of Vietnam, sat a two-drawer wood filing cabinet.

Angela walked directly to it. "Ryan called this his 'mission planning center.' He spent hours in here every night, but especially in the last couple of months before the trip. Finding out about his father meant everything to him."

From the desk, she retrieved a key and opened the cabinet. She pulled out the only file in the drawer, a six-inch brown accordion file stuffed full of papers. She had to grab it with both hands to keep from dropping it. She hesitated before giving it to Casey. Finally, with a grimace, she handed over the file.

"It's heavy, so be careful," she said.

"I've got it," Casey replied, clutching the file with both hands. She noticed the handwritten label on the top right corner. " 'Sapphire Pavilion.' Do you know what that is?"

"I don't have a clue," Angela replied. "I heard Ryan mention it a couple of times while he was on the phone, but he talked about a lot of military and airplane things I didn't understand. I'm sure there will be something in the file that says what it is. Ryan was meticulous."

"Well, this should keep me busy for a while. I promise I'll go through it as soon as I get back to Williamsburg and then I'll return the file to you in person."

"I trust you, Casey." Angela laid her hand on Casey's arm. Casey could tell she was both literally and figuratively reaching out for help. She smiled and then headed back to the living room.

"I'm really glad I came here and got the chance to meet you in person," she told Angela. "I feel like I know you now. It makes me want to solve the case that much more." Now it was Angela's turn to smile.

As Casey opened the front door, Angela held her arm to stop her. "Promise me something, Casey."

"I'll try."

"I've never believed what they said Ryan did. He would never have been mixed up with drugs—we made more than enough money with his car dealership, and my family has money, too. There was also no way he'd do anything with a prostitute. I just know it; he loved me." Angela's grip on Casey's arm tightened. "Promise me, though, if you find out anything different, don't try to protect me or sugarcoat things. I need to know the truth."

"I promise. You'll get the truth." As she started out the door, Casey added, "We all will."

Angela caught up with her at the car. "You forgot this," she said, holding up Casey's briefcase. "You left it leaning against the chair in the living room." Angela helped Casey get into the car and then waved goodbye as she drove away.

Neither woman noticed the man in the blue 2000 Ford Taurus parked along the curb. He put down his micro-binoculars, started the car, and followed Casey down the street.

15

Wednesday, 31 May 2000, 10:26 a.m.
Saigon

STEVE BROKE TWENTY-TWO YEARS OF NAVY tradition and slept in until eight thirty. After shaving, showering, and dousing himself with sunscreen and insect repellant, he put on a pair of light khaki slacks and a red golf shirt and sat down at the room's undersized desk to call Sarah. He'd intended to call her after going out to dinner last night, but at 10:05 p.m. Saigon time, he lay down under the mosquito netting to take a quick twenty-minute nap and didn't wake up until morning. Of the myriad excuses he could come up with for not calling Sarah before he went to bed, that was the one she would have no problem believing. His all-night naps followed dinner like night followed day. Unless he had something to do or drank a strong cup of coffee before relaxing after eating, the Sandman was sure to visit. Combine that with the beer he had at dinner and an eleven-hour time change, and the outcome was inevitable. He dialed the hotel operator, who helped place the call.

"Hello." It was Sarah.

"Hi, honey, it's me."

"Hi, Steve. I was a little worried when I didn't hear from you last night. Is everything okay?"

"Everything's fine. I lay down to take a short nap after dinner and didn't wake up until this morning."

"Imagine that," Sarah quipped. "Have you had any luck on the case?"

"I spoke with Ric yesterday. He's doing as well as can be expected. And he did, in fact, locate the crash site he came over here to find. He and Ryan even recovered three sets of dog tags from graves near the site. I'm gonna give 'em to the Air Force as soon as I get back. But none of that helps Ric."

Steve didn't mention his dinner with Gallagher. It wasn't important, especially since he would never see her again. There was no sense in getting Sarah riled up over nothing. "How's everything back in Williamsburg?"

"Fine—nothing's going on. It is nice, though, to have a few days in the house by myself. When do you think you'll be back?"

"I might be able to catch a plane tomorrow night, which would get me back on Thursday. I'll call tomorrow to let you know for sure."

"Don't bring any malaria back with you."

"I'm taking my pills and sleeping under the mosquito netting every night, so you don't have to worry. I'm really glad I got to talk to you this morning."

"Me too. I love you."

"I love you too. Bye."

Steve hung up the receiver. He knew he was lucky to have a wife like Sarah. He again resolved to take her to dinner in New York so he could tell her how the dog tags and Ric's situation made him realize just how much he needed her. He picked up the phone to make another call and had the operator help him dial the number from the piece of paper in his wallet. He rocked back on his chair, arching his back and stretching his free hand behind his head, waiting for Casey to answer her cellphone.

"Hello?"

"Hi, Casey, it's Steve. How are things going?"

"I just finished meeting with Angela Eversall. You caught me as I'm driving back to my hotel."

"Can you talk or do you want me to call later?"

"I can talk now as long as you don't mind me driving. I've got some incredible news to tell you."

"What's that?" Steve grabbed the notepad and pen from next to the phone.

"Did you know that the pilot of the downed plane Ryan was looking for was Ryan's father?"

"No, you're kidding me." Steve set the pen down on the notepad and just listened.

"It's true. Ryan's father was lost on a mission over Vietnam and Ryan thought he located the crash site. He tried to get U.S. officials to go after it, but didn't have enough information for them to follow up. That's why he went on his own."

"So why in the world, then, would he have gotten involved in drugs? It doesn't make sense."

"It doesn't make sense to me either," Casey said. "Maybe he thought he could use the drug proceeds to pay for his expedition. But he was independently wealthy and his wife says there was no way he would do drugs, or sleep with prostitutes for that matter. He was just obsessed with finding his father."

"Well, I've got some big news, too. Ryan and Ric found the plane and I've got Ryan's notebook pinpointing the location of the crash and describing what he found there, including five gravesites. That means at least one person likely survived the crash, which is unusual, as C-130s only had five crewmembers. Someone else must have been on the plane when it went down."

"I might be able to help with that. Ryan's wife gave me a file with all Ryan's research in it. The file is called Sapphire Pavilion, but I don't know what that means. I'm hoping its contents will tell me. Ryan's wife thinks it includes the names of the plane's crewmembers on its last mission."

"We'll see if that jives with the three sets of dog tags Ric and Ryan recovered from the crash site. We can cross-check the names after you go through the file. I'd give them to you now, but you can't write them down while you're driving."

"How'd you get the notebook, Steve? Why didn't the police take it when they arrested Ric and seized the things in his room?"

"Ryan had it and the dog tags locked in a box at his hotel's front desk. Apparently the police didn't think to ask the front desk if they were holding anything for him. So after Ric told me about it, I went by his hotel, and let's just say I 'sequestered' the notebook to be sure we'd have access to it."

"Steve, I hate to end the call, but traffic's getting really heavy and I'm not sure where I'm going. Can I call you later?"

"No problem. How about I call you the same time tomorrow night so we can exchange info again."

"Sounds good."

"Oh, just one more quick thing. When you go through the Sapphire Pavilion file, see if you find a crewmember with the initials KDH. Someone with those initials left a briefcase on the plane."

"Will do, but I've got to go, Steve. Sorry, bye."

Steve hung up. He'd seen the Sapphire Pavilion name printed on the corner of one of the pages in the notebook, but there was no explanation, and he'd concluded it was random doodling. Now it sounded significant, like a code or mission name.

He reached for the notebook and opened it to the page marked by the business card the motorcyclist gave Ric after dropping him off at his hotel. Steve studied the card. The print was Vietnamese on one side and English on the other. He read the name out loud, certain he was butchering the pronunciation, "Phan Quốc Cường." Thinking "Mr. Phan" might be able to give him some insight into where Ric had been the night he was arrested, he decided to give him a call. Better yet, he'd ask one of the clerks at the front desk to call for him and arrange a meeting.

Steve tucked the card back into the notebook, dropped the dog tags into his front pocket, and put the notebook inside his leather planner. Although he wasn't hungry, he decided this would be a good time to get another cup of coffee and study the notebook in greater detail now that he had the additional information from Casey. He opened the room safe and started to take money out of his wallet so he could leave his wallet in the safe, but changed his mind. He was only going to a coffee shop a couple of doors down from the hotel. He also realized he was running low on Vietnamese currency, so he grabbed his passport and the rest of his U.S. dollars from the safe and put them into his front pocket so he could do the exchange. Taking care that the door was locked, he headed for the lobby.

16

Same day—Wednesday, 31 May 2000, 10:51 a.m.
Saigon

FOWLER COVERED THE RECEIVER SO NO one outside his office could hear what he was saying. "Are you out of your mind? What are you doing calling me in the office?"

"I own you, Bob, remember?" The woman's voice sounded playful, like a high school girl flirting with a boy already under her spell. Fowler wasn't pursuing her, though. He was caught in her web and he felt her closing in.

"Hold on for a minute. I've got to close my door." Fowler set the receiver down, walked to the door and peered out to see if anyone was loitering in the hall. Seeing no one, he closed the door and plunked down hard in his chair. He spoke in a muffled voice, still covering his mouth and the receiver with his hand. "Remember, this is a government line. It's only for official business." He meant to remind the woman their phone conversation could be monitored by the consulate for security purposes.

"This is official as far as I am concerned," the woman said with deceptive lightness. "You need to contact Steve Stilwell. His client had a notebook with details about the crash site. It was locked in a box at the front desk of his hotel. Stilwell got to it before we could. You need to tell him to turn it over to you. Then you'll give it to me. I don't want that notebook to get into the wrong hands."

"You can't be serious," Fowler said. "Even assuming I'm able to get it from him, if I give it to you, I'll be compromised as soon as I'm asked where it is. There's no way I can do that."

"You're a resourceful Yale grad," the woman sneered. "I'm sure you can figure it out."

She had him cornered and he knew it. He'd taken her money because all she'd wanted him to do was discourage Steve Stilwell's efforts in Vietnam. He'd had no problem with that. What he'd told Stilwell about Stokes' chances was true, and he thought there was no way anyone would ever find out about the payment. Now, if he refused to do her bidding, she might compromise him, or worse yet, turn her thugs loose on him. He had to escape but wasn't sure how. His best bet was to agree to contact Stilwell and then flee. At least that would buy him some time.

"All right," he said. "I'll contact him. But no more calls in the office. I'll reach out to you as soon as I have the notebook."

"Thanks, Bob," the woman said as if talking to an old friend. "As always, it's a pleasure doing business with you." She hung up.

Fowler started to panic. He rooted through his desk drawer and grabbed his wallet and diplomatic passport. He already had multi-visit visas for Laos, Cambodia, and Thailand, so his diplomatic passport would be his ticket out of Vietnam. He rushed out of his office, leaving the light on so people would think he'd be back. Then he passed through security and out of the compound, jogging most of the way to his apartment.

He arrived at his building sweat-drenched. He ran up the stairs to his flat on the third floor, unlocked the door, and burst in, heading directly to his bedroom. Pulling a black suitcase out of the closet, he flung it open onto the bed and threw in clothing and toiletries. When he could jam no more in, he zipped it and dragged it to his makeshift study. He pulled a book on economics from a stack on the shelf next to the desk and plucked twenty hundred-dollar bills from its pages. Stashing the money in his pockets, he made his way to the door and carried his suitcase down the stairs. He went out the back exit into an alley where his car, a white Toyota Corolla, was parked under a shabby, corrugated-steel shelter.

Unlocking the trunk of the Corolla, he threw the suitcase inside and slammed it shut. Then he dashed back to the driver's door, unlocked it, and jumped in. But when he turned the key in the ignition, the vehicle wouldn't start.

"Start, you bastard," he shouted, realizing that every second he delayed left him that much closer to being caught either by Consular officials or Gallagher. He tried turning the key again, but the engine wouldn't turn over. All he heard was a clicking sound.

When he looked up from the dashboard, he was startled to see a bald Vietnamese man he didn't recognize standing in front of the car and glaring at him through the windshield. Afraid he was about to be attacked, he reached with his right hand to push down the manual door lock button, but was shocked to see a Vietnamese man with bangs standing next to his door staring down at him. He jammed the door lock down and tried again to start the car. All he got was more clicks. He pushed on the horn with both hands, hoping to scare the men off with a loud, long blast. Instead he got silence.

The man standing next to the door tapped on the window to get his attention. Resigned to the fact that he was at their mercy, he looked at the man to see what he wanted.

"Open window," the man commanded.

"What do you want?"

"Open window."

"We can talk through the window. What do you want?"

The man reached into his jacket and brandished a pistol, then bashed the gun butt into the windshield, cracking the glass. "We can do this easy way or hard way. Last chance. Open window."

Fowler's stomach convulsed and he felt himself sucking in oxygen like a marathon runner. It was hotter than hell in the car, and opening the window looked like the only way he could keep from being shot. When he tried to open it, though, it wouldn't open. Nothing that required battery power worked.

"It won't open," Fowler yelled. "You've done something to the battery."

"Get out of car." The man next to the car stood back so Fowler could open the door. Fowler saw this as his only chance. He flung open the car door as hard as he could and struck the gunman in the groin. The man dropped his gun and it fell under the car door. Fowler reached for the gun, grabbed it, and poked his head above the car door to see where the men were. A gun went off.

A single bullet pierced Fowler's skull, splattering the side of the car with blood. The shooter standing by the driver's side headlight holstered his gun and helped his companion onto a motorbike parked a couple of spots down. Then he got onto his own motorbike and they sped off, blending into Saigon's late-morning traffic.

17

Same day—Wednesday, 31 May 2000, 12:31 p.m.
Saigon

STEVE LABORED TO CLIMB UP THE white marble stairs after the short walk
back from breakfast. The brilliant Southeast Asian sunshine reflected off
the glass front of the Le Dey Hotel and pounded down on him, intensifying
the already oppressive heat. Although there were no more than fifteen stairs,
it felt like climbing the steps in front of the Philadelphia Art Museum with
Rocky Balboa riding on his back. When he reached the top, he brushed the
streams of sweat away from his eyes just in time to see the bellhop open the
door for him.

"Hello, Mr. Steve," the bellhop announced. A blast of cool air from the
lobby surrounded Steve, breathing life back into him.

"Hello," Steve said, smiling. He quickly shifted his eyes from the bellhop to
his intended goal: the front desk and the lobby. "Thanks for—"

He couldn't believe his eyes. There stood Gallagher in a short, lime-green
spaghetti-strap sundress cut low in front. She looked enticing and it bothered
him that he thought so. What was she up to? Was she trying to play him for
information like she played Asian businessmen for contracts? He would have
to be careful. He couldn't let her get close enough to kiss him again.

Steeling himself, he noticed both young female front desk clerks watching
him. They were the same two clerks who saw him and Gallagher leave the
elevator together the evening before, and they saw the kiss in the lobby on
her way out. He would make sure they'd see nothing of the sort this morning.

"Hi, Steve," Gallagher said with a pleasant smile. As Steve got closer, a delicate musky fragrance wafted in his direction. The scent was intriguing and alluring, but when the lobby door opened again, a hot breeze blew the fragrance in the opposite direction. Gallagher continued to smile, unaware her bait had been neutralized.

"Wendy, what are you doing here?" he asked, making no attempt to call her by her preferred name or hide his surprise at seeing her.

Gallagher put her hands on her hips, feigning irritation. "You *have* been married a long time, Steve. That's no way to greet a girl. Last time I checked, you are supposed to start with hello." Gallagher stuck out her hand to shake Steve's.

"We can dispense with the handshake," Steve said, again neutralizing her attempt to take charge. "How about you just tell me what's going on."

Gallagher stiffened. "We need to sit down and talk for a minute." She pointed to the leather sofa where Steve had tried to get her to wait for him the night before.

Steve sat on the corner of a large cushion with Gallagher about two feet away, her knees close to his but not touching. "So, what's this all about?" he asked, placing his leather planner with the concealed notebook on his lap.

"You're not going to believe this, but you know how we were talking yesterday about the information your friend hid at the front desk of the Mountain Flower Hotel?"

"You didn't go get it, did you?" he asked. "I want to be sure it's there for the embassy to retrieve."

"You told me not to, and I certainly don't have any need for it. But that's not what I came to tell you."

Gallagher's cheeks were hollow with tension. She looked older and driven, like a businesswoman who needed to close the deal to make her sales quota. "Somebody shot and killed the front desk clerk at the Mountain Flower Hotel early this morning."

Steve was shocked. The shooting had to be linked to Ryan's death and Ric's case, but how?

Gallagher went on, "I heard about it through the expat community this morning. I came over to tell you as soon as I could. It's got to be the work of the drug cartels. You better be careful, Steve. If they know you're working your friend's case, it might be dangerous for you to stay in Vietnam, especially if they think you've got information they don't want others to have. Look what happened to Ric."

Steve thought for a second before responding to Gallagher's warning. Did she know he had the notebook? How could she, unless she was connected to the drug cartels, too? But why would the drug cartels want the notebook?

Why would they care about a C-130 downed over thirty years ago during the Vietnam War? It didn't add up.

Deciding not to divulge that he had the notebook and the dog tags, he built on his earlier lie. "The consulate's got to run with this. I'm not getting involved."

Gallagher reached over to put her hand on his knee, and he pulled away. Her face tightened as she withdrew her hand after the rebuff. "You've got to work with me, Steve. If you have something they want, let me know and I'll tell them you'll give it to them. Nothing in Vietnam is worth dying over."

He was taken aback by Gallagher's threat. She sounded like she had connections to the underworld and was offering him a chance to buy his safety. It still didn't add up. If the drug cartels had no problem killing people, why wouldn't they just kill him if they thought he had the notebook? Either they didn't know he had it, which still might not stop them from killing him, or it wasn't the drug cartels that were involved. But if not the drug cartels, then who? And who was Gallagher working for? He decided to be blunt.

Rising to his feet, he looked down at her and asked, "Who are you, really?"

Gallagher stood too and looked him straight in the eye. "What do you mean?"

"I mean it seems strange that you would know people who hold sway with drug cartels—like you're part of some elaborate ruse." Steve tucked his planner under his arm.

"We're not in Virginia anymore, Steve. This is the third world. There are no bright lines between good and evil. Everything is a shade of gray. Whether it's the drug cartels or the Vietnamese police, there are back-channel ways to get things done, and I know how to do them. If you don't want my help, fine. But you better watch your back, because if you have the notebook, they're gonna take it from you one way or another. You'll never get it out of the country." She leaned forward, and he took a step back.

"Got it," Steve said, now certain that Gallagher was on the wrong side, whatever side that was.

"Goodbye, Steve," she said, backing away toward the front door. "You know how to get in touch with me. But don't wait until it's too late. I really do want to help you." The bellhop opened the door and she walked down the stairs and disappeared around the corner.

Adrenaline pumped through Steve's veins. He'd warded off Gallagher's attempt to intimidate and seduce him, but now he was concerned he might be a target. He looked around the lobby to see if he was under surveillance, but didn't notice anything unusual. He would return to his room, check out, and transfer to another hotel so he would be harder to track. But first he had to check to see if the clerks at the front desk had any luck arranging for him to meet Phan Quốc Cường, the young man who gave Ric a ride on his motorcycle the night he was arrested.

Steve walked over to the front desk and rested his arms on the counter. The two clerks saw him coming and began to give him the broad smile they reserved for the hotel's foreign guests. "Hello, Mr. Steve," the taller of the two clerks said. Neither woman weighed more than a hundred pounds, but both looked polished and professional in their navy-blue business suits and heels. The taller clerk continued without giving Steve the chance to respond. "We were able to contact Mr. Phan and he can meet with you. He said he would pick you up out in front of the hotel at two o'clock and take you to where he found Mr. Ric. Is that okay?"

"That's perfect. Thank you very much," Steve replied, backing away from the counter and turning toward the elevator. Looking back, he added, "I'll be down at two."

As he rode the elevator to the fourth floor, Steve started to formulate a plan. He'd pack up his belongings so they'd be ready to go as soon as he returned from his interview with the motorcycle operator. Then he'd check out quietly and take a cab to the Sheraton, where there'd be a larger contingent of Westerners to blend in with. That would make it harder for anyone to cause him trouble.

A single ring announced the elevator's arrival on the fourth floor. Steve took a left and headed down the hallway to his room. As he approached, he saw the door was ajar. He hesitated; the last time he'd disregarded a partially open door, it led to him being shot in the shoulder by an international assassin. He was sure he'd locked the door when he left. Either one of the maids had left it open, or there was an intruder in his room.

Recalling Ric's problems with the police, he decided to check out the room himself. He approached cautiously, tiptoeing toward the door. He tried to look in, but the door wasn't open far enough. He'd have to push the door open to see who or what was inside. He looked around for something he could use as a weapon in case the room turned out to be occupied, but the hall was empty except for the red and gold oriental carpet on the floor and the paintings of tranquil Vietnamese landscapes on the walls. All he had was his leather day planner, and scheduling an appointment with his foe was not an option. As he tucked his planner inside his pants at the small of his back, he realized the buckle at the end of a swinging belt was a better weapon than his bare hands. He took off his belt but left the planner tucked into his pants. Then he inched the door open, carefully scanning the room.

The widening arc of visibility revealed no intruder, but someone had definitely been there. His room was in a shambles. Ceramic lamps lay broken on the floor, the few clothes he'd brought were strewn about the bed and table, the mirror over the desk was shattered, and the television lay broken on the floor with a chair leg spiked through its back. One of the doors to the wardrobe hung by its bottom hinge, the top one having been ripped off, and the room's safe was open and empty. Steve couldn't see into the bathroom, but he dared not go in. He decided his best move was to leave everything in the room, ease back into the hallway and retreat to the lobby, where he would report the damage and check out. Then he'd ride away with his two o'clock appointment and head to the Sheraton for one last night in country. He just hoped he could get out before someone, whoever it was, got to him.

18

Same day—Wednesday, 31 May 2000, 2:07 p.m.
Saigon

STEVE WAITED IN THE SEARING SUN on the sidewalk in front of the Le Dey Hotel, clutching the leather planner that concealed the notebook. He wished he could have changed into shorts and a t-shirt prior to his motorcycle excursion, but the break-in to his hotel room made that impossible. His red-collared shirt, khaki pants, and penny loafers were the only choice of attire he had for the foreseeable future—not the best combination for the tropics. As if to prove the point, he'd only been outside ten minutes and sweat already drenched his shirt—his back, under his arms, and across his stomach.

He scanned the ebb and flow of motorbikes up and down the street in front of the hotel, searching for his ride. Eventually, a red and black Honda pulled over to the curb in front of where he stood. It looked bigger and more powerful than most of the two-wheeled vehicles on the road, more like a motorcycle than a motorized bicycle or Vespa scooter. The driver took off his helmet, revealing dark-brown skin and matted black hair.

"Are you Mr. Steve?" he called out. He had to shout to be heard over the din of traffic and the incessant blaring of car and truck horns.

"I am," Steve yelled. Although the driver's use of his name made him confident this was the person he'd arranged to ride with at two o'clock, he wanted to be sure. Motorcyclists plied the sidewalks to give Westerners overpriced rides, and it was always possible someone at the hotel had arranged for a hook-up. Now that his room had been ransacked, he needed to be especially wary. The direct approach seemed like the way to go.

"Who are you?"

The driver rolled his motorcycle close to Steve so they could hear each other better. "My name is Phan Quốc Cường. You call me Phan. I gave your friend ride to his hotel about two weeks ago."

That information wasn't specific enough. Steve wanted more precision. "Do you remember what he looked like?"

"He was big Black American and he paid me twenty dollars, just like he said he would. I give him my card." That was all the confirmation Steve needed. He was talking to the right man.

"Can you tell me what happened that night?"

"It too hot to talk here. You get on bike and I take you to park. It just over there." Phan pointed to a green area on the other side of the road about five blocks down the busy Saigon thoroughfare.

"Good idea. Let's do it."

Phan put on his helmet and straddled the seat of his motorcycle. He had no extra helmet, so Steve hopped on behind him and grabbed onto the bottom edge of the seat with his left hand while gripping his planner with his right. He flashed back to his ride with Gallagher, but before he could give it a second thought, Phan revved up the engine and surged onto the street, slipping into an opening that would never pass for one in the United States. Steve felt himself sway backward and instinctively tightened his left bicep and clamped his fingers around the seat's bottom edge. A living pipeline of riders surrounded them as they streamed toward the park.

When they came to Lê Lai Street, Phan made a gradual left turn through oncoming traffic, not waiting for an arrow or a break in the flow. Like water around a branch poking through the surface of a swollen stream, motorbikes heading in the opposite direction parted and let him inch through until he escaped the intersection. About twenty-five meters farther down the street adjacent to the park, he pulled to the side of the road and cut the engine, allowing the bike to roll to the curb. The park was crowded with people seeking shade, but there was a recently vacated wooden bench under a large tree just up ahead.

"We go sit on bench," Phan instructed, pointing that way.

"I'm following you," Steve replied, watching Phan set the kickstand on the motorcycle. Phan put his keys in his pocket and led Steve along a cracked cement sidewalk crisscrossing the park to the other side. They passed a wrinkled old woman wearing an olive-drab long-sleeved linen shirt and pants, sitting on the back of her calves Vietnamese style. Her weathered face and concave cheeks hid the few teeth she had left. She glared at Steve as he walked by, making him feel uncomfortable. Her black eyes penetrated his, like she could see deep inside his soul and discern he was an American military man, a representative of the force that had caused her and her family great pain. She didn't ask for money, nor did she move, but her eyes followed him, convicting him of a crime he hadn't committed. He looked away as they neared the park bench, but the woman's hostile glare stayed with him, reminding him Americans weren't the only ones scarred by the Vietnam War.

"We talk here," Phan said.

"Okay," Steve replied, sitting at the far end of the bench and resting his leather planner on his lap. Phan, who sat angled toward him, was much younger than Steve, his straight black hair parted on the side and combed across his head in stark contrast to Steve's graying hair, cropped close in a tapered post-military cut. What struck Steve most, though, was how their appearances reflected their relative affluence. Maybe it was Phan's sandals and sundried brown feet, or maybe it was the light-blue short-sleeved shirt and dark pants so many Vietnamese men wore, but whatever it was, it made him keenly aware that he was insanely wealthy compared to Phan. It wasn't like there was anything he could or should do about it, but it made him appreciate Phan's willingness to reach across their divide to help him even more. It would have been easy to just let the rich American figure it out for himself, but Phan put cultural and economic differences aside and offered to help at a basic human level. His apparent genuineness made Steve trust him; he just hoped the younger man had information that might help Ric's case.

"What can you tell me about the night you gave my friend a ride?"

"Not so much," Phan admitted. "Why you need to know?"

"Because after you dropped my friend off, he went back to his hotel room and found drugs planted in his room. The man he was staying with died and a woman was there. She left when my friend arrived. The police came and arrested my friend, and now he's in jail awaiting trial. I've spoken with him and I know he had nothing to do with the drugs."

"I sorry for your friend. He sound like he in world of shit. But what can I do? I didn't see anything. I just gave him ride."

As serious as the situation was, Steve couldn't help but laugh. Phan's grammar was basic, but he'd already mastered four-letter-word idioms. He'd obviously learned some of his English from American movies or Vietnam veterans on reunion tours. Steve was not one to criticize. He didn't speak a single word of Vietnamese. But he pictured a bored English teacher, like Harold Ramis in the movie *Stripes*, in front of a classroom of Vietnamese students getting them to repeat the phrase "world of shit" in unison over and over again until they had it memorized.

Hearing Steve laugh, Phan gave him a puzzled look. Steve squelched his laughter. "I'm sorry, Phan. You said something that made me think of a funny old movie. I'm back on track now. Do you remember where you picked my friend up?"

"Yes, but that not help too much. He walk there to get ride. I not know where he come from."

Steve rubbed his chin, now moist with perspiration and a little bristly with invisible gray whisker stubs. What could Phan do to help him? He hadn't seen anything in the hotel room and didn't know where Ric's alley was. He just gave Ric a ride from a street corner to the Mountain Flower Hotel. Steve decided to see if a few questions might shake some useful information loose.

"So what condition was Ric in when you picked him up? Was he drunk?"

"No, but his face messed up. Someone hit him in face and his eye *verrrrry* swollen. I tried to take him to hospital, but he say no. He say take him back to hotel, so I did."

"Did you notice anything else unusual?"

"He say he lose his wallet, so he have to get money from hotel. He give me twenty dollars and I leave."

Steve knew all of that already, so Phan was looking like a dead end. The only other thing he could think of was to have Phan drive him to where he picked up Ric, just to see if the area suggested anything at all. Without seeing it, he didn't even know the right questions to ask.

"I tell you what," Steve said, "how about you take me to the corner where you picked up Ric? We'll see what it looks like, and if it's nothing, I'll pay you and you can drop me off at the Sheraton Hotel. Is that okay with you?"

"Okay with me. I take you there."

The two men got up from the bench and headed back to Phan's motorcycle. The old woman Steve had seen earlier was gone, and he was relieved he didn't have to deal with her penetrating gaze again. There was, however, something new to deal with. In the short period they had been sitting down, the sky to the east had grown ominous, with dark clouds jutting out from behind the tall buildings and heading their way. It didn't look like a good time for a motorcycle ride, especially since he was carrying his planner with the notebook inside. Although it zipped closed, he didn't want to risk getting the planner, or more importantly, the notebook wet.

"It looks like it's going to rain," Steve said. "Should we go someplace to wait out the storm?"

"No need," Phan said, not looking at Steve, his head turned toward a man standing near a light post about twenty feet down from where Phan's motorcycle was parked. "I give you raincoat." Lightning flashed over the skyline as he finished speaking, with a gigantic boom of thunder reverberating through the air. As if on cue, all the motorcycles pulled off to the side of the road, their drivers and passengers donning plastic ponchos and raincoats before the storm hit. A few seconds later, the masses were all heading on their way again, their ponchos flapping in the wind behind them.

When they got to Phan's bike, Phan lifted the seat and pulled two green plastic ponchos with hoods from the cargo compartment. He handed one to Steve and started to put the other on himself. "You put on," he instructed. Then he drew close to Steve, his back to the man under the light post, and spoke quietly.

"That man under light post behind me was at hotel when I pick you up. I think he following us. You know him?"

Steve peered at the man out of the corner of his eye. He was now leaning up against the light post, nonchalantly smoking a cigarette and seemingly indifferent to the coming storm. After blowing a big puff of smoke over his head, he looked directly at Steve. Steve pulled the poncho over his head and pretended to show no interest. Phan was right; they were being followed.

"I don't. Do you?"

"Me either. You get on bike and hold tight. Phan very good driver. I lose him."

Another movie phrase, but this time Steve didn't laugh. First someone tears up his hotel room; now some thug follows him. Although not exactly the way Phan would describe it, Steve knew it was his turn to be in for a world of trouble. The drug cartels or whoever else framed Ric were after Ryan's notebook, but why? And once they got it, would they be content to take the notebook, or would they want to silence him as they had Ryan and Ric? The only way to avoid finding out was to keep them from getting the notebook. He straddled the bike as another bolt of lightning flashed across the sky and the rain started to blow in. He hoped Phan knew what he was doing.

19

Same day—Wednesday, 31 May 2000, 2:38 p.m.
Saigon

"**W**HAT THE HELL IS GOING ON there?" the man with a Boston accent asked.

"You know very well what's going on," Gallagher retorted, pressing the telephone receiver tight against her face so she could speak softly and still be heard. "You're the one who's paying me to get it done."

"I was also paying you to keep things under the radar, remember?"

"We're being careful. You know how I work."

"Yeah, well then your idea of being careful is hosed up. Why am I seeing CNN reports about the embassy official handling the Navy officer drug case being shot and killed in Saigon?"

"It was necessary."

"Necessary my ass. What were you thinking?" The man's voice grew louder and more animated. "Before, it was a private citizen peddling drugs. Now it's a dead diplomat. There'll be a full investigation and they'll start digging under rocks."

Gallagher remained cool, not letting her contact's agitation rile her. "He was getting cold feet and he tried to flee. We caught him in the act. We had to silence him."

"That's bullshit and you know it. You should have worked with him. He listened to cash the first time; he would have listened again. If not, you could have helped him realize his family might be at risk. Now, not only do we have a major investigation in the works, we also lost our insider. This is the same bullshit that cost you your Agency position. You didn't think things through then and you're not thinking them through now. The difference is they just fired you; free agents don't always get treated so leniently."

The last comment pissed Gallagher off. She wasn't some newbie he could scare into submission. She knew what she was doing—her actions were cold, calculated, and correct. She fired back, "Listen, asshole, you're the ones who let the Navy officer live when I told you not to. You're the ones who didn't think things through, so don't come whining to me now that some necessary collateral damage wasn't thought through all the way. What do you think would have happened if Fowler had gotten cold feet and flipped on us?"

The man with the Boston accent dialed back his tone and started talking more coolly. "It's your job to make sure that doesn't happen."

"Precisely, and that's exactly what I did. So what are you complaining about?"

"If you can't see it, then you are worse off than I thought." He paused. Gallagher let the silence build, waiting for the man to continue.

"So what's the status of the notebook? Do you have it?"

"Not yet. We went through Stilwell's room, but it wasn't there. He must have it on him, so we're preparing to take it away."

"Don't screw this one up, Gallagher. Your pretty face might help you get things done, but it won't be worth a damn if this notebook gets away. I'm telling you, the boss is hot and losing his patience. I had to talk him off the wall when you demanded the additional five hundred K to get the notebook, and he's really going to lose it when he sees the headlines. If you don't produce results soon, you'll need to start watching your back. I'm not threatening you, Gallagher. I'm just telling you the way it is. *Capisce*?"

Gallagher restrained herself. "I got it, but you better keep talking reality to people. I'm not the one who made this harder than it needed to be." She hung up the phone, not caring if her contact was through with his tirade. Couldn't these assholes see this was a mess of their own making? If they had listened to her, there would be no American lawyer to hunt down and no notebook to retrieve. They thought they could keep this whole thing under the radar. What idiot came up with that idea? A former senior Navy JAG framed in Vietnam was not going to go down without some waves. They would just have to deal with them as they arose, like she had done with Fowler and like she was doing with Stilwell. She still had some tricks up her sleeve, and she would use them and win. She always did.

She would, however, start to look over her shoulder, just in case.

20

―⁓―

Same day—Wednesday, 31 May 2000, 3:02 p.m.
Saigon

PHAN GUNNED THE ENGINE AND THE bike leapt onto the road, nearly throwing Steve to the pavement. He grabbed the seat with his free hand and held on for dear life, the rain pelting him in the face and making it difficult for him to see. His hood blew back and soon his entire head was drenched, with rain running down his neck and soaking his shirt. He didn't dare let go of the seat to put his hood back on. If he did, he'd find himself rolling on the street, battered by a million motorcycle tires while Phan flew away, not even realizing he was gone.

Steve looked over his shoulder and saw the man under the light pole jettison his cigarette and dash for his motorcycle. He gave it a kick-start and darted into traffic, well behind them. When he opened the throttle to give his bike some gas, it let out a high-pitched whine Steve could hear over all the other traffic. Nudging in between tightly packed motorbikes flowing down the roadway, the man reached out with his right foot and pushed the motorbike next to him, causing the rider to swerve to the right and crash into the motorcycle next to him. The result was a pile-up of epic proportions as motorcyclists tried in vain to steer clear of the wreckage but were too tightly packed to maneuver safely. The man repeated the move on his left, opening a wedge in the traffic and causing a pile-up to his rear. Steve heard the shrill shriek of the man's motorcycle engine being throttled to perform after each territorial advance.

"He's gaining on us," Steve yelled, sounding much like a character in one of the movies he was sure Phan had watched to hone his English skills.

Phan turned his head and shouted, "You hang on." Giving his bike some gas, he veered the now screaming motorcycle to the curb, causing angry drivers to utter unintelligible Vietnamese phrases Steve was sure had universal meanings. Phan hopped the bike onto the sidewalk and jammed down the horn, blasting a warning to pedestrians and street vendors to get out of the way. After zigzagging around parked bikes and a makeshift café, Phan turned down an alley and kicked it into high gear.

Phan's bike lurched forward, tearing down the side street. Gray concrete and faded brick three-story walls blocked the sunlight and cast a shadow across the pavement, making the alley seem dark and grotesque. On one side were the dilapidated backs of shops and on the other, open entrances to rooms with barefoot children sitting on mats or playing with makeshift toys.

Ancient alley dwellers spun around to watch Phan's motorcycle with a Westerner on back zip by. As Phan zoomed around the bend and turned down an even narrower pathway slicing off from the right, Steve could hear the high-pitched screech of their pursuer's motorcycle racing down the first alley after them.

Phan slowed the bike as they neared a corner with a stack of wet, empty cardboard boxes sticking out into a mud puddle on what passed for pavement. He made a sharp ninety-degree turn to the left, causing the motorcycle to list as they went around the turn. Steve's head nearly hit the outermost box. After rounding the corner, the motorcycle righted and Phan sped to the end of the alley, where they emerged on a major thoroughfare. Steve couldn't find a street sign—not that it mattered. He wouldn't have known where they were even if there had been a billboard with a red arrow on a large map stating, "You are here."

Phan stopped the bike at the corner and jumped off, still holding onto the handlebars. "Quick," he instructed. "Give me your raincoat."

Steve hadn't even noticed that it had stopped raining or that the sun was now visible over Saigon's skyline. A dim rainbow could be seen to the east, just over a bank building several blocks away. He pulled off his poncho and handed it to Phan, who crammed it with his own poncho into the motorcycle's storage compartment underneath the seat.

"Let's go," Phan shouted, jumping back on the bike and revving the engine. Steve hopped on and had just managed to grab onto the underside of the seat when Phan pulled forward, crossing the flow of traffic and making a left turn onto the main road. He then began weaving as fast as he could in and around the cars, buses, and motorcycles heading west on the congested roadway.

"I think he gone," Phan shouted over his shoulder. "Now I take you where I pick up your friend. You watch out for us."

"You got it," Steve said, his pulse slowing to something close to normal. He was sure the drug cartels were after him, or at least after the notebook. Based on what had happened to Ric and the front desk clerk at the Mountain Flower Hotel, they would not settle for the notebook—they'd want to take him out as well. Had it not been for Phan, they would have already succeeded. But he didn't know how much longer he could count on Phan, especially once the man realized his own life was in danger. In fact, he didn't know if he wanted to let Phan help him any longer, knowing he would be at risk. He had to figure out a way to extricate himself and the notebook from this predicament while letting Phan drift back into anonymity. He just hoped they both lived long enough to come up with a plan.

PHAN VEERED HIS HONDA OUT OF traffic and idled slowly to the curb adjacent to an intersection swollen with commuters heading in every direction. When he got to the curb, he gave the throttle a little extra gas and the bike spurted onto the sidewalk, where Phan shut off the engine. He put down the stand, pulled off his helmet, and turned to Steve, who had finally let go of his death grip on the seat and was sliding off the back end of the bike.

"This where I pick up Mr. Ric," Phan announced, now referring to Ric Stokes as if he knew him well. "He walk up street here," he continued, pointing to the street coming to the four-way intersection from the left, "but I not know where he come from. He ask me to take him to hotel. I tell him his eye messed up and I take him to hospital. He say no, I take him to hotel." Steve had started to inspect the intersection when Phan added, "This corner not special. Same like other big corners."

Steve shook his head. If the intersection looked ordinary to Phan, Steve certainly couldn't distinguish it from every other major intersection he had seen: thousands of wires bundled on the ends of wooden light posts, cars and buses honking irreverently to claim their section of the road, and motorbikes everywhere. It was like someone had hit the green button on a copier and reproduced the same intersection over and over again. He realized he was wasting time looking for clues, not only because he wasn't sure what he was looking for, but also because his Western eye blinded him to Saigon. The smoking gun could be right in front of his face and he would never see it. It would take a Vietnamese observer, or better yet, a Vietnamese detective, to uncover the truth in Ric's case. But he didn't know how to hire one or whether there was even such as thing as a Vietnamese private eye.

The only realistic option was to swallow his pride, call Robert Fowler, and turn the notebook over to the consulate. Maybe by working with Fowler and the consulate, and by keeping the pressure on them to produce results rather than accept Ric's conviction as a fait accompli, he could help Ric mount a reasonable defense. That would mean getting past his dislike of Fowler and trusting him to do the right thing. If Fowler didn't give off the right vibes during the call, Steve could change his mind and keep silent about the notebook.

"Phan, is there a telephone around here?"

Phan pointed to a stainless-steel payphone under an awning in front of a restaurant just down from where they were standing.

"Thanks," Steve said, heading to the phone and studying the directions at the top of the unit. There was no way he was going to successfully place a telephone call at a Vietnamese payphone. He gave in quickly, feeling no shame. "Phan, if I give you the number, can you dial it for me? I'll pay you whatever it costs."

"They not teach you how to make phone call in United States?" This time it was Phan's turn to laugh. He reached into his pocket and pulled out a black leather wallet, retrieving a phone card from a pocket jammed with bent, mangled business cards and creased and cracked family pictures. He swiped the card in a slot on the payphone and then asked Steve for the number. Phan dialed the number and handed Steve the receiver, backing away a few steps to give him privacy. The phone rang twice before someone answered.

"U.S. Consulate, may I help you." The voice was a woman's. She spoke with no accent, so Steve assumed she was not a local hire. That meant he could speak at a normal speed and not worry about his diction.

"Yes, may I speak with Mr. Robert Fowler, please? This is Steve Stilwell calling."

"Mr. Fowler is not available," the woman replied in a neutral voice. "If you tell me what you are calling about, I can direct your call to the appropriate person."

"Mr. Fowler was working with me on a case involving a retired American Navy officer. I think it's best if I speak with him directly. Can I leave a message for him?"

"I'm afraid not," the woman replied. "Mr. Fowler was shot and killed earlier today. The embassy had just issued a statement about a half hour ago. I'm afraid someone else will have to help you."

The news jolted Steve and he gasped out loud. "That's dreadful news," he said, not knowing what else to say. His mind jumped to what the implications might be for Ric's case. Were the drug cartels strong enough to murder U.S. Government officials? If so, they would not hesitate to kill him. The case was getting worse by the minute. "I'm gonna have to call back after I've had the chance to think about this," Steve said. "I'm just not sure—"

Before he could finish, the Vietnamese man from the light post punched him in the gut, knocking the wind out of him. When he dropped the receiver and hunched over to try and catch his breath, the man wrenched his planner lose from under his arm and started to run away. With no air in his lungs and pain radiating from his stomach throughout his torso, Steve couldn't even shout for help, let alone resist or pursue his attacker. In an instant, the notebook was gone.

The next thing Steve heard was a loud "Whahaaa!" as Phan launched a karate kick that caught Steve's attacker squarely in the groin. The attacker screamed and grabbed his crotch with both hands as he melted to the ground. Now it was Phan's turn to snag the notebook from the sidewalk as he ran over to Steve, who was still doubled over trying to breathe. Phan tugged on his arm, dragging him toward his motorcycle.

"Mr. Steve, Mr. Steve, we have to go. Get on seat and we go." Phan jumped on his bike and started the engine as Steve struggled to get on. Phan twisted around and handed Steve his planner. "You be more careful and hold notebook tight." Then Phan pulled the motorcycle out into traffic to put some distance between them and the attacker, who was by now stumbling to his own motorcycle.

Phan weaseled over to the centerline dividing the flow of traffic. Taking advantage of the narrow gap down the middle, he guided his bike through the undulating hole. When they came to the first major intersection, he didn't stop for the red light, but instead clawed a passage through the crossing vehicles. Steve's left arm cramped from clutching the bottom of the seat so tightly, but he dared not let go. He dug his planner into his lap, resolving that if someone tried to get the notebook from him again, they would have to pry it loose from his cold, dead hands.

Phan banked the motorcycle first left and then right as he careened through the tangled web of Saigon's streets and alleys. Old shops, new buildings, deteriorating tenements landscaped with power poles whose wires substituted for branches and leaves, and plush villas with young women in colorful silk tunics looking on from balconies, flew by in a blurred blending of Vietnamese culture and urban society. Phan finally came to a stop at a bustling intersection too crammed to cross while the light was red.

"Where are we going?" Steve asked, having demurred to Phan on the escape plan.

"Notre Dame just up ahead," Phan shouted. "You go in door after I drop you off. You go through church, come out back, and I pick you up. We got to go, that man still follow us." When the light turned green, Phan bolted through the intersection and headed for Notre Dame.

When they rounded the next corner, Steve saw the two unmistakable bell towers of the imposing red brick cathedral built by French colonists in the nineteenth century. Phan pulled up to the curb at the entrance to the church and Steve hopped off. "You go now," Phan directed. "Man very close." Phan then sped away, leaving Steve at the mercy of his pursuer. He turned and walked quickly to the entrance to the Cathedral, noting the inscription above the door, *Deo Optimo Maximo*, as he went inside. He thought it unusual that the inscription caught his eye, particularly given that he didn't speak Latin. He knew *Deo* meant God and assumed the other words loosely translated to optimal and maximum, but whatever they meant, the inscription and the beauty of the stained-glass windows inside reminded him that his fate was now in God's hands.

He thought about hiding in a confessional until his pursuer gave up and left, but he was afraid the man would not respect the sanctity of the confessional and would open the doors looking for him. Besides, Phan's plan seemed plausible, provided he could get out of the building before his pursuer saw him. He started to run under the cream-colored vaulted ceiling of the long aisle to the right of the nave and was just about to sprint to the open door at the end of the right transept when he heard a calm, steady voice call him from the altar.

"Where are you going in such a hurry, my son?"

Steve stopped and turned to see a middle-aged Vietnamese priest dressed in a traditional black suit with a white starched collar. He spoke with a high-pitched nasal voice and a distinct Vietnamese accent. Otherwise, his English was flawless, although the echo in the empty cathedral made understanding him a challenge.

Given that he was a priest, Steve took the time to answer him. "I'm sorry for running, Father, but someone is after me. I've done nothing wrong, I promise you, and I mean no disrespect to the Lord's house. I'm afraid I must go now." In his haste to make good his escape, he didn't see the priest make the Sign of the Cross in his direction, nor did he hear the priest call after him, "Bless you, my son." He disappeared out the door and headed down the cracked sidewalk to the road. Now he had to find Phan.

* * *

THE MAN PURSUING STEVE SAW HIM dismount from Phan's motorcycle and make his way into the cathedral. He thought it typical of a Westerner to seek sanctuary in a church. The church meant nothing to him; he was Buddhist by birth and agnostic by practice, so he could do whatever he needed to do in the church without feeling constrained by the nature of the building or anyone inside.

He parked his bike at the curb and ran up the sidewalk to the *Deo Optimo Maximo* entrance, paying no attention to the inscription above the door. Stopping behind a reddish-brown railing at the back of the Cathedral, he looked across the vast, pew-filled nave. At the far end was the altar, with a center aisle leading from the back and cutting the pews into bride and groom sides. The pews were empty, except for four nuns in black and white habits kneeling and praying near the left side of the altar. The Westerner was nowhere to be seen.

He began to trot up the black and white geometrically tiled center aisle, his head pivoting from side to side, searching under and along the wooden pews to make sure his target didn't slip past him. When he saw the confessionals under an arch leading to the right-side aisle, he slid down the pew to the first door and yanked it open, only to find it empty. As he started to open the second door, one of the nuns, who looked to be in her seventies, scolded him in Vietnamese and asked him what he was doing. He ignored her berating and opened the second and third doors, finding nothing. He then returned his attention to the cathedral at large and continued up the right-side aisle, the nun continuing her verbal chastisements. When he reached the transept, the priest who had earlier blessed Steve approached him from the altar. He spoke in Vietnamese.

"Are you looking for something, my son?" The priest continued walking toward the man. The man looked askance at the priest and didn't answer him. Instead he turned his attention back to the right side of the transept, scouring the area for the Westerner. As the priest drew closer, the man pulled a gun from his pocket and held it at his side, leaving just enough visible to warn the priest to leave him alone.

"Please put that away and let me help you," the priest said calmly, as if gun-toting thugs were an everyday occurrence. "You won't need that here. No one will harm you." The priest walked on an intercept course that took him directly toward the advancing gunman. When the priest was almost upon the man, he once again implored him to put the gun away.

"Please, my son, this is a house of peace. There is no place for guns here." The priest halted just short of the man, who stopped and turned to face him.

"Where is the Westerner who just came through here?" the man demanded. His voice spit contempt. He had no time for Western religions or their lackey Vietnamese agents. The elderly nun approached from the left, but when the clicking of her shoes on the tile floor alerted the priest to her approach, he held up his hand like a traffic cop, making it clear she was to come no closer. She kneeled at the closest pew and began to pray.

"Many people come into this building," the priest responded. "It is the house of the Lord."

"I haven't got time for games," the man growled. He lunged forward and grabbed the priest by the hair with his free hand while he brandished the pistol with the other. He dragged him over to the nun kneeling in the pew near the altar and pointed the gun at her head, while still holding the priest by the hair. She looked up at him without fear, a single tear trickling through the furrows of her wrinkled cheek. "Now tell me, where did the Westerner go? If you lie, I will kill her while you watch."

The priest choked out a response, his voice strained by pain and the twisted posture forced on him by the man grabbing his hair. "I saw him walk through the main entrance but I didn't see him leave."

The man yanked the priest's hair, pulling him closer and jamming the pistol's barrel into his forehead. "Try to remember better," the man instructed. He dug the barrel into the priest's skin, drawing blood and causing him to writhe in pain. The nun kneeling next to them looked on stoically, her eyes conveying sadness, the sadness of someone who has seen much horror in her life but can no longer react to fear. The other nuns had vanished from the sanctuary.

"My memory is good," the priest asserted, not resisting the gunman's grasp. "I did not see him leave."

"You are a liar!" the gunman yelled. He pistol-whipped the priest to the ground and kicked him in the head, knocking him unconscious. The elderly nun rose to her feet and threw herself on the priest, shielding him with her body. The gunman laughed. "I should kill you both," he scoffed, aiming the weapon at the nun's head. "But I don't want to waste the bullets."

Realizing that the other nuns were nowhere to be seen and that the police could be on their way, the gunman walked quickly around the remaining interior perimeter of the building. Finding no one, he glanced back at the altar from the main entrance at the opposite end of the building. All he saw was the nun attending to the priest, who was slumped over in the first pew. The Westerner and his notebook had escaped for now. This would not be a pleasant report to his boss, but he really didn't care. She was just another Westerner who needed to go back to her own country. Maybe his target's escape would convince her to do so. That is, after she paid him for his services.

21

***

Same day—Wednesday, 31 May 2000, 5:01 p.m.
Saigon

STEVE SCANNED THE FLOW OF TRAFFIC from the left, searching for Phan. Given the multitude of riders, all wearing helmets and all moving in a tide of two-wheeled vehicles, it would be next to impossible to recognize him. He might not even show up. Phan owed him no loyalty or commitment, and he'd already put himself in grave danger by helping Steve. Perhaps Phan was having second thoughts about playing the Good Samaritan.

"Mr. Steve," came a familiar voice from a Honda as it pulled up to the curb about fifteen feet from where Steve stood. "Hurry up! You get on bike and we get out of here."

"Phan!" Steve yelled, thrilled to see his guardian. He ran to the motorcycle and hopped on the back, clamping his left hand on the bottom edge of the seat using muscle memory rather than conscious thought. He had become a veteran Vietnamese motorcycle passenger. All he needed now was his own helmet.

Phan started the bike and shot back into traffic, now at the height of rush hour.

"Thank you for coming back," Steve shouted, not sure if he could be heard over the orchestra of engines and horns.

Heavy traffic at the next red light forced Phan to come to a complete stop. He twisted around toward Steve and smiled, his cigarette-stained teeth already a deepening brownish-yellow. "When Phan say he be there to pick you up, Phan be there. You tell your friends, Phan best driver!" Phan smiled again at Steve, but turned back around to drive when the increasing drone of engines forecast that traffic was moving again.

"Where are we going?" Steve shouted as they started to inch forward.

Phan yelled back over his shoulder, "I take you to police."

Remembering how Ric's ordeal played out with the Vietnamese police, Steve was not inclined to go that route. Now that Fowler was dead, he wasn't sure the police could protect him. There was no way he was going to risk staying at the Sheraton, or any other hotel for that matter, as the assault at the payphone told him the drug cartels would find him, wherever he tried to hide. There was only one alternative left if he hoped to stay alive and get the notebook back to U.S. authorities.

"Take me to the airport," Steve shouted. "It's time for me to go home."

This time Phan didn't turn around. Traffic was just too heavy. Instead, he took his left hand off the handlebar and gave Steve a thumbs-up. All they had to do was get to the airport alive.

SURPRISINGLY, THE RIDE TO TAN SON Nhat Airport proved uneventful. Phan's ruse at Notre Dame had worked and whoever had been following them was gone, or he was lying back and waiting for another opportunity. There was nothing Steve could do about it either way, so he kept to his plan to get out of Vietnam and back to the safety of the United States.

Heavy traffic on every street leading to the airport made *slow* too fast a word to describe their progress. Although the trip was no more than five or six kilometers, they crawled every step of the way until the final kilometer, when traffic started to move at a normal speed. Phan took advantage of the lighter volume, darting into gaps and weaving around slower vehicles until they entered the airport grounds and made their way up to the terminal. He pulled over in the first available slot to let Steve off.

"We make it," Phan announced. "I told you Phan good driver."

"You're the best," Steve replied, smiling broadly at his new friend. "I can't thank you enough for all you've done." Steve reached out to shake Phan's hand, a gesture that made Phan smile, as well. "You saved my life, Phan. How can I ever repay you?"

"How about you be my American friend?" Phan asked. "Maybe I visit America some day and stay with you?"

"I'd really like that," Steve said, pulling his wallet from his front pants pocket and flipping through the bills inside to see how much money he had. He pulled out all the Vietnamese Dong, including sixteen 100,000-Dong notes, and handed it to Phan. Although only about seventy-five dollars, it would be a fortune to Phan. Then he reached into another pocket and removed four of the five hundred dollars he kept in reserve. He wanted to give Phan all his reserve money, but he didn't know what he would need in the airport and on the way home, so he kept a hundred-dollar bill just in case. He handed the rest of the money to Phan. Phan didn't say anything right away, but the look on his face told Steve everything he needed to know. This was manna from heaven. It had to be about half a year's wages. Maybe it would allow Phan and his family to live large for a while, as long as the driver remained safe from whoever had been pursuing them.

"Mr. Steve," Phan said finally. "This too much money. I give you ride on my motorcycle, maybe I save your life. You give me fifty dollars, no more."

Steve couldn't help but laugh. At least now he knew what his life was worth in Vietnam.

"Why you laughing?" Phan asked. "Did you think of American movie again?"

"I'm laughing because I have found a new friend in Vietnam who makes me smile." Feeling guilty for having to leave Phan behind he added, "You're a good man, Phan. I am lucky I met you. Thank you for all you've done and for helping my friend. You must take the money. Fifty dollars is for your driving and for saving my life. The rest is a gift from one friend to another." Steve reached out and shook Phan's hand again. He tucked his planner under his arm and then used his left hand to double-grasp Phan's hand.

"Okay," Phan said. "I take money because I your friend."

"Phan, you've also got to be careful now that you've helped me. The people that were trying to get this planner may come after you now. I don't think they will, because you don't have what they want, but you need to be careful."

"I take care of myself," Phan said proudly, standing up a little straighter and puffing out his chest. "Remember, I kick bad guy who take your planner. I A-Number One driver. You tell your friends when they visit Saigon."

"You know I will," Steve promised, dwelling on Phan's last words. They gave him an idea. It wasn't something he was thrilled about, but if Phan was up for it, it was worth a try. Phan sounded confident and unafraid, so he might be just the right guy for the job.

"You know, there is one more thing you might be able to do for me." Steve paused, as second thoughts already bubbled to the surface. But with no other real options, he plowed forward. "Remember I told you that when Mr. Ric went up to his room after you dropped him off, his friend was dead and there was a girl in the room?"

"Yes," Phan said, his eyes focused intently on Steve's.

"I need to talk to that girl."

"I find her for you. What's her name?"

"That's the hard part, Phan. I don't know her name or anything about her. All I know is that she's a prostitute. I can't even tell you what she looks like. I just know she was in the Mountain Flower Hotel on the night Mr. Ric was arrested and his friend died. I need her to tell me the truth about what happened in the room that night."

Phan didn't hesitate. "I find girl for you, but how I tell you when I find her?"

Steve reached into his wallet again and produced one of his business cards. "You call me at the number on the card," Steve instructed, "and I'll pay for the call."

Phan looked at the card and read Steve's telephone number back to him. "Is that right number?" he asked.

"That's it, you've got it right," Steve confirmed. "Are you sure you want to do this? It could be very dangerous."

Phan took the card and tucked it in his wallet. "I find girl for you because you are my American friend." Phan smiled, but not quite as broadly as before. Steve sensed a degree of apprehension in his response.

"Thanks, Phan. Promise me, though, if things get dangerous or you or your family feels unsafe, you'll stop looking for her. I'd never forgive myself if anything happened to you."

"I promise, Mr. Steve," he said earnestly. "Now you go. Maybe you miss plane if you keep talking."

Steve had one more thing to say. "After this is all over, Phan, I want you and your family to visit me in the United States as my guests. You've earned a nice vacation in America."

"Is that true?" Phan asked, buoyed by the prospect of a trip to the United States.

"It's true, I promise you," Steve reassured him. "I've got your card so I know how to get in touch with you." Steve looked at his watch; it was almost seven p.m. "I better get going," he said, shaking Phan's hand one last time. "You be safe."

"Goodbye, Mr. Steve," Phan said as he finished shaking hands. Putting on his helmet, he jumped back on his motorcycle and disappeared into the traffic heading away from the airport. Steve watched him go, wondering whether he had signed Phan's death warrant by asking him to find the girl. He promised himself he would reward Phan and his family, whether or not Phan found the girl, and he fully intended to bring them to America to visit. Phan just had to live long enough so he could keep his promise.

22

Same day—Wednesday, 31 May 2000, 7:11 a.m. CDT
Houston, Texas

ALTHOUGH IT WAS BRIGHT AND SUNNY outside, the hotel room was dark—morbidly dark. A few errant rays of sunlight seeped around the edges of the opaque, plastic-backed curtains, but the room remained black. Even the LED display on the alarm clock was invisible, the unit having been turned around so its red glow dissipated on the burlap wallpaper. The air conditioner, cranked to high, blew frigid air across the room. Nothing moved.

Casey lay in a semi-fetal position in the bed closest to the air conditioner. Her arms and legs felt heavy, far heavier than she had the strength to lift or swing out of bed. Her head felt heavy too, sinking deep into the pillows. She'd pulled the covers over herself as the room chilled. Now she felt like their captive, unable to throw them off, but more importantly, not wanting to. She lay there, motionless, waiting for time to pass.

She was having second thoughts about her new job. She'd thought what she was getting into was a small trusts and estate practice where she could litigate cases and deal with the past on her own terms. She wanted safety, she wanted simplicity, and she wanted to get lost in her case files. She needed time to work its slow magic and heal her, chipping away at the memory of the day in Iraq that mutilated her body and changed her life forever. Instead, her first case had brought her military memories front and center. She found herself consoling a woman who just lost her husband, even though Casey had yet to find consolation for what she'd lost during her own aircraft disaster six years before.

She could deal with getting Ric Stokes out of the drug charges if that was all there was to it. But as far as she was concerned, this case was no longer about drugs. It was about the five souls onboard the plane that crashed into the Central Highlands in 1968. She could only remember one of their names, Lieutenant Colonel Ray Eversall, because he was Ryan Eversall's father. But in a strange way, their names didn't matter. Each assumed the identity of her late copilot, reminding her that she had caused the death of her friend and colleague.

She had intended to wait to read the Sapphire Pavilion file until she returned to Williamsburg. But after meeting with Angela Eversall and speaking with Steve on her cellphone, she couldn't sleep. Rather than toss and turn in bed, she pulled the contents from Ryan Eversall's accordion file and replaced them with her notepad and some other background research she'd brought with her from Williamsburg. Then she climbed into bed and started to read.

The papers gave her a snapshot of the doomed plane's final flight. Five men boarded the C-130A on 18 January 1968. They took off from Ubon Air Base in eastern Thailand on a Top-Secret mission designated "Sapphire Pavilion." If details of the Sapphire Pavilion mission had been declassified, Ryan Eversall had been unable to find them because there was nothing in the file explaining what the mission entailed. Only the five crewmen were on the flight manifest, making it impossible to explain from the official record how there could be five graves near the wreckage of the aircraft. Who could have buried the fifth crewman if only five men were on board? The North Vietnamese or Viet Cong would not have done so—they would have let the bodies rot. But if friendlies had found the wreckage, why was it not reported or investigated by U.S. authorities? Something didn't add up.

The thought of the five souls buried alone on the mountain ate at her. Who could have survived the crash? How long had they survived? Did they feel lucky they were alive, or guilty because the fates had selected the others to die? Soon she had transposed her analysis of their situation with that of her own crash experience, driving her into a deep and impenetrable funk, the likes of which she had not experienced since right after she learned her leg had been amputated. It was all she could do to shove the papers under the covers behind her, hit the master light switch, and pull the blankets over her head. Unable to sleep, unable to cry, unable to scream, she lay there frozen in time, experiencing her own crash and her copilot's death over, and over, and over again, until she was too exhausted to go on.

Ringhhh. Ringhhh. Ringhhh. The high-pitched screech of the room's telephone pierced the morning quiet. Thinking it was Steve calling to update her on his progress, she fought to pull herself closer to the edge of the bed. When she pushed back the covers and reached for the phone, goose bumps erupted on her exposed skin from the ice-cold air streaming out of the wall unit. She mustered all her strength to answer the phone without tipping off Steve that something was wrong.

"Hello, this is Casey Pantel."

"Ms. Pantel, this is the front desk. Can you come down for a moment? There's a problem with your credit card that we need to straighten out with you right away."

The unexpected reason for the call distracted Casey from her depression, prompting her to rally enough strength to continue the conversation.

"I'm sorry, but I'm still in bed. I'll need some time to get ready. Can you tell me what the issue is?"

"I'm sorry, but we prefer not to talk about credit card issues over the telephone. We'll give you a full explanation as soon as you come to the front desk."

Casey thought it sounded like the clerk was reading the response to her question, so it was clear she wouldn't be able to get anywhere on the phone with the clerk. "Okay. I'll be down as quickly as I can."

"Thank you, Ms. Pantel. We'll see you shortly."

Casey hung up. Curious as to what the situation might be, she crawled out of the covers to the side of the bed. No longer protected from the arctic air pumping from the air conditioner, she shivered and reached for her prosthetic leg. She liked to keep it at the foot of her bed in the event of an emergency, although more than once she'd found it on the floor next to the bed, having launched it during a stray convulsion in her sleep. This morning she found it right where she'd left it and was able to put it on with little effort. As it was now almost seven thirty, she decided to throw on a pair of jeans and a t-shirt, do some minimal work with her hair, and see what the issue was. Then she'd come back to her room and get ready to go. She thought it funny how something as simple as a call about a credit card problem had helped pull her back from the edge. Then she thought about it again. There was nothing funny about it at all.

CASEY EXITED THE ELEVATOR AND WALKED through the lobby of the Executive Suites Hotel. She didn't look bad given that she'd taken only ten minutes to get ready. She'd never see these people again anyway, so it really didn't matter. What did matter was finding out about her credit card. It was the only one she had, and if there was an issue with it, she wasn't sure what to do. With no one standing in line in front of her, she walked right up to the counter where a young man waited to help.

"Are you checking out?" the young man asked.

"No, not yet. My name is Casey Pantel in Room 502. Someone called me about ten minutes ago and asked me to come to the front desk because there is an issue with my credit card."

"I'm sorry, no one told me about it. It was probably our accounting section. Let me check and I'll be right back." The young man disappeared through a doorway behind the front desk on Casey's left. He was gone about two minutes before he re-emerged. "I just checked with accounting and there's no problem with your credit card. The charge went through fine, so you're okay."

Casey looked perplexed. "So who called me then?"

"I don't know, but I didn't call you and neither did accounting."

"Could anyone else from the front desk have called?"

"Nope. I'm the only one here this morning. Maybe the call was a mistake."

Then it hit her. "The file!" she shouted.

"What file?" the front desk clerk asked.

"I'm sorry, but I've got to get back to my room right away."

Casey hurried to the elevator and pushed the up button. Both elevators were on the fifth floor. She banged on the "up" button over and over, but nothing happened. The elevators remained on the fifth floor.

Casey turned and shouted to the front desk clerk, "Is there a stairway to the fifth floor?"

"If you wait for a minute, ma'am, I'm sure the elevators will come down."

"Look, damn it, that's not what I asked." Casey reverted to her Army officer training and took control. "Where's the stairwell to the fifth floor?"

The young man raised his eyebrows. Before he had a chance to object, he found himself pointing in the direction of the stairwell and saying, "There."

"Thanks," Casey yelled over her shoulder as she bolted for the door. Then she turned to look back at him as she prepared to enter the stairwell. "If you don't hear from me within ten minutes, call the police."

A second later, the door to the stairwell swung closed behind her and she rocketed up the stairs as fast as her legs—both real and prosthetic—could carry her.

23

───∿∿───

Same day—Wednesday, 31 May 2000, 8:28 a.m. EDT
State Department, Washington, DC

THIRTY-THREE-YEAR-OLD PEGGY ALTMAN SAT IN THE anterior room on
the Seventh Floor of the Main State Building waiting to brief Secretary
of State Susan McDermott and Assistant Secretary of State for East Asian and
Pacific Affairs, Elrod Benfield. It didn't matter that Peggy, as the Country
Officer for Vietnam, had briefed the Secretary numerous times on other
matters. She still experienced waves of nausea and perspired heavily in
anticipation of the briefings because Susan McDermott—the first woman to
hold the office of Secretary of State—was her hero.

Peggy had the information about Robert Fowler's murder memorized
and could recite it backwards and forwards. The problem was, Secretary
McDermott was never satisfied with facts; she wanted insight. What did
the events mean and what did they imply? Those were the questions Peggy
dreaded because her answers were little more than speculation. She'd caveat
everything she said, of course, but she couldn't control what the Secretary did
with her opinions. She hoped major foreign policy decisions weren't hanging
on the best-guess assessment she'd formulated on her elevator ride to the
Seventh Floor.

As Peggy thought through the Secretary's possible questions, the
receptionist entered the waiting area. Peggy was so deep in thought that
she didn't notice the woman looking her way, so she had to announce her
presence. "Ms. Altman, the Secretary will see you now. Please follow me."

The fiftyish receptionist manufactured a smile, did an about-face, and started walking to the Secretary's office without waiting to see if Peggy followed. Peggy flattened the rolled-back pages of her yellow legal pad and jumped out of her chair to catch up. The receptionist was already waiting at the door of the Secretary's office by the time Peggy rounded the corner. She paused for a second to tuck her short blonde hair behind her ears. Since her pregnancy, her hair had lost all its bounce and there was little she could do with it other than push it out of the way. Whatever it looked like now would have to do.

"Madame Secretary, Ms. Peggy Altman is here to see you." The receptionist stepped back to allow Peggy to enter.

"Hello, Peggy," Secretary McDermott said, rising from her chair behind her broad, dark cherry desk. "It's so good to see you again." She stepped forward and the two shook hands. "You've met Elrod Benfield, haven't you?"

"Oh, yes, of course, Madame Secretary," Peggy responded. Benfield approached Peggy from the plush red leather chair he was sitting in opposite the Secretary's desk.

"Hello, Peggy," Benfield said, shaking her hand.

"Why don't we have a seat at the table to discuss the situation in Saigon," the Secretary suggested, motioning for everyone to head toward a large oval conference table at the rear of her office. "And I hope you don't mind if I keep calling it Saigon. Old habits are hard to break."

Peggy waited for Benfield to choose his seat before she opted for hers. The jockeying gave her a moment to study the two senior diplomats. Secretary McDermott radiated professionalism from head to toe. From her highlighted shoulder-length hair, to her blue tailored suit and cream chiffon blouse, to her black high-heel shoes, she looked like a woman who could simultaneously grace the cover of *Vogue* and the front page of the *Wall Street Journal*. Though in her late fifties or early sixties, she was so fit and trim she could pass for a woman fifteen years younger. She carried herself with panache. She could just as easily converse at the staff level about the Washington Redskins as she could talk about nuclear nonproliferation on the floor of the United Nations. To Peggy, she was the epitome of a leader, able to guide people to difficult objectives and make them feel good about their endeavors.

Benfield was not quite the opposite, but he was definitely different. Although he also wore a blue tailored suit, his white shirt was wrinkled behind his tie and his oxblood wingtip shoes scuffed. His hair curled on top, with gray infiltrating the black all around. He looked as brilliant and eccentric as he was, much like a stereotypical mathematics professor at a New England college. There was nothing malevolent about him, but he lacked the Secretary's polish and charisma. As a result, people followed his orders because they had to, not because they wanted to, and it gave them no satisfaction. No doubt he had reached the final rung on his ladder, whereas Secretary McDermott still had two more possible rungs to climb.

"Would either of you like coffee or tea?" the Secretary asked. Both her guests politely declined.

"All right, then let's get down to business," the Secretary began. "Peggy, what's happening in Saigon?"

"We don't know much more than we did earlier this morning. Robert Fowler was found shot to death in Saigon. He was either getting in or out of his car at his residence, and he had a gun in his hand. The Vietnamese police have the lead on the investigation, but we've got a Diplomatic Security Special Agent inbound to assist.

"That reminds me," the Secretary interrupted. "Didn't we invite DS to this meeting? Where's Sam Bowers?"

"We did," Benfield said. "I'll have Madeleine track him down. Excuse me for a second." He got up, was gone less than a minute, and hurried back to his chair. "Madeleine says he's on his way. He got waylaid in traffic."

"It's pretty sad when you say you're stuck in traffic and people know you're telling the truth," the Secretary quipped. "You've really got to love Washington to live here." She put her game face back on and resumed questioning Peggy. "Was there anything else?"

"The Vietnamese police found a packed suitcase in the car, so it looks like Fowler was heading out of town."

"That wouldn't be unusual for a Consular Officer," Benfield interjected. "They travel around the area as part of their responsibilities."

Peggy chose her words carefully so as not to embarrass Benfield in front of the Secretary. "Normally that would be the case, but this was unusual, because it was a Wednesday afternoon and he wasn't scheduled to be out of the office. According to the Chargé, Fowler should have been in his office when this happened." Benfield nodded, which Peggy took as tacit acceptance of her position.

"So, what does this mean?" the Secretary asked, moving to the line of questioning Peggy knew was coming but dreaded nonetheless. Precision word choice from here on out was critical.

"Well," Peggy began. "The Chargé thinks—"

"I'm sorry I'm late." A gruff hulk of a man entered the office. His dark-brown suit and wide yellow tie looked too small for him, although given his size, just about anything would have looked too small. His slicked-down gray hair made him look even bulkier, and his slightly enlarged stomach bulging over the top of his belt didn't do him any favors. His backwoods accent completed the picture.

"Come in, Sam," the Secretary beckoned. "Peggy Altman is filling us in on the Robert Fowler case. Grab a seat and chime in whenever you need to."

Sam Bowers, the Assistant Secretary for the Bureau of Diplomatic Security or DS, walked behind the Secretary to the chair next to Benfield. To accommodate his girth, he had to pull the chair well away from the table to slide in. Peggy waited until Bowers settled into his chair before answering the Secretary's question. She began by bringing him up to speed.

"The Secretary asked about the significance of Robert Fowler being found out of the office with a suitcase packed when he wasn't scheduled to be anywhere."

"Not to mention with a gun in his hand," Bowers drawled.

"Exactly," Peggy said. "Maybe I'm stating the obvious, but I think he was trying to get away from something. You don't just walk away from your desk at the consulate without telling anyone, let alone take a trip somewhere. I don't care how new he was to the Foreign Service; he would have known that. I think he was running."

"What level of security clearance did he have?" the Secretary asked.

"He had a Top-Secret clearance—all our junior Foreign Service officers do," replied Bowers.

"Any chance he was passing classified information to someone?" continued the Secretary.

Bowers took this question, as well. "There's always that possibility, but we don't think so. He didn't have access to anything in the Consular Section that would be of significant interest to anyone. We're checking now to see what he accessed recently on his classified computer, but the embassy in Hanoi doesn't think we'll find anything out of the ordinary."

The Secretary continued to press for a motive. "So what was it if not classified information?"

Peggy jumped back into the conversation. "Hanoi thinks it might have been drugs, Madame Secretary."

"What makes them think drugs? Do they have any evidence?" The Secretary didn't wait for an answer. "I don't want him tarred with drugs, or anything else for that matter, until we're reasonably sure. Are we reasonably sure it was drugs?"

Peggy continued to take the lead. "It's speculation at this point based upon a case he was working."

"What case was that?" asked Benfield, joining the conversation.

"It's a case involving a former Navy JAG, Captain Ric Stokes. He's in jail pending trial on possession of heroin charges. Fowler was the liaison between the Vietnamese government and Stokes' attorney, another former Navy JAG named Steve Stilwell. In fact, Stilwell is over there now and met with Fowler before he was killed."

"I don't get it," the Secretary said. "How does being a liaison in the case connect Fowler with drugs? Do we have any evidence at all?"

"The embassy doesn't," Peggy admitted. "But that's the only unusual thing Fowler was working on. Plus, the drug cartels in Vietnam are known for their violence."

"Again, I don't see how any of that connects Fowler with drugs," the Secretary insisted. "Maybe it would help if you reminded me about the Stokes case. What's that about?"

Peggy was ready for that question, too. "Stokes and another man, Ryan Eversall, went to Vietnam at the beginning of May to find an airplane lost during the Vietnam War."

"Were they legitimate?" The Secretary asked. "I mean, if they were legitimately looking for an airplane, how did Stokes get mixed up with drugs? Was the airplane story a cover for a drug purchase?"

It was Benfield's turn to answer. The case was part of his portfolio as the Assistant Secretary for East Asian and Pacific Affairs. "It's a strange case, Madame Secretary. Ryan Eversall believed he located an airplane downed during the Vietnam War, but refused to disclose its location. He hired Ric Stokes, a retired Navy JAG specializing in international law, to handle the bureaucracy and make sure they did things right—which they did. Stokes says they found the plane, but on their final night in Vietnam, Eversall died of a heroin overdose and Stokes was found in possession of a kilo of heroin. The Vietnamese theory is that they were celebrating before they returned to the United States, but the events are so out of character for both of them, we don't know what to believe. Eversall was a respected businessman in Houston and Stokes a former senior Navy officer. Neither had any financial problems or history of misconduct. Stokes claims they were set up, but doesn't know why or by whom. He's sitting in a Vietnamese jail waiting for a trial that will likely result in the death penalty."

"Excuse me for a second," the Secretary broke in, shifting forward in her chair and sliding her elbows on the table. She picked up the phone in the center of the table and used the intercom to call her receptionist. "Madeleine, would you please bring me a cup of coffee? Thanks." The Secretary hung up the receiver, eased back into her chair, and asked, "Are we doing anything to help Stokes?"

"That's where Fowler came in," Benfield continued. "He was making sure the Vietnamese treat Stokes properly, and he arranged for Stokes' American attorney to see him in jail. And one of our lawyers talked to Stokes' attorney before he went to Vietnam to see his client. In other words, we're doing all we can, but right now the Vietnamese are holding Stokes, and I'm afraid in this case, that gives them the upper hand."

Benfield paused, but his perplexed expression communicated he had one more thing to say. "Honestly, I can't blame the Vietnamese. I'm not sure we'd do anything differently." Bowers nodded in agreement. As he did, Madeleine produced the cup of coffee.

"Thank you, Madeleine," the Secretary said. Turning to Peggy, she asked, "Do you have anything to add?"

"Only that Stokes hasn't told us where the plane is, so we haven't been able to verify whether they found it. If there's no plane, then maybe they were there to purchase drugs. You'd think that Stokes would have told us where the plane is to buttress his credibility."

"You would think that, wouldn't you," agreed the Secretary. "Just out of curiosity, what kind of plane was it?"

"I don't know," Peggy admitted, "but I can find out."

"It was a C-130 lost in January 1968," Benfield said. "Eversall's paperwork says it was lost just before the Tet Offensive and that there were no survivors."

The Secretary picked up her coffee cup and leaned back in her chair. She blew on the hot, black liquid and then took a small sip, followed by a much longer, deeper swig. The silence stretched out. She took a third drink from her cup, deep in thought. Peggy felt the tension rise but dared not say anything, particularly as the most junior person in the room. After one final sip, the Secretary leaned forward, placed her coffee cup on the saucer, and gave her final direction.

"Okay then," she began. "Sam, you and your Security team get to the bottom of Fowler's murder. Leave no stone unturned. The investigation needs to withstand Congressional scrutiny—I don't want the President embarrassed on this. And keep me apprised. I want weekly status briefs, as well as when there are any significant developments."

"Got it," Bowers responded.

"And don't we have a private security contractor that's supposed to be protecting our personnel in Vietnam?"

"We do," Bowers confirmed.

"Then talk to them and find out what went wrong. The taxpayers are going to want to know why we're paying for security and not getting it. I want to know that, too."

"We'll get that for you, Madame Secretary," Bowers said.

The Secretary continued, "Elrod, I need you to prepare a memo on Fowler's murder and the Stokes' case. Keep it short—no more than two pages. Get with Sam's folks to put it together. I need it ASAP for the President."

"I'll take care of it," Benfield responded.

"Hold on a minute, Elrod. I'm not finished with you."

"Yes, ma'am," Benfield added.

"Get with Public Affairs and put together a statement of what we know. I want facts, only facts. I want the public to know our embassies overseas are safe."

"They are," Bowers asserted. "I'm confident of that. This was a one-off event."

"Well, it better be if that's what we're saying. But unless you are one hundred percent sure, don't say it. Public Affairs will know how to couch it. We can't be second-guessed here."

"I've got it," Benfield said.

"One last thing, Elrod."

"What's that, Madame Secretary?"

"Have your folks get with Stokes' attorney. What did you say his name is?"

"Stilwell. Steve Stilwell."

"Okay, have your folks get with Steve Stilwell. Find out everything you can from him about Stokes' case. Maybe it will help with the Fowler investigation. Also, if he needs any help with Stokes, give it to him. I don't want an innocent American military officer rotting in a Vietnamese jail, or worse yet, executed for something he didn't do."

"Will do," Benfield said.

Secretary McDermott turned toward Peggy, who picked up her pen. "Nothing for you, Peggy. You did a good job on the brief and I appreciate your insight."

Surprised but happy to have evaded a tasking from the Secretary, Peggy smiled wearily and responded with a simple, "Thank you, ma'am."

"Oh, there is one more thing, Elrod."

"Of course, ma'am," Assistant Secretary Benfield said awkwardly. Peggy assumed his "of course" meant he would do anything the Secretary asked, but it sounded like a cheeky response to yet another tasking. Peggy was glad it was the Assistant Secretary's gaff and not hers.

"I want more information about the plane Stokes says they found and where it is. If there are Americans out there that haven't come home yet, we need to go get them." She paused and took one final long drink of coffee, draining her cup. Then she added, "Now let's get going. We've got work to do."

24

Same day—Wednesday, 31 May 2000, 8:41 a.m. EDT
Washington, DC

THE PHONE RANG TWICE BEFORE THE man with the Boston accent picked up. "Hello."

"Why am I seeing a televised statement about the investigation into the diplomat's death?" The caller's every word expressed anger and contempt.

"It's to be expected after a diplomat is murdered," the man with the Boston accent answered matter-of-factly. He didn't want to convey any sense that the operation was out of control.

"What do you take me for, a fool? Of course that's what is expected! It should never have come to this. What about the notebook? Do we have the notebook yet?"

"Not yet, I'm afraid." The man with the Boston accent didn't try to explain Gallagher's efforts. This wasn't a time to make excuses. It was a time to take direction and assuage the boss's anger. Nothing he said was going to help. He hoped short, direct answers would minimize the blowback.

"What do you mean you're 'afraid'? I don't put people in charge of operations to be afraid. Perhaps I need to replace you with someone who's not afraid to do what it takes to get the job done."

"It's an expression," the man with the Boston accent declared, not wanting to get backed into a corner. Sounding weak now could have serious repercussions. He had to come off as firmly in control without assuming blame for the operation's failures. "Besides, you don't want to replace me. I've got the network to get this done. You take me out of the picture and you'll be starting from scratch. By the time you get things back on track, it'll be too late."

"So what's your plan?"

"Stilwell's on his way back to Williamsburg. We believe he has the notebook with him. We'll get it from him there."

"That's bullshit. He never should have been allowed to leave Vietnam with the notebook. That's mission failure. I should remove you for that alone."

The man with the Boston accent pushed back. "No. If something had happened to him in Vietnam, that would have been bullshit. You think there's an investigation now? It would have been mammoth had Stilwell been killed. They would have linked all the incidents together naturally until they found a common denominator. It would be just a matter of time."

"And what would that common denominator be?"

The man with the Boston accent knew this was not a rhetorical question. It was calculated to drive him toward a course of action. With each day the operation continued and the more complex it became, the chance of discovery grew exponentially. Now tracks would have to be covered. If he didn't make the decisions, the decisions would be made for him. Then he might become part of the tracks requiring corrective action. This was not the time for mercy.

"Gallagher."

"I'm glad we understand each other." The caller paused before continuing, as if to let the response sink in. "What about the investigation into the diplomat?"

"They won't find anything, so it won't go anywhere."

"They'll have to find *something*; otherwise this incident will be a political liability for the President. Your job is to make sure they find something that ends their inquiry."

"We'll link him to drugs."

"I don't care what you link him to as long as it's not us and it resolves the matter."

"Got it," the man with the Boston accent responded. "Is that all?"

"You tell me."

"No, there's one more thread." He hadn't reported this segment of the operation yet. He would have preferred to bring it up under different circumstances, like when he already had the file in hand. But his mouth started to answer the question faster than his mind could formulate the optimal strategy for disclosure. It was too late for strategy now; he couldn't wind back the clock.

"We think Eversall may have kept some papers on Sapphire Pavilion in his home office."

"What do you mean, you *think*? And why are you only thinking now?"

PS-BX068651B5

CreateSpace
222 Old Wire Rd
Columbia, SC 29172

Question About Your Order?

Log in to your account at www.createspace.com and "Contact Support."

06/30/2017 07:17:05 PM
Order ID: 1765418827

Qty.	Item

IN THIS SHIPMENT

1   Sapphire Pavilion
     1603816038

The caller sounded outraged. "I can't believe I'm just hearing about this for the first time. It's been over two weeks since Eversall died. This is more bullshit! Someone get into the house and take the papers. Why am I making these decisions?"

"You're not," the man with the Boston accent said coolly, trying to defuse the caller's fury. "I'm making them." Now he opted for full disclosure to show he had command of the situation. "Stilwell's got an associate working the case with him. She's in Houston and she's already got the papers. We'll have them in our hands shortly."

"In case it isn't clear, I'm not pleased with how this operation is progressing. The next time I call, I better not hear any of this 'we *will*' bullshit. I pay you for results. That means you plan, you worry, you execute, and I get results. Do we understand each other?"

"We do."

"Good."

A slamming receiver ended the call. The man with the Boston accent's course was clear. He needed action on three fronts—Stilwell, the diplomat, and the Sapphire Pavilion file—and he needed to eliminate anything that might be traceable to him. This last part was unfortunate because he liked Gallagher, but she had no one to blame but herself. Her carelessness had allowed things to go awry, so she would have to be held accountable. But not just yet. He still had a couple of jobs for her to complete.

25

Same day—Wednesday, 31 May 2000, 7:45 a.m. CDT
Houston, Texas

CASEY RAN ALL THE WAY UP the stairs to the fifth floor and exited the stairwell adjacent to the elevators. Their doors were locked in the open position, preventing them from servicing other floors. Out of breath from the climb, she eased her way to her room, which was just down the hall to the right. The hall was otherwise empty, and it was deathly quiet. She stopped in front of her room and tried to push the door open, but it was locked. That was a good sign.

She pulled the card key from her pocket and slid it through the electronic lock. A tiny green light glowed. The door was now unlocked, but only for the time it took her to enter. In an abundance of caution, she opened it slowly and scanned the room. The queen-sized bed was as she left it with the covers pulled up loosely to the pillows. The slacks and blouse she'd taken off the night before lay neatly across the chair at the far end of the room. It was safe to enter.

She walked in, closing the door behind her. It was warmer than when she got up, which made sense. After all, she had adjusted the thermostat upward before she left. She looked to her left. Her leather briefcase was still there, leaning up against the metal leg of the desk. Then she looked at the top of the desk: the Sapphire Pavilion accordion file was gone. Someone had been in her room and stolen the file.

"What in the world is going on?" Casey said aloud. "Why would someone want that file?" Suddenly Angela Eversall's paranoia didn't seem so crazy. In fact, now that Casey thought about it, she must have been under surveillance from the time she arrived at Angela's house, if not before. Her Army self-preservation instincts kicked in. She needed to get the Houston police involved and report the stolen file. She also needed to make sure nothing else was missing and get ready to catch her flight at noon.

She walked over to her bed, lifted the covers, and chuckled. Whatever the burglar thought he got, it wasn't the contents of the Sapphire Pavilion file. Those papers were still safe and warm beneath the sheets and blankets. She pulled the covers back over the papers and slid a little closer along the mattress to the nightstand, where she used the phone to call the front desk. The same clerk she'd spoken to in the lobby answered.

"Front desk, may I help you please?"

"Yes, you can. This is Casey Pantel in Room 502. I believe I spoke with you just a couple of minutes ago about my credit card."

"Yes, ma'am. How may I help you?"

"While I was in the lobby talking to you, someone broke into my room and stole a file from my desk. I'd like to make a police report."

"Are you okay?"

"Yes, I'm fine. But a file is missing."

"Do you know how they got in?" the clerk asked. "I mean, is the door broken?"

"No, the door's fine and I don't know how they got in. I'm sure it was locked before I came down to the lobby if that's what you're getting at."

"No, I was just checking to see if I needed to send a repairman up."

Casey could feel her patience dwindling. She had a plane to catch, yet she couldn't get past the condition of the door. "We'll it might not be a bad idea to have it checked. Obviously somebody was able to get into my room and they must have come through the door."

"Okay, I'll have someone come by to look at the lock."

"Thank you. Now will you call the police for me?"

"Is a file the only thing missing? No money, credit cards, or other valuables?"

It finally occurred to Casey that the clerk was going down a checklist. She hoped he was near the end. "I'll have to check, but all I've noticed so far is the file. It was from a legal case I'm working on, so it's very important to me to get it back."

"And again, no one was hurt or injured?"

"Yes, that's correct."

"All you have to do is fill out a hotel loss report and give it to me. Then just mail or fax a copy to the Houston police."

"So the police won't come and check out the room?"

"Not in our experience, unless someone's hurt or there's a significant property loss."

Casey's irritation boiled over. "You've got to be kidding me! Someone breaks into my room and steals a file and the police won't come and check it out?"

"I'm sorry, Ms. Pantel. You're certainly welcome to call them and try for yourself. All you have to do is dial 9 for an outside line and then 911, and maybe they'll come out for you. But like I said, in our experience, the police are satisfied with a copy of our loss report."

"Well can you at least send someone up to my room with the form? I may be in the shower, so it's fine if they just slip it under the door."

"Of course, Ms. Pantel. We'll send someone right up. And I'm sorry you've had a problem with your room. I can assure you we take security here very seriously."

"I'm sure you do. Thanks for your help." Casey hung up the phone more than a little perturbed. She couldn't believe someone had broken into her room and the only investigative effort was a hotel loss report. She wasn't sure if she should accept that answer or call the police to see for herself, but since the only things missing were her notes and background research and she had to catch a plane in a few hours, it would be easier to just fill out the form and be on her way.

She stood up and walked over to her carry-on suitcase sitting open on a stand across from the bed. Retrieving some undergarments, she walked into the bathroom to take a shower. She flipped on the light and set her clothing down on the counter; then she leaned forward to get a closer look at a faint red splotch on the side of her nose. She hadn't noticed it before, so it must have appeared overnight. She touched it with her finger as if exploring it would tell her what it was.

As she started to lean back from the mirror, the shower curtain burst out of the bathtub toward her, ripping rings from the rod and pulling short screws out of the mounting brackets securing the rod to the wall. The shower curtain enveloped her and a man's arms wrapped it tightly around her body. She screamed as loud as she could, but couldn't turn around or see her assailant because the shower curtain blocked her view. He started to throw her to the floor. Though powerless to resist from inside the shower curtain, she again screamed at the top of her lungs and reached for the counter, having managed to keep one arm outside the curtain's sheath. As she felt herself falling, she grabbed a hair dryer from the counter to hit her assailant, but the downward pull was too much and she slammed onto the bathroom's tile floor. She landed on her right shoulder and arm, still wrapped in the shower curtain. She screamed again and flung her arms out to free herself from the cocoon. As she did, she felt the man kick her in the back. She flung off the shower curtain and looked up just in time to see a white male with dark hair, wearing a t-shirt and jeans, open the door and run outside. He had the Sapphire Pavilion accordion file in hand as he slammed the door behind him.

Casey picked herself up off the floor and ran to the door. She didn't try to pursue the man; instead, she locked the deadbolt and fastened the chain lock. If the intruder realized he didn't have the file's original contents, she didn't want him to be able to regain entry and surprise her again.

She limped over to the bed and sat down next to the telephone, again calling the front desk. As she waited for an answer, she felt a throbbing pain emanating from her upper right shoulder, which bore the brunt of her fall on the bathroom's tile floor. She hoped nothing was broken.

"Front desk, may I help you please?" It was the same clerk.

"Yes, this is Casey Pantel in Room 502 calling back."

"Yes, Ms. Pantel."

Casey sensed the clerk's frustration, as if he were saying, "What now, Ms. Pantel?" She could picture him rolling his eyes in anticipation of her latest complaint.

"You're not going to believe this, but it turns out that burglar was still in my room when I called you. I must have come back before he had the chance to escape. He was hiding in my shower."

"Oh my God!" the clerk exclaimed, any hint of frustration gone. "Are you all right?"

"This time you better call the police. He shot out of the shower when I went into the bathroom and threw me on the floor. He also kicked me on his way out. I'm a little bruised and the shower curtain and rod were ripped from the bathroom wall."

"Of course, Ms. Pantel. I'll call the police right away. Are you sure you're okay? Would you like me to call an ambulance?"

"No, but I do need you to call the police ASAP. I want them here in case he comes back."

"Of course, Ms. Pantel."

"Thanks," Casey replied. "I'll be in my room."

Casey hung up the phone and massaged her right shoulder and arm, mentally reviewing everything that transpired. She couldn't believe she'd allowed herself to be surprised like that. She should have checked out the entire room, or better yet, insisted on a police investigation once she was sure her room had been burglarized. She was angry with herself for letting her guard down. She wouldn't let it happen again.

She was also angry with whoever was trying to deter her from finding out about Ryan Eversall and Sapphire Pavilion. What could they possibly be after? The plane crashed during the Vietnam War—ancient history by today's standards. Planes crashed and crewmembers died during wars; she knew that all too well. There had to be something unique about this plane, its crew, or its mission to warrant breaking into an attorney's hotel room thirty-two years after the crash to steal a file about the plane. And if the break-in was linked to Ryan Eversall's death and trumped up drug charges against Ric Stokes—as it certainly had to be—that unique something was apparently worth murdering for.

Casey looked at her watch. It was almost 8:10 a.m. Two things had changed in the hour since she'd dragged herself out of bed. First, the intruder's bungled burglary had bought her time. He'd stolen the Sapphire Pavilion file all right, but he'd gotten none of its original contents. Until someone who knew what to look for realized that, she might be able to pursue her leads unhindered by snooping eyes.

Second, she knew what her next step had to be: a visit to Maxwell Air Force Base and the Air Force archives. She'd seen in Ryan Eversall's papers that he'd been there, but he'd never been in the military, so he might not have known the right questions to ask or gotten the access he needed to dive deep. She was a veteran and had the scars to prove it. If something was hidden in the archives, she'd find it. A distinguished naval officer's life depended on it, as did her own sanity. She would not take no for an answer.

Oh, and there was one more thing driving her forward. Now she was fired up.

26

Thursday, 1 June 2000, 12:42 a.m.
Saigon

PHAN NEVER CONSORTED WITH CRIMINALS. ALTHOUGH poor and struggling to earn enough money to support his wife and baby girl, he always found a way to do it legitimately. His pay from working at a travel agency catering to Western tourists provided a steady though meager income. It did him no good to ask for more money. Too many people waited in the wings to take his job. So he invented ways to supplement his wages.

His goal was to work in a restaurant frequented by Westerners so he could earn the tip money his friends talked about, but those jobs were hard to get even though he spoke English well. He taught martial arts for a while, cashing in on a skill he'd learned during his mandatory stint in the Army, but his employer went out of business still owing him three months' wages. This left him trolling the streets to give Westerners rides on his motorcycle, like he had Mr. Ric and Mr. Steve. Most Westerners didn't trust him when he pulled up on his motorcycle and asked them if they wanted a ride, but sometimes he got lucky and it paid off handsomely.

The money Mr. Steve gave him was beyond his wildest dreams. He'd already gone back to his house and showed it to his wife, who just cried. They had never seen so much money and they reveled in their good fortune. But then Phan told her what Mr. Steve asked him to do, and she warned him against it. It was dangerous enough having helped Mr. Steve escape. But in her mind, his trying to find an unnamed prostitute who had witnessed a possible drug-related murder was ludicrous.

"Let's keep what we've got already and be happy," she told him. "We don't need any trouble."

Phan saw things differently. He saw the assignment as his family's ticket to America. But what if Mr. Steve forgot his promise or never called again because Phan couldn't find the prostitute? He didn't want to take any chances. To him, going to America was like going to heaven. And maybe, just maybe, once they got there, Mr. Steve might help them stay forever. How wonderful it would be for his baby girl to grow up in America.

That hope was worth betting his life on, so he set out to find the prostitute. Before he did, though, he gave his wife one hundred dollars and Mr. Steve's contact information. The rest of the money he split into separate pockets to avoid handling all of it in public view. He told his wife that if anything happened to him, she should call Mr. Steve and he would take care of her.

"I am not taking the money for me," she said angrily. "Because if you do not come back, the money means nothing. I am taking the money for our daughter, because she will need it if she does not have a father." Then she turned her back on him and let him go.

Although a stranger to the criminal underworld, Phan had a friend who was not. His friend grew up in his neighborhood and went to school with him, but after that their paths diverged. While Phan pursued work and family, his friend shunned family and worked just enough to feed an insatiable heroin addiction picked up in seedy bars. Phan hadn't seen his friend in years but knew where to find him. His friend still lived with his parents in their old neighborhood house. Phan also believed his friend's parents would welcome him because they had always considered him trustworthy. Tonight he would put their trust to the test.

Phan rode his motorcycle to his friend's house and arrived just after 11:30 p.m. A strung-out skeleton with dark, recessed eyes and broken teeth tarnished from years of chain-smoking unfiltered Indian cigarettes met him at the door. The apparition scared Phan, reminding him of the hell he was about to enter. But the prospect of taking his daughter to America made him push ahead. This might be his only chance.

"Hello," Phan said to his friend. They stood facing each other at the ground-floor entrance to the three-room apartment. A tired incandescent bulb in an uncovered fixture hung from the center of the ceiling, casting a shadowy glow that barely interrupted the night. Phan discerned the outline of a wooden table, three wooden chairs, and a small television in the background. The only other items in the room were a hotplate and a charcoal grill. The revolution hadn't done much for his friend's family.

"Why are you here?" the friend asked.

"I need you to help me."

The friend pulled an almost empty pack of cigarettes from the breast pocket of the dirty blue and white striped cotton shirt he wore. He took a cigarette and stuck it in his mouth, then stuffed the pack back in his pocket without offering one to Phan. Pulling a disposable lighter from his pants pocket, he lit the cigarette, sucking the smoke in so deeply that the tip of the cigarette burned brighter than the light bulb. He tried to tilt his head away from Phan when he exhaled, but whatever he was high on skewed his aim and the smoke engulfed Phan's face. Phan didn't back away.

"How can I possibly help you?" the friend asked, an undertone of derision in his slurred words.

"I need you to help me find a woman."

"Oh," the friend smiled. He took another drag on his cigarette. "That didn't take long." The friend withdrew inside, pulled up one of the chairs near the table, and sat down. "You can sit down too, you know."

Phan followed his friend inside, then grabbed a chair and sat backwards so he could rest his elbows on the chair back. "It's not what you think."

"What is it then?" He drew again on his cigarette, already half its original length.

"I have an American friend," Phan explained. "He's a lawyer working on a case. He's asked me to find a butterfly girl who might know something. The girl was in a hotel room where an American died of a heroin overdose about two weeks ago. Another American was arrested and is in jail for possessing heroin in the hotel room. The American lawyer thinks the butterfly girl can explain what happened."

His friend sneered. "You'll never find her, and even if you do, why would she talk to you? The dealers will kill her and then they'll kill you. I don't want to be a part of that."

"I will pay you." Phan hated to offer money because he knew what his friend would do with it. For the same reason, his friend would never turn down money. His friend's America was another heroin fix.

"How much?"

"One million Dong."

His friend laughed. "Do you think I would risk both of our lives for one million Dong? I want twice that—two million Dong."

"Okay," Phan said. "I'll give you half now and the rest when we find the girl." Phan reached into one of his pants pockets and retrieved the Dong Steve gave him. He counted out one million and gave it to his friend, who looked greedily at the full stash.

"All right, but I hope you know what you're getting into. These people may kill you just because you're asking questions. It's not some schoolboy game."

"Then let's get going before I change my mind."

"We can't go tonight. I need to make some inquiries first. You meet me here Friday at midnight and be ready to go. Once I make the inquiries, there will be no turning back."

"I'll be here," Phan declared.

"One last thing." His friend's eyes and lips formed a subdued but deranged smile.

"What's that?" Phan asked.

"Be sure to say goodbye to your wife."

27

⎯⎯∿∿⎯⎯

Same day—Thursday, 1 June 2000, 5:52 p.m. EDT
Williamsburg, Virginia

STEVE TRUDGED INTO HIS OFFICE AND plopped down on his chair, which rolled backwards on the plastic floor mat with the momentum of his aching body. He was running on fumes after the long flight back and wasn't even sure if he could stay awake long enough to drive the short distance back to his house. But he wanted to check in with Casey to see what she'd found out since he'd spoken with her last. He also wanted to give her a heads-up about the trouble he'd had in Vietnam in case it followed him back to Virginia. He leaned back and rested his eyes, the leather cushion compressing just enough to hold his head in place.

"Mr. Stilwell," Marjorie barked, shaking his arm. Steve opened his eyes, not sure where he was. "I'm sorry to wake you, but Casey's on the phone."

Steve looked around the room to get his bearings and slid forward in his chair. "How long was I out?"

"Only about five minutes. Why don't you hurry up with the call and I'll take you home. You shouldn't be driving when you're this tired." Marjorie gave him a stern look, underlining her position. "I won't take no for an answer."

Steve knew there was no sense arguing, especially when she was right. "Okay, you win," he said wearily. "I'll make this quick." He rolled his chair forward until his knees tucked under his desk and then picked up the phone.

"Casey? You still there?"

"I am, Steve. Welcome back." Steve gave Marjorie a thumbs-up. With the connection confirmed, she left the room.

"It's good to be back. I must say I had a very interesting time. Someone in Saigon went to great lengths to get Ryan's notebook from me. In fact, I barely got out of Saigon with the clothes on my back. I'll give you all the details when you are back in Williamsburg, but you should be careful, just in case."

"Well, I've had a pretty rough go of it myself," admitted Casey. "Someone broke into my hotel room in Houston yesterday and stole the Sapphire Pavilion file. I surprised the intruder, but I'm afraid he got the best of me. Filing the police report and seeing a doctor delayed my departure until this morning."

"Are you okay?" Steve couldn't believe Casey had been victimized. This took the case to an entirely new level.

"Don't worry, I'm fine," Casey reassured him. "Just a couple of bumps and bruises. Nothing serious."

Steve started to think out loud. "Something big's going on here. The fact that someone was able to orchestrate attacks against us in both Vietnam and the United States tells me they're well funded and connected."

Steve leaned forward and switched his phone on speaker so he could add hand gestures to the conversation, even if Casey couldn't see them. Meanwhile, Marjorie entered his office with a can of Diet Coke and a glass of ice. She set it on his desk and started to leave, but he motioned for her to stay. More than once her insights had helped with a case.

"It's got to be the Vietnamese drug cartels," he continued, advancing his first theory. "But why in the world would they care about a C-130 that crashed during the Vietnam War? I went through Ryan Eversall's notebook on the trip home, and there's no indication the flight had even a remote connection with drugs. I suppose it's possible that the search for the plane was just a cover and that Ryan and Ric Stokes were mules on a drug-smuggling trip gone wrong. I can't buy that, though, as I'm one hundred percent sure Ric Stokes wouldn't have had anything to do with the trip if he thought drugs were involved. I'd bet my life on it."

Casey jumped in. "After talking with Ryan Eversall's wife, I'm also certain he wasn't involved with drugs. He'd become obsessed with finding out what happened to his father. He was already independently wealthy and didn't care about money. Drugs were the furthest thing from his mind."

"If that's all true," Steve said, "why would the drug cartels want information about the plane?"

Marjorie spoke up. "Maybe they don't want the plane to be found."

"Take that a little further, Marjorie," encouraged Steve, hoping to draw out her reasoning. "Why wouldn't they want the plane to be found?"

"I don't have the foggiest," Marjorie said. "Maybe it was on a drug smuggling route and now that the plane's been found, they're afraid of being exposed."

"Wow, that's really good, Marjorie," commented Casey.

Marjorie grinned. "That's why Mr. Stilwell pays me the big bucks."

"I think you're on to something, Marjorie," Steve added. The discussion injected him with new life. He stood up and started to walk around his desk. As if he were arguing to a jury in a courtroom, he said, "We know drugs are involved because of Ryan's death and Ric's arrest. But what if the drugs are a red herring? In other words, what if the drugs' only purpose was to frame Ryan and Ric, and the cartels were not otherwise involved?"

Casey pressed Steve on the point. "Doesn't that get us back to where we were when we started asking who could orchestrate these actions on two continents?"

"Not quite," Steve reasoned. "Now we've got a different question—Marjorie's question. Perhaps we should be asking who would be willing to kill in order to keep the plane from being discovered. If we approach it from that angle, we might figure out the why."

Casey pushed back again. "If that's the case, it might not have nothing to do with the plane. It might be the location of the plane. I don't see how that points us in anyone's direction. It essentially makes everyone a suspect."

"Not quite everyone," Steve said. "It's got to be someone with either an interest in the plane or the location of the crash. I don't know why anyone with an interest in the plane would want to prevent its discovery, but that may be because there's something we don't understand. But somebody or some company might have an interest in where the plane is. Take mineral rights, for example. The plane's discovery might impede the exercise of those rights. Someone might want to make sure the plane isn't discovered until they get the chance to exploit the land."

"That makes sense," Casey conceded, "but I don't see how we're any closer to identifying who's behind all this."

"It doesn't identify anyone," Steve said, "but it does dictate our next moves. I can use my contact at the State Department to see if anyone's got an interest in the land around the crash site. If they do, they'll be our prime suspect."

"And if no one has an interest in the land?"

"That's why you need to keep pursuing what happened to the plane."

"You know," Casey said, "there is one more possibility we haven't talked about."

"And what's that?" Steve asked.

"What if it's our own government?"

"I'm not sure I see it. Run your logic by me."

"Well," Casey began, "it's really not thought through yet. But we do know the plane was on a Top-Secret mission. Maybe there's something about the flight the government doesn't want discovered. And didn't Ryan say there were reports about the crash site's existence, but the U.S. government never followed them up, claiming insufficient information? There were five Air Force crewmembers on that flight. You would think the government would have pulled out all of the stops to investigate the rumors."

"Okay," Steve said, "let's explore that possibility, as well. Speaking of possibilities, were you able to glean anything from the Sapphire Pavilion file before it was stolen?"

"I'd leafed through it quickly, but I learned enough to know what I need to do next." Casey didn't mention that she still had the complete file, or that the intruder had really only stolen her own notes and background material.

"Don't leave us hanging," Steve said. "What will you do next?"

"I don't want to sound paranoid, but just in case someone's listening, how about we save that for when I return to Williamsburg in a couple days?"

"Great idea," Steve said, impressed by Casey's instincts. He couldn't imagine finding another young attorney, or a more experienced attorney for that matter, with her foresight and composure. "Let's limit the information we pass via telephone to emergencies and time-sensitive data. Everything else, we communicate in person. I do still want to check in, at least with Marjorie, so we all know everyone's safe."

"That works for me," Casey replied.

"Okay, then. I'll see you when you get back to Williamsburg."

"Goodbye, Steve. Goodbye, Marjorie." Casey terminated the call.

Steve reached over and pushed the speaker button to make sure the call actually ended. "By the way," he added, looking toward Marjorie. "I'm really glad you stayed. I think your insight may have put us on the right track."

"Like I said, that's why you pay me the big bucks." Marjorie smiled and put her hands on her hips. "And, Mr. Stilwell, feel free to make those bucks even bigger any time you want."

Steve grinned, hoping Marjorie was joking. "No fair kicking a man after he's been in an airplane for over twenty-four hours." The temporary jolt of energy from the planning discussion wore off quickly, leaving him ready to drop in his tracks. "How about I take you up on that ride home," he said. "I may be asleep before we get there." He picked up his planner and started for the door.

"I'll lock things up and be ready to go," Marjorie responded. Steve didn't really hear her; her voice was a distant buzz. Mentally he was already pulling the covers back on his bed. Whatever he needed to think about would have to wait until morning.

28

Friday, 2 June 2000, 6:38 a.m. EDT
Williamsburg, Virginia

S TEVE SQUIRMED ABOUT, TRYING TO GET comfortable, his bloodshot eyes
propped open by jet lag. Instead of resigning himself to remaining awake
and possibly getting something done, he convinced himself that if he stayed
in bed long enough, he would eventually drift back to sleep. But as he lay there
trying to doze off, every creak or crack of the walls, every muffled brush of
a leaf-filled branch against the side of his house, and every tick and tock of
Sarah's alarm clock reverberated even louder. He tried covering his ears with
his pillow, only to hear the feathers crackling like a bowl of Rice Krispies. His
alarm finally sounded at six forty-five, signaling the end of his futile quest for
a little more sleep.

After getting ready for work, he sat in the kitchen waiting for his morning
feast. Sarah liked to make him a big breakfast after he returned from trips
so she could find out how things went. Although he loved the breakfast, he
dreaded the post-trip ritual because it inevitably ended in conflict. Sarah
wanted him to describe everything that happened, day by day, while he
tended to breeze through the details because in the back of his mind, he could
hear the thud of probate files dropping onto his already mountainous inbox.

Today was different. Since he already had the one file he needed to dissect
sitting in his planner next to his steaming hard-fried eggs, sausage, and
English muffin, he didn't feel the tentacles of his office files pulling him back
to work. Today he could give Sarah the attention she deserved.

"So how does it look for Ric?" she asked, shifting the conversation from background noise to a subject she was interested in.

"I wish I could say it looks good, but I'm afraid it doesn't. It would break your heart to see him. He's trapped in a Vietnamese hellhole."

Sarah cut to the chase. "Did he do it?"

"No way. I looked into his eyes, Sarah. His eyes can't lie to me. I've known him too long. He's innocent, but so far I've found nothing to help him. He's just a few months away from a kangaroo trial and a death sentence, and all I'm gonna be able to do is read about it in the newspaper."

"I know you too, Steve Stilwell, and I'm sure you came away with something. You wouldn't have left Vietnam if you thought there was still information there you could use to help Ric."

"Actually, I think the key to the whole case is right here in my planner." Steve moved the plate of no longer steaming eggs to the side and pulled his planner in front of him. He unzipped it, revealing Ryan's notebook. He started flipping through the pages. "Ric and the guy he was traveling with found the plane they were looking for. It crashed somewhere in the mountains of Vietnam's Central Highlands. It's all here—the map coordinates for the location of the plane, a description of the debris field, and the names and dog tags of three of the five crewmen who were buried at the crash site. I'm just not smart enough to know what to look for."

"Well then, you need to hurry up and get that file to someone who is."

"Are you trying to rush me through my eggs?" Steve looked at Sarah and grinned. She still captivated him, even in an old William & Mary workout t-shirt and pajama pants whose cuffs dragged on the floor. No makeup, no finely coiffed hair at 7 a.m., just the confident, self-reliant woman he married. He knew she wanted to hear more about his trip, but instead of pressing him, she was encouraging him to get on with it because she knew and respected what was important to him. As far as their marriage was concerned, she was a team player in every sense of the word. Unfortunately, he often took advantage of that fact, leaving her feeling used. But this time she was giving him her blessing to get on with his case, and get on with it he would. The thought did cross his mind that work could wait a little while longer and he could fill her in on everything that had transpired, but with his workaholic wiring, he bypassed that option by rationalizing that his mind would be elsewhere, intent on solving the case.

"Just go and get Ric out of jail and let me know when you're done." This time it was Sarah's turn for a weary smile. "It's taken twenty years of marriage, but I've finally given up."

"Don't give up," Steve protested as he cut a piece of fried egg, added it to a sausage patty, and used his fork to set the cholesterol bomb on his English muffin. "I need you to keep me from running amuck." He stifled his smile by shoving the breakfast concoction into his mouth and following it with a sip of coffee. Sarah waved her hand in protest, but she smiled anyway. He could always make her smile, even when she didn't want to.

"How about as soon as this is over, we fly to New York for dinner and a play?" he asked, recalling the promise he'd made to himself during his trip to Vietnam.

"We'll see," she said, noncommittal, even though he could tell she wanted to go. "A lot can happen between now and then, you know."

She was right; she nearly always was. Better to dive into his work now and get it over with as quickly as possible, and then work on their relationship down the road. Although not an optimum game plan for a marriage, it had worked for them so far. He needed it to work at least one more time.

29

Same day—Friday, 2 June 2000, 8:45 a.m. EDT
Law Offices of Steve Stilwell, Esq.
Williamsburg, Virginia

ALREADY ON HIS SECOND CUP OF coffee, Steve loosened his tie, unbuttoned his shirt collar, and rolled up his sleeves. Better able to focus now that he was comfortable and hyped on caffeine, he parsed the notebook word by word one more time. He wanted to analyze every syllable Ryan wrote just in case it provided a clue as to the downing of the plane or the demise of its crew. He'd already read it twice on the trip back from Vietnam, but the cramped, dimly lit airline seats weren't conducive to a forensic analysis of an airplane crash, so he hadn't uncovered anything particularly helpful.

As he got near to the end of the notebook and Ryan's hand-drawn schematic of the debris field, he paused. He'd glossed over the last several pages too quickly. He reached over and picked up the dog tags recovered from the crash site and set them in front of him, aligning them in a row so he could read their names. Notifying these men's families and finally bringing them home was a top priority, along with getting Ric out of prison and back to the United States. Marjorie had already blocked out an hour at two o'clock so he could call Joint Task Force-Full Accounting in Hawaii to report what he'd found. He'd tried to call as soon as he arrived in the office, but with the six-hour time difference between Williamsburg and Pearl Harbor, he'd been unable to talk to a live person, and he didn't want to leave a message on such an important matter. This meant the Airmen's families would have to wait a few more hours.

Recognizing that Joint Task Force–Full Accounting would want Ryan's notebook, he had Marjorie make several copies, each held together with a plastic spiral binder spine. He also instructed her regarding securing the original, just in case he needed it as evidence in Ric's case. He didn't want to turn the original over to the Joint Task Force and then not be able to get it back right away if the Vietnamese Government demanded it as part of the terms for releasing Ric. He knew the Joint Task Force and the U.S. Government would want to cooperate to gain Ric's release, but after twenty-two years of working in the military's bureaucracy, no way was he going to hinge Ric's freedom on some overworked civil servant's desire to cooperate. Besides, the Joint Task Force could get all the information they needed from a copy.

Marjorie poked her head into his office. "I'm doing the bank run now. I should be back in half an hour. I'll get everything taken care of." She held up the papers she was carrying to show Steve what she was taking with her. "And it's such a nice day out, I think I'm gonna walk."

"Roger that," Steve replied as if he were responding to the captain on the bridge. "I've got the phones while you're gone." Steve gave a quick salute to Marjorie, who smiled.

"Bye," she said, drawing out the word so it had a distinct Southern flavor. With that, she disappeared into the lobby and a moment later, Steve heard the front door close. Now he could get back to work on the notebook. He began by pulling his computer keyboard toward him and running a web search for VF-101, the F-14 Tomcat jet fighter training squadron on the East Coast. He wanted to see who the commanding officer, or CO, was, hoping he might know him. Since the F-14s were being phased out as the Navy's front line jet fighter, he also hoped the CO would have some time to do him a favor. The website identified the CO as Captain Roger "Zip" Thornton, whom he unfortunately didn't know. But the Navy officer brotherhood was close knit, so he hoped Zip would take his call. He dialed the squadron's telephone number displayed on the website.

The person answering the telephone spoke rapidly, making it hard for anyone with an untrained ear to understand. "VF-101 Grim Reapers, this is a non-secure line, Petty Officer Bulgona speaking, may I help you please."

"Yes, hello, Petty Officer Bulgona. My name is Steve Stilwell. I'm a retired Navy JAG and I'd like to speak with your skipper, if he's available."

"One moment please." Music began to play on the line while Steve waited on hold. Petty Officer Bulgona interrupted with a follow-up question. "What did you say your name was, sir?"

"I'm a retired Navy JAG, Captain Steve Stilwell. I only need a couple of minutes of the skipper's time." Steve knew he was going through the filtering process. By now, Petty Officer Bulgona was in Captain Thornton's office, seeing if he'd take the call. Steve knew the answer could very easily be no, but he hoped Zip's curiosity about a retired Navy JAG calling him would overtake his desire to channel the call to someone else.

"I'll put you through now, sir," Petty Officer Bulgona announced. Before Steve could say thank you, Zip Thornton picked up.

"Hello, this is Roger Thornton."

"Roger, hi. My name's Steve Stilwell and I'm a retired Navy JAG working a rather convoluted case that involves the crash of a C-130 during the Vietnam War. My client, retired Captain Ric Stokes, and his associate discovered the crash site and took some notes describing what they found, and I was hoping you or someone in the squadron might be able to take a look at them to see if you can tell me anything about what might have caused the crash."

"Did you say your client is Ric Stokes?"

"I did. He's one of the two men who found the crash site."

"Is he a retired JAG officer?"

"He is."

"Well, hot damn," Zip said enthusiastically. "He and I served together on board *Nimitz*. What's he up to these days?"

"Actually, he's in jail in Vietnam. Somebody planted drugs on him while he was in country looking at the crash site, and now he's in jail awaiting trial."

"No way. He's the straightest arrow I know."

"I couldn't agree more," Steve replied. "But I need evidence to present to the Vietnamese government. Right now, all I've got is speculation, and not even much of that. That's why I need you to examine the notebook. It's a detailed description of everything they found at the crash site."

"Bring it over and I'll take a look right away. Any problem with me showing my XO? He's actually got some cockpit hours in C-130s."

"You can show it to anyone you want. I just need to get an answer back from you as soon as possible. I've got to get to the bottom of this before Ric goes to trial. He's facing the death penalty."

"You've got to be kidding me."

"I wish I was. Right now, all I've got is Ric's word and this notebook. Whatever you can do would be greatly appreciated."

"Bring it here today and I'll have something back to you by COB tomorrow."

"That would be great, Zip. I'll deliver it myself this afternoon."

"Do you know where I am? I don't even know where you're calling from."

"Sorry about that. My practice is in Williamsburg, so I'm only about an hour away from Oceana. As long as traffic through the Hampton Roads Bridge-Tunnel isn't bad, I should be able to make it to the Naval Air Station no later than twelve hundred." Steve reverted to military time without thought or effort.

"I'll alert the Quarterdeck and they'll escort you back to my office," Zip promised. "And tell Ric I said hello and that I know he's innocent. There's just no way he's involved."

"I will," Steve promised. "I'll make sure he knows how much you're helping him. I'll see you this afternoon."

Steve hung up and checked his watch. It was almost 9:45, and he would have to be on the road no later than 10:30 to make it to Zip's office by 12:00, assuming the tunnel cooperated. He still had to call the State Department to follow up on who might be interested in the crash site, and he needed to be back by 2:00 to call the Joint Task Force. His schedule was suddenly chockablock.

Steve heard the front door open and someone come into the lobby.

"Marjorie, is that you? That was a pretty quick bank run."

"Is that how you welcome visitors to your office?" The voice was familiar, but it wasn't Marjorie's. It was distinctly more feminine, more pleasant, more enticing. Hearing the voice out of context, he couldn't place it at first. But when he looked toward the door and the woman walked into his office, he couldn't believe it was her. There she stood, wearing a short yellow sundress speckled with green, pink, and white flowers, the wide neckline dipping low across her chest—not too low, but low enough to attract a man's interest. White leather sandals, a Kate Spade handbag, and a chiding smile finished the look. Steve thought her smile awkward, given the way they last parted company. Still, it disarmed him. He couldn't force himself to be unwelcoming, even though his guest had to be up to no good.

"What are you doing here?" he asked as he rose from his chair and started walking toward her. He didn't return her smile or try to hide his surprise.

"Looks like you haven't learned since Saigon," Gallagher replied. "Still not offering a girl a chair."

Steve wasn't as gracious this time around. Now she was on his turf, and he intended to control the conversation. Before this meeting went any further, she would have to level with him about what was going on.

"I can be a slow learner sometimes," Steve said. "But if you give me some straight answers I might be a little more hospitable."

Gallagher strolled farther into his office and gripped the back of one of the tub chairs facing his desk. "So what is it you want to know?" she asked, her expression daring him to challenge her.

"I want to know who sent you here and why."

"I like you, Steve. You're different from most of the other men I know. You've got an innocence about you I find attractive. Besides ..." Gallagher began as she eased around to the front of the chair and sat down, not waiting for an invitation. She set her bag on her lap, crossed her legs, and began to bounce her right foot as if to draw his attention to her smooth, bronzed legs. "I had to come back to DC anyway, so I thought I'd swing by Williamsburg to see where things might go."

Steve shook his head and laughed. "Nice try, but I'm not letting you 'facilitate' me this time. I want to know the truth. Why are you here?" Realizing Gallagher had already won Round One by maneuvering herself into a seat, he walked back behind his desk and sat down in his chair, sliding it as far forward as it would go until his stomach pressed against the edge of the desk. This put a barrier between him and Gallagher and blocked his view of her legs. He didn't need any distractions.

"You want it straight?"

"I don't have time for games, Gallagher. I've got a friend who's facing the death penalty and I've got work to do. If you won't tell me what's going on, then I'm gonna have to ask you to leave." Steve surprised himself with his bluntness, but something about her drew it out of him. He didn't want to lose Round Two.

"Then I think we'll see eye to eye, as I don't have time for games, either." She reached into her bag and pulled out a five-by-seven-inch manila envelope. She put her purse on the floor and set the envelope in her lap, again leaning forward to speak. Her voice was quiet but firm. "I need you to give me the notebook, Steve."

Steve continued to look into her eyes. He hoped she couldn't see his facial muscles tighten. He had to keep his cool. Her direction confirmed his suspicions that she was somehow involved in the case, but he didn't want his expression to convey his reaction, positive or negative, to her revelation. He also wasn't ready to admit he had the notebook. When they last met, she was still offering to help him get it.

"Shouldn't you be asking the Mountain Flower Hotel about that?"

"Cut the BS, Steve. Like I said, I don't have time for games either. You don't know what you're getting in to now. It would have been much easier for you if you'd just let them have it in Saigon. You're making it harder for them to take the notebook and let you go."

Steve didn't like being threatened. "Who are you really, and who are they?" he demanded.

The last vestige of a smile vanished from Gallagher's lips. "People who don't care who dies or goes to jail. They just take what they want, and they want the notebook." Gallagher paused, allowing her words to sink in. "I want to help you, Steve. I'm not them. Like I said, I just facilitate things."

"Like getting them the notebook they want?"

"Exactly."

"Well, you can tell them to pound sand. That notebook's going to the U.S.

government so they can find the crash site and repatriate the crew. There's nothing you can do about that."

"Then you'll be signing Ric Stokes' death warrant."

Her response caught Steve off guard. He'd thought possessing and analyzing the notebook was the key to getting Ric off death row and out of prison. But what if turning over the notebook to Gallagher could bring about Ric's release? He had to at least explore the possibility. "What do you mean?"

"They'll make sure the Vietnamese never get any evidence that might set Ric free." When Steve didn't respond right away, Gallagher went on, "Look at me, Steve. Look into my eyes. I want to make sure you understand what I'm about to say." She glared at Steve and Steve glared back, losing focus until her entire head started to blur. "If you don't give me the notebook, Ric Stokes' blood will be on your hands. Right now, you're the only one who can prevent his death. All you need to do is cooperate with me."

"How do I know you won't just take the notebook and let him die anyway? You yourself said your people don't care who dies or goes to jail."

"They don't, but I do. You give me the notebook and I'll see to it he's released. I know the prosecutor, and I'll visit him myself." Gallagher's expression softened, her lips moving in the direction of a grin but not quite getting there. She was somewhere between serious and seductive. "I can be very persuasive, you know."

Steve looked away and leaned back in his chair. His primary responsibility was to get Ric released, but he had to do it ethically. If he gave the notebook to Gallagher, he'd be condoning the seduction and/or bribery of a Vietnamese judge. Whether or not the judge was already corrupt didn't matter; he'd still be actively encouraging the unlawful manipulation of Vietnam's legal system. He saw this as different from his bribe of the prison guard. The guard was not an officer of the court; he was just Ric's custodian and his payment bought nothing more than time. This payment, or whatever it was, would affect the outcome of a trial.

Beyond the ethical concerns, turning over the notebook would mean the families of the five crewmembers buried in the mountainous hinterland of Vietnam might never learn the fate of their loved ones. Surely Gallagher would make him turn over the copies he'd made of the notebook. If he didn't, and the U.S. government searched for the plane, he expected her to renege on the deal. That also meant she would be unlikely to pursue Ric's release right away. Once Ric was released, she would lose her leverage. For that matter, once she had the notebook, she had no incentive to gain Ric's release, and Ric was likely to face the executioner in any event.

He had one more option: he could promise to give her the notebook as soon as Ric was released from jail and out of the country. This satisfied his obligation to Ric, but it compromised him ethically and left the families of the crewmembers in the dark. He could go back on the deal at that point, as well, and turn the notebook over to the U.S. government, but he anticipated retaliation would be swift and severe.

"I can't," Steve announced.

"You can't what?" Gallagher replied.

"I can't give you the notebook. I can't betray those families, and I can't condone manipulating a court, even if it's a corrupt one." Stating his reasoning out loud and actually hearing the words made him more comfortable with his decision. "As I said earlier, you can tell 'em to pound sand. I'll get Ric released, and it'll be legit."

"Don't fool yourself with your ethical self-righteousness." Gallagher spoke with insight and eloquence far beyond that of a business-deal facilitator. Steve wondered what she had done before she'd sold her soul. She tossed a manila envelope onto Steve's desk. It skipped over the blotter and fell into his lap. He picked it up and held it out in front of him, his right arm resting on the desktop.

"What's this?"

"Open it," Gallagher insisted. "And we'll see just how ethical you are."

30

Same day—Friday, 2 June 2000, 9:13 a.m. CDT
Maxwell Air Force Base, Montgomery, Alabama

"May I help you?" the woman asked as Casey set her purse on the counter in the reading room of Fairchild Memorial Hall, home of the Air Force Historical Research Agency. The woman spoke with a drawl so drawn out that Casey thought she'd have to come back later in the day to hear how the sentence ended.

"I hope you can," Casey said. "Here's my situation. I'm representing a Navy captain who found the wreckage of a C-130 in the mountains of Vietnam. We think something about the plane holds the key to a murder, but we know nothing about it or its mission. I was hoping you could help find out what the plane's mission was on the day it crashed and who was on board. Does that make sense?"

"My goodness," the woman responded. "I must say I haven't heard that one before." The woman slid a form under the window bars for Casey to fill out. "That's a Form 1297. Fill it out the best you can by telling me everything you know about the airplane. Then we'll see what we've got that might help."

"Thank you so much," Casey said genuinely. She didn't have much information about the plane so it didn't take her long to complete the form. She slid it back to the librarian, who had watched her write everything down. She perused the form's contents while Casey looked on.

"Mm-hmm. I'll be able to find something on this. I'm going to need a little time, as I've got to retrieve the unit history and the aircraft record card.

I'd suggest you look around and come back in half an hour. I should have something by then."

"That sounds great," Casey replied. "I'll see you soon."

Casey loitered near the counter because she didn't want to miss the librarian returning with her research. When the woman reappeared well ahead of schedule, Casey was ready for her. This time, though, the woman had a couple of extra folders in hand. She was sure Ryan Eversall would have seen the same documents during the course of his research, but maybe with her military perspective, she would note something he'd overlooked.

"That was quick," Casey remarked, not attempting to hide her appreciation for the librarian's efforts.

"Things are pretty orderly here," the librarian responded. "Although it doesn't look like it, we do work for the military."

"I think that's one of the reasons I was excited to come here," Casey continued, partly to ingratiate herself to the librarian and partly because it was true. "It just feels good to be back around people who understand flying."

"Oh, were you in the Air Force?"

"No, ma'am. I was an Army helo pilot."

"Gracious sakes alive," the librarian exclaimed. "That must be so exciting—certainly a lot more exciting than working behind bars in a library." The librarian chuckled at her own joke, causing her reading glasses to slip down her nose. Pushing the glasses back in place, she went on, "Are you still flying?"

"No, I'm afraid not. I got out of the Army a few years ago and went to law school. Now I'm just flying a desk."

"Well, at least you had the opportunity. Most of us can only dream." The librarian sighed and then got down to business. "Well then. Here's what I was able to find." She set two folders on the counter in front of her, opening the top one with the care of an elderly woman finding a diary from her teenage years in the bottom of an old chest in the attic. She began to read information from the folder out loud.

"The plane card for Tail Number 70467 indicates the aircraft was a C-130A assigned to the Twenty-First Tactical Airlift Squadron at the time it was lost. The squadron was known as the *BEEliners*. There's a copy of the squadron history in the file. It looks like the squadron supported special operations during the Vietnam War. The history isn't classified, so I can make a copy of it for you when we're done."

That would be great," Casey said.

The librarian continued disclosing the folder's contents. "This plane flew its final mission on 18 January 1968. It took off at night from Ubon Air Base in Thailand on a Top-Secret mission, code-named Sapphire Pavilion. The mission name is unclassified, but the mission itself still hasn't been declassified, so I'm unable to tell you what the mission was. In fact, it was so highly classified that we don't have a file on it." The librarian stopped looking at the papers inside the folder and shifted her attention to the inside of the folder jacket itself. "Wait a minute," she said. "This is odd. I've never seen this before. There's a handwritten note in pencil on the inside cover of the folder. It doesn't say whether it's classified, so I guess I can tell you what it says." She hesitated, though, apparently rethinking her decision to disclose the comment.

Casey could hardly control herself. She wanted to know whatever was written on the inside cover, even if it was meaningless. But if the librarian decided to confirm whether it was classified, they would most certainly err on the side of non-disclosure and she might lose access to a critical clue. She weighed in to keep the disclosure decision moving in the right direction.

"Given the classification involved for the mission, I'm sure if the information on the folder were classified, it would have been properly labeled," Casey asserted. "Otherwise you'd have to report a security violation for not properly securing the classified information." Casey knew the librarian would not want to report a security violation. There would have to be an investigation and the librarian's name would be associated with it, even if her only involvement was reporting the discovery. Casey hoped the universal fear of red tape would work in her favor.

"I'm sure you're right," the woman agreed. "The file says, 'Contact State Department.' "

"Is there any indication what information that relates to in the file? I mean, does it say what to contact them for?"

"Nope. It just says Sapphire Pavilion, then a dash, then 'Contact State Department.' "

"I wonder why Ryan Eversall wouldn't have seen that?" Casey said out loud, although the question was actually intended to spur on her own thinking.

"Maybe because it's written on the inside cover of the folder, which we may not have given him. It's entirely possible that the librarian who helped him only gave him the contents of the folder after confirming there was no classified material mixed inside. Sometimes we keep the folder at the counter when it's busy because it helps us remember what documents are out in the reading room."

"That would explain it," Casey said, nodding her head. "I never would have thought of that. Thanks."

The librarian beamed at her apparent success and then moved to the second folder, opening it with the same care. "This one's got a copy of the flight manifest in it. It shows there were five crewmembers on board. Would you like their names?"

"Yes, I would. That's one of the most important things I'd hoped to find."

"Their names are Lt. Col. Ray Eversall, Captain John Peke, Captain Joe Scalpato, Master Sergeant David Dugan, and Staff Sergeant Jose Medeiro. The file also lists them as missing in action. The folder says the plane didn't return from its mission. I can make you a copy of the manifest so you don't have to write their names down. It only costs ten cents."

"I would like a copy of that, along with the unit history," Casey said. "Is that all you've got?"

"I'm afraid that's it. You might try the State Department, but unless the mission's been declassified, they won't be able to tell you anything. I hate to say it, but it can take a long time to get something declassified—years, even. Or they may not want to declassify it at all. You can never tell."

"Well, I can't tell you how much I appreciate your help. Maybe I'll get lucky at the State Department just like I did here." Casey started to walk away.

"Don't leave just yet, miss," the librarian called out. "I've still got to make you your copies."

"Oh, yes, of course. Thank you."

Casey returned to the counter for the copies. She couldn't wait to tell Steve what she'd found. More than that, she couldn't wait for Steve to follow up with the State Department to see if they could tell him what Sapphire Pavilion was.

31

Same day—Friday, 2 June 2000, 10:27 a.m. EDT
Law Offices of Steve Stilwell, Esq.
Williamsburg, Virginia

THE MANILA ENVELOPE WASN'T SEALED, so Steve folded back the flap and pulled out a small stack of photographs. "What are these?"

"I wanted you to have something to help you remember your trip to Vietnam," Gallagher replied. "Why don't you take a closer look and tell me what you think."

Steve brought the first picture more clearly into the light from the recessed ceiling lamp directly over his desk. It showed him eating dinner with Gallagher at ZACCA's in Saigon. Both of them were smiling and Gallagher was holding a full glass of red wine. Steve shifted to the second picture after moving the first one to the back of the stack. Steve was on the back of Gallagher's motorbike with his legs straddling her. He couldn't believe what he was seeing.

"This isn't funny." Steve's face flushed red with anger. "Who took these pictures?"

"Does it matter? All they did was capture us spending a little quality time together. Pictures don't lie."

"I can't believe you did this. This could give someone the wrong impression. You know everything was completely innocent."

"Was it, Steve? You didn't seem to resist too hard snuggling up against me on my motorcycle. Don't worry though. I'm sure your wife—Sarah, isn't it?—Sarah will understand." Gallagher wasn't smiling now. She had found a weakness in his defenses.

"Leave her out of this. This is between you and me." He stopped to look at the rest of the pictures. The next showed him and Gallagher coming out of the elevator into the lobby of the Le Dey Hotel, and the next showed Gallagher kissing him with the two front desk clerks watching in the background.

Now he was really pissed. Pissed at Gallagher for playing him the way she did, but more pissed at himself for letting it happen. He'd done nothing wrong, but he also had not done the right thing. He'd allowed himself to be put in a compromising position by a pretty face and now the pretty face was backing him into a corner. He spoke out of frustration, already knowing the answer to his question. "It was all a set-up, wasn't it?"

"That's such an ugly way to describe it, Steve. Like I've said from the start, I facilitate things. One of the things I'm facilitating is getting Eversall's notebook to my client. Sometimes that means taking a few liberties." Gallagher gave Steve a coquettish grin, as if this really were a game.

Steve flipped to the final picture. "This is outrageous!" he exclaimed, standing up and shoving his chair behind him with his legs. "This never happened. It's staged and you know it." He threw the stack of pictures on his desk, scattering them across his desk calendar.

"You've got to be careful about leaving your room unattended in a foreign country, Steve. You never know what might go on in there while you're gone."

Now Steve understood why Gallagher was waiting for him in the lobby at the Le Dey Hotel the last time they met. It was no chance encounter. Nothing had been left to chance. "So I take it you want to trade the pictures for the notebook. Am I seeing things right?"

"It seems like a fair deal. And because I like you, I'll also see what I can do about getting your friend out of jail. Sounds to me like you'll achieve everything you set out to do when you took the case. All you have to do is give me the notebook and it's a done deal."

"And if I don't?"

Gallagher looked at her watch. "Unless I make a call within the next six minutes, then Sarah gets a copy of the pictures and Ric Stokes will die at the hands of a Vietnamese firing squad. Seems like a pretty clear choice to me." Her gaze was compelling and unapologetic.

"If I give you the notebook, how do I know you won't keep a copy of the pictures and use them against me?"

"Just like I won't know if you'll keep a copy of the notebook to use against me. I'd say it's trust, but that's really not the right word." Gallagher cupped her chin in her hand as she pondered her word choice. "I'd say it's more like détente, wouldn't you?"

Steve was in an untenable position. What was more valuable to him, his integrity or his marriage? His honor or his friend's life? It angered him even more that he considered her offer a viable option. If he accepted it, Sarah would never know of Gallagher's existence and Ric would either be released from jail and return home or be no worse off than he was now. The same could be said for the families of the lost Airmen—turning over the notebook to Gallagher would make them no worse off. And if Gallagher tried to double-cross him, he'd still have a copy of the notebook he could disclose to the Joint Task Force–Full Accounting so they could find the plane and recover the Airmen's remains. The cost: hiding from Sarah misleading evidence of an affair that never happened, and improperly influencing a judicial system that was corrupt already and that had wrongfully arrested Ric in the first place. The answer was all too obvious.

"Steve, I hate to rush you, but if I don't make a call in the next two minutes, Sarah's going to see some interesting pictures from your trip to Vietnam. So what's the verdict, Counselor? Do I get the notebook, or does Ric die?"

As Steve was about to give his answer, he heard the door to the outer office open. A moment later Marjorie poked her head in. She started to say something, but when she saw Gallagher sitting in front of his desk, she mouthed, "I'm sorry," and backed out.

Gallagher put her phone back into her purse and started to get up to leave. "I'm sorry it had to come to this, Steve. I hope you can live with the consequences."

"Wait a minute," Steve announced. Standing up, he put both hands behind his head and looked up at the ceiling. His teeth were clenched and his eyes squinting with tension. "I can't believe I'm saying this, but go ahead and make the call." He dropped his hands to his sides, slapping both his thighs as he did. His legs were shaking, the way they had when he made split-second decisions advising Navy admirals ready to employ lethal force. He tried to steady them by putting his hands into his pockets, but that did little, and it certainly didn't help with his nausea. He felt like he had just sold his soul to the devil.

"You're making the right decision," Gallagher reassured him. As she began to press the buttons on her cellphone, Marjorie came to the door again.

"Mr. Stilwell, I'm sorry to interrupt, but Casey's on the phone. She says it's important and that I should interrupt you."

"I'll wait outside while I make this call," Gallagher said. As she went out to the lobby, Marjorie came into Steve's office. He saw her glance at the photos scattered across his desk. Her eyes widened.

"Who's that?" Marjorie whispered, tilting her head back toward the lobby.

"It's someone I met in Vietnam," Steve replied. "And it's not what those pictures would lead you to believe."

Marjorie acted unfazed, but Steve could see disappointment in her eyes. "Casey's on hold and you better pick up," she stated in a flat voice.

Steve didn't have time to go into it any further. Without saying his usual "thanks," he picked up the phone.

"Hello, Casey," he said. "I hear you have some news for me."

"I'm sorry to interrupt, Steve, but I do have something you'll want to follow up on."

"What have you got?"

"As we suspected, Sapphire Pavilion is somehow associated with the C-130's final mission. My guess is it was the code name for the mission."

"That doesn't move the ball very far down the field," Steve said, his tone more critical than usual. "Were you able to find out anything else?"

"Well … yes," Casey replied, a little hesitant after Steve's admonition. "I don't think it's a Department of Defense mission. There's a handwritten note in one of the Air Force's historical files that says 'Contact State Department.'" Casey paused, but when Steve didn't say anything, she continued, "I know this is pure speculation, but maybe this flight had some kind of diplomatic connection. Maybe the State Department had someone on the flight. That would explain why there are five graves at the crash site—because there were six souls on board the aircraft and at least one of them survived the crash."

Casey's theory brought a flicker of life back to Steve. Until he'd told Gallagher that he'd give her the notebook, he'd intended to call his friend Tad Schwartz at the State Department Legal Adviser's Office to find out if anyone had an interest, legal or illegal, in the region where the plane crashed. Now he'd have something more specific to ask: what was Sapphire Pavilion? If the answer was still classified, Tad might not be able to tell him, but he knew Tad would pursue the lead if it would help gain Ric's release. It was a long shot, but twenty minutes before, he'd had no shot at all. He probed a little further.

"Is that it?" he asked with a little more inflection in his voice.

"I was able to get the names of all five crewmembers on board the flight. I cross-checked the names with the ones you gave me from the dog tags Ric recovered. All three matched. This will finally bring closure to their families and allow them to be buried with the honor and dignity they deserve."

Casey's observation cut deep into Steve's marrow. Here he was, a twenty-two-year Navy veteran, and he was willing to deny these brave men who died serving their country a proper homecoming. He rationalized his decision to turn over the notebook was to get Ric out of jail, but was it? Or was it to keep Sarah from seeing some pictures that might destroy his marriage? Not only that, Gallagher hadn't guaranteed Ric's release—she'd only promised to *facilitate* it. What did that mean?

Steve felt his face and ears turning red hot. He was at a crossroads and had to decide which way to go. Once he turned over the notebook, he could never go back. His integrity would be compromised forever. Now, with the State Department lead, maybe, just maybe, a door would open leading to Ric's release. But he would never know unless he opened the door, and that meant keeping the notebook and allowing the pictures to be delivered to Sarah.

"Oh, there's one more thing," Casey added. "None of the crewmember's names matched the initials Ryan found on the briefcase. I'd be willing to bet they belong to a passenger arranged by the State Department. That could be the key to finding out about Sapphire Pavilion."

"Thanks, Casey," Steve said, back to his usual quiet and genuine tone. "Your report couldn't have come at a more opportune time. I'll call my contact at the State Department and see what I can learn." Then he added, "We'll talk about it another time, Casey, but you saved me. I cannot tell you how grateful I am."

"You're welcome, but I really didn't do anything."

"Oh, yes you did," Steve reassured her. "Now get back here so we can finish this case up and get Ric out of jail. And be careful on the road."

"Will do," Casey said. "Goodbye."

Steve hung up the phone without saying anything more. Now he knew what he had to do. He had a plan.

STEVE HURRIED OUT TO THE LOBBY to snag Gallagher. She was standing by the window with her back to him, flanked by Marjorie's plants on both sides. Marjorie sat at her desk staring at her computer, avoiding eye contact with both Steve and Gallagher. She fidgeted with a pencil and moved some papers around, but Steve could tell she was disappointed in him and didn't know how to handle it. He would sit down with her later, but first, he had deal with Gallagher.

"Wendy, why don't you come back into my office for a minute," Steve said, summoning her from just outside his office door. She turned toward him and smiled, reminding him of a lioness gloating over a successful kill. All she had left to do was grab the notebook and be on her way.

"Remember," she said, exaggerating the sway of her sundress as she walked by Marjorie's desk, "my friends call me Gallagher." She caught up to Steve, and at his invitation, walked ahead of him into his office. "You are my friend, aren't you?" She smiled at him again, daring him to flirt with her.

"That depends on how well you take bad news."

"What do you mean?" Gallagher's smile evaporated.

"I've changed my mind," Steve announced. "Take your pictures and give them to whomever you want. And you can forget about the notebook. I'll go to hell before I turn it over to you. If that works for you, then I'd say I'm your friend." Now it was Steve's turn to smile.

"You don't know what you're doing, Steve. Things are going to get a lot worse for you. I know these people—they're ruthless."

"You talk about 'them' like they're someone else. Don't you see? You're one of *them*."

"Whatever. I can see I'm wasting my time here." Gallagher clutched her purse and did a pirouette toward the door. "It's too bad this didn't work out, Steve," she said, loud enough for Marjorie to hear her. "I really did like you."

"Aren't you forgetting your pictures?" Steve gathered them up from his desk.

Gallagher was already in the lobby. She stuck her head back in his office. "Keep them as a souvenir of your trip to Vietnam. Goodbye, Steve. I wish you luck. You're gonna need it." Then she turned and made her way past Marjorie, ignoring her frigid stare. A few seconds later, she was gone.

Steve walked as far as his office door and took a position in the middle of the doorframe. Marjorie ignored him and went on with whatever she was pretending to do behind her desk.

"Marjorie, you've got to stick with me on this." Marjorie didn't look up or acknowledge his presence. "Have I ever lied to you?"

"Not that I'm aware of," Marjorie conceded without looking toward him.

"Well I'm certainly not going to start now." Steve walked over and stood directly in front of her desk. "You can look me in the eye, Marjorie. My eyes won't lie. Nothing went on between that woman and me. She had something to do with framing Ric Stokes and now she's trying to blackmail me into turning over the crash site notebook. I'll explain the pictures later, but trust me, it's a set-up and nothing happened between us."

Marjorie looked up at him with eyes that said, *I want to believe you, but I'm not one hundred percent sure.* Then she broke her silence.

"Okay, Mr. Stilwell, I'll stick with you for now." She still sounded disappointed. "But I'll be honest. If it doesn't turn out like you say, I won't be able to work for you anymore." She opened her desk drawer and pulled out a "Received" stamp to begin processing the incoming mail. Then she added, "It's a sisterhood, you know. Women don't take kindly to men who cheat on their wives."

Marjorie looked back at him as if to gauge his reaction, but he didn't flinch. He was telling the truth, so he knew things would eventually work out.

"Fair enough," he said, "but we've got to get right to work. I need to take a copy of the notebook out to Oceana to have an aviator review it. I've also got to stop by and see Sarah right away to warn her about those pictures." He stretched out his left arm and checked his watch. It was almost eleven fifteen. "Holy cow, I'm running way behind. Marjorie, can you give the CO of VF-101 a call and let him know I'll be late? I probably won't get there until one or one thirty. Also, if you can set up a call for me around three with Tad Schwartz at the State Department, I'd appreciate it. He's in the Legal Adviser's Office. Just tell him it's about the case in Vietnam and he'll know what I'm talking about."

"Got it," Marjorie said, albeit with less than full enthusiasm. "What about your call to the Joint Task Force in Hawaii at two?"

"Oh, that's right. I forgot. We'll have to put that off until I've got a window of free time."

"Okay. I'll take care of it."

"Thanks, Marjorie. Just help me hold this together until we get the case wrapped up and then we'll sit down and talk. But for now, I've got to get on the road. I don't think we've got much time left."

Semi-satisfied Marjorie had been placated, Steve hustled back into his office and grabbed a copy of the notebook to take to Zip Thornton. He also stuffed the pictures into his suit coat pocket. The last thing he wanted was for them to start floating around. He was certain that if he left them sitting on his desk, Marjorie would look at them, and when she saw the last one—staged in his room when he wasn't there—she might get too upset and change her mind. Plus, he wanted to show all the pictures to Sarah, especially if she hadn't seen them yet, so he could take the element of surprise away from his adversaries and explain their context first hand. If she had already seen them, he wasn't sure what reception he'd receive. Still, he was certain he'd made the right decision to hold onto the notebook. He just hoped that Ric Stokes and Sarah agreed.

32

Same day—Friday, 2 June 2000, 11:23 a.m. EDT
Williamsburg, Virginia

STEVE PRESSED THE BUTTON ON THE garage door opener as the tires bounced over the curb and his metallic blue 1982 Celica bounded into the driveway. He tucked the car's wedge-shaped nose under the door's rising bottom edge and zipped inside. Sarah's car was still in the other bay, so at least she hadn't left him yet. He could only hope that she would give him the chance to explain. The pictures would hurt her; pictures like that would hurt any woman who thought the love of her life had cheated on her. The one thing he had going for him was that he hadn't actually done anything, nor had he even thought of doing so. But the photos told a different story.

He hopped out of the car, slammed the door, and hustled to the kitchen. "Sarah!" he yelled as he walked inside. "Sarah!" he shouted a little louder after not getting a response to his first entreaty. He hoped she had simply stepped outside for a few minutes. If he was really lucky, she hadn't seen the pictures yet and he could set the stage before showing them to her. He was sure that if he could explain in advance, she would give him the benefit of the doubt and this would turn out to be much ado about nothing.

He hustled through the kitchen and rounded the corner into the hall and foyer. "Sarah!" he called again as he started to climb the stairs to the Second Floor. When he got to the top, he headed straight for the master bedroom. Sarah sat alone at the far end of the room in a Queen Anne chair, looking out a closed window into the front yard. She wore a pair of summery shorts, a polo shirt, and sandals. Though she was dressed for fun, her face said otherwise.

"Hi Sarah," Steve said, his volume dialed back from the shouting of just a few minutes before. She didn't move or acknowledge his presence. She just looked out the window, like an artist studying her subject for a portrait she wasn't sure how to begin.

Steve gave the room a quick scan. On the bed was a yellow manila envelope and a handful of pictures scattered across the burgundy comforter. On the other side of the bed, a single picture lay face up on the floor. Although it was hard for Steve to see from where he stood, it looked like the picture of him riding with Gallagher on the back of her motorcycle. Given the pictures' haphazard arrangement, he surmised they had been thrown rather than set down hastily or dropped. Sarah was either hurt or angry—more likely both. He had to proceed carefully so as not to make a terrible situation worse.

"I'm sorry you had to see those pictures," he began, his voice conciliatory and just loud enough to be heard. "I promise they're not what they seem." Sarah continued to stare out the window, ignoring his apology. That meant she was very upset, but he didn't let her silence discourage him. He had to break through.

"Absolutely nothing went on between me and that woman. Those pictures were a set-up."

"What's her name?" Sarah asked, her voice quieter than Steve's but no less determined.

"It's Gallagher, Wendy Gallagher," he said softly. "But she goes by Gallagher."

"Where did you meet her?

"At a restaurant in Saigon. You saw it in one of the pictures. I was sitting alone, getting ready to order dinner, and she asked if she could join me. I told her yes because she was an American and I wanted to be polite, but I also told her I was married. Nothing went on between us. Not only did I not let it happen, I wasn't looking for anything and I didn't want anything." Steve stepped closer to her to emphasize his next point. "You know I love you."

Sarah turned her head to look at him for the first time. Her eyes had an intensity about them; Steve felt them probe deep inside him, searching for something, like evidence of innocence lost. The look made him feel distant from her, separated by a chasm he'd built but couldn't cross. Every second of silence caused the chasm to widen.

"Sarah, I swear it was a set-up. These pictures are either taken out of context or are outright lies."

Finally she spoke. "Of course it was a set-up," she said. "Give me some credit. It's obvious someone was hired to take pictures of you and that woman."

"I knew you'd understand," Steve said, relieved. "I'd never do anything to jeopardize our marriage."

"That's where you're wrong, Steve," Sarah said, catching him off guard. "You've been doing things to jeopardize our marriage for years. You've just never admitted it, even though I've tried to tell you. All those late nights working for the Navy, the deployments, the weekends preparing for the cases—all that jeopardized our marriage. I just put up with it because I kept telling myself it would get better." Sarah shifted in her seat until her entire body faced Steve. "These pictures confirm I was wrong. I've got to accept that I'm just not that important to you."

"That's not true, honey," Steve insisted. "You're the most important thing in my life."

"Am I, Steve?" Sarah's voice rose in volume but remained under control. "If I'm that important to you, why are you straddling some young tart on a motorcycle? And why is she kissing you in the lobby of a hotel, or getting out of the hotel elevator with you, or smiling in a bed with your shirt draped over a chair in the background?" Her voice cracked.

"I swear to you, I have no idea how she got into my room to have that picture taken, but whenever it was, I wasn't there. She followed me up to my room after dinner to get the name of the place where Ryan stashed his notebook because she said she could help me with his case. I never let her inside. Nothing, I repeat, *nothing*, went on."

"You don't get it, do you?"

"I know you're angry, Sarah, and you have every right to be. But I promise I didn't do anything to compromise your trust."

"Well, that's where you're wrong. A faithful husband never would have let himself be put in the position you found yourself in. You were set up all right, but you allowed it to happen. You shouldn't have been on the motorcycle with her, and you shouldn't have taken her to your hotel. I don't care what you did or didn't do. You messed up, Steve, and I'm not sure I can trust you anymore."

"I know I let you down, but I promise you can trust me. I never would have let anything happen."

"Can't you see? It already has. Maybe you weren't unfaithful—I do believe that—but I'm not sure you were faithful, either. Try to see things through my eyes for a moment. If someone gave you pictures of me straddling some guy on the back of his motorcycle and that same guy kissing me in a hotel lobby when you thought I was supposed to be working, if you're honest with yourself, you'd at least be suspicious. Add to that the years of me playing second fiddle to your job and you'll understand where I'm coming from." Sarah stood up in front of her chair. "I need time to think."

It was Steve's turn to talk but he didn't know what to say. There was more than a grain of truth in Sarah's accusation. He could have done more to avoid the set-up, but he didn't, and now there was no way he could go back and fix it. This wasn't like a late night at the office, although that was part of it. This was the culmination of years of neglect, brought to a head by pictures that magnified every blemish in their relationship, blotting out all the positives. The pictures triggered a temblor along a fault line in their marriage, damaging its foundation. This time he couldn't just ignore the damage, hoping it would repair itself—it was too severe. All he could think to do was to be honest and say what was in his heart.

"I really don't know what to say, Sarah, other than I love you and I'm sorry I didn't do more. But I swear nothing happened."

"I'm sorry you didn't do more too, Steve." She looked away from him, signaling that the meaningful part of their conversation was over. "I'll give you a call when I get things worked out." Tears started to run down her cheeks. She wiped them away as she headed for the bedroom door.

"Please, don't go," Steve pleaded, his own eyes watering. He followed her out the door and down the stairs. She didn't answer him; she just continued to the foyer and through the hall. Steve trailed close behind her.

"Where will you go?"

"I'll let you know after I get there," she said, slowing enough to pick up her purse from a kitchen chair.

"How long will you be gone?" he asked, realizing there was no way to stop her. She opened the door to the garage and started to head outside. All he could do was follow.

Sarah opened her car door, stopping long enough to look back at Steve and answer his last question, a question he'd almost forgotten he'd asked. "I don't know," she said. "I've packed what I need in the car, so don't expect me anytime soon. Besides, me being gone will allow you to focus on getting Ric Stokes out of jail, which is what you need to do anyway."

"What I need to do is save my marriage and keep you from leaving," he implored, moving closer. Before he could reach her, she'd hopped into the driver's seat of her SUV.

"Too bad it took you so long to realize it." Tears streaming down her face, Sarah closed the car door, started the engine, and backed out of the driveway. Steve watched her as she drove away without looking back. He couldn't believe she was gone.

33

Same day—Friday, 2 June 2000, 11:35 a.m. EDT
Washington, DC

"I just spoke with her. She couldn't get it," the man with the Boston accent reported.

"Why not?" asked a gravelly voice on the other end of the line.

"Because she didn't try hard enough. I've got the mission from here."

"You've had the mission all along. She only worked for you. Her failure is your failure." A raucous, cigarette-ravaged cough barked through the telephone as if intended to be in the listener's face. "So what are you going to do about it?"

"Every minute we delay gives Stilwell another opportunity to distribute the notebook, so I'm gonna destroy it, and him, today."

"Stilwell too?"

"You have a better option?"

"I had lots of better options, but Gallagher's incompetence and your acquiescence took them away. If you don't succeed, the only option I'll have left is to cover *everyone's* tracks."

The man with the Boston accent knew what that meant—he was just as expendable as Gallagher. Loyalty or the fact that this was the first real problem he'd ever had with a mission carried no weight. All that mattered was the here and now.

"That won't be necessary."

"What about Gallagher?"

"Done."

"What do you mean, done? Is she dead?"

"We're on the phone, remember?"

"What do you take me for, a fool?" the voice shouted. "Do you think I'd even be talking to you unless I knew the line was secure?"

The man with the Boston accent glossed over the question so as not to fan the flames of anger. "Everything's in place. Like I said, it'll all be over tonight."

"For your sake, I hope so," the voice said. He terminated the call.

34

⌇

Same day—Friday, 2 June 2000, 11:40 a.m. EDT
Williamsburg, Virginia

GALLAGHER SET HER SUITCASE ON THE bed and flung it open. There was
little to pack; she only took things out when she needed them. She went
into the bathroom, gathered her toiletries, and crammed them into three
green and white Naugahyde press-and-seal makeup pouches. She tossed
them on top of her clothes in the suitcase.

Taking a step back, she surveyed the room, just to be sure she hadn't
missed anything. As she did, her sandaled foot stepped on a fountain pen
she'd dropped a few minutes before but forgotten. When she looked down
and saw what it was, she smiled. The pen was her one link to normalcy. She'd
used it to write her girlfriends from college. She always wrote them in purple
ink, a continuation of a co-ed tradition she began at the George Washington
University in Washington, DC, thirteen years before. Of course, her girlfriends
knew nothing about what she really did. They just marveled at her postcards
and letters from exotic places around the world. Their stories were much more
mundane: husbands, babies, starter-homes, in-laws, and family vacations at
Disney World. She lived out her dreams vicariously through them and they
through her. It was the perfect symbiotic relationship. She stooped to pick up
the pen.

The first bullet penetrated the sliding glass door and thumped into the
drywall just above her back. Her legs instinctively gave way and she fell flat on
the floor, just in time to hear the second bullet punch through the glass and
rip into the wall almost a foot below the first. She reached up to get her purse

from the bed, using the suitcase lid to cover her hand's movement. With one quick motion, she grabbed her purse and flung herself back down to the floor, just as two more bullets tore into the bed where her purse had been. Both lodged in the wall just above her flattened body.

She couldn't see who was shooting at her or how far away they were, but she guessed they were in the woods across the back lawn with an unobstructed view of everything in her room through the sliding glass doors. The only way out was the door to the hallway, but even if she survived long enough to get there, she'd be gunned down as she tried to unfasten the chain lock.

Surprisingly cool given her situation, she set her action-oriented mind to work in a search for options. She could telephone the man with the Boston accent to call off his dogs, but that would only confirm she was still alive and hasten the sniper's walk across the lawn. Then her face flushed red hot with anger. They'd planned to kill her all along! The sniper had to have been in position before she'd reported her failure to get the notebook. They must have had her under surveillance and known precisely when she hung up the telephone after making her report. After she'd admitted she didn't get it, the man with the Boston accent gave the order to take her out.

For the first time, she realized what she was up against. Richard would order the man with the Boston accent and the organization at his disposal to hunt her down to the ends of the earth. She pictured her cold, lifeless body washing up on the beach of Sao Paolo, if she lived long enough to get there. She'd always lived with danger, but she'd never been the target of a determined man directing a host of undercover operatives to kill her.

A new sensation charged through her neurons. Not fear, not sorrow, not regret for a life she would never live, but vulnerability. For the first time in her life, she felt vulnerable, treed by hounds and waiting for the hunter to come and finish her off.

She considered standing up and getting the inevitable over with, but then her anger returned full force. How dare he try to eliminate her! It was *his* mission failure, not hers. Richard was the one who should feel vulnerable. Then another realization hit her: he did. That was why he was trying to kill her, because he realized she could hurt him. The thought rekindled her self-confidence and she began to look for a way out.

She scrunched herself closer to the head of the bed and rolled over onto her back. Then she emptied her purse and used it as a prod to push up the lid to her suitcase. Another bullet passed through the glass door, and the purse flew out of her hand. "Just my luck," she said aloud, "a patient sniper." At least it meant he was still in position across the field and apparently content to keep her pinned down. Was that because someone else was making his way to the room to finish her off? That was how she would handle it. That meant time was running out. She needed to make her escape and she needed to make it fast. Then she had a radical idea.

35

Same day—Friday, 2 June 2000, 11:45 a.m. EDT
State Department, Washington, DC

THE INTERCOM BUZZED IN THE SECRETARY of State's office.
"Madame Secretary," Madeleine began. "Mr. Benfield and Mr. Bowers are here to see you."

"Thanks, Madeleine, send them in." Susan McDermott set aside the Secret intelligence report she was perusing, dispensed with her reading glasses, and rose from behind her desk to greet her guests.

"Elrod, Sam, please come in." She shook hands with each of the men as they stepped into her office. "Let's sit down and you can tell me what you've got." She led the way to the conference table at the back of the room, and all three sat down. The Secretary got right down to business. "So I assume this meeting has to do with Robert Fowler. Am I right?"

"You are, Madame Secretary," Bowers drawled. "We've got an update in the case."

The Secretary leaned forward in her chair and rested her elbows on the table. "So, what is it?"

"Our investigator in Vietnam has been working with the Vietnamese police to solve Fowler's murder." Bowers opened a folder, pulled out a couple of pages from an unstapled report, and set them on the table in front of him. He used his right index finger to keep his place on the bulleted page. "It looks like Fowler was involved in drug trafficking."

"Remember what I said before, Sam. I don't want this young man's reputation sullied with drugs unless the evidence clearly supports it. Do you have hard evidence?"

"Unfortunately, we do. We went back for a follow-up search of his apartment because the landlord wants everything cleared out so he can rent the place again. Fowler had a desk in a room he used as a study, and we found an unmarked envelope the Vietnamese police hadn't noticed before sitting near the top of a stack of papers. It contained a key and a business card for a local bank."

"Was it a key to a safe deposit box?" interrupted Benfield.

"It was," Bowers confirmed. "The interesting thing was, though, the bank's records didn't disclose the name of the person renting the box or when it was rented out, and no one knew or would admit knowing anything about it. Even the box's access log was blank. Anyway, when we opened it up, we found a half-kilo of pure heroin and ten thousand dollars in U.S. hundred dollar bills. There were also two Vietnamese names, together with their telephone numbers, on a piece of rolled-up paper. The Vietnamese police traced the names, and both are thugs from the Khun Sa network."

"What's the Khun Sa network?" asked the Secretary.

"Khun Sa is a former Myanmar warlord who owns the heroin market in Southeast Asia. He's under house arrest by the Myanmar government, but DEA says his organization still funnels heroin into the U.S. and Australia. DEA figures he's paying off the Myanmar government so they will let him keep his organization intact."

"So where does that leave us, Sam?" the Secretary said.

"It could explain why Fowler was gunned down like he was. It looks like he was involved with some really bad actors."

"What could he have possibly been doing with these guys?"

"DEA thinks they might have been using him as a mule to smuggle heroin through Customs."

"Will you be able to get anything from the thugs?" asked Benfield.

"Not likely," Sam replied. "The Vietnamese police are bringing them in for questioning, but they told me not to expect any answers. They've had little luck breaking Khun Sa's network. His people are either too loyal or too afraid to talk. They'd rather take their chances with the Vietnamese police, even if that means facing the death penalty."

"All right," the Secretary said, "I want you to talk to everyone in the consulate who knew Fowler and his colleagues stateside. Leave no stone unturned. I want to make sure he was the only one involved. The last thing we need is for someone else to tell us we have a smuggling ring in the State Department. And get Public Affairs in on this right away if you haven't already.

This will all be fodder for the press, so I want to make sure Public Affairs has something prepared when the news breaks."

"I'll take care of it," Bowers said. He started to collect his papers and stuff them back into the folder as if the meeting were over.

"Not so fast," the Secretary chided. "What about the case of the retired Navy captain in the Vietnamese jail? Could Fowler's case be connected in any way?"

"I suppose it could," Bowers conceded, "but we haven't found it. As far as we can tell, it was just a coincidence that Fowler was working on Stokes' case and they both have some sort of drug connection."

"Well, I don't believe in coincidences," the Secretary said. She slid her forearms forward on the table and leaned into the conversation as if she were going to address each man sitting at the table up close and personal. "It's just too odd that we'd have a current State Department employee and former senior Navy officer involved in drugs in Vietnam at the same time. I sense there's a connection, and we haven't dug deep enough yet."

"You don't think Stokes and Fowler were working together to run heroin, do you? That just sounds too preposterous." Benfield's smirk communicated how little he valued the Secretary's instincts.

The Secretary pulled her arms back into her lap and retrenched from her more intimate communication mode of a moment before. "I don't know what I think," she said, her normally even voice raised, "because you haven't given me the information I need to reach an informed conclusion. I'm in the dark here."

Benfield backed off, stung by the Secretary's quick turn of the tables. "I'm sorry, Madame Secretary. That didn't come out exactly as I intended."

"I got it, Elrod, but I still feel like the information isn't getting to me fast enough. I've not heard anything from you since you gave me the memo for the President—nothing from your discussions with Stokes' attorney and nothing about the plane Stokes found." The Secretary focused on Benfield as if he were the only person sitting at the table. "This isn't a routine request, Elrod. When one of our people is murdered, it's a big deal. This won't ever be old news to me, so don't treat it that way." She paused just long enough to let her admonition sink in, then to make sure Benfield understood the real point behind her rebuke, she added, "And don't take this out on your team, Elrod. I asked you and Sam for the update, not them."

"I'm very sorry, Madame Secretary." No longer smirking, Benfield shrank back in his chair, trying to recover from the maelstrom he'd set into motion. "We did actually try to reach Stokes' attorney, Steve Stilwell, but we haven't connected with him yet. He's the key to both the Stokes case and what Stokes knows about the plane crash. I'll make sure we talk to him right away."

The Secretary returned to a more conversational tone after learning Benfield had at least tried to contact Steve Stilwell. "I tell you what, Elrod … I can help you move things along. Get ahold of Stilwell and tell him I'd like to talk to him about the Stokes case and how we can help him. Let's see if we can get him on my schedule for tomorrow. I'd like to meet with him in my office, with both of you present."

"I'm sure we can make that happen," Benfield said, sounding more confident now that the Secretary had shifted from admonishment to assist mode. "But it seems a little unusual for you to meet with an attorney like this, not to mention that it will be Saturday tomorrow. Why don't you let me or someone from the Legal Adviser's Office meet with him?"

"I appreciate you trying to keep me out of the trenches, Elrod, but we need to get to the bottom of this. We owe it to the embassy in Vietnam and to Fowler's family. I need to be able to look them in the eye and tell them I did everything I could."

"I'll get with Stilwell and set up the meeting, Madame Secretary."

"I knew I could count on you, Elrod." The Secretary pushed back her chair and started to get up, signaling the end of the meeting. "I look forward to seeing you both tomorrow."

36

Same day—Friday, 2 June 2000, 11:47 a.m. EDT
Williamsburg, Virginia

STEVE DRIFTED BACK INTO THE KITCHEN, leaving the door to the garage open behind him. He felt confused and angry and wanted to lash out at someone or something. He bumped into one of the chairs as he wandered past the kitchen table and cursed it for getting in his way. He knew what he had to do—get the notebook to Zip Thornton so Zip could analyze the crash site data. But that task seemed trivial now that Sarah was gone.

Steve kicked the base of the antique claw-foot oak table, causing it to creak backward on its ancient wooden wheels. How could he not have seen it? Gallagher had played him and he'd let her. He never would have been unfaithful to Sarah, but this technicality allowed him no comfort. Instead, the memory of riding on the back of Gallagher's motorcycle and his failure to keep control of the situation convicted him in the court of conscience. Even though he'd had no intention of being unfaithful, he'd compromised his emotional fidelity. That was what Sarah saw when she looked at the pictures, and there was nothing he could do or say to make those mental images go away. Add to that his tendency to put job before family, and it was no wonder she'd left him. Although it was hard for his Type-A personality to admit, he'd failed her as a husband.

Steve put his elbows on the table and buried his face in his hands. How could he have been so stupid? And what was he going to tell the boys when they got back from their fishing trip in Canada next week? That he had no idea where their mother was? He assumed she'd either gone to friend's house in Washington, DC, or gotten a hotel room somewhere until she was ready to talk. Then she'd call him. Could he wait that long to talk to her, or should he call her first and try to work things out? And what about the case? His decision not to give Gallagher the notebook moved Ric Stokes one step closer to the firing squad.

He stood up from the table, hoping a change in posture might help him think more clearly. Perhaps the best thing to do was to drive to Virginia Beach to deliver the notebook to Zip Thornton. That would give him an hour in the car to get his head on straight and come up with a plan. "That's what I'll do," he said out loud, as if announcing it to the empty kitchen validated the decision.

He walked into the garage and closed the door behind him. Just seeing Sarah's empty parking spot brought back the pain of her departure, but he got into his car anyway and backed to the end of the driveway, stopping to push the garage door button on the visor. He put his right arm behind the passenger seat headrest and looked over his shoulder to make sure the way was clear before backing into the street. Then his phone rang.

"Thank God," he said as he dug into his pants pocket and pulled out his cellphone. "It's got to be Sarah." But he didn't recognize the number on the display. Disappointed but curious, he answered the call.

"Hello?"

"Steve, it's Gallagher. Don't hang up—I'm ready to make a deal."

"What the hell are you doing calling me?" He started to close the phone, but then changed his mind. He wanted to have the last word. "You're not going to change my mind. And besides, you've got nothing to hold over me. Sarah knows everything."

"Look, Steve, I don't have time to negotiate. Some guy's shooting into my room at the Colonial Inne. I'm sure he'll be here any minute to finish me off, and if I die, there's nobody else who can save Ric Stokes' life."

"What is it you want?"

"Drive here as fast as you can and come around the backside. Just drive right up on the grass until you see a sliding glass door with a bunch of bullet holes in it. When you get here, honk your horn and I'll jump in your car."

"How do I know this isn't another set-up?"

"You don't, but if you don't get here in the next three minutes, I'll be dead and so will the truth about Ric Stokes."

Somehow he sensed Gallagher wasn't bluffing this time; she was laying it all on the line. He realized he didn't secure a commitment from her regarding how she would help him. He also realized he'd be driving into the line of fire of whoever was trying to kill her. But this time, he wouldn't be compromising his integrity, just his life. And with Sarah gone, that didn't seem quite so important. What he really needed to do was save Ric Stokes.

"I'm on my way!" he shouted as he flipped his phone shut. He gave his blue Celica the gas and shot out of the driveway, straightening the vehicle out on the road. He gunned it to the stop sign at the end of the street, braking to a California stop not much below the speed limit. His house was only three or four minutes from the Colonial Inne as long as he didn't get behind anyone slow or get stuck at any lights, so he prayed his luck would hold. He also prayed the Williamsburg Police wouldn't have a trap set up to catch speeding tourists. If that happened today, he'd read about what happened to Gallagher in tomorrow's paper.

Steve rounded the corner onto Jamestown Road and blew past the three-hundred-year-old Christopher Wren Building on the grounds of the College of William and Mary. A moment later, he made another sharp right and then a left, tearing down Francis Street to the Colonial Inne. When the traffic light in front of him turned yellow, he floored it, passing a green BMW with an old man at the wheel, and zoomed through the now red light, swerving to the left to avoid a vehicle just entering the intersection. The driver laid on his horn, but it was no more than background noise. Steve wasn't going to let this opportunity slip away.

Steve made a hard right into the Colonial Inne's long, winding driveway. At the end stood the stately white hotel, full of tourists coming and going on a beautiful late-spring Williamsburg afternoon. He drove into the parking lot to the left, carefully maneuvering through the cars to avoid hitting any pedestrians. When he got to the back of the building, he looked across a long grassy yard to the lush woods on his left. With his three minutes up, he shifted his Celica into first, scaled the curb, and cruised through the velvety green backyard, searching for a glass door riddled with bullet holes.

As he rounded a corner, he saw a man crouching next to a room, like he was trying to sneak inside. Steve could see he was holding something, but couldn't tell what it was. The man was wearing jeans and a blue golf shirt, not the typical dress of a maintenance person or gardener. Hoping it wasn't a tourist playing hide and seek with his kids, he accelerated toward the man and blasted his horn. Startled, the man turned and faced Steve. He had a gun.

Steve pushed the accelerator to the floor and headed toward the man, but on a course that would take him just to the man's right. The man raised his pistol and took aim at Steve through the windshield, so Steve turned hard to the left, whipping the car's back end out of control. The man pulled the trigger. The bullet struck the upper portion of the passenger side door, but did no damage inside. Driving as if on ice, Steve jammed the wheel to the right and gunned the engine, straightening out the car and once again heading toward the man, now only thirty yards away.

Staring directly at Steve, the man planted his feet a shoulder length apart and raised the pistol to get off one more shot—certain to be fatal at this range. As the man brought the pistol into firing position, Gallagher hurtled out of the hotel room behind him. She launched an uppercut with her foot that landed solidly in his crotch and cracked him in the head with the butt of a pistol she held in one hand while still gripping her Kate Spade purse with the other. As the man reeled and fell to the ground, Gallagher grabbed his pistol and ran for Steve's car. A shot from the woods struck the wall behind her.

Steve had no intention of sticking around any longer than necessary. He skidded to a stop next to Gallagher. She yanked open the passenger door, dove in, and pulled the door closed behind her. Another bullet from the woods struck Steve's left front fender with a metallic thud.

"What was that?" he yelled.

"There's another shooter!" Gallagher screamed. "Get the hell out of here!" Gallagher stayed below the dashboard so the shooter couldn't see her, but Steve had no such option. His only defense was to make a hyper-fast exit. Rather than try to circle around and go back the way he came, he tore across the Colonial Inne's finely trimmed lawn, heading around the back of the building. Another shot hit the vehicle, this time shattering the backseat window directly behind Steve's head. He never flinched—his total focus was on escape. Finally, he rounded one more corner and saw a parking lot ahead. This time he didn't slow to ease over the curb; he hit it at speed, causing the eighteen-year-old Celica to creek and crack with aftershocks. Back on pavement and seemingly in control, he sped around the front of the hotel, looped around the oval driveway, and exited the Colonial Inne grounds with a right turn on Francis Street.

"Holy shit!" he exclaimed, a rare divergence from his usually tame vocabulary. He sped down the historic colonial thoroughfare. For the second time today, his legs shook uncontrollably. He wanted to say something profound, but his trembling generated quite the opposite result.

"That was pretty messed up," he declared.

Gallagher glared at him from the floor.

Steve's first inclination was to laugh at seeing this normally sassy woman in her designer sundress scrunched under the dashboard. A tangled mass of hair darted in every direction, as if each strand were trying to flee on its own. But most intriguing, he could see fear in her eyes. Not an all-consuming fear that would have certainly been reasonable under the circumstances, but a measured, subdued fear. She had gotten herself into a situation where she couldn't control her own destiny, and now she needed his help to get out.

Despite all she had done, seeing her this way made him feel like he could work with her.

"It's okay for you to sit up now." His voice grew less animated as his adrenaline level retreated. Without a word, Gallagher clawed her way into the seat and exhaled deeply. She dropped the two guns and her purse on the floor, adjusted her dress to get everything in the right place, and plopped her hands in her lap.

"Now that was close," she announced.

"You better put your seatbelt on," Steve directed. "It would be a shame to survive all that and then get arrested for not wearing a seatbelt."

Gallagher smiled and looked over at him. "Thanks, Steve. I owe you one."

"You owe me more than one," he said, quickly transitioning from humor to resolve. "You owe me Ric Stokes out of jail, and I'm holding you to it." He looked back down the road and shifted the car into fifth gear as the Celica's engine whined to cruising speed.

Gallagher ignored Steve's attempt to hold her feet to the fire. "By the way, where are you taking me?" Then she added as if in an afterthought, "I hope you realize turning me over to the police won't get you what you want."

"Look, I'm done playing games here. I need to know your plan to deliver on your promise to get Ric Stokes out of jail, or I will take you to the police and you can tell them your story."

"That's a pretty bold statement, given that I'm the one with the guns."

Gallagher's wry little smile seemed to indicate that she was assessing his reaction to her not-so-veiled threat. He let the statement bounce off him as he merged onto I-64 eastbound and got up to speed. That gave him a few seconds to organize his thoughts. He would roll out what he knew, or thought he knew, to rekindle the fear she had already sequestered away. He spoke without looking at her, as though his main concern was driving and she was merely a sideshow.

"You've got the guns but you've got none of the cards."

"What's that supposed to mean?" Gallagher looked directly at him, which meant he'd piqued her interest. Now he had to play the situation to his advantage.

"It means whoever we just dealt with is after you. They'll be back and you know it. So you won't kill me. You need me to help keep you alive."

Gallagher looked out the front window, as if uninterested. She didn't speak or give any indication he'd hit a nerve. He pressed further.

"So why are they trying to kill you?"

Gallagher turned her head and looked directly at him. "Because I couldn't get the notebook from you."

"Ahhh, so it's my fault?"

"From my perspective, yes." The wry smile returned as she looked at him. "But then I'm sure you see things differently."

"Hhhmph," Steve huffed. "It's so nice of you to consider my feelings."

"I thought so, too," Gallagher said. Apparently satisfied she'd made her point, she again turned away from Steve to look out over Chesapeake Bay as they crossed the Hampton Roads Bridge-Tunnel toward Norfolk, Virginia. The water was glassy smooth near the bridge, with hardly a ripple to be seen. The Bay looked like a giant swimming pool with container ships and coal haulers far in the distance.

"So can we get back to serious matters?" Steve didn't wait for Gallagher to object. "Why would they kill you over the notebook?"

"Like I said, I was supposed to deliver the notebook and I failed. That's the way it is in my business."

"I think there's more to it than that; otherwise there'd be a lot of dead operatives around. I think they're trying to cover their tracks."

"Of course they're trying to cover their tracks. They're afraid if I'm caught, I'll identify them to save my own skin."

"And they'd be right, wouldn't they?"

Gallagher hesitated. "What do you mean?"

Steve could finally see the goal line—just a few more questions and he'd have what he needed.

"That's why you called me. You know you can't keep running and that they'll catch up with you someday. Your only hope is to destroy them before they destroy you, and you think I can help you do it."

"I called you because I was pinned down in a hotel room. It's not like I had a lot of choices."

"But you also promised to get Ric Stokes out of jail, and that means telling the truth about what happened to him. So, how are you planning to do that and save your own neck at the same time?"

Gallagher sat up straighter in the seat. Her face tightened, and any semblance of a smile vanished. "Let me put it to you simply: I want a free pass. That means no prosecution, here or anywhere else. I also want protection, a new identity, and a safe house in a country of my choosing. I get to keep a U.S. Passport and come and go as I please. In return, I tell everything I know to whoever you want, including what you need to get Ric Stokes off."

"The Attorney General will never go for it. You're involved in the death of at least one American and you had another framed and left to die in a Vietnamese prison."

"Then you get the Attorney General to see it differently, or I say nothing, period. I'll either rot in jail or get taken out by my former employer, but either way, Ric Stokes dies. I'm the only one who can connect the dots in a way the Vietnamese police will believe. It's up to you."

"I'm gonna need time to think about this."

"You can think all you want, but if they get to me before you make the only real choice you've got, then you'll have both my blood and Ric Stokes' on your hands."

Gallagher was right and he knew it. He had no other option, unless the notebook had some hidden clue as to who the bad guy was.

"All right, here's what we're gonna do. We'll be at Naval Air Station Oceana shortly. I'll get out of the car outside the gate so we don't drive on base with those weapons. I've got to meet with a squadron commanding officer for a few minutes and then I'll be ready to go. I'll call you and you pick me up where you dropped me off. Then we'll drive back to Williamsburg and I'll make my decision."

"What's to stop me from just driving away?"

"Then you'll have to watch your own back to make sure they don't kill you."

Gallagher nodded. "Just make it quick. For all I know, they're after us already. I don't think we've got much time."

Steve figured she was right, but there was little he could do about it. He had no idea whether a U.S. attorney would agree to a deal, and he felt like the deal would be letting Ryan Eversall down. But then reality set in. He was ready to take the risk if it meant getting Ric Stokes out of jail alive.

37

Saturday, 3 June 2000, 1:22 a.m.
Saigon

PHAN AND HIS FRIEND RODE THEIR motorcycles deep into Saigon's squalor. Dark three- and four-story tenements—ramshackle buildings devoid of hope and promise—flanked the dimly lit alley. The smell of cooking fires extinguished hours before still lingered in the humid night air, as did the odor of refuse stacked willy-nilly in piles along their route. Phan and his friend's motorcycles splashed through puddles formed in depressions in the dirt road, soaking areas that had nearly dried after an early evening shower.

Phan's friend motioned with his hand toward a building up ahead on the right. They drove past the entrance and tucked their motorcycles up against the wall just beyond the entrance. The center section of the first floor was entirely open to the alley. A single light shone faintly through a yellow, ragged lampshade. Nothing in the room was painted, or if it was, it had been years and the colors had long since faded. Now the room's defining feature was its weathered wood. A couple of broken pallets stacked on end against the wall took up most of that section of the room, while an open fire with a pot suspended over it occupied the opposite side.

An old woman sitting on her haunches tended the fire. When Phan and his friend approached, she tossed a pallet fragment into the flames and stood to meet them. She was dressed like a peasant, in a loose-fitting light-gray pajama-type outfit. Her skin was remarkably smooth for a woman her age, but when she barked her first words through a throat scarred by nicotine, Phan lost sight of her youthful skin.

"You want girls?" she said. "My ladies are very nice."

Phan's friend did the talking, which was exactly what Phan wanted.

"Mother," the friend said to the woman, deferring to her as head of the house. "We are looking for a girl I was told works here. She saw something and my friend needs to talk to her."

Phan's lips curved upward to something short of a smile, and he nodded as a show of respect.

"What did she see?" the woman asked.

Phan took that as his cue to enter the conversation. "She saw an American die from a heroin overdose and another get arrested by the police."

"My girls have nothing to do with drugs." Looking away from them, she shooed them away with her hand. "You'll not find that girl here."

Phan turned to leave, but his friend grabbed his arm. "It's not time to go yet," he said sternly. "Give the mother an incentive to talk to us."

Phan looked at his friend, confused. He wasn't sure what his friend meant, but he had no intention of hitting or hurting the woman in any way. His friend glared at him and rubbed his thumb and fingers together. Now Phan understood.

"Mother," Phan said, following his friend's lead. "I really need your help finding the girl who knows what happened. Here's something for your trouble." Phan put five folded 100,000 Dong notes into her hand and closed her fingers around the money. She immediately opened her hand to count how much he had given her.

"You give me another five hundred thousand Dong." Her tone and expression conveyed this was not a negotiation; it was a fixed-price contract with no guarantee of satisfaction.

Phan looked at his friend for guidance. "Do you have a choice?" the friend asked.

"I guess not," Phan said, again digging into his pocket. He pulled out another pre-folded group of notes totaling 500,000 Dong and handed it to the woman, who again immediately counted it. She gripped both folds of bills and began to disgorge the information Phan came for.

"I have heard of what you say," she began. "One of my girls, Trang, may be able to help you. Come this way."

The woman reached for a curtain on the back wall that had escaped Phan's notice. She pulled the curtain open, revealing a dark hall leading to a room with a dull yellow glow permeating a cloud of smoke hovering just below the ceiling. The woman walked into the passageway and headed toward the room. Phan waited for his friend to follow her, but when he didn't, Phan entered what he was sure was a hidden passage to hell. His friend followed them into the darkness.

The hall opened into an anterior room populated by three or four strung-out, scantily clad prostitutes and a sweaty man without a shirt sitting next to a closed door at the far end of the room. His muscular forearms and biceps were decorated with intricate tattoos, but the smoke was so thick and the light so poor that Phan couldn't identify the designs. What Phan could see was a long, thick scar running above the man's beltline, as if someone had tried to disembowel him. His hair was black and long, falling over his shoulders, and he had an air of evil about him. Phan was sure he was there to keep the women in line and deal with any unruly or ungrateful customers. He also knew there was no way Trang would talk to him if the enforcer could hear what she was saying.

"Which girl is Trang?" Phan asked.

"She's not here," the woman said, "but she will come shortly. You must wait."

"What does he want?" the enforcer asked the woman.

"He paid to get Trang." She showed deference to the enforcer, but not fear. She didn't disclose why Phan wanted to see Trang, but made it sound like he wanted her for sex.

The enforcer rocked back and grabbed a longneck beer bottle from under his folding chair. He took a long swig, draining the last of the liquid, then tossed the bottle into the corner, which was littered with five or six other glass carcasses. He stared at Phan, declaring his alpha status with his coal black eyes. Phan got the message—these were his girls and his space, and Phan better play by his rules, whatever they were.

A door on the side of the room opened and a middle-aged man emerged. He tucked his ratty white knock-off polo shirt into his jeans as he walked into the room. He said nothing and made no eye contact, maneuvering through the clutter to the hallway to make his exit. As he disappeared, a young woman came to the door of the room just vacated by the man. She had on a horizontally striped skintight tube skirt so short, Phan was embarrassed to look her way. Her hips were thin and boyish, but her unbuttoned shirt left no doubt she was a woman. Her face was pretty, save for the dark circles under her eyes. Phan guessed she was in her early twenties. But what he noticed most was her dazed stare. She seemed detached from her surroundings, as if her mind was somewhere else.

"Trang," the old woman coughed. "This man has paid full price. Give him what he wants."

Trang turned and vanished into the room, leaving the door open behind her.

The enforcer laughed, then became serious. "What are you waiting for?" he shouted, starting to get out of his chair. "You don't look like the type of man who knows what to do with a woman. Why are you here?" He moved toward Phan.

Phan started for Trang's room, but eyed the enforcer to convey he was not intimidated. "I know what to do with a woman," he began, "and I paid my money. Now leave me alone."

Phan's forcefulness apparently satisfied the enforcer, who shook his head and returned to his perch on the chair. Phan went into Trang's room and shut the door behind him. She was already sitting on the bed, which was the only furniture in the room aside from a small nightstand with a candle burning on it. The candle's flame cast a dim light, exaggerating the size of Trang's shadow on the wall across from the bed. Trang started to take off her shirt.

"No," he whispered loudly, catching her before she went too far. "I don't want that. I need to ask you some questions."

"I don't get paid to answer questions," the young woman said, sounding more coherent than her appearance at the door had led Phan to believe. She sounded brazen, calloused, and jaded beyond her years. She pulled her shirt back in place, buttoning it from the bottom up. If she had been the girl next door at one time, she was no longer that girl. Now she was someone else's object, just trying to survive. Seeing her in these circumstances saddened him, as he flashed forward to what the future held for his own little girl. He would never allow this to happen, even if it cost him his life. He was now even more determined to get his family to America, whatever the cost. At the moment that meant being strong with Trang, just as he had been with the enforcer.

"If you don't answer my questions, you don't get paid."

"What is it you want?"

"I understand you may know about what happened to the American who died in his hotel room a couple of weeks ago. Is that true?"

"Maybe you didn't hear me before. I don't get paid enough to answer questions."

Phan noted the difference in wording. The first time she said she didn't get paid to answer questions. This time she said she didn't get paid *enough*. Phan took that as a not-so-subtle indication she would answer his questions if the price was right.

"I heard you this time," Phan said, digging into his pockets. He pulled out another pre-sorted pack of five 100,000 Dong notes, folded in half and held together by a paper clip. He had more money than that, including 250 U.S. dollars, but he wanted Trang to think 500,000 Dong was all he had. He took off the paperclip and stuffed it in his pocket, then he flipped the first two 100,000 Dong notes from the stack and handed them to Trang. "Here," he said, making sure it sounded like he was begrudgingly giving the money to her. "Now what can you tell me about the night the American died?"

Trang took the notes and crumpled them in her hand. "You can't be serious," she chided. "It's going to take a lot more than that to help me remember. I want one hundred U.S. dollars." She threw the crumpled Dong notes on the floor.

"Where am I going to get that kind of money? Take the rest of this. You will have five hundred thousand Dong. That's more than enough for what you know." Phan picked up the notes she threw on the floor, smoothed them out, and offered her all five.

"Do you know what could happen to me if I tell you?"

Phan didn't respond. He was willing to sacrifice anything to get his family to America, so he really hadn't given much thought to the consequences for those he was asking for help.

"I'll tell you. If they find out, they will kill me. And probably you, too."

"So what would change if I gave you one hundred dollars?"

"At least I'd have something to show for it, and maybe I could get out of here."

"So how do I know if you even have the information I need?"

"Because I do. But if you don't believe me, then maybe this will convince you. The American who died—he didn't shoot up. They held him down and injected the drugs into his arm. If you want the rest, it's going to cost you."

Now Phan knew she was the right person. He hadn't mentioned how the American died or that drugs were involved; she came up with those details on her own. He decided to take a chance and reveal that he had the money she wanted.

"Okay, I'll give you one hundred dollars—fifty now and fifty after you tell me what you know."

"I thought so," she said, standing up and pointing her finger at his face. "You lied to me. You said you didn't have the money. The one-hundred-dollar price is no good anymore." She sat back down on the bed and crossed her arms, staring at him.

Phan was angry with himself for lying to her. She was way more street-smart than he gave her credit for. But what really bothered him was that she had caught him lying. He never lied, but he lied to her because he thought he had to. He was mad at himself for not having told her the truth to begin with. Now his lie would have consequences.

Bang, bang, bang. The loud pounding on the door made Phan's heart stop. He was so startled, he let out a short "Ahhg!"

"Hurry up in there," the enforcer boomed through the door. "Your time is up or you pay more money."

Phan spoke fast, not knowing if the enforcer would barge into the room and find that he had done nothing but talk to Trang. Then he would want to know what was going on. "I'm sorry for lying to you. But to be honest, I did not trust you."

"Why, because I am a whore?" The young woman glared at him. The detached look she'd had when Phan first saw her was gone. He was surprised at how articulate she was and the way she had shamed him into a corner.

"Yes," Phan admitted. "I thought you would be happy to get five hundred thousand Dong and you would tell me what I needed to know."

Trang stood up and walked over to him. "Well, you made a big mistake. So, here's the way it's going to be. You give me one hundred dollars now and tell me where you live. Then I'll come by your home tomorrow and you'll give me another hundred dollars. Then maybe I will tell you what I know."

Phan knew he was out of time and options. She wasn't going to be able to tell him anything now; the enforcer could burst in at any moment. Plus, she had the information he needed, so she held all the cards. He dug into his left front pants pocket, the pocket with the dollars. He pulled out all five twenty-dollar bills and handed them to her. Then he pulled out his wallet and gave her one of his tattered, sweat-stained business cards. "Okay, here's the money, and my address is on the card. When will you come by?"

Trang didn't answer. Instead, she grabbed the bills and the card and stuffed them into her purse on the floor next to the bed. Then she jumped back onto the bed, unbuttoned her shirt, and started to pull it off.

"Go now," she told him, "and leave the door open behind you so they can see me dressing. You will see me again tomorrow. Now go."

Phan nodded and turned toward the door. As he did, the door came flying open and the enforcer stood there, blocking the exit. Phan could barely make out his features in the candlelight. The light in the room behind the enforcer made his face appear like a shadow.

"We're done," Trang shouted, standing up from the bed and making it clear she was only partially dressed. The enforcer backed away from the door to let Phan leave.

"Hurry up," he demanded. "Do you think you are the only one who paid for her this evening? Now get going."

As much as he wanted to, Phan didn't look back at Trang. He wanted to take her with him to keep her from having to be with more men and to get the information he knew she had, but there was no way that was going to happen. As he walked past the enforcer, he saw his friend sitting next to one of the women. He looked out of it, strung out on the same drugs the enforcer used to keep the women subdued. Phan couldn't leave him there. Who knew what he might say while he tripped into oblivion? Phan walked over to him and pulled him to his feet.

"We've got to get going," Phan told his friend.

"I don't want to go. Leave me here."

"I can't do that. Your parents would never forgive me." Phan put his friend's arm over his shoulder and guided him back down the hallway toward the exit. His friend was too high to resist. When they made it outside, Phan turned around to make sure they weren't being followed, and then he somehow managed to get his friend loaded onto his motorcycle. He pulled his friend's arms around his waist and started the engine. They slowly backed into the street, avoiding the stacks of garbage, and headed down the alley the same way they had come. They'd have to retrieve his friend's motorbike later.

For now, he was just glad they'd survived. The question was, would Trang show up tomorrow like she'd promised?

38

‹›

Friday, 2 June 2000, 2:28 p.m. EDT
Virginia Beach, Virginia

ZIP THORNTON SENT A DRIVER TO pick Steve up from the POW/MIA Flame of Hope Memorial Park on Oceana Boulevard, just outside the main entrance to the base. The sailor's crisp white uniform, impeccable protocol, and radiant self-confidence made Steve miss the esprit du corps and camaraderie of his active duty Navy brethren. Perhaps that was why he felt a natural affinity for Casey as a former sister-in-arms.

Zip Thornton was all business. As Commanding Officer of the Fleet Replacement Squadron, responsible for training newly minted fighter pilots before they deployed on aircraft carriers in the U.S. Atlantic Fleet, Zip had no time to spare. Still, he carved a hole in his schedule to meet with Steve, took the notebook from him, and promised to have his team go through it with a fine-tooth comb. It was the military brotherhood in action.

The squadron driver returned Steve to his drop-off point on Oceana Boulevard, where the quiet of the POW/MIA Memorial, broken only once by the ripping sound of a Navy jet rocketing skyward, reminded him of his own loss that day. Once again he'd gotten so engrossed in his work that he'd let Sarah's departure fade into a remote compartment of his brain while he dealt with Gallagher's rescue, her demands for immunity, and the process of turning the notebook over to Zip Thornton. For Steve, the situation was all too typical. The one person he actually loved was being crowded out by events he felt he had little control over.

Lost in thought and his eyes fixed on the black POW/MIA flag hanging limp on its pole, he didn't hear the car beeping behind him. Finally the driver laid on the horn with one long blast. Steve spun around to see Gallagher waiting in his Celica at the end of the parking lot. He gave the flag one final mental salute and then walked back to the driver's side of the vehicle. Gallagher had the window down and looked up at him as he approached.

"Since I know where we're going, how about I drive?" Steve suggested in a flat voice.

"Fine with me." She opened the door and eased out of the car. Steve slid into the driver's seat while Gallagher walked around the front and settled into the passenger seat, ready to go.

"You know, I'm lucky I didn't get stopped by a cop. The side window's broken out and there are bullet holes everywhere. I felt like I was driving a Toyota gangster-mobile."

Gallagher's attempt at humor was lost on Steve. He backed up until he could pull forward and exit the memorial onto Oceana Boulevard. Then he accelerated to fifty-five miles per hour, all without saying a word.

"What's the matter, Dr. Gloom?" Gallagher asked. "Didn't your notebook meeting go well?"

"Oh, I don't know," Steve said sarcastically. "I mean, you attempted to blackmail me this morning with pictures taken out of context, my wife left me, I almost got killed in an ambush that shot up my favorite car, and one of my best friends is in jail awaiting execution in Vietnam. I guess it's my lucky day."

"Blah, blah, blah," mocked Gallagher. "I hope you're over it soon 'cause we really don't have time for your pity party. Where are we going, anyway?"

"We're getting on the interstate here and heading back to Williamsburg. Then we're going to my office, and I'll give the U.S. Attorney a call to see what we can arrange. We can figure out the rest after we hear what he says."

"What if he won't go for it?"

"Then I'll try harder. I've also got a secret weapon I can use. I just hired a new attorney in the office. She used to work for a federal judge in Norfolk. I'm thinking that may come in handy as we try to make all the pieces come together."

That answer seemed to satisfy Gallagher. She sank back in her seat and started to watch the scenery go by. Eventually she closed her eyes. Despite her apparent resilience, she'd had a stressful day as well.

Traffic was still relatively light for a Friday afternoon. Lots of cars were heading eastbound for the beaches, but not many people were heading inland toward Williamsburg for the weekend. In fact, when they reached the Hampton Roads Bridge-Tunnel, traffic was so light Steve could concentrate a little less on the road and look over to his left to see three of the Atlantic

Fleet's aircraft carriers in port at the Norfolk Navy Base. The size of the aircraft carriers never ceased to amaze him, even though he'd seen them hundreds of times and deployed on one to the Mediterranean Sea. It was like seeing one of the Seven Wonders of the Modern World in Williamsburg's backyard. His thoughts started to drift back to his halcyon Navy days.

Wham! Metal slammed into metal, forcing the driver's side of the Celica to crash up against the tubular guardrail on the left side of the bridge. Steve fought to keep control, taking his foot off the accelerator and trying to apply the brakes. Gallagher woke up and screamed as her passenger side window shattered, an eighteen-wheeler's lug nuts drilling a circular pattern into her door and shoving the car to the left. "What's happening?" she shrieked.

"Hang on!" Steve yelled, as he jammed on the breaks and laid on the horn. But the Celica didn't slow down as the semi's tractor thrust it forward. Then, just as fast as it happened, the truck veered to the right and its wheel stopped grinding into Gallagher's door. Steve veered to the right as well, to get the left side of his Celica off the guardrail. He depressed the brake as far as he could.

Wham! The truck's cab slammed into the Celica from the right again, hurling Steve's car back into the guardrail on the left side of the bridge. This time, the truck's force didn't let up and Steve felt the Celica being crushed between the semi's cab and the guardrail. Before he could react, the left side of the Celica rode up on the guardrail, and with one strong push from the truck, jumped over and plunged twenty feet head first into the murky Chesapeake Bay.

When the wedge-shaped front end of the Celica hit the water, it began to submerge then bounced back until the car sat level on the surface. Steve was dazed, having hit his head on the steering wheel, and it took him a second to orient himself and figure out what had happened. He unfastened his seatbelt and looked over at Gallagher. She was slumped in her seat, unconscious. He could see blood streaming down her face from a cut somewhere above her hairline.

"Gallagher!" he yelled. "Are you all right?" He didn't wait for an answer—he didn't expect one anyway. He started to climb over the center console to release her seatbelt, but water came rushing in through her shattered window and the shot-out window behind the driver's side door. The force pushed him back into his seat. The cold water pouring over Gallagher's right shoulder revived her and she screamed.

"Oh my God. Help me, Steve!"

"I'm trying," he yelled back. "Get your seatbelt unfastened."

By now the water was even with the top of the doors and the car was being dragged under water. Steve tried to open his door, but it wouldn't budge. He didn't know whether it was because it had been damaged by the guardrail or because of the water pressure from the outside. He figured his best chance was to roll down his window once the car was fully submerged and then swim out to freedom. Somehow, though, he had to free Gallagher and get her out with him. He didn't have much time. There was less than a foot of space between the ceiling and the water, and Gallagher's seatbelt was making it hard for her to keep her head above water.

"Listen to me," he commanded. "I'm going to go underwater to get your seatbelt off. You take a deep breath before your head goes under and then get out through your window." Steve didn't wait for a confirmation. He tilted his head back, sucked in the biggest gulp of air he could force into his lungs, and dipped underwater toward Gallagher's waist. It was too murky to see, so he reached out and probed with his hands until he felt the seatbelt coming across her chest and followed it down to her lap. She was still struggling to release it, so he pulled her hands away and depressed the red button at the center of the buckle.

It was jammed. Maybe she'd caught a piece of clothing in it when she fastened it, but the damned thing wouldn't open. He pushed the button again and yanked on the shoulder harness with all his might, pulling it apart. He tried to push her out the window, but she wasn't taking any initiative. In fact, she felt limp. He wasn't sure if she had passed out, given up, or was too injured to save herself, but she wouldn't go out the window.

Steve exhaled some of the air in his lungs and started to feel his own oxygen reserve running out. He had two options. He could leave Gallagher, go out his own window, get some fresh air, and then come back down to get her. But if the car sank in the meantime or he couldn't get her out, he'd never be able to live with himself, so he took the other option. Grabbing Gallagher's left arm and shoulder, he forced her toward the window. Bracing his feet on the seat and pushing for all he was worth, he managed to get her torso outside the car, and then with one more push, her legs. He held on tight to one leg, just in case she didn't start to float to the surface. Seeing stars and trying not to inhale a mouthful of seawater in the quest for air, he propelled himself out the window behind Gallagher and grasped her around the waist.

Steve broke through the surface like a submarine breeching after an emergency ascent. Gallagher broke through as well and started choking as soon as she hit the air. Her mouth filled with brine and she vomited.

"Hold on to my hand," Steve said as he let go of Gallagher's waist. It was too hard to maneuver in the frigid water at such close quarters. By putting some distance between them, he could better use his legs and his free hand to swim toward one of the bridge pillars, roughly twenty-five feet away. When they arrived, he had Gallagher hang on to his shoulders with both hands while he used one hand to grasp the top of the pillar and the other to keep them from being swept into the razor-sharp barnacle-encrusted concrete.

"Are you okay?" he asked, this time better able to process Gallagher's response.

"I think I'm hurt pretty bad." Her voice was barely audible over the sound of the traffic on the bridge and the eastbound lanes a few yards away.

"Hang in there, Wendy," Steve said, thinking this might be just the right time to use her first name. "I see a boat heading our way." He waved and called out to it with all his strength.

"Help! Over here, help!"

The man at the helm of the sport-fishing boat waved back and headed directly for them. Steve could see a second man on the boat grabbing a couple of life jackets.

"They see us, Wendy," Steve yelled. "We'll be safe on the boat in less than a minute."

39

Same day—Friday, 2 June 2000, 10:18 p.m. EDT
Williamsburg, Virginia

STEVE WANDERED BACK TO HIS LAW office to meet with Casey after being discharged from the hospital. His injuries were miraculously minor—a few cuts and bruises and lots of soreness setting in. Gallagher wasn't so lucky. She'd asked him to hold her hand before she was life-flighted to Richmond, which he did, of course. After all, she had no family and no one who cared whether she lived, although there was no shortage of people eager to send her to the afterlife. She looked frail lying in the hospital bed, her ribs and right arm broken, her lung punctured and spleen ruptured, and her face bruised and swollen. Not to mention that she had a concussion and almost drowned. She was a shell of the woman who had strode haughtily into his office earlier in the day brandishing her ultimatum, yet he derived no pleasure from her downfall. He felt like she was just getting to the point where she would redeem herself by helping him secure Ric Stokes' release. The truck on the bridge had closed that window and possibly cut her life tragically short. As he watched the helicopter whisk her away, he knew he would never see her again.

Although minor in comparison but still crippling in terms of his ability to get things done, his Celica was history, leaving him without a vehicle, and his cellphone and wallet were soaked from their dip in the Chesapeake Bay. His wallet would dry and be fine, but the same could not be said for his cellphone. Hoping providence would finally shine upon him, he removed the phone's SIM card, cleaned it with a tissue, and inserted it into a spare phone he kept in his desk drawer. He then plugged the phone's recharger into the outlet next to the credenza behind his desk and the phone came on. With at least one small victory to celebrate, he sat down to decompress in the quiet, only to hear the front door swing open, followed by the sound of a rolling suitcase thumping across the metal doorsill.

"Is that you, Casey?" he shouted from his desk as he stood up and limped to the lobby.

"It is," Casey responded. "Sorry I'm a little late, but I got here as fast as I could."

Steve met her at the door to his office, stepping out of the way so she could roll her suitcase inside. "You're not late at all," he said. "How about we grab a seat at the conference table, or do you need a break first?"

"I'm good," Casey said as she walked over to the table that just one week before had been the site of her first and final interview. Steve took the seat opposite her, gripping both armrests and carefully lowering himself downward until his lower back made a soft landing against the chair's hardwood slats. He was so caught up in the task at hand that he didn't notice Casey watching his every move.

"Shouldn't you be home in bed?" she asked, quickly assuming Marjorie's role. "Marjorie told me you were in a bad car accident today, and you're clearly in pain. I really don't mind coming in tomorrow or Sunday, once you feel better."

"I appreciate that, but I'll probably be even stiffer tomorrow." Steve's half-grimace, half-smile acknowledged Casey's point while conveying he felt well enough to talk. "Besides, I've got a meeting with the Secretary of State tomorrow afternoon, so I want to make sure I'm up to speed on everything you found out."

Casey's eyes widened. "Did I hear you right—Secretary of State, Susan McDermott?"

"That was my reaction when Marjorie told me. Apparently my friend in the Legal Adviser's Office called this afternoon and told Marjorie that someone would pick me up tomorrow morning for a two-p.m. meeting."

"Wow, that's pretty cool. Do you know what she wants?"

"All I know is the meeting is about Sapphire Pavilion."

Casey grinned. "The timing is perfect. You can ask her about the State Department notation on the mission file."

"That's exactly what I thought. But I wanted to touch base with you first to make sure I'm familiar with everything you uncovered."

Casey shrugged. "I really don't know any more than what we spoke about on the phone. The mission was Top Secret and I didn't have access to anything classified, just the handwritten cross-reference to the State Department." Casey tightened her lips and tilted her head back, briefly looking beyond

Steve. He could see her mind churning, so he waited for her to reengage. A moment later, she resumed the conversation. "Come to think of it, there is one additional detail worth mentioning." She opened her briefcase and pulled out some notes from the historical center. She ran her finger down the page, then flipped it over and did the same on the other side.

"Here it is," she announced. "The C-130 belonged to the Twenty-First Tactical Airlift Squadron. That squadron did special operations, so it's entirely possible this plane was on some type of special mission. Putting two and two together, I think it was doing something for the State Department."

Steve jotted down the information so he'd remember to ask about it. "Maybe I can get Secretary McDermott to commit some resources toward mining the State Department's archives and finding out what it was."

"Do you need me to work on anything while you're in Washington?"

"Why don't you take the weekend off? If I heard Marjorie right, you're barely moved in here."

"My apartment's in pretty good shape. I don't have that much to move and Marjorie said she would help me. Besides, I feel like we're closing in on the case."

"I thought so too," Steve acknowledged, "but I'm afraid the car accident really set us back."

"You mean besides you being beat up and almost killed?"

Steve rested his elbows on the table and cupped his hands under his chin. "Did Marjorie mention that there was someone else in the car when it went over the guardrail?"

Casey's eyes widened. "No, you're kidding me. Who was it?"

"It's a long, convoluted story, but saving all the gory details for later, there was a woman in the car who I believe holds the key to getting Ric Stokes out of jail. I think she's the one who orchestrated the scenario that got Ryan killed and Ric arrested. She was ready to turn state's evidence if I could get her in the Federal Witness Protection Program."

"Holy moly!" Casey exclaimed, having adopted her boss's aversion to foul language. "Is she okay?"

"They life-flighted her to Richmond this afternoon; the docs say it's touch and go. Besides almost drowning, she's got a ruptured spleen, a punctured lung, a concussion, and a bunch of broken bones. She looks like a truck literally ran over her, which in a way it did."

"Was the FBI able to get a statement from her?"

"I don't think so. The doctors said she's in too bad shape."

"So why is she willing to cooperate? What's the catch?"

"It's her organization that's trying to kill her. I'm sure they're the ones who ran us off the bridge after their attempt to kill her earlier in the day failed."

Casey flipped her notepad to a clean page to take some notes, but instead of writing, she brought her pen to her chin and again looked beyond Steve. "Something still doesn't make sense. Why were they trying to kill her?"

"She told me it was because she wasn't able to get Ryan Eversall's notebook. But on second thought, I bet they realized we're going to figure out whatever it is they're trying to hide about the plane crash and are hunkering down. Gallagher—that's the woman's name—was a loose end they had to eliminate. Unfortunately, they got to her before we had the chance to find out what she knows."

Casey stood up and positioned herself behind her chair, gripping the back with both hands and leaning forward as if ready to argue her case from a podium in front of a jury. "And I thought I was going to be litigating Baby Boomer wills ...."

Steve nodded. "You never know what's gonna walk through the door in a practice like this."

"How about I come into the office tomorrow morning and stand by, just in case you need me to do something for your meeting with the Secretary. If I haven't heard from you by late afternoon, I'll go home."

"I'd really appreciate that, Casey. Now let's clear out of here and get some sleep."

"You go ahead, Steve. I'm going to lock up Ryan Eversall's Sapphire Pavilion file and see how many emails I've got in my inbox."

"I thought they stole the Sapphire Pavilion file from your hotel room?"

"I didn't want to say anything over the phone, but all they got was my notes. I still have the entire file."

"Wow, that's the best news I've heard all evening. Why don't you just lock it up and check your email tomorrow?"

"I'm so wide awake after a cup of coffee on the plane, I couldn't sleep now if I wanted to. Plus, if I check it tonight, I'll be able to sleep in a little longer tomorrow morning, when I will be tired."

"All right, but promise me you won't stay much later."

"I promise. Now let me get out of your hair so you can head home." Casey reached over to grab the handle of her suitcase and started to head for the door. "Oh, sorry I can't give you a ride home, but I took a cab from the airport. I was planning on calling a cab when I'm ready to go."

"Thanks anyway, but I'm gonna walk home. It's such a beautiful night and I can use the time to think about my meeting tomorrow."

What Steve didn't say was he also had to sort out his situation with Sarah. He still hadn't heard from her, and that tore at him because he felt like the longer they stayed apart, the easier it would be for Sarah to call it quits. He selfishly didn't want her to discover her life might actually be better without him.

"Enjoy your walk, and good luck with the Secretary tomorrow. Tell her I said hello." Casey smiled as she disappeared with her suitcase, her briefcase resting on the suitcase's extended handle.

Steve slid back his chair. Even though he wasn't seriously injured in the crash, his whole body ached. He pried himself off the chair and inched his way over to his desk to gather some things to take home so he could read them in the morning before he had to come to the office to meet the State Department driver. Grabbing a copy of Ryan Eversall's crash site notebook, he stuffed it into his leather planner, and made sure he had two functioning pens and a pad of paper. He also tucked a small stack of business cards into a pocket in the planner. He didn't want to look unprepared for his meeting with the Secretary.

Steve wedged the planner under his arm and headed for the door, turning out the lights just before he passed into the reception area. "Good night, Casey, and thanks for your help tonight. Remember, you promised not to stay too late."

Casey was already delving into her email. Steve saw her look away from her computer screen just enough to answer him, but he could tell she still had one eye on whatever she was reading. "Good night, Steve. I'm glad you're okay, and I hope you feel better."

With that, Steve headed out the front door, making sure it was securely locked. Even though the area around his office on North Henry Street was safe—aside from an assassin trying to kill him in his office a couple of years ago—he felt a little guilty about leaving Casey alone so late on a Friday night. He suppressed his concerns, though, rationalizing she was a former Army officer who knew how to take care of herself. In any case, she'd promised him she would be leaving soon.

***

WITHIN THIRTY MINUTES, CASEY HAD GONE through everything in her virtual inbox, so she shifted her attention to the physical inbox sitting on the front right corner of her desk. Since she was so new, there were only a few papers inside, including some case digests explaining recent Virginia Court of Appeals decisions. As a new litigator, she had to become intimately familiar with the decisions of the Appellate courts because they would teach her what she could and could not get away with when trying a case before a Virginia jury. She debated whether to start reading the digests now, but opted against it. She was starting to fade. She checked her watch to see if it was late enough to justify the way she felt. It was almost midnight.

"Holy cow," she said out loud, yawning and stretching her arms over her head. "Where did the time go?" She reached forward on the keyboard and shut down her computer. Then she opened her briefcase and put away the Sapphire Pavilion file Angela Eversall gave her, as well as some expense receipts she'd collected on her trip. She started to make her way to the door.

A cellphone ringing somewhere outside her office stopped her in her tracks—she was supposed to be alone. Her first instinct was to get out as quickly as possible, but her second instinct—to find the cellphone—won out. She opened the top middle drawer of her desk and pulled out a large pair of scissors to deal with any would-be attacker. Then she started inching out of her office, one cautious step at a time.

Once in the lobby, she could tell the ringing was coming from Steve's office. The room was dark, except for the faint glow of a streetlight on the other side of North Henry Street angling through the window. The light cast a bluish tint on the area behind Steve's round conference table, but it made the other side of the room where the ringing was coming from shadowy and foreboding.

The building was so quiet that the phone's ring pierced the darkness like a warning bell at sea. Casey repeated to herself that she had nothing to fear, but her heart wasn't listening and its pounding began to compete with the phone.

Then, as suddenly as it began, the phone stopped ringing and the silence returned, save for the rhythmic thumping of Casey's heart. Recognizing it was now or never, she reached her hand into Steve's office and flipped on the light switch, causing the lamps and light fixtures to spray light across the room. She clenched her teeth, gripped the scissors in attack mode, and thrust herself into the office.

Thank God it was empty.

Casey's emotions shifted from fear to embarrassment faster than Steve's office transitioned from dark to bright. She scanned the room to make sure she was safe and spotted Steve's cellphone sitting on the credenza behind his desk with its recharger plugged into the wall.

"He forgot to take his cellphone home," she said out loud, sighing in relief. She went over and retrieved it, thinking she would have her cab stop by his house on the way home. Out of curiosity, she glanced at the caller ID and noticed it was from Sarah.

"That's odd," she said out loud again, hoping the sound of her own voice would make the office less scary. Steve hadn't mentioned Sarah was out of town or that he was going anywhere but home, so she grew concerned something might be wrong. She recalled her days standing watch in the Army when her Commanding Officer would say, "If you can't decide if a situation warrants calling me, then it's close enough to the line and you should go ahead and call." Thinking the same rule of thumb applied here, she shoved Steve's phone in her pocket and walked back to her office to get his home number and give him a call.

Crash! The sound of shattering glass at the back door sent an electrifying chill through her that dwarfed her reaction to the ringing cellphone. Now someone was breaking into the office for sure. She eased the door closed so as not to give away her location, but the hinges squeaked as it passed the halfway point. Certain her position was no longer a secret, she slammed the door and locked it as fast as she could. Then she ran over to her desk to call 911.

She yanked the phone off the desk and started to dial, but heard nothing when she stuck the receiver up against her ear. The line was dead. She cursed and threw the phone in frustration back on her desk, where it skidded past her briefcase and went off the far end, hanging by its cord just above the floor. Then she remembered she still had Steve's cellphone. She dialed 911 and waited for an answer.

"Williamsburg Police Department, is this an emergency?" The dispatcher sounded unenthusiastic, like she had already taken dozens of routine calls that evening and figured this to be yet one more.

"Yes!" Casey hissed into the phone. "I'm in the Law Offices of Steve Stilwell on North Henry Street and someone is breaking in."

"Calm down, miss," the dispatcher instructed, suddenly sounding prepared to direct the resolution of a potentially dangerous situation. "What's the address of the building?"

"I don't know!" Casey yelled. "I just started working here. Surely you've got to know where Steve Stilwell's law office is. It's really close to DoG Street."

"Okay, I'll get a policeman right over there. Are you in a safe place?"

"I'm locked in my office." As Casey answered, she started to see light appearing under the door. "You've got to get here right away," she said. "It looks like they've turned on the light right outside my office."

"Please stay on the line while I dispatch an officer."

Casey heard the dispatcher speaking into a radio. The dispatcher told the officer a break-in was in progress at her building, and that there was a woman alone in one of the offices making the 911 call. As she listened, she kept her eyes glued to the light under the door, watching for any feet that might approach or cause a shadow. Looking closer, she noticed something odd about the light. It wasn't the sterile white light of the neon ceiling lights or desk lamps in the lobby. It was more of a yellow light that flashed in intensity and then subsided. "Oh, no," she muttered as she began to process what the strange light meant. "Officer, are you still there?"

"I am. Who am I talking to?"

"My name is Casey Pantel. I'm a new lawyer working for Steve Stilwell. But can I get you to hold on for a minute? Something strange is going on outside my door. I need to check it out."

"Casey, if you're in a safe place, you need to stay where you are. An officer should arrive in a couple more minutes."

"I will, but something isn't right." Casey started toward the locked door. She looked around for an object to club the intruder with if he came bursting through. Nothing caught her eye, but she felt strangely drawn to the door.

"Casey, can you hear me?" the dispatcher asked. Casey could, but she was so focused on the door, she didn't respond. She walked toward it as if mesmerized.

"Casey, can you hear me? Are you okay? Please answer me. The officer will be pulling up in just a minute."

Casey felt like she didn't have that long. She walked up to the door and put her hand on the knob to find out who, or what, was on the other side.

"Oouchhh!" she screamed. Her entire arm recoiled.

"What is it?" the dispatcher asked. "Casey, are you okay?"

"I think the building's on fire! I just burned my hand on the doorknob." She kept her eye on the door, but backed away until she was in the center of the room.

"Listen to me, Casey," the dispatcher instructed, "don't open that door. If there's a fire on the other side, you want to keep it there. Do you understand me?"

"Yes," Casey said as she spun around to make her way to the window.

"Is there a window you can get out of?"

"I'm heading for it now," Casey responded. En route, she had the presence of mind to throw Ryan Eversall's Sapphire Pavilion file back into her briefcase so she could keep it from being destroyed.

"Okay," the dispatcher acknowledged. "Get out of there as fast as you can. The officer's on scene and he's confirmed the building is on fire. Fire trucks are on their way."

Casey didn't hear anything the dispatcher said. She'd set the cellphone down on the windowsill so she could unlatch the window and climb out. After turning the latch, she pulled up on the two handles at the bottom with all her might, but the window wouldn't budge.

"Aghhhhhh!" she screamed, and gave the window another tug. Nothing. No movement. She tugged again. It was stuck. It looked like the last time the window was painted, the painters had allowed the paint to dry with the window closed, cementing the frame to the sill. Then she smelled it—smoke.

She turned around and saw thick gray smoke pouring under the door and streaming into the room. The lights flickered, then came back on. She reached for the phone to tell the dispatcher she was trapped, but with all her adrenaline pumping, her limbs lost their usual precision and she knocked the phone to the floor. She picked it up and started to speak, only to realize the fall had terminated her call. She coughed from the thickening smoke, trying not to suck in any tainted air. Then the lights flickered and went out.

"Please, no!" she cried. Now she couldn't even look around the room for something to smash through the window. Then it came to her. She dropped her briefcase, stood about eighteen inches from the wall, and planted her left leg on the floor. She followed up with her best Chuck Norris imitation and kicked sideways through the glass pane with her prosthetic right leg and foot. The glass shattered and cut deeply into what previously had been flesh, but this time the damage was limited to tears in and around the cuffs of her pants. Still balancing on one leg, she ran her shoe and artificial foot around the edge of the window, cleaning the glass shards from the window frame. Then she brought her leg back inside and pushed the screen out of the window.

"Help!" she yelled out the window. "Help me!" She poked her head outside to see if anyone could hear her and saw a policeman running toward the window with a flashlight.

"Help me," she yelled again. "Help me out of here!"

The policeman ran up to the window, the bottom of which was about four feet off the ground. "Give me your hands!" he yelled back at her. Casey could see the red lights of the approaching fire trucks and hear their sirens wailing through the streets.

"I'm afraid I'll cut myself on the glass," she shouted to the policeman.

"Then lean out the window and I'll lift you out."

The room was now full of smoke, which billowed through the open window as from the top of a chimney. Casey stuck Steve's cellphone in her pocket and leaned outside, simultaneously choking and sucking in fresh air. The policeman's strong arms pulled her out of the office with the ease of a father picking up his toddler. She tried to keep her body off the window frame as he lifted her outside, but both of her shins dragged over the bottom edge as he pulled her to safety. She didn't feel it, but the broken glass protruding from the window frame sliced superficially into her natural leg in a couple of places, and blood soaked her pant leg and sock. As soon as both her feet touched the ground, the policeman led her away from the building. She turned around just in time to see flames gush through the office. A minute more inside and she would have burned to death.

"Are you okay?" the policeman asked.

"I'm not sure," she replied, trying to hold back the tears. Now that she was safe, everything started to catch up with her. The entire building was in flames, casting that same yellow glow she'd first seen under the door onto everything in her vicinity. Then she realized she'd forgotten to grab her briefcase before she came out the window. "Oh, no!" she screamed. "We've got to go back there to see if I can grab my briefcase. The Sapphire Pavilion file is in it."

"Don't worry about any files, Miss. Just be thankful you're safe. You were pretty brave in there." The policeman shined his flashlight on her. When he helped her to her feet, he saw her blood-soaked pants.

"Why don't you come with me, miss? We've got some paramedics over here and they'll make sure you're okay."

Casey kept quiet. She felt so guilty about forgetting her briefcase that she just followed the officer's lead. She had to get ahold of Steve right away and tell him what had happened. The Sapphire Pavilion file was gone, as was everything else they'd collected on Ric's case. And now the office was gone too, not to mention her purse with all her identification, credit cards, cellphone, and money. She started to feel a burning sensation on her right hand and on her left leg. It wasn't a debilitating pain, but it was very uncomfortable and growing in intensity. Her throat also felt sore and scratchy.

"I need to sit down for a second," Casey told the policeman. "I'm starting to hurt a little."

"Of course, miss." He helped her sit on the cool grass a couple of houses down from the burning office. It seemed like daylight with the outside of the office now engulfed in flames. Fire trucks with their red flashing lights gyrating wildly streamed water onto the building, and the paramedics hustled toward Casey as soon as they saw her being helped away from the building.

Casey's first priority now was to call Steve to tell him about the fire, but with the way she felt, that was going to have to wait a while longer. The lights started to twinkle and get a little blurry, and she felt light-headed.

"I think I'm going to faint," she told the policeman.

"Hurry up," he shouted to the paramedics. They got there a second later, but it was too late. She'd already passed out.

40

Saturday, 3 June 2000, 2:51 p.m.
Saigon

THE KNOCK CAME MUCH EARLIER THAN Phan expected. He left his wife holding their daughter in the kitchen area of their one-room apartment and went to answer the door, peeling back a curtain from the window and looking to see who was there before he unlocked the deadbolt.

It was her. She looked like any other young woman. Tight-fitting jeans, flip-flops, and a light orangish-red short-sleeved cotton top. Her black hair was long, straight, and shiny like it had just been washed. She didn't look like the same Trang he'd spoken to earlier that morning.

"You came," he said, opening the door just enough to let her inside. She slipped into the room and reached behind her to close the door.

"I might have been followed," she warned. "You better lock it."

"Why do you think you were followed?" Phan asked. He glanced across the room at his wife and saw fear wash across her face. She pulled their daughter closer and hugged her to keep her safe. Phan locked the deadbolt and latched the chain on the door to reassure her.

"The man you saw in the room last night confronted me when I left. He asked me where I was going and I said to get something to eat, but I don't think he believed me. I don't trust him."

"Let's get on with it, quickly." Phan reached into his pocket and pulled out one hundred U.S. dollars. He handed them to Trang and she stuffed them into her jeans pocket. "Now tell me what happened that night with the Americans."

"Are you a fool? I already told you what happened to the first American.

So what if I tell you some drug dealers planted heroin in the other American's suitcase. What good is it to you? Do you think the police will believe me? I can tell you, they will not, because when they look at me, they see a whore. It doesn't matter what I say."

Phan hadn't thought this far ahead. He'd promised Steve Stilwell he'd locate the woman who saw what happened, but they hadn't discussed what to do once he actually found her. Now he had her and he didn't know what to do. He was frozen in indecision.

"Do you have a back door?" Trang asked.

"Why do you want to know?"

"Because I don't want to be here when that crazy man gets here. You can deal with him, but I'm leaving."

"Wait a minute," Phan ordered, holding up the palm of his hand. "I've got an idea." He pulled out his wallet and flipped through the business cards stuffed into the cash pocket. When he found the card he was looking for, he pulled it out and tucked his wallet back into his pants pocket.

"Okay, everyone out the back door," he commanded as he double-checked the deadbolt. "We need to get to a phone."

"I don't want to be a part of this," Phan's wife protested. "Let her go, Phan. You are putting our daughter in danger for some American you don't even know. Why do you think he will care what happens to us? He's probably already forgotten about you."

Phan didn't have time to argue. He was already committed—the danger wouldn't subside if he let Trang go. The enforcer might kill them just because Trang stopped by their house. It was time to get out of the apartment and not come back until it was safe, but they had to move quickly.

"He will remember, because his friend is still in jail here. We all must go, now." He shepherded them toward the back door and pulled it closed behind them as they walked into a dimly lit interior hallway. Thinking he heard a noise coming from behind the closed door to his apartment, he rushed them to the stairs. "Hurry, we must go quickly. He is coming!"

Phan caught up with his wife and grabbed their daughter. He was stronger and could carry her and still move quickly. He started running down flights of stairs, clutching her in his arms, while the two women followed close behind. When they got to the street, they ran under an archway and into the alley behind the building, where they had three streets to choose from. Phan chose the street to the left because it allowed another quick turn to the right. That way they wouldn't be visible for long.

"Hurry," he said, just loud enough for the women to hear. "Someone is coming down the stairs behind us." His daughter started to cry as she sensed her father's fear. Phan tried to reassure her, but it was no use. She was scared and nothing he could do would comfort her.

"Give her to me," Phan's wife directed. They paused and Phan handed his little girl over. It worked. She buried her head in her mother's shoulder and stopped crying.

"Look up ahead," Phan ordered as they neared the end of the alley, giving them a moment to regroup. "There's a bus boarding on the main street. Stick close with me and let's get on it."

The group sprinted to the bus at the end of the alley. They made it just as the driver closed the doors. Phan tapped on the window and the driver looked at him but left the doors closed. Phan reached into his pocket and pulled out a fistful of Dong notes and showed it to the driver. The door opened. As Phan climbed the stairs onto the bus, he saw the enforcer turn the corner down the alley and start running toward them.

Phan didn't bother to count the money. He jammed the Dong into the driver's hand and whispered something to him. Then he grabbed his wife's arm and started to pull her through the crowded aisle toward the back of the bus. The driver left the door open and the enforcer ran straight for it. He jumped on the bus just as Phan's little band made it to the midway point of the aisle. The driver tried to collect the fare from the enforcer but he ignored the request and started to push his way to the back where Phan, his wife and daughter, and Trang stood. As soon as the enforcer was about halfway toward them, Phan opened the door at the bus's midsection and jumped out, yanking the women and his daughter with him. The instant they were off the bus, the driver closed the doors and pulled away, taking the cursing enforcer with him.

Phan had no intention of waiting around to see where or how long it took the enforcer to get off the bus, so he led the trio in the opposite direction, hoping to disappear in the afternoon crowd. No one spoke; they just wove through the mob of commuters, randomly heading right and left as they crisscrossed intersections and ran across alleyways. Once he felt safe, at least for the time being, he finally stopped at an apothecary.

Although the business card was crumpled and sweaty, Phan could still read Steve Stilwell's cellphone number. At the counter, he purchased an international calling card and some water for the women. Then they walked over to the payphone on the wall opposite the counter so he could place the call. Phan's wife let their daughter sip water while Trang propped herself up against the wall close enough to hear Phan's conversation, which began shortly after Phan dialed Steve's cellphone number.

"Hello?" a woman's voice answered. Phan expected Steve to answer, not some woman he didn't know. He tried to adjust to the difference, but the urgency of the situation convinced him to ask for Steve.

"Hello, is Mr. Steve there?"

"No, he's not. May I ask who's calling?"

"Yes, my name is Phan. I am Mr. Steve's friend from Vietnam."

"Hello, Phan. My name is Casey and I work with Steve. He forgot his phone and I haven't been able to get it back to him yet. I'll tell him you called as soon as I see him."

"I need to talk to Mr. Steve now," Phan insisted. "Please let me talk to him."

"He's not here, Phan. In fact, it's very early in the morning and I've actually been trying to reach him to tell him I'm in the hospital. The only reason I answered the telephone was because I thought it might be him calling. Is there something I can help you with?"

Phan thought for a minute and looked at his wife and daughter. He didn't know the woman on the telephone, but she said she worked with Mr. Steve and she answered his phone. Mr. Steve wouldn't have allowed her to do that if he didn't trust her. Recognizing he had no choice, he decided that had to be good enough.

"Yes, maybe you help me," he began. "Mr. Steve asked me to find the woman in Mr. Ric's hotel room when Vietnamese police take him. I find her and she is with my family, but someone following us. I think he trying to kill us. What do I do?"

The woman who had been so quick to respond kept quiet now. Why couldn't Mr. Steve talk to him? He would know what to do.

The woman broke her silence. "I'm sorry, but I've forgotten your name. Could you tell me again?"

"Yes, my name is Phan. But you must hurry. Man may come any time."

"Okay, Phan. Where are you now?

"Saigon. We all in Saigon."

"Good. Do you have money to take a cab?"

"I have Mr. Steve's money. Where do we go?"

"Go to the U.S. Consulate. Have the taxi drop you off as close as possible to the main entrance, and go inside right away. When you get inside, give them Steve Stilwell's name and ask for temporary refuge. Tell them you have a witness to the murder of an American and someone is trying to kill you. Can you remember that?"

"I think so. We take taxi to U.S. Consulate and I tell them I know Mr. Steve. I give them Mr. Steve's card."

"Perfect, Phan. Then remember to tell them you have a witness to the murder of an American with you and that someone is trying to kill you. Tell the consulate people to call me at this number if they want more information."

"Okay, we go now. I don't want man to find us. We go get taxi now."

"Good luck, Phan. I will try to speak to Steve Stilwell and tell him what's going on. I'll also see if we can let the U.S. Consulate know you're coming. How long of a cab ride is it?"

Phan wasn't listening anymore. He was already thinking about where he could hail a taxi without being noticed by the enforcer. Instead of asking the woman to repeat what she said, he decided it was better to just end the call.

"Thank you," he replied, "but we must go. I call Mr. Steve again from American Consulate."

Phan liked the plan, as long as the American Consulate would let him in. Many Vietnamese people wanted to travel to America, so they would go to the consulate to try to get a visa. They would make up all kinds of stories to get the consulate to grant their requests. But his story was true, even though it sounded fantastic. Besides, he had nowhere else to go. His family couldn't go back to their apartment because the bad guys would surely be waiting. He also didn't know how long Trang would stick around, yet she seemed to be important to Mr. Ric's case. If he could just get inside the American Consulate and convince them to hold him until Mr. Steve could talk with them .... Without that, at best he'd be out on the streets with his wife and daughter with nowhere to go. At worst ... he didn't want to think about that. He would simply have to make the Americans help him.

41

Same day—Saturday, 3 June 2000, 5:17 a.m. EDT
Williamsburg, Virginia

STEVE HUSTLED THROUGH THE AUTOMATIC DOORS at the Williamsburg
Regional Medical Center and rounded the corner to the waiting area.
Casey sat alone in one of the lightly padded vinyl bench chairs, her hair in
disorder and her clothes torn and dirty. She looked haggard even from a
distance. He ran toward her, angling around a bank of chairs and a magazine-
covered table. She saw him coming and hobbled to her feet using crutches. His
big hug temporarily suspended the more formal office protocol he otherwise
maintained.

"Thank God you're safe," he said, releasing her from the hug. "I would
never have forgiven myself if anything had happened to you. I'm so sorry you
had to go through this."

Casey shifted her weight on the crutches and inched away from the bench
chair to steady herself, smiling awkwardly. "Thanks, Steve, but there's nothing
you could've done."

"Well, I've let you get caught up in this convoluted case and never really
asked if you were okay with the risks you'd be assuming."

"I walked into it with my eyes open," Casey countered. "Besides, I don't
think anyone could have foreseen all that's happened. I mean Ryan Eversall
dying, Ric Stokes in jail, you being pushed off the bridge, and your passenger's
death."

Steve's eyes widened. "What did you say?"

Casey's expression turned downcast. "Oh, Steve, I'm so sorry. I thought you knew. The local news covered your crash and they're reporting that the woman who was in the car with you died. It's been on the news ticker at the bottom of the TV screen."

The news hit Steve as hard as the semi had hit his Celica. The only words he was able to utter through the paralyzing shock seizing his vocal cords were, "She's really dead?"

"The news said she died from her injuries. She was in intensive care at a Richmond hospital."

Steve backed up and dropped down into one of the bench chairs. He looked up at Casey for a second, then rested his elbows on his knees and buried his face in his hands. The closer they got to solving the case, the more things spun out of control. Now Gallagher was dead, and like the captain of a ship, he felt responsible because it happened on his watch. She'd trusted him and was in the process of making things right when a truck he should have been paying attention to cut her life short. He had to admit he would miss her confident, devil-may-care personality, even though he knew she played a leading role in Ryan Eversall's death, Ric Stokes' jailing, and Sarah's departure. Now, with her gone, unraveling those actions seemed nearly impossible.

"Are you okay, Steve?" Casey shuffled over next to him, sat down, and propped her crutches against the empty seat to her left.

Steve lifted his head, his cheeks red from the pressure of the palms of his hands. "I'm fine, Casey, thanks. The news was just a little overwhelming since I was the one driving her when the accident happened."

"That was no accident, Steve. Someone was trying to kill you. At least you're safe."

Steve forced a smile. "So I came here to console you and instead you're the one doing the consoling. This isn't turning out like I planned."

"Don't worry about that. But as long as we're getting bad news out of the way, I've got something else I need to tell you."

Steve perked up and looked back at Casey. "I thought you said you were all right?"

"I am, but my files aren't. I left Ryan Eversall's Sapphire Pavilion file in my briefcase in my office and there was no way to go back and get it. I'm sure it was destroyed in the fire."

"I don't care about those files at all," Steve said dismissively. "I'm just grateful you weren't seriously hurt. Oh, and by the way, we got so wrapped up in me, you never told me about your injuries. Are you okay? I mean, I can see you're using crutches, so you must not have come away unscathed."

"My left leg and foot got cut on some glass when the policeman pulled me out of the window, but other than being a little shaken, I'm fine." Casey stretched out her prosthetic leg in front of her. Her pants were so torn from the window glass that it was easy to see the titanium shaft running from the socket liner below her knee down to her shoe. "Who would've thought my right leg would end up being my good one?" She chuckled as she looked over at Steve and he returned a half-hearted smile. "So," she continued, "where do we go from here? We've lost the key witness and the Sapphire Pavilion file, not to mention our office. And I'm sure that means we also lost the Ryan Eversall's notebook. Are we at the end of the road?"

"Not yet," Steve said emphatically. The suggestion that they might have to give up re-ignited his determination, desire, and need, to drive on. "We've still got our ace in the hole, and better yet, the bad guys probably have no idea we've got it. In fact, with Gallagher dead—that's the name of the woman who was in the car with me—and our office burned down, they may think they've won. That might have bought us some time."

"So what's our ace in the hole?"

"Ryan Eversall's notebook. After I brought it into the office yesterday morning, I had Marjorie secure the original in our safe deposit box at the bank. So that evidence is preserved. Plus, I took a copy to the CO of a fighter squadron at Oceana, and he's sifting through it to see if he can glean some kind of clue. We may hear from him later today."

Casey picked up on Steve's excitement. "We know from the Air Force archives that the State Department should be able to tell us something about the Sapphire Pavilion mission, and you're meeting with the Secretary of State."

Steve checked his watch. "Yeah, and I've got a State Department driver picking me up at what used to be our office in a little over three hours. So how about I ask the hospital staff if they can call a cab and get us back home? I'd at least like to get another hour of sleep before I talk to the Secretary."

"Better yet," Casey said, "the nice policeman who brought me here said he'd stick around to make sure I got home. Maybe he'll give us both a ride."

"That sounds good. And if I think of anything I need this afternoon, is it still okay if I give you a call?"

"That reminds me," Casey said. "You left your cellphone at the office and I got a call from a man in Vietnam who says he knows you. It was hard to understand his name; it sounded like he was saying 'fan.' He said he found the prostitute from Ric's room."

"Phan found her?" Steve blurted out in amazement. "That's fantastic!"

"That's what he said. He also said he thought someone was trying to kill him, so I told him to go to the consulate with his family right away and tell them he's got a witness to a murder."

"Perfect! Now we've got two aces in the hole."

"As long as the consulate lets him in. I told him I'd call the State Department so they could let the consulate know he's coming, but with all that's happened,

I haven't done that yet. I'll call as soon as I get back to my apartment."

Having personally experienced the danger in Saigon, Steve worried about Phan's safety. If the consulate turned Phan away, he could be killed, but Steve didn't want to say anything to Casey that might upset her. She'd been through a lot in the last few hours, and the last thing she needed was a guilt trip if anything happened to Phan. There was nothing he could do about it now, anyway. It was best to just affirm her plan.

"That sounds good," Steve assured Casey. "You call the State Department as soon as you get home and I'll raise the subject tomorrow during my meeting with the Secretary. That should cover all our bases."

"Wait a minute," Casey declared as she dug into her pocket. "That won't work. I was able to save your cellphone from the fire, but not mine." Casey produced Steve's phone and handed it to him. "Will you be able to call the State Department?"

"I'll take care of it," Steve confirmed. "Now how about we get going? We both need to get some sleep."

"Uh-oh." Casey clenched her jaw momentarily and then said, "I just thought of another problem. Now I don't have a phone, so you won't have any way of getting in touch with me when you're in Washington. I don't have a house phone yet. All I had was my cellphone."

"Then you keep my phone and you call the State Department," Steve said. "That way, if I need something, I can call you from a land line at the State Department."

"Are you sure?"

"Positive. That works best for both of us, and you'll have a phone. You can use it all you want—I have unlimited calling on weekends. Do you have a recharger that works?"

"Believe it or not, I do. I had the same phone."

"All right then, I think we're set. Let's hope your policeman friend is still here so he can give us a ride home."

42

Same day—Saturday, 3 June 2000, 1:57 p.m. EDT
State Department, Washington, DC

STEVE FIDGETED WITH THE ZIPPER ON his leather planner as he paced around the Secretary's anterior room, waiting to be called into her office. He'd never met with the Secretary of State. Not that it was out of the realm of possibility, since he'd been an international lawyer in the Navy Judge Advocate General's Corps. He had, in fact, met with the Secretary of Defense on two occasions. Not one on one, of course, but as a member of a team briefing "SecDef" on the international legal issue du jour. He'd also worked at the State Department for a couple of years, but he'd only advised mid-level political appointees. This was his first time meeting the top of the diplomatic totem pole.

The Secretary's receptionist appeared in the waiting area. "Mr. Stilwell, the Secretary will see you now," she announced. "Please follow me." Steve followed her around the corner to the Secretary's office. The receptionist announced his arrival.

"Madame Secretary, Mr. Steve Stilwell is here to see you."

"Thank you, Madeleine," the Secretary responded as she headed for the door to greet Steve. Madeleine retreated into the hallway to allow Steve to enter the Secretary's office. The Secretary met him at the door, hand outstretched.

"Hello, Steve. I'm Susan McDermott." The Secretary shook his hand, the smile on her face putting him instantly at ease. "I really appreciate you coming up here on a Saturday. I hope your wife didn't mind us stealing you away on such short notice."

"I'm very pleased to meet you, Madame Secretary," Steve responded, evading the question about his wife. "It was no problem at all. In fact, it was probably good to get away from Williamsburg. It's been a tough couple of days."

"That's what I hear," the Secretary acknowledged. "But before we get into that, why don't you let me introduce you to the other people who have come to hear what you have to say?"

"Oh, yes, of course," he replied as they walked past an end table and veered toward the waiting crowd. He'd been so singularly focused on meeting the Secretary, he hadn't noticed the group assembled around the conference table at the back of the room.

The Secretary escorted him to an empty chair to the right of her seat and then stood at the head of the table. She began her introductions by pointing to each person and reciting his or her name. "On my left is my Executive Assistant, Hanna Edwin. To her left is the Assistant Director of the FBI's Criminal Investigative Division, Campbell Drury. Sam Bowers is the Assistant Secretary of Diplomatic Security, and Peggy Altman is the Country Officer for Vietnam. To your right is Elrod Benfield. He's the Assistant Secretary of State for East Asia and Pacific Affairs. And last but not least, for everyone else, this is Captain Steve Stilwell, the attorney representing Captain Ric Stokes, the retired Naval officer being held in Vietnam on drug-trafficking charges." With introductions out of the way, the Secretary took her seat, signaling to everyone present they could take their seats as well.

"Please, everyone, help yourself to water, coffee, or tea. And while you're doing that, I'll go ahead and get started." The Secretary put both of her hands on the end of the table as if to brace herself for what she was about to say. As she did, Elrod Benfield poured himself a glass of ice water and offered some to Steve, who politely declined by smiling and mouthing *No thank you.*

"So, I understand you were involved in a very serious traffic accident yesterday."

Steve nodded. "That's correct, although I'm not so sure it was an accident. I was driving on the Hampton Roads Bridge-Tunnel when a tractor-trailer forced me over the side of the bridge. Unbelievably, I have only a few bruises and some stitches to show for it, but the woman riding with me wasn't as lucky. I understand she passed away last evening." Steve noticed that no one seemed surprised by the news; clearly they had been briefed prior to his arrival.

"We heard that, as well," the Secretary confided. "What a tragic loss of life."

"I'm still trying to come to terms with it, myself," he admitted. "Especially since I was driving the car when it happened. Although she started as a bad actor, I think she was prepared to redeem herself and testify against the organization that was trying to kill her. So not only is her loss tragic because she never got her shot at redemption, but she was my best chance to exonerate Ric Stokes."

"Not quite," the Secretary began cryptically. "Some of your other efforts have borne fruit, too."

"That's great to hear, though I'm not sure what you mean."

"Peggy, why don't you tell Mr. Stilwell what transpired at the consulate in Saigon this morning."

"Of course," Peggy said. "Someone you met during your visit to Vietnam last week arrived at the consulate with his wife and daughter. He brought a woman with him who apparently was in the hotel room the night Ryan Eversall died."

"Are they safe?"

"They are," Peggy confirmed. "In fact, they're at the consulate now."

"Thank God," Steve responded.

"My Security people have already spoken with the witness and she looks like the real deal," Sam Bowers chimed in. "She insists Ric Stokes had nothing to do with the heroin in his suitcase."

Steve couldn't contain his enthusiasm. "That should do it!" he declared. "She's the smoking gun I've been looking for. Can we use her to get Ric Stokes released from jail?"

"It's not quite that simple," the Secretary explained. "The woman is a prostitute and the Vietnamese authorities will consider her unreliable."

"So just because she's a prostitute, they don't think she can tell the truth?" Steve's disgust caused him to momentarily lose sight of whom he was speaking with.

"That's part of it," the Secretary said, unfazed. "The other part is that they question her motives. They think she'll say anything if she believes she'll get to go to the United States, even if that means lying."

Elrod Benfield leaned forward so he could make eye contact with the Secretary. "Oh, and there is one more thing. The consulate gets the sense that the Vietnamese won't be willing to let Captain Stokes go unless they have someone to try in his place. They don't want to be seen as kowtowing to the Americans by just letting him go."

"Do the Vietnamese have a strong interest in the case?" Steve asked. "After all, it was an American who was killed. Can't we work with them on that point?"

"That's the approach we'll have to take," Benfield continued, "but it won't be easy. The Vietnamese government imposes draconian punishments on its own citizens involved in drug trafficking. They won't want to be seen as being more lenient with a foreigner."

"So it sounds like the witness doesn't do much for us," Steve concluded, his frustration apparent as he sat all the way back in his chair and pulled his hands away from the table.

"That may be true as far as the girl is concerned," the Secretary interjected, "but there's more. Campbell, why don't you tell everyone what the FBI's been able to find out?"

Campbell Drury reached down next to his chair and fumbled through his briefcase. He produced a white pocket folder and set it on the table in front of him. His movements were sequential; he didn't start opening the folder until he had it positioned just the way he wanted it on the table in front of him. The folder had the FBI logo centered a quarter of the way down, with big block letters LAW ENFORCEMENT SENSITIVE emblazoned in red just below the logo. He opened the folder and pulled out some papers stapled together at the top left corner. Steve got a quick glance at the cover sheet before Campbell peeled it back to reveal the first page. He assumed it was an investigation report.

Between Campbell's methodical movements and Bowers' Southern drawl, Steve wished he could give them a caffeine infusion in hopes of speeding things up. When he saw the Secretary tapping her finger on the table waiting for Campbell to begin, he knew he wasn't alone in his impatience. Campbell perused the document before beginning, producing even more squirming.

"So tell us what you've found, Campbell," the Secretary directed, her frustration bubbling over.

"Of course," Campbell finally said. "The FBI and the DEA have had a joint investigation ongoing for over a year into a possible insider using official channels to bring heroin into the United States from Southeast Asia. The investigation had shown little progress and we were preparing to shut it down until Ric Stokes' arrest and Robert Fowler's murder. Now we've teamed up with Sam Bowers' embassy security organization to correlate the information he has with what we've been able to discover."

"So what is it you've learned?" the Secretary asked, her verbal tempo increasing with her impatience at the FBI agent's inability to get to the point.

"This has to stay in the room," Campbell instructed. "We've got a confidential informant who's opened some doors for us. Let me put it this way: the informant has filled in some of the details on the Asian operation we suspected but couldn't prove. With what we've got, we're pretty sure we'll be able to shut the Asian side of the operation down before it does any more damage."

Steve sensed the FBI director choosing his words very carefully. With all he'd been through in the last couple of days, he didn't have time for bureaucrat-speak. He needed to know where his case stood and whether the

U.S. Government was going to help him get Ric Stokes out of jail. Now it was his turn to conduct an interrogation.

"Mr. Drury, you say you've gained information about the Asian side of the operation. What about the U.S. side? Where do you stand on that?"

"It's still early, of course, but we're not where we need to be yet on the U.S. side."

Having worked in DC and also prosecuted cases for the Navy, Steve knew what "We're not where we need to be yet" meant. They either had damn little or nothing at all. He wanted to press further, but he didn't want to embarrass Campbell in front of the Secretary. He might need Campbell's help down the road. Plus, Campbell had probably told the Secretary exactly what the FBI had before the meeting, but was being more circumspect now since Steve was a civilian attorney representing a client rather than a U.S. Attorney prosecuting the case. Regardless, Steve wasn't done with Campbell, and he probed him with another question.

"So if you've got information about heroin trafficking in Southeast Asia, can you use it to get Ric Stokes out of jail?"

"Well, let me say this. We've looked at the statement the prostitute gave to Sam Bowers' team and what she says is completely consistent with what our cooperating witness says. So we are confident neither ... excuse me for a minute while I check my report." Campbell flipped back to the second page and ran his finger up the text until he found the information he was looking for. "We are confident neither Ryan Eversall nor Ric Stokes had anything to do with heroin or heroin trafficking. We believe they were targeted because they located the wreckage of a plane that someone didn't want found."

"Who exactly is that someone?" the Secretary asked, now sitting all the way at the front of her chair and leaning toward Campbell with her elbows and hands on the table as if they were supporting her.

"Richard," Campbell replied.

"Richard who?" Benfield asked, unable to wait for the Secretary to follow up on her own question.

"I'm afraid we don't know that yet, but we're working on it."

The Secretary flopped all the way back in her chair, exasperated. Steve saw her take a deep breath and noticed her cheeks turning an angry shade of red. She seemed more agitated than the others with the lack of useful information. He sensed she knew something they didn't, but wasn't comfortable throwing it on the table. He decided to press further with the hope that he might find the key to unlock her hesitation.

"So why would Richard care about the wreckage of a plane lost over thirty years ago?" Steve asked.

Campbell shook his head. "We have no idea. In fact, we have almost no information about the plane. I'm sure you know more than we do."

"Well, I can definitely help with that, as we've been able to find out quite a lot," Steve admitted. He flipped open his planner, revealing Ryan Eversall's notebook, but he didn't explain what it was. Instead, he shifted it to the left side of his planner to consult some notes he'd jotted down on a notepad in preparation for the meeting. He looked at the Secretary as he spoke.

"The plane was a C-130 Hercules transport assigned to the Twenty-First Tactical Airlift Squadron. It took off with at least five people on board from Ubon Airbase in Thailand early in the evening on 18 January 1968 on a Top-Secret mission. It never returned. We know now that it's because the plane crashed in a mountainous region of Vietnam known as the Central Highlands. We think everyone on board was killed."

Elrod Benfield spoke up. "What do you mean you *think* everyone on board was killed? Is it possible someone survived?"

Steve twisted around to respond. "I don't think so, but I can't say for sure."

"What do you mean?" said Benfield.

"Well, this may be more information than you want, but it'll help answer your question. Ryan Eversall and Ric Stokes went looking for this plane in Vietnam because Ryan's dad was the pilot. Ryan did extensive research into the crash and we had his research file until it was destroyed in my office fire last evening. But using that file, we learned the names of the plane's five crewmembers."

Steve picked up Ryan's notebook and held it up for everyone to see. "This is Ryan Eversall's notebook describing the crash site. He took extensive notes, describing the debris field in detail and cataloging everything he found, including three sets of dog tags." He shifted back in his chair to direct his comments to the Secretary. As he did, he thought he caught her dabbing the corner of her eye. Then she asked him a question in a much softer voice than before, so soft he had to strain to hear.

"Did the names on the dog tags match the crew list?"

Steve dialed back his volume as well, touched by the Secretary's compassion for the lost airmen. "I'm afraid they did, Madame Secretary. And they also found five gravesites there that would correspond to the five-man crew of a C-130."

Benfield spoke up again. This time, Steve didn't turn around, but instead sat all the way back in his chair so he could see both Benfield and the Secretary. The Secretary slumped back in her chair, her sadness oppressing the meeting.

"So if there were five aircrew, how could there be five graves?" Benfield asked. "Does that mean there were others on the aircraft, or did someone find the crash site and bury the crew? And if that was the case, why are we just finding the crash site now?"

Steve couldn't help but turn toward Benfield to respond. "I can't answer those questions right now, but I'm hoping the State Department can help us with that."

"And why is that?" Benfield continued.

"The historical file at the Air Force archives contains no information other than a reference to the State Department, so we think the plane might have been on a diplomatic mission when it was lost. The plane also had a Top-Secret code name."

"Sapphire Pavilion," the Secretary whispered.

Steve turned back toward the Secretary, not sure he'd heard her correctly. "I'm sorry, ma'am, but I didn't hear what you said."

"I said Sapphire Pavilion …." The Secretary's voice trailed off as she spoke.

"Why, that's right," Steve confirmed, amazed. "How did you know?"

The Secretary pushed her chair back and stood up. "My dear God, I can't believe this." As her eyes began to well up, she turned away and walked over to her desk.

"Let's take a short break and wait in the lobby for a few minutes," her executive assistant directed. "We'll reconvene in ten minutes."

43

Same day—Saturday, 3 June 2000, 2:16 p.m. EDT
Williamsburg, Virginia

THE LAW OFFICE BURNING TO THE ground affected more than Casey's intended Saturday workplace. Now, all her files, her research, her personal belongings, and most importantly, Ryan Eversall's Sapphire Pavilion file, had been reduced to a soupy black ash that filled every pocket and depression in the building's incinerated structure. So she sat in a cubicle at the College of William & Mary's law library, the only other place she could think of that brought within reach all the legal resources she might need if Steve called.

She scooted her chair back and glanced out the window. It was sunny and hot out, with the thermometer pushing over eighty and the humidity high. She rested her natural leg on a chair next to the desk to keep her shin elevated. If she sat normally with her natural foot on the floor, the blood flow in her leg made the stitches in her shin throb. She'd taken two ibuprofen around 12:30 and they helped, but elevating her leg chased the throbbing completely away. She thought it ironic that her prosthetic leg had saved her life the night before while her good leg now gave her trouble. She wondered if the reason she lost her leg in the helicopter crash was to prepare her for her escape through the window. Although the thought offered consolation, she hoped next time God would allow her to keep her limb and use something else to break the glass.

Ringhhh, Ringhhh, Ringhhh. The sound cut through the bookish silence, causing titles to rumble on their spines. *Ringhhh, Ringhhh, Ringhhh.* The alarm trumpeted from her purse and she lunged for it, grabbing it before a third sequence of rings escaped. Because her cellphone was destroyed in the fire, she didn't think to turn Steve's phone on vibrate. She flipped it open to stop the ringing, hoping that no one in the library would complain.

"Hello, this is Casey Pantel," she whispered, her cupped hand covering the phone and her mouth.

"I'm sorry, I must have dialed the wrong number. I was hoping to speak with Steve Stilwell. Sorry to bother you."

"Don't hang up," she said in a more normal voice, "you've got the right number. Steve Stilwell left me his phone while he's on a short trip to Washington, DC. I'm Casey Pantel, and I'm a lawyer who works with his law practice. Is there something I can help you with?" She scanned the room but didn't catch any hostile stares from the few library patrons in view.

"Hi, Casey. This is Roger Thornton. I promised I'd get back to Steve today about a project I've been working on for him. Do you know when he'll be back?"

"I don't expect him until much later this afternoon or even sometime this evening. By chance are you the CO who took a look at the crash site notebook for him?"

"That's me," Captain Thornton confirmed, "and I'd like to share our findings. Is there any way I can contact him now?"

"I'm afraid not, but you can certainly pass the results to me and I'll make sure he gets them. In fact, I'm working on the case with him, and if the results are something I can use, I can act on them now without having to wait until he returns." Casey hoped the caller wouldn't insist on talking with Steve, because it could cost her hours of valuable research time. She decided to throw her military service into the mix to assure the man she would understand whatever he had to tell her. "It's Captain Thornton, is that correct?"

"It is, but feel free to call me Roger."

"I appreciate that, Captain, but I'm a former Army Captain and that will be way too hard for me. As a former helicopter pilot, I'm pretty comfortable taking down any technical information you might have and I'll be sure to convey it to Steve accurately."

"All right," Captain Thornton replied, apparently reassured, "from one captain to another."

Casey chuckled at Captain Thornton graciously equating his rank with hers, when in fact he, as a Navy captain—the equivalent of an Army colonel—far outranked the Army captain she had been. Captain Thornton didn't give Casey time to respond beyond a laugh.

"I had my guys go through the notebook with a fine-tooth comb trying to see if we could figure out what might have brought down the plane. Normally, it's next to impossible to figure out something like that without seeing the

/reckage. But my ordnance officer saw something that may have solved the puzzle."

"That's fantastic," Casey said. "What was it?"

"Well, there was a page in the notebook that had nothing but parts and debris listed with either partial or complete serial numbers. Although most of the numbers meant nothing to us, my ordnance officer recognized one of the serial numbers as belonging to an AIM-9 heat seeking air-to-air Sidewinder missile."

"So what does that mean?" Casey had no idea where Captain Thornton was going with this.

"Well, let's just say it's suspicious to say the least. As you know from your Army days, most C-130s have no armament and they certainly weren't equipped to fire Sidewinder missiles. In Vietnam, only Navy and Air Force jets fired those."

"Wait a minute!" Casey broke in excitedly. "Are you saying a U.S. Air Force or Navy fighter shot down the C-130?"

"Not at all," Captain Thornton retorted. "In fact, we know that didn't happen. These missiles have always been strictly controlled and tracked by serial number, primarily because they're so expensive. So my ordnance officer and some old shipmates he enlisted to research the issue were able to get their hands on Navy and Air Force missile inventory records and confirm this was not a Navy or Air Force missile."

"So whose was it?"

"Before I get to that, let me mention a couple of other possibilities we eliminated. First, we thought it possible that the C-130 might be carrying the missile as cargo. But the fact that only one missile was found made that unlikely, as did the fact that the missile didn't match any Air Force or Navy serial numbers. Second, we thought the missile might have been mistakenly fired by an allied aircraft, but this was a nighttime shoot-down. No one other than the U.S. flew night fighter missions."

"Are you telling me you think this plane was shot down?"

"That's our best guess, and we think it had to be a U.S. fighter jet that did it. But we also confirmed that no U.S. Air Force or Navy fighter fired a Sidewinder missile on January eighteenth, 1968."

"Then who did?"

"Find out who was flying F-4 Phantom fighter bombers in Vietnam on that date other than the U.S. Navy or Air Force and you'll have your answer."

"Any suggestions on where I should start looking?"

Captain Thornton hesitated. Casey was just wondering if they'd been disconnected when he answered her question. "As I recall from my Naval War College studies, there were lots of black programs going on in Vietnam at the time. Most of them never became public, and most involved the CIA in some way, shape, or form. My guess is if you poke your head around the CIA in Vietnam in 1968, you'll find what you're looking for. But I wasn't kidding when I said that's my guess, because I've got absolutely nothing factual to base it on."

"I just can't believe a U.S. fighter pilot, no matter who he was working for, would have intentionally shot down a U.S. Air Force C-130."

"Slow down, there, Counselor," Captain Thornton cautioned. "I never said it actually happened, and if it did, I certainly didn't say it was intentional. You and I both know friendly fire incidents happen, no matter how hard we try to prevent them."

"I can't argue with that," agreed Casey, talking more boldly to a senior officer than she would have had she still been in uniform. "But you also told me it wasn't an Air Force or Navy fighter that fired the missile, and that none of our allies could have done it. Something isn't adding up here, and it doesn't sound very friendly to me."

"That's why you're involved in the case, Counselor. Now it's your job to make sense of it all."

"We'll see what we can do," Casey answered with Captain Thornton's words reverberating in her head. "Can you email Steve Stilwell a short summary of your findings? I'm sure we'll need something we can show people to help them see what might have happened here."

"Of course. I'll get something to him this afternoon. I've got his card with his email address on it."

"Please thank everyone for looking at the notebook for us, and I'll be sure to give Steve a full report when I talk to him later this afternoon."

"You bet. By the way, is Steve the same Steve Stilwell who was involved in the traffic accident on the Hampton Roads Bridge-Tunnel?"

"That was him. It's a miracle he's alive, let alone suffering only minor injuries."

"Well, tell Steve I'm glad he's all right, and express my condolences for the person he was with in the car."

"I'll do that, Captain. Goodbye."

Casey flipped the silver cellphone closed, then squeezed it in her hand. If Captain Thornton was right, his information was earth-shattering. She could already picture the headlines in the *New York Times*: CIA SHOOTS DOWN U.S. AIRCRAFT ON SECRET DIPLOMATIC MISSION DURING VIETNAM WAR. It wouldn't matter that the events took place over thirty years ago. It would be one more disastrous chapter in an even more disastrous war. That had to be why someone was trying to keep the wreckage from being discovered.

More difficult, though, was figuring out who that someone might be. The list of possibilities had to be short, given that the shoot-down occurred in 1968. Most of the senior leaders in the CIA in 1968 were likely dead, so they wouldn't care if the information became public. It had to be someone senior enough to direct action in 1968, but young enough to still be alive today and care about the incident being made public.

Casey knew she had to get the information to Steve as quickly as possible. She had no way other than email of getting in touch with him, and where would he check his email, at the Secretary's office? Where would she send the email from, for that matter? Besides, Captain Thornton had already promised to email. She figured she could probably find Steve through the State Department Operator; someone had to answer the phones there on a Saturday afternoon. But when she checked her watch and saw it was not quite 2:35 p.m., she assumed he would still be meeting with the Secretary and she didn't want to embarrass him by interrupting the meeting. She would just have to wait until he called to give him Captain Thornton's news.

That delay tied in, though, with something else Captain Thornton said that really struck a chord with her. "It's your job to make sense of it all." With Captain Thornton's words, a light switched on. She wasn't just working this case because it had been assigned to her; she was working it because someone was counting on her to figure out what was going on and to fix it. To Ric and Noriko Stokes, her help meant life or death, and to Angela Eversall, it meant clearing her husband's name and possibly holding his killers accountable. For the first time since she had given up flying helicopters, she felt like she had landed in the right place and was doing work that would make a difference. Now she just needed to get with Steve Stilwell and make sense of it all.

44

Same day—Saturday, 3 June 2000, 3:08 p.m. EDT
State Department, Washington, DC

WHAT COULD SECRETARY MCDERMOTT POSSIBLY KNOW? The events
took place over thirty years ago, yet the pain in her eyes reflected a
deep, recent wound. Steve sensed apprehension on the FBI director's face
as they filed to their original positions around the conference table. Did the
FBI director know more than he was letting on? Was it possible the Secretary
was somehow involved in the recent events in Vietnam? He hoped she would
provide enough information to dispel any speculation.

"I'm sorry you had to see that emotional display," Secretary McDermott
said. She sat down in her chair and pulled it forward, making an obvious
attempt to sit up straighter than usual. She dispensed with post-break
pleasantries, took a long, deep breath, and jumped right into her explanation.

"I knew in my heart this was Sapphire Pavilion as soon as I heard it was a
C-130 lost in January 1968. I guess I thought it might go away or I hoped, at
least subconsciously, that you'd come here today and prove me wrong." The
Secretary's eyes started to water again, but this time she took a sip of ice water
and the cool water seemed to infuse her with newfound strength. She went
on, speaking more forcefully, and driving any emotion out of her narrative.

"This plane was on a Top-Secret State Department mission. In fact, it was
on a Top Secret White House mission."

The Executive Assistant interrupted her. "Madame Secretary, this mission
may not have been declassified yet. Do you want me to get the files to see what
we can say?"

"Thanks, Hanna, but I'm declassifying it now. The men who died on this flight have waited long enough." The Secretary looked toward Steve as she began to speak, but Steve wasn't sure she was actually seeing him. She seemed to be gazing through him, into time and space, where she could separate herself from the reality and impact of what she was saying.

"You've got to take yourself back to what was going on in the Vietnam War to understand Sapphire Pavilion. This was January 1968, right before the North Vietnamese Tet Offensive. That offensive changed the course of the war. We knew the North Vietnamese were planning an offensive and we knew it was going to happen soon; we just didn't know exactly when or where. But intelligence reports suggested it was going to be bigger than anything we'd seen before, and we were doing whatever we could to get ready."

"I'm sorry to interrupt," Steve said sheepishly, "but you keep saying 'we.' Who is we?"

"Of course. 'We' is the U.S. Government."

"Thanks, Madame Secretary, and I apologize again for interrupting." Steve thought the Secretary's "we" seemed much more personal, but it wasn't the time to push the issue. Better to see how things played out.

"It's no problem at all," the Secretary continued, her confidence getting stronger as she continued to recount her story. "President Johnson didn't want to risk a defeat right before the 1968 Presidential election, so he was looking for a way to end the war. Politically, though, he was between a rock and a hard place. He wanted to avoid appearing weak to the hawks in Congress because he needed their support for his domestic programs. But if he kept escalating U.S. involvement in the war, he risked losing his own party's support for his Democratic reelection bid.

"Then two events converged to convince President Johnson to try something utterly radical. In late 1967, Bobby Kennedy passed him in the Democratic Presidential polls, putting his re-election bid in jeopardy. Johnson knew if he couldn't pull off something big, he'd never reverse Kennedy's momentum. At the same time, he started receiving intelligence reports that the North Vietnamese Communist leader, Ho Chi Minh, was very ill and possibly near death. The reports included rumblings that Ho Chi Minh wanted to see the war end before he died."

"Madame Secretary," Benfield interrupted. "Please forgive me, but as you can tell by my gray hair, I've got you by a few years." The Secretary smiled and Benfield chuckled, making it clear his observation was an understatement. "I also recall these events, although perhaps not with the same clarity and perspective you seem to have. As I recall, you were assigned to the U.S. Embassy in Saigon, but I don't remember exactly when that was. Were you involved in some capacity?"

"I appreciate your not-so-veiled skepticism, Elrod," the Secretary chided. "But I've been thinking a lot about this since we learned about the plane crash. It's brought back some painful memories, and with those memories comes the story behind them. If you let me continue, I think you'll understand."

"Of course, Madame Secretary. I hope you don't think I was questioning your veracity. I just wanted to better understand the source of your insight."

"Don't worry, Elrod. Your position is still safe. But let me get back on track." The Secretary paused briefly, then continued, "I believe I left off with Ho Chi Minh on his death bed."

Steve nodded.

"Johnson thought he could handle the North Vietnamese the same way he handled Congress—he was sure he could cut a deal with Ho Chi Minh if they could just sit down and talk with each other. The problem was, both sides' public rhetoric made that impossible. So, Johnson decided he would cut through all the diplomatic roadblocks, meet with Ho Chi Minh, and end the war before the election. Before he could do so, though, he had to see if Ho Chi Minh would even consider the idea. But the plan was so closely held, it couldn't go through normal third-country diplomatic channels, which were necessary because the U.S. didn't have diplomatic relations with North Vietnam. So Johnson told Secretary of State Dean Rusk he wanted a special envoy to personally deliver the proposal to Ho Chi Minh and bring back his reply. Johnson dubbed the plan 'Sapphire Pavilion,' because, I was told, those were the first two words that came to his mind beginning with the same first letters as the words 'secret peace.'

"To keep the Sapphire Pavilion plan from leaking out, Johnson told Dean Rusk and Secretary of Defense Robert McNamara to work out the details. So Dean Rusk told the U.S. Ambassador to South Vietnam to arrange the envoy's trip after certain trusted intermediaries laid the groundwork. Since the Political Counselor recommended me and I had the right clearance and was fluent in French, the Ambassador made me part of the planning and execution cell.

"Although I thought the idea was crazy at first, the North Vietnamese agreed to accept the envoy as long as he came to Hanoi in an unarmed aircraft, which they would guarantee safe passage. So the Secretary of Defense arranged for a C-130 to take the envoy from Ubon airbase, in Thailand, to a remote airfield outside the North Vietnamese capital. The crew knew nothing about the envoy until just before takeoff—he boarded the plane while it was taxiing on the runway. Even then, the crew didn't know where they were going, and wouldn't know until they were airborne over South Vietnam's Central Highlands. That's when they could open their Top-Secret orders that would take them to an airfield near Hanoi and bring them and the envoy back the following night. What we didn't count on though, was the plane being shot down."

"So who shot it down?" Steve asked, completely absorbed in the story.

"It had to be the North Vietnamese," the Secretary answered matter-of-factly. "The Secretary of Defense had prearranged to keep other military aircraft out of the Sapphire Pavilion sector, and we later confirmed that no U.S. military aircraft shot anything down over the Central Highlands that evening."

"I can't believe the North Vietnamese would do that," Steve continued. "They had to know the consequences would be catastrophic."

"You would think so, wouldn't you?" the Secretary said. "The Ambassador told me Johnson erupted when he heard the news, screaming at the top of his lungs that the 'Commie bastards' had double-crossed him. He was so furious, he told the Secretary of Defense to escalate the bombing until Ho Chi Minh and the North Vietnamese were blown into oblivion. The Ambassador said Johnson told the Secretary of State that no one double-crossed him like that and got away with it. Then, about ten days later, at the end of January 1968, the North Vietnamese launched their Tet Offensive all across South Vietnam. Although they were eventually beaten back on every front, that offensive turned out to be the beginning of the end for America's involvement in Vietnam. Those of us who knew about Sapphire Pavilion assumed the North Vietnamese shot down the plane because they didn't want Johnson's initiative to delay their offensive."

"What an incredible story," Steve remarked. "It reveals so much about why Johnson acted the way he did for the rest of his presidency. After that, there could be no peace under his administration. I'm surprised he didn't make his effort public to rally the American people behind him."

The Secretary shook her head. "He couldn't, because he knew the right would criticize him. Plus, when the Tet Offensive hit, there was no turning back. So the mission remained Top Secret and faded into history."

"Until now," Benfield said.

"Until now," the Secretary confirmed.

Steve wasn't satisfied. While the Sapphire Pavilion explanation offered insight into the strategy of the Vietnam War, it left key questions open, including about the Secretary herself. She didn't cry at the table because Johnson lost his re-election bid. There had to be more to the story. He pushed the issue.

"But none of this explains why someone is willing to kill to keep the plane from being discovered. I mean, President Johnson's long since dead, so why would anyone care?" Steve took a moment to rub his chin and frame his next thought. It had been a long time since he'd advised senior government officials, yet he felt surprisingly comfortable thinking out loud in front of these dignitaries he knew only from the headlines. His anonymity gave him license to speak without the usual filters.

"I suppose it could be the Vietnamese, as they might not want the discovery of the plane to affect the thawing of relations between our two countries. But I doubt they've got the ability to correlate the Sapphire Pavilion wreckage to the 1968 peace initiative they sabotaged."

"I agree with Mr. Stilwell," Benfield said, sliding his elbows along the table as he leaned all the way forward. "I don't see how you get from this mission in 1968 to intrigue and murder in 2000. Something's missing." Benfield looked around the table to a bunch of nodding heads. Buoyed by his silent supporters, he addressed the Secretary directly. "In fact, I'd say something big is missing. I think you should go public with the details about the flight and let the FBI launch a full investigation." Benfield sat back in his chair as if his suggestion was the Secretary's only rational choice.

The Secretary didn't respond; she just gazed around the table. This time, though, all eyes were on her, waiting expectantly for some pronouncement that would bring rationality to an irrational situation. She gave them no respite. Instead, she looked uneasy, as if she had more to say, but something was holding her back—something that had been buried deep for many years.

Steve believed he had the key to loosen the Secretary's tongue, but he had to do it in a more intimate setting. He believed she wanted to tell the rest of the story, but not to a room full of strangers. Perhaps she would be willing to tell it to a smaller group, or better yet, just to him. He'd made a career out of making people feel comfortable confessing their most personal legal troubles. He decided to give it a try.

"Madame Secretary," he began. "Could I ask to speak with you alone for a moment?"

The Secretary's eyes widened. She started to speak but stopped herself. Clearly, Steve's request caught her off guard. The Secretary's Executive Assistant jumped in to save her.

"Mr. Stilwell, I'm afraid that's not how the Secretary likes to conduct business. She prefers an open discussion where everyone gets the chance to participate."

"I understand completely, and I'm not trying to take away anyone's opportunity to contribute." Steve glanced at the young Executive Assistant, who was doing her bureaucratic best to protect her boss, then looked back at the Secretary. "I tell you what. How about you stay here with the Secretary so you can take notes on my conversation with her. When we're finished, we can bring everyone in, and if the Secretary wishes, you can brief everyone on the content of our discussion."

The Secretary's Executive Assistant was quick to respond. "I'm afraid that won't—"

"That will be fine, Mr. Stilwell," the Secretary broke in, brushing away some hair that was sneaking along her right cheek. "I'm sorry for the inconvenience, but if I could ask everyone except Hanna to wait outside for a couple of minutes, we'll bring you back in after I hear what Mr. Stilwell has to say." As the guests pushed back their chairs to make their exits, she added, "I would like Elrod to stay, as well."

"It's completely your call, Madame Secretary," Steve said. He guessed she knew what was coming, and if she felt comfortable discussing the issues in front of Benfield, he had no problem with it either. His only reason for suggesting that the Secretary clear the room was for her comfort. As the last of the attendees filed out and pulled the door closed behind them, the Secretary looked to Steve to begin the conversation.

"The floor is yours, Mr. Stilwell. What's on your mind?"

"Well, I couldn't help but remember something you said when you answered Mr. Benfield's question about your assignment in Saigon."

"Oh? What was that?"

Steve thought the Secretary's reaction seemed forced, so he turned his chair toward her, putting distance between himself and Benfield and the Secretary's Executive Assistant. He wanted the Secretary to concentrate solely on him and forget the presence of the other two people. It would make it easier for her to disclose whatever it was she had pent up.

"You said Sapphire Pavilion brought back painful memories. Yet everything you've spoken about has been rather impersonal. That makes me think there is not only more to the story, but more that involves you personally."

"That's a little presumptuous of you, isn't it, Mr. Stilwell?" The Secretary reached for her ice water and took a small sip. As she set the glass back down on her coaster, Steve noticed her hand shaking. She clasped them together on the table.

"Maybe so," Steve answered, "but there's a man's life at stake here. If you know anything—anything at all—I'd respectfully ask you to get it on the table so we can at least see if it matters. We owe it to Ric Stokes and Ryan Eversall's widow." Steve couldn't give her an easy out, so he looked directly into her eyes, imploring her to answer. If the Secretary was going to keep her secret, he had to convey to her that there would be a steep emotional price to pay. "Please, Madame Secretary. The window where we can make a difference may close soon."

The Secretary returned Steve's gaze, but he refused to back down. Her eyes looked angry—perhaps because she was being asked to recall a memory she had suppressed for thirty years. Steve was sympathetic to her plight, but she had to be forthright with him. He couldn't take no for an answer.

The Secretary looked up to the ceiling and ran her hands through her hair on both sides of her head, looping the highlighted strands behind her ears. Steve could see the fault lines around the corners of her mouth tighten as she struggled with the dilemma, although he sensed she'd already made up her mind and was just gathering the courage to begin.

"All right, Mr. Stilwell." The Secretary sounded sure of herself. "I can't believe I'm getting ready to say what I'm about to say. It's certainly nothing official, but if it helps get to the bottom of this, then it's something I feel morally obligated to do."

"I appreciate that, Madame Secretary." Steve pulled his writing pad closer and prepared to take notes. If this was a one-time disclosure, he wanted to be sure he copied it accurately.

"As you surmised, I had more than just a professional interest in this mission. The envoy on Sapphire Pavilion was the embassy's Political Counselor. We'd worked together for nearly two years, and the night before the flight, he asked me to marry him."

Although Steve had no idea what he'd expected the Secretary to say, her actual disclosure had never entered his mind. He tried not to look shocked, as he didn't want to do or say anything that might dissuade her from continuing. However, there was a question she clearly wanted him to ask, so he asked it.

"Were you …" Steve took a short breath, feeling uneasy about getting too personal but aware he had no other choice, "engaged to him?"

"I didn't give him an answer," the Secretary replied, the assertiveness now gone from her voice. "Although we'd seen each other discreetly, he was ten years older and I worked for him. How could I say yes? So I sidestepped the question and told him we'd talk after he returned from the mission." The Secretary pushed back her chair and stood up, walking over to the window. She looked outside, her back to everyone in the room.

"I made up my mind after we said goodbye that night, but we never got the chance to talk about it again. I went with him to the airfield in Thailand and he waved to me as he boarded the plane. That was the last time I saw him." The Secretary reached out and touched her reflection on the glass. She didn't say anything further and just stood there as if she were searching for her lost lover's spirit somewhere outside.

"I'm so sorry," Benfield exclaimed.

"I am as well, Madame Secretary," Steve added. "If you don't mind me asking, what was his name?"

"Kenneth Hollins," the Secretary said, whirling around to face her interrogators. "We assumed he was killed when the plane went down. The embassy had a cover story that he was killed during a restaurant bombing."

The Secretary returned to her chair and continued in a dispassionate tone, as if to show she was long since over the pain, despite her earlier assertions to the contrary. "I've got to admit, at the time it was hard for me to deal with. I completed my tour at the embassy, but then left the Foreign Service for corporate America. I put Vietnam and Kenneth behind me."

"Until now," Steve commented, borrowing a phrase from Benfield.

"Until now," the Secretary confirmed. "But I don't think there's anything I've said beyond the nature of the mission that might be helpful. It's just a lot of history."

"Maybe and maybe not," Steve said. "This may seem far-fetched, but what if someone survived the crash and is trying to keep the plane from being discovered?"

"I don't think we need to be smearing the reputation of the dead, Mr. Stilwell." The Secretary rolled her chair up under her desk, closer to his seat. "You know as well as I do that the plane crashed in the middle of the Vietnamese mountains and was lost without a trace for thirty years."

Steve felt compelled to defend his theory. "I know it's a long shot, but someone could have survived."

"And then made his way back to civilization and hid his identity from the world for the last thirty years? That's preposterous, Mr. Stilwell. And that's all I'm going to say on the matter." The Secretary crossed her arms in front of her chest, her tone and body language permitting no argument.

"I've got no other leads, Madame Secretary," Steve confessed. "We'll just have to see if we can identify someone who doesn't want the plane discovered." Although Steve gave the impression that he'd discounted the possibility that one of the plane's passengers was behind the intrigue, he still intended to explore the option. He had nothing else to go on.

"Then why don't you meet with the others out there and see if you can come up with something," the Secretary directed. "You can tell them everything I told you, but I don't see the need to sit through it again myself. I've disclosed enough deep, dark secrets for one day."

"We'll take it from here," Benfield assured her. He stood up and positioned himself behind his chair while Steve and Hanna followed suit. "I'll brief you on Monday morning with whatever we're able to come up with."

"Thanks, Elrod," the Secretary affirmed. "And thanks for meeting with us on such short notice, Mr. Stilwell."

"It was my pleasure," Steve replied. "Before I go, can I ask you to have the embassy see if what we have now is sufficient to either secure Ric Stokes' release or at least delay his trial until we can get additional evidence? Now that you know he's innocent, we can't let him stand trial. If he does and he's convicted, the Vietnamese will never back down. They would lose face."

"We'll take that for action, too, Madame Secretary," Benfield volunteered.

"Get on that right away, Elrod," the Secretary directed. "We can't let Sapphire Pavilion claim any more lives."

45

———✦———

S TEVE EMERGED FROM THE SECRETARY'S OFFICE feeling optimistic. Now that Secretary McDermott had a personal interest in his case's outcome, he was certain it would get the attention and effort it deserved. In fact, he was convinced that the meeting bought Ric Stokes time. The full weight of the U.S. Government would now be brought to bear on the Vietnamese prosecutors, not in a destructive way, but in a positive way to save an innocent man's life. Surely the Vietnamese Government, which also had to consider the impact non-cooperation might have on improved trade relations with the United States, would see it that way. But the Vietnamese would need another suspect to blame the drug heist on, and Steve wasn't sure they had a viable candidate.

After confirming his assessment of the meeting results with his State Department escort Tad Schwartz, he asked to use a telephone to share his news with Casey. He was sure she would be standing by until she received the all-clear. He dialed his cellphone number and waited. She picked up after the fourth ring.

"Hello, this is Casey Pantel." Casey's voice was muffled and hard to understand.

"Hi Casey, it's Steve. Hey, I'm having trouble hearing you. Can you speak up a little?"

"I'm so glad you called, Steve," she said excitedly, louder but still restrained. "Can you hold for a minute until I get outside? I'm in the stacks in the law library, and although it looks deserted, I'd feel more comfortable talking t you from outside."

"Sure," Steve replied, curious as to why Casey seemed so eager. "Just let me know when you're ready to talk." He rolled the chair he was sitting in closer to the desk and opened his planner in case Casey said something he needed to jot down. She came back on the line a minute or so later, her voice no longer hushed, but strong and confident.

"Sorry about that, Steve, but I'm so glad you called. I found out something amazing."

"You go first then," Steve said.

"You're not going to believe this, Steve, but it sounds like the CIA might have shot down the C-130."

"What?" Steve couldn't hide his skepticism. "How in the world did you come up with that?"

"You got a call from Captain Thornton, the squadron CO you gave Ryan Eversall's notebook to. His ordnance officer was able to match up a serial number found on debris at the crash site with an air-to-air Sidewinder missile. He also confirmed that it wasn't an Air Force or Navy missile, or one fired by our allies. He thinks it might have belonged to some CIA black-ops program."

"Holy smokes! You've got to be kidding me. That's huge."

"I know. It could be front page news."

"It's way bigger than you think."

"What do you mean?"

"The Secretary told us what Sapphire Pavilion was. The plane was on a Top-Secret mission directed by President Johnson himself. It had an emissary onboard who was going to meet with Ho Chi Minh to set up direct talks with the President to see if the two leaders could agree on terms to end the Vietnam War. So if what you're saying is true, somebody in the CIA sabotaged the President's peace proposal and extended the war. The political implications are enormous. No, they're beyond enormous." Steve couldn't believe the direction this case was taking, or how fast it was unraveling. The downed plane and its secrets were finally coming to light after over thirty years.

"We still don't know who in the CIA might have done it," Casey admitted. "Captain Thornton had no way of identifying the culprit. In fact, he stressed he had no proof the missile was CIA. That was just his best guess."

"The CIA will be able to trace the missile, and even if they can't, the manufacturer probably can. It may take time, but they'll do it. This is the beginning of the end, Casey. I see the light at the end of the tunnel."

Casey continued to inject reality into the discussion. "But can we really go to the CIA? I mean, if we know there's someone in the CIA, or at least with CIA connections, behind all this, won't we tip them off?"

"Wait a minute," Steve said. "We know who it is!"

"The CIA connection?"

"Yes! It's Richard."

"Richard who?"

"We don't know that yet, but now we'll be able to find out. We just need to find Vietnam-era Richards with CIA connections and we'll find our man."

"How are we going to do that? The CIA doesn't make its operatives' names public."

"We can't, but the Secretary of State can. Let me see if I can get back in with her before she leaves the building. She'll definitely want to hear what you've come up with."

"Do you need me to do anything for you?"

"No, you've done enough, Casey. Why don't you go home and get some sleep? We'll regroup in the office on Monday."

"Um, we don't have an office anymore."

"Oh yeah ... how quickly we forget." Steve was getting antsy—he needed to catch the Secretary before she departed the building—but he didn't want to be rude to Casey. After all, she was the one who provided the information he had to relay to the Secretary. He just needed to wrap up the call quickly. "Well then, how about we meet at my house at nine o'clock on Monday morning?"

"Okay, I'll see you then, Steve. Give me a call if you need anything."

"Don't worry, I will," Steve promised. He hung up the phone, hurried out to Tad Schwartz, and told him he needed to meet with the Secretary and Elrod Benfield again right away if they were still available. They were, but only if Steve could be back in the Secretary's office in five minutes. Steve was riding the elevator to the Seventh Floor less than a minute later.

When Steve and Tad Schwartz arrived in the Secretary's waiting area, Madeleine escorted them into the Secretary's office, where Elrod Benfield was already at the conference table in his usual seat.

"Please, have a seat, gentlemen," Madeleine instructed. "I caught the Secretary just as she was climbing into her car to leave for the day. She asked that I have everyone staged in her office and ready to go by the time she gets back. She's got an engagement later this afternoon, so you'll have to be quick." Madeleine left the room, leaving the three men to wait for the Secretary's arrival.

"So what's this all about?" Benfield asked, perturbed at being summoned back to the Secretary's office at the whim of an unknown civilian attorney.

Steve pulled out the chair opposite Benfield and sat down. "I've got some new information about the case," he said matter-of-factly, without offering what that information might be. If Benfield was going to put on airs in the

Secretary's absence, he would have to wait for the Secretary to return to find out what was going on.

Secretary McDermott strode back into her office and headed straight for her seat at the end of the table. Steve, Tad, and Benfield all stood as she approached. She sat down, slid her chair forward, and exhaled deeply, as if she had run all the way up the stairs from her car to the Seventh Floor. Then she turned her attention to Steve, smiled politely, and got down to business. The small smile, even if perfunctory, contrasted with Benfield's grumpiness and put Steve at ease.

"Okay, Mr. Stilwell. I understand you've got some additional information. What do you have?"

Steve also slid his chair forward and put his arms on the table. "I've got some incredible news."

"Okay, let's have it then," Benfield admonished, his impatience getting the best of him. "The Secretary doesn't have much time."

Steve didn't give the Secretary the chance to jump in and defend him. He got right to the point. "It looks like Sapphire Pavilion might have been intentionally shot down by the CIA."

Susan McDermott's eyes widened, and she drew her hands into clenched fists. Even the corners of her mouth tightened, raising her lips into the furthest thing from a smile. She didn't move or respond verbally to what Steve said, but her body language spoke volumes.

Steve continued, "Yesterday, I gave Ryan Eversall's crash site notebook to the commanding officer of a fighter squadron at Naval Air Station Oceana in Virginia Beach. He analyzed the notebook and made what I've got to admit is a startling discovery. Some of the debris found at the crash site contained the serial number of a U.S.-made air-to-air missile. He was also able to confirm the missile didn't belong to the Air Force, the Navy, or an ally. His instinct tells him it must have been assigned to a black-ops program run by the CIA."

The Secretary's creamy complexion turned pink, then red, as anger won out over her need to stay neutral. "Do the records go back that far?" she asked. Even her diction seemed crisper than during their earlier meeting.

Steve had thought this question through since speaking with Casey. "That's going to depend on who was behind this. If very senior, they'd have the wherewithal to cover their tracks. But if it was a lower level official doing some freelancing, then the records are likely still intact."

"I don't buy it," Benfield retorted. "Why in the world would the CIA shoot down a U.S. military plane on what they had to know was a Presidential mission?"

The Secretary glared at Benfield and spoke to him in an icy tone that made Steve glad Benfield was the object of her wrath and not him. "That's precisely why they shot it down," the Secretary asserted as if she had reached that conclusion long before. "There were certain elements of the government that didn't want peace because they thought we could bring the North Vietnamese to their knees if we just had the courage to stick the war out." She looked back at Steve and then down at her hands, still clenched in white-knuckled fists. "So who do you think did this, Mr. Stilwell?"

"I don't know how high this might have gone, Madame Secretary. It seems like there had to be some senior CIA involvement, given how closely held the mission was. You'd be a far better judge of that than me. But my guess is the person we're dealing with now was a mid-level CIA official at the time, either at CIA Headquarters in Langley, or more likely, in country."

"Why do you say that?" asked the Secretary.

Steve couldn't tell whether she knew why and was just testing him, or she just wanted to hear his logic. Although she looked stern, the icy glare was gone, so he assumed it was the latter.

"Because executing the shoot-down required someone tactical, who knew about Sapphire Pavilion and had access to secret CIA air assets in country. Say, for example, the CIA Station Chief or Deputy Station Chief. If they were in their mid-forties during the war, they'd be in their seventies now. That's young enough to worry about being tried for murder if someone found the plane and figured out what happened, and old enough to have the financial clout to keep the crash site from being discovered."

"I didn't know the CIA flew anything that could fire an air-to-air missile," Benfield said cautiously. "I thought they only flew transport missions under the guise of Air America."

"That's a question the CIA will have to answer," Steve replied. "I doubt we'll find that type of information in the public domain."

"Dick Phillips," the Secretary announced, pounding the table. "I'll bet it's Dick Phillips. How could he have done such a thing?" The Secretary gasped, clapping her hand over her mouth. "He was my friend and Kenneth's friend, and he killed him. I can't believe it. He killed Kenneth."

"I'm sorry, Madame Secretary," Steve apologized. "But I'm not following you. Who is Dick Phillips?"

The Secretary's ruddy glow vanished with her revelation, her face suddenly ashen and drawn, her expression more vulnerable. She spoke quietly, but with the conviction and certainty of a jury announcing guilty findings after a thirty-two-year trial. "Dick Phillips coordinated CIA air operations at the embassy in Saigon. He'd been in country since at least 1965 and was the Agency's Number Three man at the embassy. He had to know what was going on and he would've been in a position to direct the mission. He was a fervent anti-Communist and despised the North Vietnamese. He was sure that if South

Vietnam fell, the rest of Southeast Asia wouldn't be far behind."

"Wait a minute," Benfield declared. He seemed to be coming around to their way of thinking. "After Robert Fowler was murdered, I personally spoke with the contractor providing security for embassy personnel in Vietnam, Cambodia, and Laos." Benfield looked up at the ceiling lights and rubbed his chin, deep in concentration. "I think his name was Richard Phillips. That can't be the same person, can it?"

"Richard!" Steve and the Secretary exclaimed in unison.

Steve waited for the Secretary to complete the thought. When she didn't, he did the honors, hoping he wasn't just stating the obvious.

"The FBI rep at our earlier meeting said they were looking for a man named Richard. That was the name their confidential informant gave them."

"It all makes so much sense," the Secretary said, putting the remaining pieces of the puzzle together. "He probably used his contract with the embassy and his Agency contacts to stay plugged into the area. So he would have known when Ryan Eversall was coming to Vietnam to look for the plane."

Steve picked up where the Secretary left off. "Exactly. And when Ryan Eversall and Ric Stokes found the plane, Richard used his contacts to set them up and make it look like they were involved in drug smuggling. What he didn't count on was Ryan's notebook. When he found out about that, he pulled out all the stops to try to get it back before it got into U.S. government hands, knowing that as soon as it did, the military would launch a recovery mission. If that were to happen, it would only be a matter of time before someone figured out about Sapphire Pavilion and traced everything back to him."

"I'm calling the FBI Director," the Secretary declared. "I want this asshole arrested, exposed for the traitor he is, and tried for murder."

"I suggest they act quickly," Steve warned.

Benfield urged caution. "I'm sure they'll take this seriously, Mr. Stilwell. They can't help but do that. But they also aren't going to want to act recklessly and arrest someone without sufficient evidence."

"I'm not recommending they do. But Richard must know by now that Ryan Eversall's notebook is in government hands, so he's also realized there's nothing he can do to stop the government from locating the plane. Plus, the FBI already has the confidential informant and the witness at the consulate in Saigon. They may want to execute a search warrant right away at Richard's home and office, before he has time to destroy the evidence. I'm afraid there's no time to waste."

"Okay, gentlemen," the Secretary concluded. "I've got what I need. I think the FBI Director's going to be very interested in what we've uncovered. I'll give him your name and contact information, Mr. Stilwell, so his investigators can follow up with you."

"That sounds good," Steve said, nodding his head, "and if it turns out like we've discussed, I'd appreciate it if the consulate could coordinate with the Vietnamese government to get Ric Stokes released. Now we can show that not only is he innocent, but we know who the guilty party is." Steve stood up to make his exit and let the Secretary make her call. Benfield and the Secretary rose as he did.

"You bet, Steve," the Secretary said, extending her hand to thank him. "I really appreciate your help with this case, more than you can ever imagine. And I know the families of the downed airmen will as well."

Steve shook the Secretary's hand and then Benfield's. No one smiled or said anything else—all that needed to be said had been said. All the evidence was on the table, albeit scattered around the globe and including testimony from persons unknown. Moreover, their collective efforts, together with those of Casey and Phan, had stitched the case together into a coherent mosaic. Now it was up to the FBI to bring Richard and his organization to justice.

That was the most unsettling part for Steve: the case was now completely out of his hands. All he could do was wait.

46

Monday, 5 June 2000, 10:17 a.m. EDT
Elizabeth City, North Carolina

THINGS HAD MOVED QUICKLY SINCE SATURDAY afternoon's brief to the
Secretary of State on the status of the FBI's investigative efforts. Now, less
than forty-eight hours later, Campbell Drury, the Tactical Team Leader—or
TAC—and the Search Team Leader stood by two FBI vehicles parked along
a secluded narrow two-lane blacktop road leading to the headquarters of
Ajax Global Security Inc., the private security firm owned by Richard "Dick"
Phillips. Campbell, who was now personally overseeing the investigation,
listened as the TAC rattled off orders into his radio, coordinating the efforts
of over twenty FBI agents poised to secure Phillips' home and the Ajax Global
Security headquarters complex so the search teams could follow on and
collect evidence.

Located adjacent to the Great Dismal Swamp in the vicinity of Elizabeth
City, North Carolina, the complex comprised over ten thousand muggy,
mosquito-infested acres of challenging terrain. Not the setting one would
expect for most corporate headquarters, the site was perfect for preparing
prior military, former spies, and soldiers of fortune for wide-ranging private-
and public-sector security assignments in harsh environments around the
globe.

Starting immediately after the Secretary of State's telephone call to the FBI
Director on Saturday afternoon, Campbell's investigation team shifted into
overdrive to research Phillips and his security firm. By late Sunday morning,
they had kluged together a dossier on Phillips using open-source material and

information provided by Secretary McDermott, the CIA, Steve Stilwell, Casey Pantel, the Vietnamese witness holed up at the U.S. Consulate in Saigon, and a confidential informant. The mosaic they assembled was both telling and damning for Phillips, particularly when viewed through a law-enforcement lens.

The team's research disclosed that Ajax Global Security Inc. was Phillips' brainchild after he left the CIA in 1975, the same year the South Vietnamese government fell and the victorious North reunited the country under Communist rule. With no competition to speak of, Ajax soon monopolized the U.S. private-security market, protecting expatriate executives, drilling platforms, factories, and even U.S. embassy personnel living overseas. As the threat from international terrorism grew in the early 1990s, Ajax dominated the world market. And when the U.S. and Vietnam reestablished diplomatic relations in mid-1995, Phillips came knocking at the State Department's door, offering to protect the embassy's residential compounds in Hanoi and Saigon, a contract he personally secured and executed with unusual vigor.

Phillips' contract gave him access to classified embassy threat briefings for all of Southeast Asia and afforded him a special vantage point from which to detect even the slightest interest in Sapphire Pavilion. Campbell surmised this was how Phillips learned about Ryan Eversall and Ric Stokes' expedition to find the downed C-130, and Phillips then used the connections he'd developed over his long association with Vietnam, including with the drug underworld, to keep the plane's discovery under wraps.

Armed with the information from his various sources, Campbell's team swore out an affidavit and secured a search warrant from a federal judge in the Eastern District of North Carolina. The warrant covered Phillips' home and cars, as well as Ajax Global Security Inc.'s headquarters complex. Campbell was now on scene to observe the headquarters' portion of that search, albeit from a distance so he wouldn't get in the way of his agents. Other FBI agents prepared to undertake the search of Phillips' residence.

Not wanting to give Phillips any more time to destroy evidence—he had to be aware the FBI was on his trail—Campbell staged his tactical and search teams on the outskirts of both the house and headquarters properties, hoping to capitalize on the element of surprise. Once the TAC informed him that both teams were in position, Campbell gave the TAC the thumbs up. The TAC nodded and barked "Execute, execute, execute!" into his radio, setting the tactical teams in both locations in motion.

The next sound Campbell heard was two helicopters flying overhead toward the headquarters complex. Both were FBI aircraft, and they took station at opposite corners of the building in a show of force designed to convince anyone that escape would be futile. At the same time, a column of

SUVs filled with FBI agents sped by him and approached the headquarters complex. They fanned out once they reached the parking lot and quickly blocked all the egress points. Two vehicles parked as close to the front door as they could and eight agents jumped out of their cars and prepared to enter the building. A young man in a light-gray suit came out the doors and started to angle to the parking lot, but the agents quickly detained him and directed him to a processing station being set up in the rear.

Another SUV pulled up behind Phillips' Jaguar, blocking it in its parking spot. Three agents emerged from the vehicle and one jimmied open the driver's side door and then popped open the hood and the trunk. Agents and evidence technicians in a white van quickly converged and began their search of the vehicle.

"Mr. Drury," the TAC called loudly over the semi-distant whirring of the helicopters. "SWAT One is preparing to go in."

Campbell's eyes were glued to the agents as they approached the front door. Six went inside, while two stayed back to make sure no one slipped in behind them. Now there was nothing to do but wait for status reports. Within seconds, the TAC received a call on his radio.

"They're inside the residence now," the TAC reported. "There was no one at home, so they let themselves in. They've secured the residence and the search team is heading in."

"Sounds good," Campbell replied. "Tell 'em to keep us informed." The TAC nodded.

The TAC looked back at Campbell and pointed toward the parking lot to the right of the front door. "SWAT Two just reported in. They're preparing to enter the building. You can see them heading toward the door from the right."

Campbell nodded but didn't say anything. There would be a lot of insignificant reports today, but he didn't want to squelch them because then his agents would hesitate to report things that did matter. He couldn't risk that outcome.

"SWAT One is on the fourth floor just outside of the executive suite. They're getting ready to go in now." The TAC smiled. "I wish I were there to see the look on Phillips' face. The rich ones always think they'll get away with it."

"You'll see it soon enough when they bring him out in handcuffs," Campbell remarked.

"Yeah, well it's too bad those Air Force guys on that airplane won't get to see it." The TAC's comment added an unexpected dose of melancholy to the event.

"That's why we're here," Campbell said with unusual passion, "to see it for them."

The TAC half-nodded as he put the radio up to his ear to take another call. "There's a problem," he said excitedly.

"Where?"

"In the executive suite."

"Is everyone okay?" This was Campbell's overriding concern. Casualties would be devastating.

"I've lost 'em," the TAC announced. "SWAT One, SWAT One, this is TAC, do you read me over?" He paused for a moment and evidently got no response. "SWAT One, SWAT One, this is TAC, do you read me, over?"

"What's going on?" Campbell demanded.

"I can't tell," the TAC replied. "I'm sending SWAT Two to the fourth floor to check on them."

"Do whatever you have to do," Campbell snapped, fighting the urge to head into the building himself. That was precisely what he should not do. His TAC needed to remain here and control whatever emergency had developed in the building while Campbell personally handled the back and forth with Washington that was sure to follow. To involve himself in the tactical situation was to invite disaster. For all he knew, though, disaster had already arrived.

47

Same day—Monday, 5 June 2000, 3:07 p.m. EDT
Williamsburg, Virginia

STEVE HAD HELPED CLIENTS DEAL WITH fires before, but he'd never experienced their catastrophic effects firsthand. His files, his computer, his furniture, even his favorite picture of Sarah, were now indistinguishable amid a soot-black carbon wasteland soaking in the fire-hose-drenched aftermath of what used to be his office. Although he'd only been in private practice a shade under three years, he'd grown attached to the creaking of the floorboards in the hall leading to the kitchen and the outer office where Marjorie's plants basked in the sunlight through the bay window. As bad as he felt with just his office gone, he couldn't fathom the loss people felt when fire destroyed their family's residence.

Despite having to work out of his house, he'd had a much busier day than anticipated. Casey showed up right on schedule at 9:00 a.m., ringing the doorbell together with Marjorie, whom Steve had called the night before. They set up a temporary office in the dining room, running a telephone line along the floor from the kitchen and positioning themselves equidistant around the oval dining room table. They then divvied up the responsibilities and set about getting the law office back on its feet. Steve knew his clients would be understanding of the fire unless it impacted their cases; then they would expect him to get everything done and filed on time no matter how difficult it might be. They were right, of course, which is why Marjorie immediately set about obtaining three new computers and arranging for the off-site backup data to be reinstalled. She had the office calendar up and running by one o'clock and started to cancel appointments for the current week with a vengeance.

Steve tasked Casey with finding available office space so they could re-open as soon as possible. They both enjoyed working near the restored area of Colonial Williamsburg, so Casey left the office to meet with a realtor to see what might be on the market. Her mission was to find two or three options they could discuss at the end of the day. She departed the house around 11:15 a.m. and popped back through the front door just past three. Both Marjorie and Steve called out to her.

"Hi guys," Casey replied, in keeping with her Midwest upbringing. "How are things going?"

"We're making progress," Steve announced. "The key, though, is were you able to find anything?"

"I was, and you're not going to believe it, but there's a perfect four-office suite right down from us on the corner of North Henry and Prince George Streets. It's that beautiful white-painted brick colonial office building. I've set up an appointment for all three of us to walk through tomorrow morning at ten thirty, if that works for you."

"It works for me," Marjorie declared.

"Me, too," Steve said. "And I'm sure it's reasonably priced?" He knew full well that historic office space that close to the Duke of Gloucester Street would command a premium.

Marjorie hammed it up to counter his concern. "A man of your stature needs an office like that, Mr. Stilwell."

"I think you deserve it," Casey added, laying it on as thick as Marjorie.

"Why does this sound like Sarah telling me I'm about to save money as she's heading out the door to go shopping on Black Friday?" Everyone laughed, although Steve's smile trailed off the fastest.

"By the way," Casey continued, still chuckling from Steve's comment. "What does Sarah think about us setting up the office in your dining room? She can't be too thrilled."

Steve's face fell and he lapsed into momentary silence. Marjorie looked down and broke eye contact. Casey's question drove home the stark reality that he hadn't seen or heard from Sarah since she'd left him last week. He'd intended to call her parents to see if she was there, but with the car wreck, the trip to the emergency room, the meeting with the Secretary, and then the fire, he'd neglected to make the call. Not only did his silence confirm all Sarah's contentions, but it also made it almost impossible for him to convince her he'd really missed her since he hadn't even taken the time to call. Her cellphone register wouldn't lie.

"I'm sorry, did I say something wrong?" Casey looked bewildered by the sudden change of mood.

"No, not at all," Steve said. "Why don't you sit down? I'll fill you in on yet another casualty of this case."

"Uh-oh," Casey gasped. "I did say something wrong. I'm sorry, Steve. You don't owe me any explanations."

"Yes, I do," Steve said. "How about you and Marjorie both sit down for a second so we can assess where we are, including on this case." As Marjorie was already seated, she just scooted her chair to the right to make room for Casey to pull up next to her. Casey clasped her hands, her forearms on the table, and waited for Steve to speak. Marjorie looked like she was trying to make herself invisible.

"Okay, this is hard for me to say, but I just need to get it out so we're not all dancing around the subject. If we're going to work together as a team, then we've got to be able to talk about the tough issues. So here goes." Neither woman made eye contact, so he could tell this was just as uncomfortable for them as it was for him. He took a deep breath and started to talk.

"This case has been pretty rough on Sarah." He found himself sitting all the way forward in his chair, his shoulders curving toward his captive audience. Trying to relax, he said, "I didn't realize it at the time, but when I was in Vietnam, a woman set me up to blackmail me with Sarah. Actions that seemed innocent at the time—and I can assure you they were innocent—don't look quite as innocent when taken out of context in photographs. When I wouldn't turn the crash site notebook over to the woman, even after she threatened me, she gave the photographs to Sarah."

Steve paused to wait for a reaction, but there was none. Either Casey and Marjorie didn't know what to say, or they imagined the worst and thought he was lying. Hoping it was the former, he continued with his explanation.

"Sarah knew when she saw the pictures that I had been set up."

"How could she tell?" Casey asked.

"Because the pictures were taken from a distance by a third party—like me having dinner with the woman or riding on the back of her motorcycle, or her leaning over and kissing me without warning in the hotel lobby. Marjorie's seen the pictures. She knows what I mean." Marjorie looked over at Casey and nodded her head. "You can see the pictures, too, Casey. I've got nothing to hide."

"So why did Sarah react the way she did, if she knew you'd been set up?"

"Just like a veteran cross-examiner, going right to the heart of the matter." Steve gave her a rueful smile.

"I'm sorry, Steve," Casey said. "You really don't owe us an explanation."

"Like I said, I think I do. And I'm glad you asked the question. It actually makes it easier for me to talk. So let's just say I've been a workaholic all my life and I poured my heart and soul into the Navy, often at the expense of Sarah and my family. My time away from home in Vietnam on this case and my interaction with this woman to try and get the information I needed to get Ric Stokes out of jail convinced Sarah that things haven't changed post-Navy. So she's taken some time off from me to think things over. I haven't heard from her since she left on Friday morning."

"The woman I saw in your office on Friday morning—was she the same woman who was killed when your car went off the bridge?" Marjorie had a knack for calling it like it is.

"She was," Steve said. "And she was the woman from Vietnam who was in the pictures. Her organization turned against her when her attempts to get the crash site notebook failed. She knew they were trying to kill her, so she agreed to turn state's evidence and help get Ric Stokes out of jail. She was killed before she had the chance to talk to the police."

Steve paused again to let the information sink in. "I guess that's a long way of saying, Sarah won't mind if we work in the dining room for a while." The corners of Marjorie's mouth rose ever so slightly, so Steve knew she was back in his camp. He wasn't sure where he stood with her until that moment, and her trust was important to him. He needed her support to get his feet back on the ground both personally and professionally.

Ringhhh. Ringhhh. Ringhhh. Steve's cellphone sounding off in the middle of the table cut the conversation short.

"Uh-oh," Casey gasped again as Steve reached for his phone. "I just remembered something I forgot to do."

"Hold on to that thought," Steve said. Opening the phone, he said, "Hello, this is Steve Stilwell."

"Hello, Mr. Stilwell," a very efficient sounding female voice began. "This is Assistant Secretary Elrod Benfield's office. Are you available to speak with the Assistant Secretary?"

"Of course, anytime it's convenient for him."

"I'm going to put him on the line now."

Steve covered the cellphone microphone with his hand and whispered to Casey and Marjorie, "It's Assistant Secretary Elrod Benfield at the State Department." Before he could say anything else, Benfield came on the line. Steve shook his head and pointed at the phone with his free hand, signaling he couldn't talk anymore.

"Hello, Steve, this is Elrod Benfield."

"Hello, Mr. Benfield. How are you this afternoon?"

"I'm doing fine, Steve. I hope you are as well. Anyway, the Secretary just received an update in the Sapphire Pavilion case and she asked me to give you a call."

"I really appreciate you keeping me in the loop, Mr. Benfield. I hope it's good news." Steve imagined it must be. His bureaucratic experience told him that senior people only called when they had good news. If it was bad, they let their staff make the call.

"Well, it's a little of both," he admitted. "I guess the most significant news is the FBI locked down Dick Phillips' house and company headquarters this morning in Elizabeth City, North Carolina."

"Wow, that was fast," Steve gave Marjorie and Casey a thumbs-up. "Did they arrest him?"

"Well, before I answer your question, there's a little more to it. The FBI went there to search his house and headquarters. They intended to make the arrest decision based upon what they found."

Steve could tell where the story was heading. "I take it that means they didn't find anything."

"It wasn't just that they didn't find anything—everything was gone. When they arrived at his headquarters this morning, it looked from the outside like everything was normal. His car was parked in its usual spot and the parking lot was filled with employee vehicles. The search team headed straight to Phillips' office on the fourth floor to present their warrant and assert control over the evidence. But when they got there, they found out he hadn't come into work this morning. In his office, everything appeared in order, except that his computer's hard drive was missing and its components were ripped out. Two file drawers that Phillips' secretary says were normally locked were open and empty. They also uncovered a safe hidden under the floorboards beneath his desk. Once they got it open, it was empty too."

"I trust that's the bad news?"

"Hold on to that thought," Benfield said. "There's more. The FBI also found nothing at Phillips' house. He was divorced and had no kids, so he lived by himself. The FBI is tracking down his housekeeper to see if she can provide any insight into when he might have left or where he might have gone. From what clothing is missing from his closet, she might at least be able to give the FBI an idea of the climate where he was headed."

"Can't they check with the airlines to see if he's flown anywhere?"

"Of course," Benfield replied curtly, as if he believed Steve was trying to dictate the FBI's investigation techniques rather than just advance the conversation forward. "They've already done that and found nothing. They are sure, though, that given Phillips' past, he's got a new identity and a forged passport. They're also sure he's left the country by now, no doubt with a substantial sum of cash in hand and some Swiss bank accounts to set him up nicely for the rest of his life."

The information angered Steve. From Benfield's account, the FBI seemed content to let Phillips go. Could it be that the CIA was covering for one of its own, even after all these years? The crew of Sapphire Pavilion was dead, as were two diplomats. Ryan Eversall was dead and his reputation ruined. Ric Stokes was awaiting trial on charges everyone knew were trumped up. And Sarah was still gone, the least violent but most personally painful of all of the consequences of Phillips' actions. Despite the devastating fallout, all Benfield could say was it looked like Phillips was set up nicely for the rest of his life.

"I'm not going to let them drop this," Steve stated flatly. "Phillips may think he's gotten away and is going to live out his days like a king, but I'm going to find him and make sure he's held accountable for what he's done."

"Hold on there, Mr. Stilwell. I'm not sure where you got the idea that anyone is going to let Phillips get away with this, but I can assure you that's not going to happen. The FBI has already notified Interpol, so police around the world are looking for him. It's just a matter of time before he makes a mistake and someone notices him."

"Ric Stokes doesn't have a lot of time," Steve insisted, raising his voice. "We can't wait for Phillips to make a mistake. We need to get Ric Stokes released now, before he goes to trial and it's too late." Steve looked up and saw Casey putting her finger to her lips to get him to quiet down. He'd become so engrossed in the conversation, he'd forgotten she and Marjorie were there. He nodded in acknowledgment.

"Well, that's where the good news starts," Benfield continued. "A representative from the FBI and I just met with the Vietnamese Ambassador to the United States to discuss this case, and frankly, that's the real reason for my call."

"That sounds promising," Steve said in a more reasonable tone, hoping the Vietnamese would delay Ric Stokes' case until the United States could present enough evidence to get them to drop the charges.

"It's more than promising," Benfield declared, sounding like someone making a press announcement. "It's game changing."

"What is?" Steve asked excitedly.

"I'm getting to that," Benfield said. "As I'm sure you can imagine, the Vietnamese Ambassador is well versed on this case. We've discussed it with him regularly ever since Stokes was arrested. We presented him with all our recent discoveries, including the information your team uncovered, as well as the full story of Sapphire Pavilion. We also committed to use additional information provided by the confidential informant to assist Vietnam in dealing with drug trafficking in and throughout Vietnam. When we added that we have alerted Interpol to help us arrest Phillips, the Ambassador was very impressed. He believes his government will be very receptive to the information we provided, and he thinks they will actually consider releasing Stokes by the end of the week if everything we said checks out, which we both know it will." Benfield paused to let his previous statement sink in. "In other words, Mr. Stilwell, it looks like your efforts and Vietnam's desire to continue our countries' rapprochement have combined to free your client. Congratulations, Mr. Stilwell."

Steve couldn't contain his excitement. "That's unbelievable!" he shouted, holding the phone away from his mouth to avoid deafening Benfield. He looked up at Casey and Marjorie. "Ric Stokes should be released this week!" Big smiles broke out around the table. Casey clapped her hands silently, but then pointed back at the telephone to remind Steve he was still speaking with Mr. Benfield.

"Sorry about that outburst, Mr. Benfield. But that's the best news I've had in a long time."

"I'm glad we're able to end on a happy note."

"Before you go, will someone from the State Department call Noriko Stokes?"

"I'll be calling her right after I'm done speaking with you. My office will notify you as soon as I talk to her. Then feel free to contact her yourself."

"And what about Ryan Eversall's widow?"

"We'll be calling her as well, Mr. Stilwell. Rest assured we have the case in good hands. Now, I've got to get going so I can make the other notifications. You know the level of visibility this case has received."

"Certainly, Mr. Benfield. And thanks so much for your call."

Steve ended the call, ecstatic with the news. The troubles of the discussion before Mr. Benfield's call were light years away. He couldn't wait to share the great news with Noriko Stokes. He also couldn't wait to get Ric Stokes released and back in the States before the Vietnamese government changed its mind. Then he realized he also wanted to share his success with Sarah, but she wasn't around. He could almost hear her say "I told you so," because once again, calling her was an afterthought. But he sensed that, under the circumstances, she would forgive him the oversight.

Thinking of Sarah took the edge off the victory, which Casey must have sensed, because she returned to where she'd left off before Elrod Benfield called.

"Steve, I'm not sure this is the right time to tell you this, but there probably won't be a better time."

Steve could tell Casey was concerned; in fact, she looked like she was dreading what she had to say. He hadn't seen such trepidation in her eyes since the day of her interview when she confessed she sometimes needed to see a doctor at the VA. She had him worried.

"What is it, Casey?"

"I'm so sorry, but I forgot to tell you something." She seemed on the verge of tears.

"What was it?"

"I'd completely forgotten about it, but when you were talking about Sarah before the phone rang, it suddenly occurred to me. On the night of the fire, I was in my office when I heard a cellphone ringing. It scared me at first, because I thought maybe there was someone else in the office. When I went to explore, I found it was your cellphone in your office. I could tell from the caller ID that it was Sarah, but I didn't think anything of it at the time because I didn't know she'd left you. Then the office caught fire and you were gone the next day at the State Department, and the call completely slipped my mind. I'm so sorry, Steve. I'm so, so sorry."

Steve didn't hesitate. "Don't worry about it, Casey. That's actually wonderful news. I'll give her a call right away. Please don't give it a second thought. I'm amazed you remembered it after all you've been through, and I'm even more impressed that you had the courage to tell me. If you'd said nothing, I never would have known. So I really appreciate you telling me, and by the way, you did a fantastic job on this case. Ric Stokes will be a free man because of your insight and investigative work. I can't believe how lucky Marjorie and I are that you came along."

Steve walked over to her and offered to shake her hand. Casey pushed back her chair and stood up, her smile relieved but proud.

"You too, Marjorie," Steve said, moving around Casey to congratulate her. "We win as a team, and we lose as a team. And this team couldn't do it without you." He reached out to shake Marjorie's hand, but she stood up and gave him a big hug instead.

"I don't shake hands, Mr. Stilwell. When my team wins, I hug."

"All right then," Steve declared. "We're done for the day. I've got a couple of phone calls to make, which I can do on my own. Then how about we meet for dinner tonight at the King's Tavern on DoG Street. I could go for a little colonial dining and celebration."

"I'm in," announced Casey.

"Me, too," said Marjorie. I'll make reservations for six thirty."

"I'll see you both there," Steve said as they headed for the door. "Thanks again for all you both did."

"Go make your phone calls," Marjorie reminded him. "And call Sarah first."

"Will do, Marjorie. Will do."

48

Same day—Monday, 5 June 2000, 4:18 p.m. EDT
Williamsburg, Virginia

STEVE'S HAND SHOOK AS HE DIALED Sarah's number. Sweat formed on his scalp and his head itched, so he raked a hand through his hair as he waited for Sarah to answer. He hadn't been this nervous since he'd asked Sarah out on their first date. If she made this very difficult for him, she would be justified in doing so. He had lots of failings she could cite, ranging from his recent trip to Vietnam to his long hours at the office getting sucked into his clients' cases. But his greatest failure lay in his inability to make his family a priority. It was for this sin he was now on trial, with Sarah sitting as his accuser, judge, and jury. He knew she would not tolerate bluster; she would demand substance, and he had only a few precious minutes to make his case. When she answered the telephone, the stopwatch started.

"Hello?"

"Hello, Sarah. It's Steve."

"Hello, Steve."

Sarah's curt reply communicated that the call was all his responsibility. If he wanted the ball to move down the field, he had to carry it.

"So, how've you been?"

"I'm doing fine."

"Can I ask where you're staying?"

"At the Palmer's beach condo. It was vacant this week, so they let me use it."

"That was nice of them." Sarah didn't respond, so he knew he had to get to the point. "I didn't know you called me on Saturday night until today." Sarah still didn't say anything, so he continued, "I plugged my cellphone in at the office and then left it there. Later that night, Casey was working late and saw that you called, but she forgot about it when the office caught fire and didn't think of it again until just a few minutes ago. So I'm sorry I didn't call you back earlier." The apology cracked Sarah's response code.

"I called after I saw your accident on the late-night news. I wanted to make sure you were okay."

"I had a few bumps and bruises and was a little shaken up, but I was otherwise okay."

"The woman in your car who died … was she the woman in the pictures?"

"She was, Sarah. Her organization was trying to kill her because she'd failed to get a notebook I had. She was ready to turn state's evidence and help get Ric Stokes out of jail in Vietnam. Unfortunately, her organization got to us before I could get her to the FBI. She was on the side of the car where the eighteen-wheeler hit, and she bore the brunt of the impact."

"So, what do you want, Steve?"

"I want you to come home. The case is over and Ric Stokes should be released from jail this week. We can put our lives back together again."

"Nothing's changed, Steve. You could've called me to let me know you were okay after the accident or after your office burned down. But instead, you were so preoccupied with your case that you didn't think about it until Casey told you this afternoon that I called."

Steve had no choice but to tell the truth. Silence would be damning and anything else would just be an excuse. He laid it on the line. "You're right, Sarah. Damn it, you're right. But it doesn't mean that I don't love you and that I don't want you back. Will you please forgive me and work through this with me? There's no way I'm going to have another case like this, so we'll be able to settle down and lead a normal life."

Sarah laughed, but it wasn't the type of laughter he wanted to hear. It was bitter, devoid of humor and chock-full of sarcasm. "You're still living in a dream world, Steve."

"I am, you're right about that. But I'd rather live in a dream world with you and at least have a chance of happiness, than live anywhere else without you. Won't you take another chance, Sarah? I know things have gotten better since I retired from the Navy. So we've had a few rough times. We just need to keep working at it."

"We've been over this ground before, Steve. And we always end up in the same place."

"Yeah, but the bottom line is I love you and I know you love me. Otherwise, you wouldn't be wasting your time right now talking to me. We both want our marriage to get better. It's worth it, Sarah. We're worth it."

"You talk a good game. You always have. But I need more than words. I need actions that show I matter to you."

"You know you matter to me."

"So do lots of other things, and that's the problem. You better move me up on the priority list, right now."

"Does that mean you're coming home?"

Sarah paused before answering, raising Steve's hopes. "No, I'm not ready for that and I don't think you are either. I want you to take some time to think about us and what you really want. When you figure that out, then we can talk again."

"When will that be?"

"I don't know, but I know it's not now. This is something that's been building up for years. It can't be resolved overnight."

"I think this is a mistake, Sarah. It makes more sense to think this through together. It's too easy to walk away once we're apart."

"I guess that's the point, isn't it? We need to find out if we have what it takes to stay together. I feel very strongly about this."

Steve could tell Sarah wasn't going to change her mind, and further attempts to persuade her would only reinforce her decision. As much as he hated to admit it, she was probably right, anyway.

"Okay, we'll take some time, but I'm not going to let you down, Sarah, I promise. I really do love you, you know."

"I hope so, Steve. I really hope so. Goodbye." Sarah hung up before he could reply.

Steve walked into the living room and flopped down into a soft, brushed-leather chair. He was shaken after his talk with Sarah, not to mention physically and emotionally drained from working Ric's case. He had a lot of work ahead of him to win Sarah back, but that was exactly what he intended to do. Now he just had to figure out how.

EPILOGUE

Six months later
Arlington National Cemetery

CASEY HAD NEVER ATTENDED A FUNERAL at Arlington National Cemetery; that was the problem. Since her helicopter crash, she'd obsessed over what it would be like. She'd heard the hooves of the horses clopping on the pavement as they slowly pulled the caisson to the finely manicured gravesite. She'd pictured the family walking at the rear of the procession, their mournful eyes fixed on the flag-draped coffin rolling along the narrow road in front of them. She'd heard the sermon, flinched at the Ceremonial Guard firing its volleys, and grew blurry-eyed at the thought of the bugler playing his singular salute to her departed brother-in-arms. Everything was there, down to the last detail. Everything, that is, except Casey.

Her preoccupation with military funerals began in the weeks leading up to her copilot's funeral at Arlington. She was the one at the controls when their helicopter went down, so she felt responsible for his death. Although it helped that the official investigation cleared her, the findings didn't alleviate her guilt. She wanted—no, she needed—to tell him she was sorry, that she was proud of him, that he was a good soldier and a good man, and that she would never forget him. But fate hadn't granted her that opportunity, nor had it allowed her to attend his funeral.

Her guilt gripped her like a curse, manifesting itself through her injuries. Every prosthetic step she took reminded her of her failure. She'd developed coping mechanisms with the help of her counselors at the Veterans Administration. Immersing herself in the law worked best. But the aftermath of the nighttime crash was never far from the surface, and the moment she lost focus on her casework, visions of the missed funeral reappeared.

Today was a fitting day for a military funeral, right out of Casey's dream. The December wind blew cold but not biting, forcing tree limbs devoid of leaves to convulse as if their contribution to the ceremony was to reinforce death's closure. In collusion with the wind, the gray, overcast skies drew the mourners to the gravesites. The Pentagon loomed in the background, its pale concrete walls framing the long procession as it wound its way to the gravesites.

All five families had requested that the crewmembers be buried at Arlington at the same time and in the same place. They agreed that since the men had flown together, died together, and waited together on the Vietnamese hillside for over thirty years until they could finally be brought home, they should be buried together in the nation's highest place of honor. Now the families of Lieutenant Colonel Ray Eversall, Captain John "Pikes" Peke, Captain Joe Scalpato, Master Sergeant David Durango, and Staff Sergeant Jose Medeiro stood side by side, bound together by common loss and common purpose, bidding a final and long overdue farewell to their fallen heroes.

The families also issued a special invitation to Steve and Casey in recognition of their efforts to make sure the U.S. government learned of the plane's location. Casey drove from Williamsburg with Steve and Phan, who stood silently next to her. Phan's presence was a testament to Steve's promise fulfilled, for he and his family were now staying with Steve, hoping to make a new life for themselves in America. Ric and Noriko Stokes were there as well, as was Ryan Eversall's widow, Angela, and her two children. Secretary of State Susan McDermott also attended, not as a VIP, but as a fellow mourner, acknowledging the loss of her former suitor—whose body had yet to be found—from so many years before. Casey noted that Secretary McDermott's eyes appeared red and puffy; she was sure the Secretary had been crying. Now, however, McDermott assumed the stoic demeanor of a senior political leader guiding the funeral's participants through the final chapter of a tragedy.

The event was even bigger than Susan McDermott, as the media's presence made clear. The airmen's story gained national prominence as soon the Pentagon's Joint Task Force–Full Accounting used Ryan Eversall's notebook to find the crash site. The details of Sapphire Pavilion flooded the media, bringing the failed peace attempt and the Vietnam War back into the public spotlight, with political pundits arguing "what if" the mission had delivered the State Department's envoy to Hanoi as originally planned. But those discussions mattered little now. Everyone but the tabloids just wanted the crewmembers to rest peacefully, knowing they now had the blessings of a grateful nation.

As the gravesite eulogy closed, the ground shook from the roar of four

U.S. Air Force F-16 fighters soaring overhead. Casey looked up to watch the jets flying the missing-man formation—one jet peeling away, leaving a gap in the lineup of the remaining three to symbolize their lost Sapphire Pavilion comrades. But to Casey, the gap morphed into something intensely personal. It was the tribute to her copilot she had missed seven years before. A shiver ran down her spine. So much of the funeral was exactly as she'd imagined it in her dream.

Casey's emotions roiled inside her as she realized she'd been given a rare second chance. She could finally give her copilot the salute he deserved. Oddly, it didn't matter that it wasn't his funeral. He would understand. Now the crack of the Honor Guard's rifles was every bit as much for her copilot as it was for the Sapphire Pavilion crew.

Casey's funeral dream and the reality of the moment began to merge, until the sound of "Taps" echoing across the cemetery completely replaced her dream. She dabbed at her eyes to hide her emotion. "Army helicopter pilots don't cry; they fly missions," she repeated to herself over and over. She had to compartmentalize her feelings and keep her game face intact.

When the bugler sounded his last haunting note, she stood at rigid attention. She couldn't remember her dream anymore. Only today's funeral remained. She felt drained, but at peace. Finally, at peace. Then she felt Steve grasp her arm.

"Casey, are you all right?" Steve's voice sounded distant but concerned. "The ceremony's been over for a couple of minutes."

"Oh, I'm sorry," Casey responded, feeling like she had to dial back into her surroundings. "I just got caught up in the funeral. It's so tragic. These men were on a peace mission and they were killed by a fellow American. I can't even imagine how the families must feel."

"None of us can," Steve said, shaking his head. "But at least they've got some closure now. How about we go to the reception for an hour or so to extend our condolences? Then we can head back to Williamsburg. Does that work for you?"

"Can I meet you after the reception? I've got something to take care of."

Steve looked puzzled. "Where, here? I can drive you someplace if you need me to."

"No thanks. It's here. But I do need to go to the reception with you and Phan to get a little information first."

"You're being cryptic, Casey. Are you sure you're okay?"

"I'm fine, I promise." Casey smiled to reassure Steve. "I've got some unfinished business. There's somebody here I need to see. He's waited a long time for this."

Steve smiled back. "And so have you, Casey. And so have you."

Casey gave Steve a hug. Steve understood her. She had definitely come to work for the right person. Although one of the main reasons she sought him out was because she knew he would be flexible in dealing with her appointments at the VA, she somehow felt those appointments wouldn't be necessary anymore. Sapphire Pavilion had brought peace after all.

* * *

Six months later
Rhodes, Greece

IT WAS JUST AFTER EIGHT P.M., and the ancient stone street through the walled city sounded like a carnival. Lamps, lights, and candles beamed hundreds of gold-star halos from their assigned positions in the warm medieval night, a night only just getting underway. Mostly German vacationers moved along in chattering crowds, searching for the right restaurant to satisfy their cravings for Mediterranean food and Greek libation. They strolled in both directions until one or more in their party split off to investigate a random shop or restaurant, hoping to find some unique treasure or priceless artifact squirreled away for centuries among the hordes of mass-produced souvenirs from China.

One such woman diverged from the stream of people as they passed a two-story café on the corner of the street. The café's yellow-arched portico, supporting a black-rail flower-covered porch on the second floor, served as the demarcation line between the outside café and the interior of the restaurant. The woman entered the café at the far end, adjacent to a less inviting establishment. She walked hurriedly to the back until she passed under one of the archways and entered the restaurant proper. She headed directly to the polished, wall-length bar, invisible from the street. Anyone observing might conclude she had been there before.

"I'd like two glasses of champagne," she said to the first male bartender to notice her, which didn't take long. She was an attractive woman, probably in her mid-thirties, trim and athletic. She wore a light-blue sleeveless summer top, unbuttoned enough to attract interest, and a lacy white cotton miniskirt that fluttered as she walked. She caught the bartender giving her a quick once-over, his eyes lingering longer than they should have on her tanned legs.

She called him on it. "Is there something wrong?"

The bartender, who had to be older than she was, grinned. "No, nothing is wrong," he replied with a thick Greek accent, making no apology. "What kind of champagne would you like, my dear?"

"Give me the best you have by the glass," she instructed, reaching into her purse to retrieve her wallet.

The bartender poured the first glass and set it on the counter. "So, you celebrate with someone special?"

"You could say that," she replied. "How much do I owe you?" She knew how to take control of conversations and keep them from heading in unwanted directions, which anything delaying a quick departure from this bartender would be.

The bartender got the message. "Wait a moment, please," he requested, the wide grin of a moment before replaced with a smile expressing no more than common courtesy. He finished pouring the second glass and set it on the counter. Then he rang the sale up on the cash register and looked back at her. "That will be forty-three Euros."

"Very well," the woman said, pulling a fifty Euro note from her wallet. "You've been so … kind." She slid the note on the counter, tucked her purse under her arm, and picked up both glasses of champagne. The bartender said something in reply, but she paid no attention; she was already turning away from the bar. She walked onto the portico, stopping at a counter briefly before she strolled to a table for two with an older gentleman sitting alone. She came up from behind him, glided past close enough to ensure he could smell her fragrance, then turned slowly to face him.

"Do you mind if I join you?"

"Of course not. Please sit down." He looked startled at first, but recovered quickly. "You've already got two glasses of champagne. Did you expect our conversation to be that difficult?"

"It's nice to see you, too, Richard." Her voice blended elements of sarcasm and seduction, concealing both her purpose and mood. "You don't really think I'd ask to join you without being prepared to share, do you?" She slid one of the glasses across the table. "So how long have you been in Rhodes?"

"For about two weeks," Richard replied. "But then, I'm sure you know that already, don't you?"

"I wouldn't be a good operative if I didn't, now would I?" She smiled and sipped her champagne.

"So the reports of your death were premature?"

"I guess so. Does that upset you?"

"It was business, Gallagher." He smiled. "Now, I'm glad you're alive. So where have you been hiding?"

"I don't like to think of the Federal Witness Protection Program as 'hiding.' The U.S. Attorney at the hospital described it as a 'fresh start.' I like that better." Gallagher smiled and leaned forward, making sure wandering eyes could see what they wanted to see. "Shall we toast to both of our new beginnings?" Gallagher picked up her champagne glass and tilted it toward Richard. He picked up his champagne and they clinked glasses. They kept their untrusting eyes on each other, each trying to predict what the other's next move might be.

"So, how did you find me?"

"You're not the only one with friends in the Agency, Richard. And frankly, I'm a lot better looking than you are, so it wasn't too hard. It just took some time." Gallagher took another sip of champagne, as did Richard.

"Well, I for one am glad you're doing well," he said unconvincingly. He eyed Gallagher while he swirled the champagne around in his glass. When he started to drink it, Gallagher matched his effort, nearly draining what she had left.

"The next round is on you," she said, sitting back in her chair and crossing her legs to the side of the table. She bounced her foot as if keeping time to a slow, rhythmic melody.

"Are you trying to get me drunk to take advantage of me?" Richard asked, downing the last of his champagne. He raised his hand to summon a waiter. A young man in black pants and a white, collared shirt scurried over as if he had been waiting all his life for this moment. Richard spoke before the waiter could ask what he wanted.

"A bottle of champagne. The best you have."

"Is that all?" the waiter asked.

"For now." The waiter nodded and then disappeared beneath the portico.

"So why did you do it, Richard?"

"Why did I do what?" Richard began to squirm. He looked restless.

"Don't play games with me, Richard. I know you tried to kill me. I know it was your people who forced my car off the bridge."

Richard took the napkin from his lap and wiped the perspiration beading on his brow. Before he could speak, the waiter returned with the champagne. He showed Richard the bottle, which Richard approved with a hurried nod. The pop of the cork prefaced the fresh bubbly spilling into their glasses.

"How about we toast to a long life, Richard? For both of us." Gallagher leaned forward again, holding out her glass and waiting for Richard to reciprocate. His movements were slower and more deliberate, as if a champagne-induced lethargy were setting in. After the toast, they each took another sip of champagne and nestled in their chairs.

"As I recall, Richard, you said it was because I was incompetent. That was it, wasn't it?"

Richard leaned forward, grimacing. "It was business, Gallagher, and you didn't do your job. I just called it like I saw it. You should understand that."

Richard sat back, attempting to get comfortable. "You know in this business we can't afford to show compassion. It's just business."

"Well I'm glad you see it that way, Richard. I'm so glad you see it that way. Because I want the last thing you think about today to be who was really incompetent." Gallagher slid her chair up closer to Richard to be sure he could hear; she could tell it was becoming more difficult for him to focus on their conversation. "Because you were the one who planned the mission, and you were the one who tried to kill me twice but failed." Then she stood up and started to leave, but sat back down again to deliver her closing line. "Oh, and there's one more thing." She paused to make sure he could comprehend what she was about to say. "You were the one who drank champagne out of a glass given to you by a woman you tried twice to kill … unsuccessfully."

Gallagher looked at Richard with victory in her eyes. "Now you tell me, Richard, who's the incompetent one?"

Richard's breathing was becoming more labored; he had only a few more seconds to live. It was time to make her exit.

Gallagher smiled and said goodbye politely so it would sound like she was leaving her guest on good terms; then she disappeared into the human traffic curving away from the café through the crowded streets of Rhodes. An ambulance's siren a few minutes later from the direction of the restaurant told her what she needed to know.

After thirty-three years and the senseless deaths of both heroes and hacks, Sapphire Pavilion had come full circle. The mission was finally closed.

Photo of David E. Grogan by Bob Bradlee

DAVID E. GROGAN WAS BORN IN Rome, New York, and raised in Cleveland, Ohio. After graduating from the College of William & Mary in Virginia with a BBA in accounting, he began working for the accounting firm Arthur Andersen & Co., in Houston, Texas, as a certified public accountant. He left Arthur Andersen in 1984 to attend the University of Virginia School of Law in Charlottesville, Virginia, graduating in 1987. He earned his master's in international law from the George Washington University Law School and is a licensed attorney in the Commonwealth of Virginia.

Grogan served on active duty in the United States Navy for over twenty-six years as a Navy Judge Advocate. He is now retired, but during his Navy career, he prosecuted and defended court-martial cases, traveled to capitals around the world, lived abroad in Japan, Cuba, and Bahrain, and deployed to the Mediterranean Sea and the Persian Gulf onboard the nuclear-powered aircraft carrier *USS Enterprise*. His experiences abroad and during his career influence every aspect of his writing. *Sapphire Pavilion* is his second novel. His first was *The Siegel Dispositions*.

Grogan's current home is in Savoy, Illinois, where he lives with his wife of thirty-three years and their dog, Marley. He has three children.

You can follow Dave on Twitter (@davidegrogan) and Facebook (davidegrogan), and learn more about him at: www.davidegrogan.com.

BOOK 1

THE STEVE STILWELL THRILLER SERIES

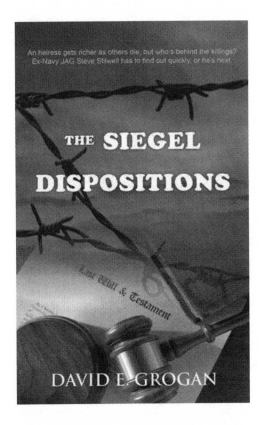

An heiress gets richer as others die, but who's behind the killings? Ex-Navy JAG Steve Stilwell has to find out quickly, or he's next.

The first assignment Steve Stilwell faces in his new law practice is to update the will of Prof. Felix Siegel, who wishes to leave a part of his estate to his wartime friends and the rest to his adopted daughter. Then Siegel dies violently. To Steve's dismay, his efforts to distribute these legacies bring Siegel's heirs nothing but death and misfortune.

Keep reading for an excerpt from

THE SIEGEL DISPOSITIONS

1

———⁓⁓———

Tuesday, September 30, 1997
Düsseldorf, Germany

EMIL WEISENTROPE CLUTCHED THE BROWN PAPER package with both hands as he shuffled past the shuttered shops on Malpelstrasse. He had to get to a mailbox. Twisting old bones no longer able to move without pain, he looked over both shoulders, certain he was being followed. All he saw were the preoccupied faces of early-morning commuters hustling anonymously off to work. Still, something told him death lurked nearby.

He couldn't report his suspicions. The authorities would hear nothing but the ramblings of a crazy old man. They might even put him in a home. But he knew. He'd witnessed death from every angle. In Auschwitz, though, there had always been others—some with names, some without—who held his hand whenever death drew near. Now he faced its foul presence alone.

He quickened his pace toward a mailbox up ahead. As he focused on his goal, a figure slammed into him, nearly causing him to drop his precious cargo. Gasping, he pulled the package close to his heart to shield it with his body.

"Watch out!" a young man yelled without bothering to look back or slow his stride. A commuter late for work couldn't be bothered to make way for an ambling old man taking up more than his share of the sidewalk.

Emil exhaled in relief and trudged the last fifty steps to the mailbox. Yanking the flap to the drop shoot open, he paused. Could he be wrong? Once gone, his package could never be retrieved. It was so final, like death itself. Tears moistened weathered cheeks and his frail five-foot, eight-inch frame trembled to its core. He had no choice. Felix Siegel would take care of it. There was no one else he trusted more.

Gnarled fingers relaxed and the package slipped away into darkness. Feeling both profound despair and inner peace, he wiped away his tears with the gray wool sleeves of his overcoat and took a deep breath. It was time to go home.

FROM CAMEL PRESS AND DAVID E. GROGAN

THANK YOU FOR READING *SAPPHIRE PAVILION*. We are so grateful for you, our readers. If you enjoyed this book, here are some steps you can take that could help contribute to its success and the success of this series.

- Post a review on Amazon, BN.com, and/or GoodReads.
- Check out David's website and send a comment or ask to be put on his mailing list.
- Spread the word on social media, especially Facebook, Twitter, and Pinterest
- "Like" David and Camel Press's Facebook pages.
- Follow David and Camel Press on Twitter.
- Ask for this book at your local library or request it on their online portal.

Good books and authors from small presses are often overlooked. Your comments and reviews can make an enormous difference.

Made in the USA
Columbia, SC
30 June 2017